THE FATEFUL
MARRIAGE

Published by Sapere Books.

20 Windermere Drive, Leeds, England, LS17 7UZ,
United Kingdom

saperebooks.com

ISBN: 978-1-913518-29-5

CHAPTER ONE

Ottilia Fanshawe, thankfully removing the bonnet from her head and handing it to the maid, Joanie, moved to the front of the parlour and peered through the open double casement upon the flagged walkway comprising the main thoroughfare of Tunbridge Wells.

"At least Sybilla secured us an apartment overlooking the Walks, Fan. It promises one source of amusement."

Her husband, busy overseeing the removal of their various pieces of luggage to appropriate accommodations, did not answer for a moment.

"Leave the writing case here, Tyler. And that valise is full of books. Take her ladyship's portmanteau." He called after the burdened footman, who was about to follow Joanie and the black steward, Hemp Roy, both equally laden with the paraphernalia necessary to a protracted sojourn in the popular watering place. "And see if you can rustle up coffee from the landlady."

"Right you are, my lord."

The servants having exited, Ottilia again claimed her spouse's attention. "Fan, do come and look. It is a droll sight, I promise you."

Lord Francis Fanshawe blew out a breath and crossed to join her. "It had better be, or my esteemed mother may expect a growling reception. Didn't I warn you she would drag us into the business?"

Ottilia slid an arm about him as he reached her, leaning in to rest her cheek against his shoulder for a space. "My poor darling. Such a good son as you are, too."

Francis only grunted, though he gave her an answering hug.

Ottilia released herself and dipped her chin towards the walkway below. "Do but look, Fan. Is it not the oddest thing for everyone to be in dishabille like this? See that gentleman in the banyan there? He has curling papers in his hair, Fan!"

"Good God!" Francis set his hands on the sill and leaned out. "Is it curling papers? Decidedly odd. Lord above, is that stout female wearing nothing but a dressing gown?"

"Yes, and scarlet, if you please." Ottilia bubbled with merriment. "What does it mean, Fan? It is not as if they are going sea-bathing."

Francis was watching the parade of semi-dressed individuals and abruptly leaned further out, looking along the street. "Ah, it must be the ceremony of taking the waters. There's a woman filling glasses at a pump down the end there."

Ottilia glanced along and noted several of the walkers were indeed sipping from thick tumblers and making faces withal. She had to laugh. "Well, if it tastes as horrible as their expressions seem to indicate, I shall not indulge."

Francis straightened, lifting an eyebrow. "Wasn't that my mother's suggestion?"

"A justification rather, I suspect. She had to provide some legitimate reason for the summons."

"Other than filial obedience? Pish and tush, as my revered mama would say. She knew you wouldn't be able to resist when you heard she was bringing my abominable niece here."

The Dowager Marchioness of Polbrook had vowed, after the trying events in March's fateful London season, to take in hand her granddaughter, the Lady Elizabeth Fiske whom, she declared, had been spoiled by her over-indulgent parents. Ottilia's liking for the girl notwithstanding, she had been dismayed when her mother-in-law wrote to demand the attendance of herself and Francis. She moved away from the window and looked across the chairs for one comfortable enough yet not too upholstered in the high warmth of the room. Not that she minded the heat after a three-day journey plagued by almost incessant rain in this summer of apparent endless wet.

"If you truly wish to know, Fan, I would far rather have gone back to Weymouth as we intended. Not that we would see much of George and Cecile."

Francis followed her, stripping off his coat as he went and throwing it over the sofa back. He shook out the ruffles to his shirtsleeves and took up a stance at the fireplace.

"I imagine he will be tacking back and forth along the coast now France is at war with our friends across the Channel."

Ottilia was trying a high-backed straight chair, but deciding it was too hard, she rose and moved to one with cushioned arms. She sat down, found it satisfactory and looked across at her spouse, her mind harking back to a secret but deep-laid apprehension.

"Do you hanker for the life, Fan?"

A startled look leapt into his eyes. "Soldiering? Dear Lord, no, Tillie!"

"I wondered if you have thought of taking another commission."

"I? You jest. It was at best uncomfortable, at worst distressing beyond words. To watch men scream in agony and have to force their fellows on to face more gunfire?" He shuddered. "It was salutary and enlightening of the best and worst of one's fellow man, but it's not a life I crave, Tillie."

She eyed him in some degree of doubt. He rarely spoke of his days in the military. "You do not miss the company of friends such as George, or the excitement?"

"The camaraderie perhaps a little, yes." His lip twitched. "As for excitement, I defy any battle to offer me as much of it as I've seen since marrying you, my loved one."

Ottilia had to laugh. "You refer, I collect, to my propensity for attracting the puzzling dead."

His eye gleamed. "Yes, and how would you manage without me?"

A shadow grazed her heart. "Not that spectre, Fan, I beg of you. I could not manage. I could not live!"

She held out a hand to him and he came across to take it, dropping a kiss on her fingers and another on her hair for good measure.

"Have no fear, sweetheart. I am a fixture."

She smiled up at him as he straightened. "I am relieved."

"Have you truly been worrying I might join up, Tillie?"

She felt her cheeks grow warm. "Oh, must I confess? If you will have it, I agreed to come here because I was afraid George might enthuse you."

He looked incredulous. "You did not! And here I was certain you could not wait to involve yourself in whatever crazy scheme Lizzy may come up with."

"No, indeed. I admit I like her very well, but it was hard to bear the pain of my responsibility in her actions. And don't try to mitigate it, Fan, for you blamed me, you know you did. Sybilla too."

"Yet Mama has called upon you again. Come, Tillie, don't fret. The girl can hardly run into trouble here."

The words were scarcely out of his mouth than the door opened to admit Tyler, armed with the accoutrements for coffee, who stood to one side with the tray as the female under discussion tripped lightly into the room, all smiles and mischief.

"Uncle Francis! Aunt Ottilia! Oh, you are not ready for visitors, are you? But you must not mind me. Besides, everyone is informal in the mornings. I saw you at the window and could not resist. Thank heavens you are come at last for Grandmama is driving me mad!"

Lady Elizabeth Fiske, a youthful brunette with a piquant countenance that matched her slight form, untied her bonnet and threw it off with an air of meaning to remain for some time. Ottilia watched the pretty confection land in a corner on the floor and gave a gurgle of laughter. "Sybilla has not managed to change much in you, I see."

"Not a whit." Lizzy's throaty laugh sounded as she descended upon Ottilia and enveloped her in a perfumed embrace. "You cannot imagine how badly I have wanted you, dear Lady Fan."

Torn between dismay and gratification, Ottilia submitted to be kissed on either cheek. "You flatter me, child."

Lizzy straightened. "I don't at all. You are just the person needed to call Grandmama to order, for of course she will not listen to a word I say."

"The boot," cut in Francis on a dry note, "was supposed to be on the other leg." He was moving to the table where the footman was setting down the tray. "Another cup, Tyler, if you please. I will pour."

Lizzy, waiting only for the servant to leave the room, crossed to him with another trill of merriment upon her lips. "Now, Uncle Francis, you are not to be my mentor, for I won't bear it. Give me a hug, for heaven's sake, for I am missing Papa dreadfully and you will have to do."

Ottilia could not forbear a laugh as Francis complied, observing as he released her, "If I am to replace poor Gil, I fear you may be obliged to have me as mentor too."

"Not in the least, for you know well Papa indulges me in a perfectly ridiculous fashion." The twinkle in her eyes belied the words. "I have it on the best of authority, you know."

Francis quirked an eyebrow. "Lady Polbrook senior?"

Another peal greeted this sally. "Who else? But, Uncle Francis, you must intervene. She has gone perfectly demented, I promise you."

A look of foreboding was cast at Ottilia and she made haste to rescue her spouse. "What in the world do you mean, Lizzy? What is afoot?"

"Oh, it is disastrous, Aunt." Lizzy flew across the room again, throwing herself into a chair near Ottilia. "Grandmama's arch enemy is here and they are at daggers drawn. Mind, I don't say she has not reason, for the Dowager Lady Wem is a most dreadful woman and seems to tyrannise over the whole of her family. You should see them attending her. They are all scared to death."

Feeling somewhat battered by the hail of words, Ottilia sought enlightenment of her husband. "The Dowager Lady Wem, Fan?"

A faint frown creased a line between his brows. "I've heard Mama speak of her, but she is scathing of so many individuals, I confess I paid little attention."

"But who is she, Fan?"

"The Dowager Viscountess Wem of the Brockhurst family. Her son has the title with estates in Shropshire, if I recall correctly. Harriet would know, but I am barely acquainted with them."

"Well, that is about to change, sir, for you cannot help but meet them here. Everyone knows everyone. You cannot avoid it. Besides, we have been crowded into the Assembly Rooms while the skies drizzle on the Pantiles."

Ottilia fastened upon the pertinent point. "But what makes her Sybilla's arch enemy?"

Lizzy fluttered her hands. "Oh, she refuses to divulge the reason. She declares it is ancient history, though it seems to me she is as greatly rubbed by it as if it had happened yesterday. You should have heard them at the ball last night."

"But do you say they are quarrelling openly?" Francis's frown intensified as he asked and Ottilia's dismay increased.

Lizzy giggled. "Yes, but only with exquisite politeness. It is quite a comedy. Or it would be if Grandmama did not break out in a fury every time we return to the lodgings. I declare, I am ready to scream if she says one more time that the creature is poison from her head to her heels." She added, in a creditable imitation of the Dowager Lady Polbrook's voice and manner, "'Poison through and through, I tell you. If one of them does not poison her back one of these days, you may call me a Dutchwoman.'"

Relieved to see her husband relax into laughter at this, Ottilia was about to speak when Lizzy forestalled her, turning with an earnest look.

"That, dear Lady Fan, is why you are so desperately needed."

Ottilia exchanged a startled look with Francis. "You don't mean to say someone has poisoned her?"

Lizzy broke into laughter. "Good gracious, no! But it can't be long before they do. It seems the Dowager Lady Wem's grandson, Daniel, has defied the match set up by his family and been secretly married these three years to the daughter of a draper. The family are all in an uproar over this misalliance and rumour has it Daniel Brockhurst swears he will kill his grandmother before he gives up his wife."

CHAPTER TWO

It was after noon by the time Ottilia managed to induce her spouse to wait upon his mother. She could not but suspect he was delaying the inevitable after Lizzy's revelations, for he loathed having to endure Sybilla's rants.

"She can very well do without us for a little longer. We've been on the road since dawn and I'm going nowhere without first washing away the travel stains and changing out of this shirt. Besides, I refuse to enter the lion's den on an empty stomach."

Ottilia thought it prudent to soothe. "I will arrange for something to be brought in, Fan."

He picked up his coat and seized a hand bell on the table, ringing it with vigour. "Meat, Tillie. A substantial pie will do the trick."

"Yes, my darling hungry one, it will be ready when you are done changing. There are chop houses enough, I dare say. The landlady will know."

"And ale," he added. "Hemp can see to it while Tyler organises food."

Ottilia conveyed her request to Joanie who answered the bell as Francis left the room, shouting for his valet. "And when you have told them, Joanie, pray bring hot water to the bedchamber."

These dispositions in hand, Ottilia took opportunity to refresh her person, reflecting it was just as well to effect these preparations since her mother-in-law was likely to keep them occupied for some time.

Lizzy had engaged to inform the dowager of their arrival and ensure she was at home in the lodgings she had taken for her sojourn, which were situated in another house in the same bank of buildings that fronted the Upper Walks, so to be handy for the Assembly Rooms across the way. Entry to the lodging houses was behind the row and a few steps would have taken them to the house in question, but Ottilia requested first to take a look at the thoroughfare affectionately dubbed the Pantiles from the slabs of paving stones that provided a substantial walkway for visitors.

"We had best take our chance while we may in case it begins again to rain."

She looked about with interest as they strolled under the shade of the long colonnade. The whole bank of little shops appeared given over to the tradesmen serving those who came here, mostly for their health. From what she could see in the windows, there appeared to be a variety of merchandise, everything from foodstuffs to the sort of toy shop stocking useful knick-knacks, or those merely ornamental. A cleverly arranged collection of prettily decorated wooden boxes caught her eye.

"Is that Tunbridge ware, I wonder? I must say I look forward to peeking into these intriguing little shops."

"But not now, Tillie. We have no time."

"Mr Sprange," she said, paying scant attention.

"Mr Who?"

"On the sign there, above that shop. Look, he has playbills, Fan."

"We are not now concerned with theatrical performances, Tillie. And I may say, after the fiasco at Weymouth, I am little inclined for such events."

Ottilia let out a giggle, recalling the previous summer spent at the seaside resort when she had been called upon to aid Colonel Tretower in unravelling the murder of a beautiful actress. Obedient to the pressure on her arm, she allowed herself to be urged out onto the Upper Walk. The earlier parade of water drinkers had disappeared and the wide paved way that comprised the main attraction of the small town was more or less deserted. Driven indoors by excessive heat? Or were they merely dressing in preparation for the next activity of the day. Sybilla had written in some detail, outlining a programme altogether busy for a watering place that had long outlived its heyday, which sounded to Ottilia like a recipe for tedium.

After the ceremony of drinking the waters, the company in general repaired to their lodgings to dress and break their fast, unless a breakfast party was in train in the Tea Room. Then it was necessary to attend morning service in the chapel, take an airing in a carriage or on horseback or, weather permitting, stroll about the Upper Walk to the accompaniment of music from the gallery. Following dinner, everyone paraded the Walks before repairing to the Assembly Rooms for idle chatter or gaming, unless a theatrical performance or one of the two balls held each week intervened. For the male element, debating the news of the day in the Coffee House might be preferred at any time, and for diehard gamesters like Lady Polbrook, foregoing other amusements for the turn of a card.

It was a programme Ottilia viewed with scant enthusiasm, but the surroundings were indeed pleasant, although she surveyed them with a critical eye. "Is this the extent of the place? No wonder Lizzy says one must become acquainted with everyone."

"A prospect," drawled her spouse, "that fills me with horror."

"Yes, but it is pretty, Fan."

There was a small musicians' gallery, with trellis barrier and pretty columns. Across the way ran an avenue of graceful trees concealing to some degree the buildings on the other side, where the land dropped to the unpaved area of the Lower Walks, as decreed by the first Master of Ceremonies Mr Nash, so said Sybilla, for the accommodation of lesser beings while the Upper Walks were reserved for the gentry. The entrance to the Assembly Rooms for the main gatherings was visible behind the trees. Leading down to where the water dispensers plied their trade at the pump that served the well were wide steps, which also ran along the colonnade side where Ottilia, with a spurt of interested relief, spied the circulating library. Salvation!

"Let us just see a little more."

Her husband submitted to walk down the steps into the square where they had earlier seen the water drinkers. The bath house stood at the back and the square led on through an avenue of more shops and also opened out into a large space opposite the library where a small building stood prominently in the centre.

"Ah, that must be where Sybilla said one might obtain information at need. Really, this place has everything all in one street. Cleverly done, I think, don't you, Fan?"

"Yes, but there must be more to it than this. We saw houses along the hill above as we came in and there are permanent residents here. I dare say the back streets stretch a goodly way too."

"But it would seem everything one needs is here, Fan, as far as one can ascertain. Though I cannot see the church Sybilla mentioned. King Charles the Martyr, was it?"

"Speaking of whom," said Francis, looking up at a window above the colonnade in the upper area, "we had best make haste. Lizzy is waving at us."

Ottilia perforce submitted to be led around to the back again and up into the dowager's small parlour. Within a short time of greetings being exchanged, it was plain that Lady Elizabeth had not exaggerated. Sybilla broke into complaint at the first opportunity.

"Had I known that vile creature was here, I should have ignored Pellew and refused to set foot in the place."

Her doctor having advised a course of treatment at the Wells, drinking the waters and taking in a change of scene, had been the occasion of the Dowager Marchioness of Polbrook inviting Lizzy to accompany her in place of her companion, Teresa Mellis, left to manage the Dower House in her absence. A spurious excuse, as she had explained in her letter to her son, which gave her opportunity to take the girl in hand as she had sworn to do. But that scheme, it appeared, had been abandoned for a battle royal with the nemesis of her youth.

Ottilia tried for a neutral note. "Is the Dowager Lady Wem also here for her health?"

Sybilla snorted. "If she is, it can only be in hopes of sweetening her disposition, and she may whistle for that. It transpires she has taken up residence here, at least for the greater part of the year. No doubt her family are delighted to see the back of her, although the Wells crowd must be wishing her safe underground."

Here Ottilia was obliged to stifle a laugh as Lizzy, seated a little behind and thus out of sight of her grandmother, rolled her eyes in an expressive fashion. Fortunately, Francis took up the baton, in a tone of suppressed exasperation.

"What in the world is the cause of this enmity between you, ma'am?"

From her comfortable chair placed near the window to catch the air, for the parlour was stuffy and stifling, Sybilla turned a glare upon her son.

"She knows well what she did."

"Yes, but we don't, Mama."

"And you won't. I will take it to my grave, but rest assured it is not forgotten."

Ottilia received one of her husband's violent looks and hastily interposed. "May we at least know when this quarrel took place?"

Lizzy cut in to repeat the litany. "It is ancient history, is it not, Grandmama?"

Sybilla turned her head with a flare of her black gaze. "I can speak for myself, I thank you. Keep your tongue, Miss!"

Lizzy subsided with a grin and a look towards Ottilia that clearly said, 'I told you so.'

Ottilia tried again. "We won't pry, Sybilla, but is it true the Dowager Lady Wem has her family here and there is a scandal of sorts?"

"Ha! My granddaughter has been gossiping, I take it. If you ask me, the creature has come by her desserts. A misalliance with a tradesman's daughter is what they are saying. One of that appalling crew must have talked for the tale is all over the town."

"Appalling crew?" Francis cocked an eyebrow. "Do you say *all* partake of the Dowager Lady Wem's character?"

The dowager Lady Polbrook snorted again. "I say no such thing. They are all so crushed and subjugated they daren't say boo to a goose. The elder girl — I forget her name —"

"Berta, Grandmama," cut in the wholly unchastened Lizzy.

"Berta, that's it. A sour female, embittered I shouldn't wonder, as who would not be, obliged to run hand and foot after a vicious mother. She looks a very scarecrow and if she was not disposed to emulate the woman, I should be sorry for her."

Ottilia could not help a sliver of sympathy. "Poor girl."

"Girl? She is forty, if she is a day."

Ottilia made haste to turn the subject again. "How many of them are there?"

"Heaven knows! She has called the lot of them in and there are Brockhursts crowding every corner. Both sons are here with their wives and sons, though I have seen no granddaughters as yet. The second daughter is here. Annis Maplewood. About the only one with something to smile about — and she does smile, for a wonder — for she escaped, it seems."

"Yet she answered the summons?"

"She did." Lizzy had taken this, a faint colour rising in her cheeks as she spoke, which at once drew Ottilia's attention. "But not her husband. Her son is with her. He's … an artist."

"Indeed?" Ottilia eyed Lizzy with interest. Did this consciousness betoken an attraction? She had no time to explore it, for Sybilla broke out again.

"If you mean the fellow who is forever sitting apart and sketching, he is here to prepare for making a portrait of a family group. That, if you please, is the excuse Protasia has put about for the gathering of the clans. But that mask is blown, for everyone knows the true reason. And it serves her right, vile-tempered witch as she is."

"Vile-tempered?" The incredulous inflexion in Francis's tone passed his mother by, though it forced Ottilia to choke on a giggle.

"She was so from a girl," declared Sybilla, speaking as if compelled, her tone low and vibrant. "We were in the same set when we came out and every girl among us detested Protasia Alcester. A more two-faced, foul-mouthed female I have never met. Oh, she could charm with the best when she chose. But we knew, if our elders did not, what she was underneath. And she dared..." Sybilla faded out, half starting as if she was not aware she spoke aloud. She gave a little shake of the shoulders and her voice grew stronger. "But mum for that. Suffice it, I know her for what she is. Poison, through and through. And if she is not taken at fault in this business, then God is beyond merciful."

It had not proved difficult for Lizzy to persuade her aunt and uncle to embark upon a sight-seeing expedition to the renowned ancient monument of High Rocks.

"It is only a matter of a couple of miles, Uncle Francis, and one cannot be at Tunbridge Wells without seeing them. There are centuries of names carved into the rocks, you know, so it is like a history of visitors."

Sybilla had predictably protested. "Clambering about rocks in this heat? It will be far too exhausting. I am astonished you have the energy after capering so much last night."

Lizzy ignored the rider. She was not to be prostrated by a ball that ended at eleven. "Well, but you may remain in the carriage, Grandmama," she said, hoping this programme would find no favour, as indeed it proved.

"What, trundle all that way merely to sit and stifle while the rest of you wander about for hours? I can very well do as much at the Assembly Rooms, I thank you."

"But you won't mind if we go? We ought to seize advantage while the weather holds, for we cannot go tomorrow and there is no saying it may not be raining again by Monday. Do say yes, Uncle Francis!"

He was eyeing his wife. "I'm game, if Tillie wishes for it. Would it tire you too much, my love?"

To Lizzy's joy, her aunt had acquiesced with a mischievous look. "I need not emulate Lizzy's antics. She will no doubt scramble everywhere she can."

Which Lizzy had every intention of doing. She said as much as they sat in the landau Francis had hired for the duration of their stay, the hoods down since the day was fine and a trifle cooler than it had been since the Fanshawes' arrival on Wednesday.

"I mean to climb up to the biggest rock, for I have discovered there is a safe path leading up to the summit."

Francis gave her a minatory look. "Well, for pity's sake, take care! We don't want you twisting an ankle or falling off this rock of yours."

"Don't suggest such a thing, Fan. How in the world would we face Harriet if she came to grief?"

"You need have no fear, ma'am. I shall be circumspect, I promise." Lizzy giggled. "Confess now, Aunt. You are only too happy to be spared Grandmama's plaints, even for half a day."

Ottilia smiled, casting a rueful look towards her husband. "I fear your poor uncle is more in need of the respite than I."

Francis rolled his eyes. "At least we may be free for a space of these ubiquitous Brockhursts."

Various members of that family had indeed been in evidence upon the two occasions Francis and Ottilia had visited the Assembly Rooms but having eschewed Friday's ball they had not been obliged by Mr Tyson, the Master of Ceremonies, to endure formal presentations.

"At least you have not had to bear the Dowager Lady Wem and Grandmama gobbling at each other like a couple of turkey hens."

Ottilia went into a peal of laughter. "Lizzy, you dreadful child! Though I confess I am a trifle disappointed not to have seen the arch enemy."

"Trust me, Aunt, you will see all too much of her in short order. She has likely recovered from her indisposition and will be haranguing her unfortunate family even as we speak."

But when they arrived at the High Rocks, having had the benefit of enjoying the sight of the massive boulders growing larger as they approached, a party of Brockhursts was seen to be among the visitors already wandering around the site.

Lizzy groaned. "Oh, no! How in the world did we come to choose the same day as this lot?"

Francis had jumped down and was preparing to help Ottilia to alight. "It makes no matter. The place is vast enough for us to be able to avoid them."

Ottilia was craning her neck as she looked up the high space of the largest rock, still some yards away. "There are several people brave enough to venture up there. Look!" She pointed.

Lizzy paused on the step, her hand in her uncle's, proffered to help her down. "Gracious! Then I can go up too."

"It will be as well to get out of the carriage first," said Francis on a dry note.

Lizzy laughed and complied, stepping down and turning at once to him. "You don't mind if I go? I promise I will be careful."

He looked wry. "I ought to accompany you."

But Lizzy had no wish to be hampered by the restrictions her uncle would doubtless impose. "I should not dream of taking you away from Aunt Ottilia. I am sure she needs your support more than I." She looked after Ottilia, who was walking towards the largest rock and must be out of earshot already. "What if she takes it into her head to go up to the top?"

Consternation leapt in Francis's face. "That is all too likely. Very well, off you go, Lizzy. But—"

"I know, sir. Take care! I will. I have no wish to be laid up, I thank you." With which, Lizzy scampered away, heading for a gap between the massive rock and one a trifle less grand near to it. She had taken the precaution of enquiring at the office of information in the square and had discovered the layout of the rocks and the route advised for ascending to the summit. It took her through an awe-inspiring gap between two elevations, and wound around into a rocky, but steady ascent readily accomplished in one of her natural agility and strength.

Arrived at the summit, she halted to catch her breath, gazing across the expanse of an uneven plateau to where a small group stood. Were they close to the edge? If so, it must indeed be dangerous to crowd together so.

Lizzy watched where she set her feet as she picked her way towards them, happy to realise there were a couple of women among them. She was not the only venturesome female, which indicated it was safer up here than one supposed. A light breeze cooled her cheeks and she paused, a thought drifting into her mind. If the wind got up, one might be in danger of being blown over. Faint alarm kept her motionless as she noted one of the gentlemen ahead holding on to his hat. Was it windier where he stood? He turned slightly and she recognised Lord Wem.

A riffle of impatience went through Lizzy as her gaze slid across the rest and she detected several more features belonging to the Brockhurst family. Must they choose this precise moment? Unwilling to parley with any of them, Lizzy opted to shift direction, heading instead for the back of the rock which did not promise the same vista since there was a deal of foliage and the tops of some tall trees intervened behind. Recalling there was another way down, if rather more precarious, she thought it was worth exploring until the Brockhurst party removed themselves.

The back end of the rock proved extensive, with dips and cracks through which a deal of vegetation grew, while mounds of more bare rock gave evidence of a much bigger edifice than was visible from the front. With extreme caution, fearing a sudden invisible drop, Lizzy made her way as far back as she dared before realising she had lost her bearings.

She turned therefore, looking across the way she had come. In some degree of relief, she saw the cut between rock and sky through the intervening foliage and was about to start back that way when another sight she had missed impinged upon her consciousness. The artist of the Brockhurst family, Mr Vivian Maplewood, was seated on a projecting mound a little to one side, his sketchbook on his knee, head down with hat discarded, his pencil scratching busily across the paper.

A little fillip disturbed Lizzy's heartbeat and the exclamation escaped her without intent. "Mr Maplewood!"

He looked up, a frown leaping to his brow. It cleared in a moment. "Ah. The unfortunate granddaughter."

He did not rise, but Lizzy barely noted this as indignation rose to her breast.

"Unfortunate? I take it you refer to Lady Polbrook? How dare you, sir! You are far more unfortunate in your grandmother than I."

His lips twisted. "It is quite a contest."

"Not according to mine. She has no doubt which of them is worse. And if the demeanour of the acolytes that surround her is anything to go by, the Dowager Lady Wem must be perfectly horrid. We are not cowed by Grandmama, I do assure you."

Mr Maplewood did not appear to resent the charge. On the contrary, amusement crinkled the corners of the light bright eyes that had first drawn her attention, making Lizzy's breath catch.

"A just observation, Lady Elizabeth. I would point out, however, that not quite all are absolutely cowed."

Lizzy eyed him, consciousness overtaking her as she took in all over again the strong jaw, the lean cheeks and the energetic vigour that seemed to come off him in waves. Not that he was athletic, she had decided, but it showed in the way he plied his pencil. She felt warmth rise in her cheeks and hastened to find an uncompromising explanation for her blushes.

"I beg your pardon, sir. I should not have spoken so rudely."

He smiled and Lizzy's bones melted. "Oh, I don't mind it. Besides, it is just as uncivil of me to remain seated as you address me, is it not?"

Lizzy had to laugh. "Yes, it is. But I don't mind it either."

His eyes gleamed. "Then we are well suited as we are. Pray don't hesitate to air your opinion of my grandmother and I shall do the same."

"Of yours or mine?"

He laughed out. "Both, I imagine. Don't tell me you are not rubbed by Lady Polbrook, for I would not believe you."

"Well, I am, if you must have it, but she is not always quite as abrasive as she has been since discovering the Dowager Lady Wem to be living here." Without thinking of the propriety of such a disclosure, she added, "I wish I knew what caused the enmity between them. Grandmama will only say it is ancient history…" Recollecting herself as the frown reappeared on his face, she clammed up. "But enough of that. Are you taking a view? I would have thought you might take a better one from the summit. At least there is a vista from there."

The frown vanished in a grin. "But the summit, my dear Lady Elizabeth, is populated by far too many members of my family at this moment." He looked down at his book. "I have been sketching that root. I like the way it sprouts from a crack in the rock and snakes along like a malevolent serpent, ready to trap the unwary."

Lizzy looked where he pointed and saw there was indeed a vine-like root protruding out of the crack, its passage along the rock meandering and creating little loops and swirls where one might indeed set a foot and trip. "You have an eye for detail, Mr Maplewood."

"A necessary adjunct for my calling, ma'am."

Lizzy was swept with a sense of fascination, not entirely to do with his artistic endeavours. "May I see?"

He pursed his lips. "I don't know. Your tendency to criticise may wholly unman me."

"Why should you suppose I might be critical?"

His lip twitched again and Lizzy's mind clouded. "Did you not just now provide me with the benefit of your opinion on my grandmother without the slightest provocation?"

Flustered, Lizzy stuttered in response. "I d-did not! I mean, it w-was not… You provoked me indeed!"

He looked amazed. "I did?"

"Yes! You called me the unfortunate granddaughter." Thoroughly ruffled, she eyed the burgeoning amusement in his face in rising dudgeon. "Oh, you are an impossible teasing creature, Mr Maplewood."

"Alas!"

Lizzy almost stamped her foot. "Really, I can't think why I am standing talking to you." She made to leave, but he detained her with a touch upon her bare arm. A flitter disturbed her pulse.

"I thought you wished to see my sketch." He held up the wide book, the pencilled drawing open to where she stood.

Caught at once by the bold strokes and the uncanny depiction of — what had he said? Yes, malevolence — in the root he had drawn, Lizzy moved to look at it more closely, her distresses forgotten. She put out a finger and traced along the paper.

"It looks positively evil. How do you do that?"

She looked back into his face as she spoke and descried such warmth in the eyes trained upon her face as startled her momentarily. But it vanished in a haughty stare.

"Are you asking me to reveal the secrets of my trade, madam?"

For an instant, Lizzy felt quite alienated and could not answer. Then his features relaxed into a grin.

"Don't look so dismayed. If truth be told, I am not sure how it is done. I have some knowledge of the general craft, you must know, but for the most part I have an idea in my head and my pencil does the rest."

He spoke in a natural tone, neither teasing nor affected, and Lizzy felt curiously privileged.

"You have an extraordinary talent, sir."

His brow flew up. "You can judge that from one sketch?"

"If it is representative of the rest, yes." But his resumption of the former manner pricked at her. "Just as I judge you a perfectly irritating individual who cannot resist making game of everything."

Mr Maplewood gave an elaborate sigh. "And she is up in the boughs again. What is to be done?"

"Nothing! I shall leave you to your sketching and pursue my—"

A high-pitched scream cut her off. Lizzy jumped with some violence, her gaze flying towards the sound.

"What the devil—?"

She had no chance to answer the artist, nor to formulate the dread thought at the edge of her mind, for the scream was followed on the instant by a long-drawn-out wail and the unmistakeable yell of a man's voice, lifted in horror.

"Oh, my God! Isabel!"

CHAPTER THREE

Snatched from contemplation of an intriguing message etched into the surface of the rock, Ottilia looked up just as a solid body hurtled down and landed with a sickening thud not a dozen yards away.

Instinct, and the instant frozen hollow in her bosom, sent her steps hurrying to the fallen figure. In a vague corner of her mind she heard the shouts and shrieks, the buzzing of many voices raised in protest and question, yet they failed to penetrate against the growing certainty of death. She reached the spot ahead of most and knelt at once to the woman, ignoring the gathering throng.

Woman it was, from the bloom and tangle of lemon-coloured petticoats splashed about the broken form. She lay half folded to one side, limbs flung out, young face open to the skies in a blank-eyed stare. Below a straw bonnet, askew upon the pale riot of curls, an ominous red stain seeped into the hard and rocky ground, her fateful resting place.

"Make way! Give room, if you please. Don't crowd around."

Francis? Grateful for his prompt response just where it was needed, Ottilia found the wrist and felt for a pulse, an action purely mechanical for the evidence told its own tale.

"Is she … is she dead?"

A hushed voice, close. Ottilia raised her eyes and encountered another female squatting on the other side of the corpse. Of middle years, pallid and drenched with shock.

Ottilia wasted no softening words. "Yes. There is no pulse."

The woman's breath dragged and she looked up to the height from where the girl had fallen. "They are all still up there."

Ottilia twisted, craning her neck to follow the line of sight. A sea of faces peered down. She brought her gaze away and found Francis standing close, his eyes trained upon the fatal ledge.

"Dear Lord, I think that's Lizzy up there! What is she thinking?"

Ottilia looked again but could not distinguish among the faces. "Go, Fan! I will manage here."

A nod, a curt word, and he was gone, pushing through the chattering knots of visitors Ottilia only now took in. She brought her gaze to bear upon the woman across from the body. "Do you know her, ma'am? Who is she?"

The woman's lips were trembling and her hands shook as she made a futile attempt to straighten the disarrayed gown, its folds caught fast under the legs, thrown ungainly out of kilter. "She is my nephew's wife. Isabel. Isabel Brockhurst."

The dread surname fell upon Ottilia's ears like stones into a pool, the ripples rapidly expanding in her mind as the implication lodged there, rock hard with foreboding. She did not hesitate. "Is she the girl of whom the Dowager Lady Wem so heartily disapproves? The misalliance?"

The woman bit her lip and her brows drew together. "What are you suggesting?"

Ottilia turned it back again. "How did she come to fall?"

The woman's face blanched the more. "No. Not that." A whisper, hardly to be heard.

There was time for no more as a man appeared above them both. "Give me leave, ma'am. I am a doctor."

Ottilia pushed to her feet. "It is too late, sir. She died on impact, I fear."

The doctor, a spare individual of a few more years than Ottilia herself, exhibited a prissy manner. "You will allow me to be the judge of that. Are you a relative?"

"Not at all, but I believe this lady is."

He turned to the woman, who had also risen, although she looked none too steady on her feet to Ottilia's sympathetic eye. "I am Doctor Heather, ma'am. I was exploring farther off or I should have presented myself at once."

The woman took his hand. "Annis Maplewood. I am one of her aunts."

He responded suitably and knelt to his pointless task. Ottilia, standing back, became aware of the world around them. The shouts and murmurs. Was someone crying? A bare few minutes had passed, she realised. There was still shock. And those above had not yet had time to come down. She remembered Francis was on his way there and looked again, in vain, for her own niece.

Her gaze dropped without will, passing over the dead girl from a better perspective. The face was quite lovely even though the waxy tinge of death was just beginning to overlay the skin. Pity bloomed in Ottilia's bosom, ousting the horrid spectre at the forefront of her mind. Snuffed out in an instant. Of inattention? Or had she lost her footing as the result of a judicious push?

Lizzy watched Vivian Maplewood rush to the scene of chaotic shifting bodies, too close to the edge. She was shaking but could not draw her eyes from the scene.

"What has happened?" Mr Maplewood asked his cousin, Marcus.

"Isabel fell. Daniel is out of his senses."

Mr Maplewood thrust a path to the figure lying prone along the rock, his bared head protruding over the gap, hideous groans issuing forth. He tapped the shoulder of a man bent over the figure and Lord Wem looked up, impatience in his features. "Allow me, sir."

Mr Maplewood's uncle looked sour. "He won't listen."

Mr Maplewood persisted. "Let me try, sir."

Lord Wem got ponderously to his feet. "Don't know why you think you'll have more success than his own father but do as you please."

Mr Maplewood knelt to his cousin, speaking softly. "Dan! Dan, it's me."

Daniel rolled over, clutching at his cousin, his dark hair awry under ravaged features. "She's gone, Viv! She went over. I've lost her. She's gone… She's gone…"

"Hush now, hush. I know, Dan, I know."

Daniel threw his arms about his cousin, buried his head in Mr Maplewood's breast and gave way to grief.

Lizzy's gaze was riveted to the scene, as she listened to the murmurs around her.

"*Is she really dead, do you think?*"

"*She cannot have survived.*"

"*If not dead at once, she soon will be.*"

Vivian Maplewood called out to her. "Lady Elizabeth!"

Lizzy started, with a shifting gaze, as if she knew not whence the call originated. Then her eyes found his. He spoke gently, but in command withal.

"Go back, ma'am! You are too close to the edge."

She looked, not at where he sat with Daniel, right over the precipice which had taken Isabel, but at the break between rock and sky. She wafted a hand.

31

"P-pray be careful, sir. You are much c-closer than I."

He pointed his chin towards safety. "Go back, Lady Elizabeth."

Lizzy wrenched her gaze off Daniel's heaving shoulders, and stepped back.

Mr Maplewood returned his attention to his cousin, whose sobs were muted now. "Dan, come. It is time. Let us go down to Isabel."

A groan issued from Daniel's throat. "I cannot."

"You must." Mr Maplewood spoke with authority, at the same time raising his cousin by force. "Will you let strangers take care of her person?"

Daniel sucked in a despairing breath and dashed a hand across his face, streaking moisture over his pallid cheeks. "Yes, I have to go down."

Lizzy watched as he stumbled at the first step and Mr Maplewood slid an arm under his shoulder, taking his weight. Lizzy followed them down. Just as he reached the path down, Daniel leaning heavily upon his support, Mr Maplewood turned back to face her.

"Lady Elizabeth."

"Mr Maplewood?"

He paused. "Would you do me the great kindness to find my sketchbook and bring it down?"

Lizzy was bewildered. "Your sketchbook?"

"I left it where we were talking. My hat too, if you please."

"Yes. Yes, I will find them. Of course, sir. Do you go on with … with poor Mr Brockhurst?"

Her voice hushed on the name and Daniel shivered in his hold. Mr Maplewood started off at once, calling back his thanks. "I am obliged, ma'am."

"Poor man! Poor, poor man! Oh, Uncle Francis, it is all so horrid!"

Francis, a trifle out of breath from his speedy climb, set a comforting arm about Lizzy's shoulder. "I know, child. A terrible thing to witness." His relief upon spying his niece as he arrived at the top had been palpable and he lost no time in pulling her back to safety. "Let us give place, my dear."

He drew her apart from the persons attempting to make their way down from the rock's summit, following the stricken young man. The dead woman's husband, he surmised.

"Who is the fellow who bade you fetch his belongings?"

He could feel the tremors that still shook her, and her voice was unsteady.

"Mr M-Maplewood. He is Daniel's c-cousin."

Francis wanted to know why Lizzy was on such terms with the fellow that he could ask her for this service, but he refrained from asking while she was still upset. Besides, there were more urgent questions Ottilia would expect him to ferret out.

He waited until the last of the company started down the path and the two of them were alone but for a straggler who had chosen to return to the edge and peer over. Francis could not see his face and doubted he would know the man in any event. He kept his voice low. "Who is that still up here, do you know?"

Lizzy lifted her gaze, seeming to squint a little against the sun which had risen high to glint against the surface of the rock. "Marcus Brockhurst, I think."

"Which one is he?"

"Another cousin. His father is Godfrey, Lord Wem's brother." She added, on a near whisper, "I don't like him much."

Francis's senses pricked. "Why? What manner of man is he?"

"I think he's false. Smooth-tongued. Too much so."

Taking due note of this, Francis ventured to pursue a line running in his head. "Who else of the family was up here, Lizzy?"

Her head turned sharp about and she looked up at him with a frightened expression. "Why, sir? Why do you ask?"

Francis did not enlighten her. "Do you not recall?"

She drew a shuddering breath and looked away, shifting out of his hold. Her voice came low. "I am not certain." She brushed the back of a hand across her cheek in a gesture that showed her agitation. She turned, pain in her eyes. "Not Mr Maplewood. He was with me. We — we were talking when…"

She faded out and Francis became brisk. "Go on. When?"

"Someone screamed." Her breath was catching as she spoke. "We heard — I heard shouting. Isabel. Her name. Then we ran. He ran, Mr Maplewood, I mean. I followed as fast as I could, and…"

"What did you see?"

"Backs. A lot of backs. They were all looking. Mr Maplewood pushed through. I couldn't see him anymore, so I went after him."

Francis might have asked why, but he had learned from Ottilia when to leave well alone. Such questions could come later. Let her tell it first.

"What happened then?" And the pertinent point. "Did you see who was there?"

"Lord Wem. His brother." Lizzy was calming a little with the concentration. "Mr Maplewood took Daniel in his arms. They were sitting at the edge. The others moved away."

"Which others, Lizzy? Try to remember, if you please."

Her glance went to the man now standing tall, a silhouette against the sky. "Him."

"Evidently. Come, think!"

"I am trying." She drew a breath, her tone impatient. Much more like the confident girl he knew. "The elder son, Julius. Daniel's brother. Those are all the men I can remember to have seen."

"The women?" Easy enough for a female to accomplish such a deed, if there had been foul play.

"I am not certain of the women. There may have been two. Oh, I did see Berta Brockhurst. And one other, but I could not swear to her identity."

At this point, the fellow who remained was seen to be returning across the rock and Francis hushed her. "No more now."

He took stock of the man as he neared, surprised he appeared to be heading in their direction. The fellow moved with grace and his dress, Francis recognised, was of fashionable cut and fit. The buckskin breeches fitted closely to his thighs, with several dangling fob ribbons and decorated knee-bands above gleaming top-boots; the coat moulded to his form with double-breasted waistcoat beneath and neckcloth tied in a bow.

Reaching within a few feet of where Francis stood with his niece, he swept off his round beaver hat, revealing glossy brown hair cut daringly short, and executed an elegant bow.

"Lady Elizabeth, your servant."

Lizzy's curtsey was sketchy, and Francis noted she stiffened. "Mr Brockhurst."

He pursed his lips and fetched a sigh. "An ill day. I am sorry you had to witness such a tragedy."

"I did not witness it, sir. I only heard the aftermath, which drew me hither."

"You are fortunate, ma'am." He gave a shudder in which Francis placed no belief whatsoever. "Dreadful. I was moved to contemplate the scene again." He gestured back towards the edge. "I could scarce believe such a thing had occurred."

Lizzy said nothing and the fellow turned his eye upon Francis, faint question in it.

"Forgive me, sir, but do I have the inestimable pleasure of speaking to Lord Francis Fanshawe?"

The urbanity was total. Was he utterly unmoved by the loss? Francis inclined his head. "You do, sir."

Another elaborate bow. "Marcus Brockhurst, my lord. I am relieved Lady Elizabeth has a protector in this sad hour. A terrible thing, shocking indeed to the fair sex."

The resumption of a look of spurious sorrow fairly disgusted Francis, but Lizzy beat him to the post.

"Should you not go down, sir? Your presence must be wanted."

He gave a sad little smile. "Oh, I will not be missed, ma'am. With my cousin Maplewood at his beck, dear Daniel can be in want of no other comfort. They are close, you must know."

Francis took a hand. "Nevertheless, sir, I must suppose your family will be gathering in preparation for removing the unfortunate lady to a more appropriate location."

Marcus gave an exaggerated start. "You are very right, sir. Remiss of me not to realise it." He bowed again, addressing himself to Lizzy. "Again, my regrets for your presence on this disastrous occasion, Lady Elizabeth. I can only hope it will not give you a distaste for the amenities of Tunbridge Wells."

Lizzy contenting herself with a curtsey, her lips firmly closed, with a word of farewell to Francis, he at last took himself off.

The moment the man had started down the path, Francis was treated to a low-toned tirade.

"You see! So false. Does he care a whit? You can see he doesn't. I should doubt any of them do. And that poor girl lying there all this time! Poor Daniel distraught. Oh, they are a vile set of people, Uncle Francis. Even if they did not wish for the marriage, can they not have a grain of pity? It is shameful. Evil! I wish I had not been here to see this."

Francis took one of the flailing hands. "Steady, my girl. You have seen only one behave in such a fashion. There is no saying they are all as callous."

Lizzy was not appeased. "But they are. Oh, not Mr Maplewood. Nor yet his mother, who is a pleasant woman from what I have seen." Her brow creased. "Was she up here? No, I cannot think she was. Mr Maplewood must have spoken to her."

"Speaking of whom, where is this sketchbook and hat you agreed to find for him?"

This ploy successfully diverted his niece's attention. The annoyance died out of her face as she turned about. "Along here, sir. I was exploring when I came upon him." She began to walk into a little sort of wilderness, oddly appearing at the back of the huge rock. "If I had not been dismayed by seeing all those Brockhursts crowding about the edge, I might have been there to see what happened."

"Then I am thankful for that at least," said Francis, following as she led the way. "Take care, Lizzy. This is particularly uneven."

"Oh, I know it. And there is no prospect from this side." She paused, looking this way and that. "I hope I can find the spot again."

"Look rather for that fellow's belongings, Lizzy. They must be out of place and thus noticeable."

It was not long before she uttered a cry and the sketchbook was found, a leather-bound volume, open to a page upon which Francis, taking it from Lizzy's hand while she hunted for the hat, discovered a sketch executed by a hand clearly master of its art.

"This is well done."

Lizzy was scouting the area. "He is very good, is he not?"

Francis began turning the pages, finding a plethora of drawn faces, a couple of which he recognised. "Your Mr Maplewood has been drawing his family members, it appears."

Lizzy turned, somewhat red in the face. "He is not *my* Mr Maplewood!"

Surprised, Francis eyed her, closing the sketchbook. Lizzy avoided his gaze, moving away to peer over a protruding stone. He toyed with asking what she meant by such vehemence, but she cut in before he could think how to word an enquiry likely to be taken amiss.

"Here it is!" She moved around the stone. "I have it. We had best go down, Uncle Francis, so I can restore them to Mr Maplewood."

Privately, Francis doubted the fellow would have any attention to spare for a mere hat and a sketchbook. He was like to be fully engaged when Daniel was confronted with the sight of his wife's dead body.

"Murder? Poppycock, child! If you are minded to emulate your aunt's propensity for discovering a crime in every death, I am done."

Receiving one of her mother-in-law's irascible stares, Ottilia, seated by the window the better to watch the comings and goings of the parading crowds on the Walks, was unable to withstand a smile of merriment. Not that there was matter for amusement in the tragedy. She was glad Lizzy had opted to pour out the tale to Sybilla but grieved to note how shaken the girl still was by her experience, as evidenced by the vehemence of her protest.

"You were not there, Grandmama. Those dreadful Brockhursts were nearly all upon the summit. Any one of them could have pushed that girl off."

"Steady, Lizzy." Francis put up a warning hand from where he stood at the mantel. "Throwing your tongue in this fashion can get you into all sorts of trouble."

"Only in the family, sir. I am not stupid enough to say it to any of the Brockhursts."

Sybilla snorted. "You had better not."

"And that vile Marcus creature had no true sympathy," pursued Lizzy, unheeding. "You may bear me out for that, Uncle Francis."

"He was certainly a trifle too smooth for one who had just lost a member of the family."

"But that does not make him a murderer, Francis. The child is raving."

Lizzy turned on Sybilla. "I am not, Grandmama. Any man must be careful of his wife's safety, or indeed any female. Both Mr Maplewood and Uncle Francis warned me away from the edge. Daniel must have done the same. Why should she fall?"

Ottilia caught a glance from her spouse. Had he a notion? Having no wish to encourage her niece's conviction, she said nothing. But her sharp-eyed mother-in-law had seen it.

"Why do you look at her so, Francis? What do you know?"

He looked down into his mother's face and gave a faint sigh. "There is no denying there were a number of Brockhursts at the scene, for I saw them after the event. From what Lizzy tells me, they were crowded at the edge."

"Yes, they were, all in a huddle." Lizzy threw a hesitating look at Ottilia. "At least, I confess I only observed that after Isabel fell."

Ottilia smiled at her. "Very good, Lizzy. Accuracy in these things is essential."

She received a black look from her mother-in-law. "You deign to enter the discussion now, do you? I suppose I may next hear you are bent upon discovering which of these wretched Brockhursts did the deed."

Before Ottilia could respond, Lizzy broke out again. "Oh, no, no, Grandmama. Pray don't blame Aunt Ottilia. She warned me several times not to jump to conclusions."

"To no avail, it would seem," Ottilia said, throwing her an amused look.

Lizzy sat down abruptly. "I can't help it. If you had only seen poor Daniel weeping in his cousin's arms! It was so affecting." She turned swimming eyes upon Ottilia. "I could not move from the spot, I promise you. Only when Mr Maplewood implored me to remove from the edge…"

She whipped out a pocket handkerchief and buried her face in it, and Ottilia glanced from her husband's rolling eye to Sybilla's exasperated expression. She got up and went to the girl, setting a hand upon her shoulder.

"You are overwrought, Lizzy. It is a horrid thing to be so close to such a dreadful accident."

Her niece looked up with a tear-stained face. "But it was not—"

"Let us assume it was exactly what it seemed, until and unless we have reason to suppose otherwise."

"But we have reason, Aunt."

Ottilia put up a finger. "No, we have not. We have only supposition and speculation. Even if it was a deliberate act, there is no possible way to prove it."

"My thought exactly."

Ottilia threw her husband a mischievous look. "I might have known you would be ahead of me."

His eyebrow quirked. "I had the advantage of you this time by virtue of chasing up that rock after Lizzy."

Sybilla banged her closed fist on the arm of her chair. "Cease and desist, the pair of you! Is this a moment for levity?"

"Pardon me, Sybilla, it is serious enough." Ottilia patted her niece's shoulder. "Try not to fret too much, Lizzy. It is tempting to put a worse construction upon what happened, and I confess I did wonder myself."

Sybilla pounced on her. "Aha! I knew it. Pray what made you think of it when you were not even a witness?"

"Unfortunately I was." Ottilia winced at the memory. "The girl fell almost at my feet."

"No!" Sybilla put a hand to her mouth. "How perfectly foul for you, Ottilia."

"Yes, it was."

Lizzy's eyes were round. "You never said so, Aunt."

"I did not wish to add to your distress." Ottilia moved to a chair. "I went to the girl at once, but it was obvious her death was instantaneous. Well for her, if I am honest, for her injuries were extensive. I could not wish anyone to survive such a fall only to endure a wholly crippled existence."

Sybilla blew out a loaded breath. "Just the sort of pragmatic view I should expect from you, Ottilia."

"Is it callous?"

"No, merciful," cried Lizzy. "It is the Brockhursts who are callous."

"Not Mrs Maplewood. She was there when I examined the body. She told me the girl's identity and she was indeed grieved." Ottilia did not mention the woman's instant comprehension of the possibility the fall had not been accidental, although she had rejected it with horror.

"I suggest we talk no more of the business," said Francis, moving to the bell-pull. "Shall I ring for refreshments, Mama?"

"Yes, do so, Francis. But it is of no use to try and suppress the subject. Nothing else will be talked of in this town for an age, you may count upon it."

"True, but we need not emulate the world and his wife."

Recognising her husband was trying to divert Lizzy's attention, Ottilia seconded his efforts. "You are quite right, Fan. We have aired it all sufficiently today. I think Lizzy in particular can do with some other diversion."

Lizzy fetched a sigh. "Well, I won't stop thinking about it. And I must find an opportunity to return Mr Maplewood's sketchbook and hat to him."

Sybilla stared and Ottilia was relieved when Francis took it upon himself to explain.

"Lizzy happened to have met the fellow just before the accident. He asked her if she would kindly retrieve his belongings, but everything was at sixes and sevens when we came down off the rock and Lizzy had no chance to give them back to him."

"Give them to Francis, Elizabeth. He may more readily do the business than you."

But Ottilia, seeing the dismay enter her niece's features, intervened. "I think Lizzy should be permitted to complete the commission. She was entrusted with it, after all."

"Thank you, Aunt."

The blush that accompanied the words told its own tale. Ottilia resolved to keep an eye out for this Mr Maplewood who had awakened Lizzy's dormant heart. Was he as interested?

Sybilla's maid entering in answer to the bell, she put in a request for Madeira to be served. "I dare say we can all do with fortifying."

Ottilia would have preferred coffee as was her wont. More so, since the suggestion to abjure the subject of Isabel Brockhurst's fatal fall had left an uncomfortable silence. But Sybilla was twitty enough without making an issue of it. She was trying to shake the inevitable questions in her mind in favour of some innocuous subject, when Sybilla let out a snort.

"This is ridiculous. We are all obsessed and I for one can think of nothing else."

Ottilia had to laugh. "I am quite of your mind, ma'am."

A sigh came from Lizzy. "Does that mean we may talk of it?"

"Not if you mean to continue with pointless speculation." Francis eyed his niece, who was biting her lip. "I don't mean to be severe upon you, Lizzy, but it is well to learn to think before you speak."

Lizzy looked abashed and Ottilia's sympathies were caught. "I believe Lizzy is learning."

She received a grateful look before Lizzy turned to Francis. "I know I am impulsive, sir. Papa always says it is my besetting sin. But…" With hesitance she glanced from one to the other, her gaze reaching Ottilia in an unmistakeable plea for help.

Ottilia smiled at her, braving the admonitory look on her spouse's face. "But?"

Lizzy avoided Francis's gaze. "Well, does it not set one wondering when one thinks of the circumstances? Isabel was a problem to the Brockhursts, was she not? Does it not seem horribly convenient that she died in such a way?"

Yes, and an unlikely coincidence. But Ottilia dared not encourage the supposition. To her astonishment, her husband capitulated.

"You are right, of course, Lizzy." Francis emitted a sigh in which Ottilia recognised the same resignation with which he so often greeted her pursuit of a like suspicious death. "That is precisely why I urged you to recall which of the Brockhursts were present while the image was fresh in your mind."

"Then you do think—"

"I don't think it, Lizzy," Francis interrupted. "Your aunt will caution you against making any such judgement without properly examining the evidence. And we have none."

"On the contrary. We have cogent evidence in an incontrovertible motive." Sybilla's black gaze swept over him, passed across Lizzy and came to rest upon Ottilia. "*If* there was foul play — and I stress the if — *if* there was, there is no shadow of doubt in my mind the Dowager Lady Wem ordered it."

CHAPTER FOUR

The Dowager Viscountess Lady Wem greeted her well-wishers with a politeness Ottilia considered spurious. Under the conventional veneer, her eyes were cold and a tell-tale muscle twitched in her cheek as she surveyed her alleged arch enemy. Urged thereto by Sybilla, Ottilia had accompanied her to pay her respects and condole with the Dowager Lady Wem's supposed loss. Their reception was frosty, among a party of female acolytes, the phrases of sympathy clearly unwanted.

"It is indeed tragic," stated the Dowager Lady Wem, sucking in her mouth and cheeks as if she had tasted a lemon.

She was a surprisingly small woman, enthroned in state upon a high-backed chair set in a prominent position. Three younger women were seated about her in the spacious though dark-panelled parlour, none of them as yet in mourning but, presumably for the sake of appearances, dressed in sober colours. To do them justice, it had been only two days since the tragedy and none of them were seen in church on the Sabbath, although the pastor had made mention of it, dedicating prayers to deceased and bereaved both.

The Dowager Lady Wem was regally attired in purple silk, which suited ill with a pallid complexion but set off her jet-black hair, worn banded under a small lacy cap and touched at the wings with streaks of grey. Ottilia struggled to find a trace of former beauty in the hollow cheeks, pointed nose and a face wholly lacking in animation. An upward slant to the eyes, of a dull grey, lent a faintly reptilian air to her countenance.

"A sad loss to you all, I make no doubt." Ottilia could not acquit Sybilla of relishing her words. To score off the rival dowager?

Sybilla's next utterance confirmed it. "Especially as I hear the victim was exceptionally lovely. You must have been so proud of your grandson's choice."

Oh, Sybilla. With a faint hope of checking her, Ottilia cleared her throat. Sybilla threw her a glance and gestured to draw her forward.

"May I present my daughter-in-law, Lady Francis Fanshawe."

Ottilia had been announced along with Sybilla, but the Dowager Lady Wem had paid her no attention. She turned at this and a serpentine glance traced Ottilia from her head to her heels.

"I have heard of you."

Detecting a note of contempt, Ottilia sketched a curtsey, but before she could formulate a suitable response, Sybilla cut in.

"I'll be bound you have, Protasia. My daughter-in-law is renowned in certain circles."

The Dowager Lady Wem's thin lips stretched in a friendless smile. "Indeed? I dare say such circles are outside my experience."

The studied rudeness of this remark provoked Ottilia to play it down. "Lady Polbrook exaggerates, ma'am." She produced her time-honoured excuse. "If I have a knack, it is merely in noticing what others might not."

Ottilia met the Dowager Lady Wem's blank stare, but in the periphery of her vision she noted two of the other women, who were sitting almost side by side, exchange a glance. The third, taller and thinner, but otherwise almost a copy of the dowager, stared likewise from a position a little behind the matriarch.

"And you noticed what?"

No appellation? Was Ottilia deemed unworthy even of a simple "ma'am"? Her ire rose and she retaliated without mercy.

"Oh, I noticed a great deal, Lady Wem. Your unfortunate relative fell but a few feet from me. Such a fall as destroyed her limbs and cracked her head open." A concerted gasp emanated from the three companions, but the dowager did not move a muscle. "A violent fall, to cause such damage, do you not think?" A pause ensued, in which she felt positive the company around held their collective breaths. Ottilia was conscious of Sybilla's tension beside her. But the Dowager Lady Wem proved equal to the challenge.

"The High Rocks are greatly elevated."

"So I observed," Ottilia retaliated, deliberately omitting any appellation, "but height is of less consequence than the manner of the fall."

The Dowager Lady Wem's lips stretched again. A smile or a sneer? "A scientific observation, Lady Francis. Are you qualified to make it?"

"My brother is a doctor, Lady Wem. I have learned of his lore."

"Indeed?"

"Indeed."

The Dowager Lady Wem's lips remained tight shut. Her temper cooling, Ottilia began to regret having said so much. But she was not willing to apologise. Fortunately, Sybilla entered the lists.

"Protasia, I trust you will not object to it if I present Ottilia to your daughters?"

Did a spasm cross the Dowager Lady Wem's face? She gestured towards the pair sitting near each other. "My daughters-in-law. Mary Ann, wife to my elder son."

The current Lady Wem, a scared-looking, mousey woman gave a short bow with a murmured 'how-do-you-do'.

"Lillian is married to Godfrey, the younger."

The second, a stout dame with a prideful air, merely inclined her head.

Lady Wem senior gave a dismissive jerk of the chin towards the woman sitting behind. "My daughter Berta."

Ottilia received a supercilious smile which did not reach the woman's eyes. But she chose to speak, in a reedy whine of a voice.

"We have heard the rumours, ma'am. People always talk. We pay no heed, do we, Mama?"

The Dowager Lady Wem's gaze passed over Ottilia and on to her arch enemy. "Sticks and stones, Sybilla. I make no truck with disparaging words. I never have."

"And who shall blame you, as prevalent as they have been? In your place, I should disregard them with equal disdain."

"In *your* place, Sybilla, I should not have attracted any. A pity one has so little authority over one's dependents. They are apt, once out of leading strings, to behave unbecomingly, don't you agree?"

As this was manifestly a dig at the marital antics of Sybilla's elder son, Ottilia expected a stinging reply. However, just as Lizzy had described, it came with a show of politesse.

"I agree implicitly, Protasia. Unsuitable marriages may cause a deal of unpleasantness within a family. Although I protest I am not so cruel as to wish the fate of my son's first wife upon his second."

The meaning of this was quite plain, as Sybilla's first daughter-in-law had been brutally murdered. Ottilia saw the impact in the flash of the Dowager Lady Wem's eyes, which were suddenly and startlingly afire. The expression sank rapidly, however, and a thin smile replaced it.

"To wish death upon one's direst enemy goes against any natural law. A nearer connection, and one fortunate enough to have gained the affections of one's grandson, must of necessity be immune to any such desire. Poor, innocent Isabel. I pity her with all my heart."

The words were accompanied by a dark malice in the dowager's grey eyes. Repulsion gripped Ottilia, together with a strong desire to be gone from the woman's presence. She acted on it without thought. "We have intruded long enough upon this stricken household, ma'am. Shall we take our leave?"

The Dowager Lady Wem made no motion to detain them, barely glancing at Ottilia before returning her gaze to the Dowager Lady Polbrook. "I must thank you for taking the trouble, Sybilla."

"And I must thank you for your hospitality, Protasia. I take it we shall not see you in the Assembly Rooms?"

The Dowager Lady Wem put up her chin. "I do not believe in making a parade of misfortune. We shall appear as usual."

"That will provide the gossips with fodder to keep them happy for days," said Sybilla, the moment they were safely out of the huge house on the hill with the door closed behind them.

Ottilia felt it proper to enter a protest. "I am surprised at you, Sybilla. I had not thought to see such disgraceful conduct on your part."

Her mother-in-law snorted, pausing before stepping up into the carriage. "You can talk. I knew how ruthless you could be, Ottilia, but you put me in dread, speaking to the horror in such a fashion."

"She *is* a perfect horror, I grant you."

A crack of laughter escaped Sybilla and she took her footman's hand to climb up. Ottilia followed her into the hired landau, unfurling a sunshade reposing on the seat and handing it to Sybilla. She took it but saw fit to grumble.

"I suppose you are too hardy to need protection."

"What I need protection from, Sybilla, is not the sun which, for a wonder, remains with us today, but the battle royal engaged in by two stubborn dames."

Another comprehensive snort greeted this complaint. "Did you see how she evaded the issue? Pity poor Isabel forsooth! She could scarcely keep the satisfaction from her face. If she did not order it, which I do not for a moment believe, she is glad enough the girl is dead. Prating of tragedies and such. Poppycock!"

A shiver crept up Ottilia's spine, despite the warmth of the day. "Yet it is tragic indeed. So young, so lovely. I am sorry for her husband."

"How do you know he did not push her off himself?"

"To avoid further confrontation? To free himself of a burden that threatened the reputation of his family? It is possible, I suppose. Although by Lizzy's account his grief was genuine."

"Well, if that hideous female is bent upon thrusting them back into the public eye, you may judge for yourself."

Seizing opportunity while her grandmother's eye was not upon her, Lizzy retrieved the errant hat and sketchbook from her bedchamber where she had secreted them. She had already ascertained that Mr Maplewood, like the rest of his family, was not in evidence in the usual morning haunts. Truth to tell she had hardly expected it, but just in case, she had kept a watch upon the Pantiles with the excuse of needing to sit by the window for air. But with Sybilla out of the way and the weather so compliant, she must seize opportunity.

If she walked up the hill by way of the Common, she might expect Sybilla's expedition of condolence to be over before she reached the Brockhurst residence. Francis had not accompanied the party, she knew, for Ottilia had left him breakfasting. Thus, Lizzy reasoned, she ought not to waste a rare moment of freedom.

"I am going for a walk, Nancy," she told her maid. "If her ladyship should return before me, pray tell her I needed to stretch my legs."

She then hastened down the stairs and was out of the door before Nancy could make any objection. Since the lodging house backed onto the road that ran alongside the Common, it was an easy matter to step onto one of the paths criss-crossing the well-used expanse of green. Occasional fairs were held here, she had been informed, and in high summer there was dancing on the Common with lanterns set into the trees. This morning, however, the place was notably free of persons but for a man with a dog, a party of children playing at bat and ball and two gentlemen in earnest conversation moving at a slow pace along a path further up the hill.

Lizzy set off in that direction, stepping briskly but without hurry. She did not wish to arrive while her grandmother was still with the Dowager Lady Wem. Closing upon the path above she noticed the two gentlemen turn to come back again and experienced an instant catch at her breast. One of them was Mr Maplewood.

She stopped where she was, watching him approach. Her pulse became flurried and she was glad to think she was carrying his belongings, which gave her a ready excuse for accosting him. More so, because he was not wearing a hat. Nor was his companion, in whom she recognised as her gaze turned upon him, Mr Maplewood's bereaved cousin Daniel. Everything else but the horrid event at High Rocks went out of her head and she blurted his name before she could think of the unwisdom of drawing attention to herself.

"Mr Brockhurst, good heavens!"

The good-looking young man jerked up his head, showing Lizzy a countenance upon which his suffering was etched clear. He did not speak, but Mr Maplewood, spying Lizzy's burdens, drew him forward.

"Good day to you, Lady Elizabeth. Is that my sketchbook you have there?"

Lizzy's heartbeat went into disarray and she struggled both with embarrassment at her outburst and the breathlessness that attacked her in his presence.

"Yes, I have it. Your hat too. I was — I was coming to the house to give them … to deliver them." The two had come up to her during this and Lizzy found herself face to face with Daniel. "Mr Brockhurst, I am so sorry. It must be perfectly dreadful for you…"

His lips trembled visibly and he opened his mouth, but nothing came out. The pain at his eyes cut Lizzy to the heart. Impulsively, she put out a hand and clutched his sleeve.

"Do not answer if you had rather not. It must be hard indeed to respond to expressions of regret from strangers."

He gave a brief nod and a tight smile, and Lizzy saw his cousin had an arm about him. Mr Maplewood chose to speak for him.

"I've dragged him out, you see. It does no good to dwell on it and brood."

Lizzy released her hold, real concern in her bosom. "But perhaps he needs to talk of it. Do you, sir? Do you let him talk if he wishes, Mr Maplewood?"

Mr Maplewood's brows rose. "Are you a mind doctor, Lady Elizabeth?"

She felt her cheeks grow warm. "I don't mean to criticise, sir, only I hold a contrary view."

"Do you indeed? To what, may I ask?"

Goaded, Lizzy was moved to retort. "To your notion it is no good to dwell on it. How can he help dwelling on it? And if he is not allowed to express his feelings—"

"I do wish to," interrupted Daniel. "I want to shout of the injustice of it to all the world."

"Steady, Dan. There is no need to—"

"There is, Viv, there is. This lady sees it, if you don't." Daniel threw a wild gesture towards Lizzy, his tone passionate and low. "You bid me to quiet and try to make me eat, and I can't. I can't eat and I can't be quiet, don't you see?"

"Well, I wish you would at this moment, Dan," snapped Mr Maplewood with more asperity than Lizzy had before heard him use. "We are attracting attention."

"So what if we are?" Daniel pulled away from his supporting arm. "Do you think it is not known to everyone about that my Isabel is lost to me? Isn't the world and his wife talking of it?" He turned on Lizzy. "You know, don't you? They talk of it everywhere, do they not? You were there. You talk of it. Why must everyone talk of it but me?"

Moved, but yet conscious of Mr Maplewood's kindling eye, Lizzy stepped closer. "Oh, hush, sir. Talk of it yes, but we must find a more private spot."

She came under the ironic eye of Mr Maplewood. "*We?*"

Lizzy met it with challenge. "Why not? I am at leisure and happy to lend a listening ear." And to Daniel, "If you are willing. Sometimes it is easier to unburden to one who is not nearly connected."

Another wild gesture came from Daniel. "Anyone other than my near connections. They are all against me."

"Hey! Have I said aught to deserve this from you, Dan?"

"Not you. I know you stand my friend, Viv. You are not like the rest. Even Julius pinched at me, although I acquit Clarissa of complicity. She at least was kind to my Isabel."

Clarissa? Did Daniel mean Julius's wife? Lizzy had spoken to the Honourable Mrs Julius Brockhurst once or twice, and to the Wem heir not at all. This was hardly the place to ask for enlightenment. She looked about and spied one of the little copses away to the further end of the Common and remembered the bench set there. It must be dry enough and they would be out of the way of anyone but passers-by for it was situated well beyond the paths leading down to the Pantiles.

"I have it, Mr Brockhurst." Lizzy pointed towards the copse. "Let us go to the bench there and we may talk in relative privacy."

Mr Maplewood regarded her with a hint of exasperation. "You hold by this scheme, do you? When I have just managed to persuade him to quiet?"

Lizzy's gaze went to Daniel, who was looking subdued and sulky. Impulse took over and she swept a gesture with her free hand to encompass him as she spoke. "Does he look satisfied? You are making him bottle it all up. Let him get it out, sir, for heaven's sake! He will be the better for doing so."

Daniel grasped her hand. "What angel sent you here just when I need you? Thank you, thank you a thousand times."

Lizzy threw a triumphant look at Mr Maplewood, who rolled his eyes.

"Do as you please, though anyone less angelic I have yet to meet."

She put up her chin. "Your opinion, Mr Maplewood, is of no consequence."

To her chagrin, amusement crept into his eyes, but he did not retaliate, instead taking the sketchbook out of her clutch. "Allow me to relieve you of those burdens, thoroughly despised by this time, I make no doubt."

Incensed, Lizzy thrust his hat at him. "I am not going to bandy words with you, Mr Maplewood. Your cousin's needs are exercising me more at this moment than your propensity to provoke me."

His amusement deepened, but he thankfully refrained from retort. "Lead on, then, Lady Elizabeth."

She turned pointedly to Daniel, who was frowning as he watched the give and take of words. It seemed to Lizzy he could not take it in. Perhaps nothing registered with him that did not pertain to his trouble. She smiled at him and tucked a hand in his arm.

"Come, Mr Brockhurst. Walk with me."

His condition made him biddable and she found it easy to draw him in the direction of the copse, conscious nevertheless of Mr Maplewood trailing behind. Her attention was reclaimed immediately as Daniel burst out again: "I can't believe she's gone. I saw it and still I don't believe it. It's like a dream. A nightmare."

His voice was rising and Lizzy cast an apprehensive glance behind her. Mr Maplewood caught her eye and flicked an eyebrow upward as if to underline his disagreement with the whole proceeding. She squeezed Daniel's arm. "Wait only one moment, Mr Brockhurst. We will be secluded in a space and you may speak freely."

She heard him draw in a half-sobbing breath, but he was obediently silent. They gained the place she had selected in a moment and Lizzy quickly checked the wooden bench.

"There, dry as a bone." She thrust him down and took her seat beside him. "Now, sir, you may say anything you wish."

He did not avail himself of this permission immediately, but sat bent forward, his arms on his thighs, hands clasped between them as he stared at the ground.

Mr Maplewood stood a moment, watching him, and then sat on Lizzy's other side, set the hat on his bare head and resting the sketchbook on his knee, opened it to a fresh page.

All too aware of him, Lizzy could not avoid sneaking a look as he withdrew a pencil from an inner pocket and held it poised over the pristine white sheet. He turned his head and caught her staring. "What? I may as well use the time while you minister to the patient, Doctor Fiske."

A giggle escaped her. She choked it off, dropping to a whisper. "Be quiet, you wretch!"

She was treated to a grin, followed immediately by a dig from his elbow and a nod towards his cousin. Lizzy turned to find Mr Brockhurst's shoulders heaving, breathy sobs emanating from his chest. Without thinking, she set an arm about him, moving closer, soothing words on her lips.

"Daniel, Daniel, don't … pray don't grieve so."

A mutter reached her. "So much for letting him get it all out."

Lizzy threw Mr Maplewood a glare, but she changed tack, setting a hand to Daniel's arm and patting. "There, poor man, weep if you wish. I shall not prevent you."

Her words had an opposite effect, for Daniel dashed a hand across his eyes, straightened up and dug out a pocket handkerchief. He made use of it; his husky speech muffled. "I beg your pardon. I did not mean to break down. It was only thinking of it again, you see. I had forgot." His voice grew stronger as he crumpled the handkerchief in unquiet fingers. "I thought I had her fast. I was holding her hand as she looked over. I can't think how it happened. My hold must have loosened, or she let go. I don't know. Next instant, she was gone." He thrust his fists against his head, agony in his voice. "I didn't even think to grab her. So fast … so fast… How? How?"

He turned to Lizzy; his countenance once again ravaged. "One of them did it, I swear. One of them, I don't know which. I can't see any more. I try to picture who was there, behind her, and I can't. Someone. One of them must have pushed her. She couldn't just fall like that."

The images he was conjuring formed themselves in Lizzy's horrified imagination. It was just as she suspected. She did not hesitate.

"I thought that too, Daniel. Do you suppose it was because your family disapproved of poor Isabel?"

"They hated her!" A vicious note entered into his vehemence. "*She* most of all. She would have done anything to be rid of my Isabel. She wanted to annul the marriage."

"You are talking of your grandmother? But she was not there, Daniel."

"She did not have to be. My father was there. My uncle. My aunts too." His eyes flared. "You know what they are saying? They are saying she jumped. Put a period to her existence."

Shock hit Lizzy all over again and she turned on impulse to Mr Maplewood, who was busy with his pencil, apparently

57

divorced from his cousin's present anguish. "For two pins I would seize that pencil and fling it into the bushes, Mr Maplewood. How can you calmly sit there drawing?"

He flicked her a glance but kept on with his sketching. "I have heard it all already, ma'am. Several times. From several mouths."

"Yes, my father's," Daniel broke in. "He said it first. He said I could not deny Isabel was unhappy. Of course I don't deny it. She was wretched. How would she be anything else with such a reception as she received at their hands? At my grandmother's hands?"

"Why did you come here, Daniel?"

"I was summoned. One of the rats betrayed me." He wafted a hand as Mr Maplewood's head shot up. "Oh, not you, Viv. I know you had no hand in that. I don't know who told her, but I would not put it past Marcus."

Nor would Lizzy, but she did not feel it incumbent upon her to say so. "But did you have to obey such a summons?"

He gave a defeated sigh. "I thought it would be for the best. I supposed, naively, a manly confession might win me absolution."

"Ha! From Grandmama? You were raving, Dan."

Mr Maplewood again, his pencil still driving across the paper even while he spoke. Momentarily distracted, Lizzy watched it travel, astonished by the outline vista appearing on the page mirroring the view below the Common, the lane beside it and a scattering of buildings beginning to take shape.

"Isabel urged it too," said Daniel, still heavily involved in his gloom-ridden tale. "It is our chance, Danny, she said. We may at last live in the open, she said." He fisted his hands on his thighs, tension in every line of his body. "She wanted to be accepted. Not for herself, or me. We were happy in our retreat, except that I had to leave her alone there too much. But once we had Pretty…" A low groan escaped him. "And how will Pretty fare now?"

Still with an arm across his back, her heart wrung, Lizzy yet caught at this new name. She turned her head to Mr Maplewood and half mouthed a whisper.

"Who is Pretty?"

He lifted his eyes from the growing sketch, casting a glance at Daniel's bowed head. "Pertesia. His daughter."

"Daughter!" His elbow dug her again and Lizzy dropped back to a whisper. "He has a daughter?"

Mr Maplewood's bright gaze found her face. "You are a little young to be suffering from incipient deafness, are you not?"

"I am not deaf!" But she was obliged to bite her lip. "I was merely surprised. And it is unbecoming in you to be trying to make me laugh at such a moment."

"I wasn't. It was a genuine enquiry."

"Oh, stop it, you provoking man!"

That glint of amusement reappeared and he returned to his sketching. Really, he was perfectly irritating. Why in the world she found him remotely attractive Lizzy could not fathom. Daniel's muttering threw guilt into her bosom. A good thing he was too lost in his own misfortune to pay the slightest attention to the little byplay. She broke into his murmurs. "Where is Pretty now?"

"Hepsie has charge of her, thank the Lord, poor motherless babe. Isabel was anxious for Pretty to be accepted, even if she was not. But Grandmama wouldn't even see her. She was furious when she learned we had a child. Isabel cried and cried. She begged me to take her home and I wish I had."

"Why did you not?"

"Clarissa said we should wait."

That name again. As of instinct, Lizzy threw a glance at Mr Maplewood. Annoying he might be, but he responded at once, rather to her surprise, but in a murmur.

"Julius's wife."

"Ah, I thought so." Touched by his tact, her feelings veered, but she was distracted by recalling the young woman as a flighty sort of female with whom she'd had little conversation beyond the commonplace.

"Clarissa came to our room. She was the only one of them to be kind. She kissed Isabel and said Grandmama had not been pleasant to her either at the start."

"Pleasant!" A snort came from Lizzy's other side. "That reptile has never been pleasant to anyone in her life."

Startled, Lizzy turned back to him. "Reptile?"

One eyebrow flicked up. "Crocodile. Snake. Lizard. Take your choice. Our esteemed grandmother fits them all." Amusement creased Mr Maplewood's mouth. "I do not scruple to say so to you as we have already exchanged views on our respective ancestors."

"I never spoke of Grandmama in such terms. Is Lady Wem so very bad?"

"Worse. If Clarissa supposed she might relent towards Daniel's wife, she has windmills in her head."

Daniel cut in with vehemence. "Clarissa was kind. Aunt Annis too, but Clarissa made an effort. She said we should wait a while, let Grandmama cool. She said I should take Isabel out of the house, go for drives."

Mr Maplewood abruptly rose from his seat, dumped the sketchbook on the bench and moved to confront his cousin. "Tell me this, Dan. Was High Rocks Clarissa's suggestion?"

Daniel stared up at him, a frown gathering. "I don't remember. I may have said it. Or she did. One of us. I only meant to go with Isabel."

Lizzy's mind was whizzing with conjecture. "But then they all decided to go?"

"Not then. I took Isabel for a drive. It was good to be out of there for a space. We talked of whether to stay or go. Isabel was calmer then and we did decide to stay for a day or two. God help me, I should never have persuaded her into it. I should have taken her away there and then. I should have——"

"Useless regrets, Dan. You could not have known what would happen."

Lizzy grasped the sufferer's arm with both hands. "He is right, Daniel. You cannot blame yourself. It will haunt you if you do."

"It haunts me now! Oh, Isabel, my Isabel!"

He broke down again and Lizzy, despairing, looked up at Mr Maplewood.

He met her eyes. "You still think talking of it helps, Doctor Fiske?"

She closed her lips upon a sharp retort, but the thought could not but obtrude she had blundered in where she had no right. He must know his cousin better, she supposed, aware the thought was grudging. She looked up again and found him watching her. "Must I say you were right? I don't know why you must needs pinch at me in that horrid way."

A faint grin showed. "Irresistible, my dear Lady Elizabeth." She made a face at him and he laughed. "Come, don't pout at me. It was worth a venture."

"What was?"

"This." He gestured towards her and his cousin.

Gratified, Lizzy found herself smiling at him. Mr Maplewood's expression did not change, but he stared at her for a moment in silence until Lizzy began to fidget. Then he took his cousin by the arm and hoisted him up.

"Come, Daniel. Dry your eyes. We are going to walk again and you won't talk."

Submissive, Daniel made use of Mr Maplewood's handkerchief and tucked it away. He turned to Lizzy as Mr Maplewood bent to retrieve his sketchbook.

"I thank you, Lady Elizabeth. Despite what Viv says, you have helped me."

Surprised, Lizzy took his proffered hand. "I did not think you heard all that."

"I am not deaf either." A tiny smile wavered for a moment and disappeared. He squeezed her hand. "You are a kind lady, ma'am, and I need kindness. Viv is a rough and ready taskmaster, but I need that too."

He released her hand. Impelled, Lizzy seized it again, speaking from the heart.

"I have no comfort for you, Mr Brockhurst. You must grieve. But it will pass. In time, it will pass."

He gave a nod but said nothing more and Lizzy saw his eyes were wet again. Mr Maplewood urged him forward and the two began to walk away.

What, no word of farewell from Mr Maplewood? That she would not endure.

"Mr Maplewood!"

He looked back over his shoulder. "Yes?"

"Do you not say goodbye to a person?"

A flick of that infuriating eyebrow. "To you, Lady Elizabeth? No, indeed. I say only *au revoir*." With which, he waved the sketchbook over his head and proceeded on his way, Daniel firmly back under his control.

Lizzy watched them go, torn between annoyance and a fillip of hope. And a niggling remembrance of the part played by Clarissa.

Ottilia found her husband in his shirtsleeves, ensconced in a comfortable chair, his feet resting upon a footstool, a jug of ale on the table at his elbow, absorbed in reading a daily journal.

"You look just like one of the valetudinarians haunting this town, Fan."

His eyebrow twitched. "A foretaste of things to come, Tillie." He struck the sheet with his hand. "The locals are up in arms at the notion they may expect a company to be billeted upon the Common here."

"Dear me, is that imminent?" Ottilia went to pick up the hand bell on the mantel and gave it a shake. "I am gasping."

"I'm not surprised if you insist upon visiting Mama's gorgon. And no, of course it's not imminent. The military may be preparing to assist Austria and Prussia, but the powers on high won't act rashly. Nevertheless, there are grumbling letters from residents."

"Is there nothing in there about this horrid death?" She sank into a chair opposite, thankfully untying the strings of her bonnet and setting it aside.

"A brief account only. There is far more attention upon this business of the mob attacking the Tuileries in Paris last week, although one cannot yet trust to its truth."

"If it is true, heaven help the Royal Family there. But what does it say of the fall?"

"Not much, despite the rumour mongers, my revered mama amongst them. You will find no lurid speculations in a respectable Tunbridge Wells newspaper."

He handed the sheet across and Ottilia found and read the snippet that told of the unfortunate fall from High Rocks of a member of a prominent family in the town.

"Did you mark the sequel in the last paragraph? *The tragedy has once more drawn to the attention of our readers the oft mentioned need for barriers and signposts warning of the dangers.* Too late for poor Isabel."

Francis took a draught of his ale. "How did you find the gorgon?"

Ottilia set the newssheet aside. "She is a very gorgon, Fan. Oh, she made a pretence of feeling the loss, but it was obvious she cared not a jot. You should have heard how she and Sybilla spoke to each other. Such barbed speeches, but politely done. Lizzy judged that to a nicety."

"I am thankful to have been spared," said her spouse with feeling.

Ottilia let out a laugh. "Yes, it would have driven you up into the boughs, my darling lord."

At this moment the footman entered, armed with a tray. "Coffee, my lady?"

"Ah, you have anticipated me, Tyler. What a prescient creature you are. Thank you."

The footman smirked a little as he set the tray down and proceeded to pour black liquid into a cup. "Your preference is well known to the household, my lady."

Aware of her husband's ironic eye upon her, Ottilia accepted the offering, laced with just the right amount of cream and sugar, and smiled up at Tyler. "I am well served by you all." The footman reddened a trifle, bowed and withdrew, what time Ottilia threw an admonitory glance at Francis. "Don't say a word, you fiend."

He raised his brows. "I wasn't going to. Not about your addiction, in any event."

Ottilia set her cup down in the saucer and shook a fist at him. His smile was both rueful and affectionate.

"Tell me about the gorgon. Have you decided she ordered this killing?"

"She is certainly capable of it. I found her abhorrent and she provoked me sadly." A sigh escaped her. "I'm afraid I behaved badly, Fan. You would have been ashamed of me."

"I doubt it, but try me."

Ottilia wriggled with discomfort and took refuge in sipping her coffee. "My only excuse, and it is a poor one, is that she was dismissive towards me. Even rude."

Francis sat up abruptly. "What? How dared she? I wish I'd been there."

"Pray don't get upon your high ropes, Fan. I retaliated."

"Good."

"Yes, but it wasn't good. I hinted at the proposition it had not been an accident. And I paraded my knowledge of medical lore. It was not well done of me and it has likely made it impossible to make any sort of headway with them all. Or at least, with the women who were present."

Francis, though he relaxed again, was still looking displeased. He was always jealously protective of her status. She found it gratifying, if restrictive at times.

"Why should you wish to make headway with them? The less we are obliged to hobnob with that crew, the better pleased I shall be."

Ottilia watched him over the rim of her cup as she sipped. Should she pursue this? He was bound to dislike it if she seriously took to looking into the death. Not that she supposed it possible to prove there had been foul play — if there had been. She hesitated too long.

"What is going on in that head of yours, light of my life?"

She prevaricated. "Why, nothing, Fan."

His gaze narrowed. "Don't fib, Tillie. I know that look."

To gain time, Ottilia concentrated on drinking. But the urge to speak of what had passed grew too strong to be denied. "Sybilla put forward the notion Daniel might himself have pushed his wife off the rock."

A startled expression leapt to Francis's face. "What? Surely not. Why in the world should he dispose of his wife?"

"My thought exactly, Fan. I could not satisfy myself that any motive of his would hold water."

"I should think not indeed. My mother must have got a touch of the sun."

"Oh, I don't think she meant it seriously. She is convinced of this Protasia's guilt, if anything."

She received a shrewd look. "But you are not?"

Ottilia had to smile. "I wish you were not so easily able to read me."

"I've said it before. You are transparent, wife of mine."

"Only to you, I hope, Fan."

He gave a rueful smile. "Tillie, you are a warm and open being. Duplicity is not in your nature."

"You would not say so if you had heard me speaking to Sybilla's enemy. I was disgracefully cryptic."

"Cryptic you often are, my dear one. But that is not the same as showing your true self to the world, which is what you do and I love you for it."

Gratified and touched, Ottilia felt warmth rising in her cheeks. "I think you hold a rather biased view of me, my dearest."

He smiled but refused the bait. "Tell me why you don't think Lady Wem enjoined someone in her family to rid her of this Isabel."

Ottilia was not quite sure of her reasons, but before she could answer, her mother-in-law's strident tones sounded in the outer corridor, speaking to one of the servants.

"Tell me at once, fellow. Is my grand-daughter within?"

Ottilia set down her coffee as Francis cursed, swinging his legs off the footstool and rising.

"Drat that niece of mine! What the deuce has she done now?"

No less exercised, Ottilia felt a trifle of exasperation rise in her bosom. Was the girl to be given no leeway? She could sympathise with the desire of a lively mind to explore outside of the humdrum existence open to females.

Sybilla was talking almost before she got into the little parlour. "If the wretched child is not with you, then where in heaven's name is she? One cannot trust anyone these days. I turn my back for a second, and what happens?"

"Well, what happens, ma'am?"

With a sinking heart, Ottilia heard the impatience in her husband's tone.

Sybilla threw her hands in the air as she marched up. "Gone! Vanished! That idiot maid of hers let her go off for a walk and she has not come back. Nor is she in the Assembly Rooms — not that I would sanction her going there alone — because I sent Nancy in search of her there and upon the Pantiles too. The wretched child is nowhere to be found."

Francis rolled his eyes and Ottilia made haste to intervene.

"If she has gone for a walk, Sybilla, I don't doubt she will be back presently."

"Yes, but why could she not say where she is going? She is in my charge. What am I to say to Harriet if I lose her?"

The querulous note betrayed her real agitation and Ottilia was about to soothe when an explosive sound came from her spouse.

"In Tunbridge Wells? For pity's sake, Mama, the place is scarcely a rabbit warren. She can't be lost."

"Then where is she?"

"I don't doubt she will be back in short order, Sybilla," cut in Ottilia. "You cannot expect a girl of her stamp to sit quietly at home with such stirring events on hand."

A glare came her way. "You mean Elizabeth is following in your footsteps? God help us all!"

"That will do, ma'am!"

Sybilla bridled, but to Ottilia's relief, a light footstep was heard in the corridor beyond, and Lizzy's voice calling out her name prevented the onset of a squabble. Sybilla's irate gaze veered to the doorway where her errant grand-daughter appeared.

"Aunt Ottilia, I must tell you— Oh!" Lizzy stopped dead, a comical look of consternation leaping into her face as she caught sight of her grandmother.

Sybilla lost no time. "And just where have you been, Miss? How dare you go off without a word to a soul? I have been worried sick!"

Typically, Lizzy became at once defensive. "I did say, Grandmama. I told Nancy I was going for a walk."

"Alone? Why did you not take your maid with you?"

"I was only going to walk on the Common."

Sybilla became icy. "Indeed? Then why, may I ask, did you have that sketchbook thing with you?"

Exchanging a startled glance with Francis, Ottilia stepped in. "You never said so, Sybilla."

Sybilla flicked a dismissive hand. "A detail. I had forgot it, as it happens." Her ominous gaze returned to Lizzy's now scarlet countenance. "What have you to say for yourself, Miss?"

Lizzy fidgeted, looking away. "It — well — it seemed a good opportunity to — to return Mr Maplewood's belongings."

"Did it indeed? You went to call upon the gentleman?"

"No! At least, not directly."

"What do you mean, not directly?"

Lizzy's agonised glance went from Sybilla to Ottilia. She at once came to the rescue. "You meant only to leave them at the house, I dare say. Is that it, Lizzy?"

A grateful glance was cast upon her. "Exactly so, Aunt. I thought, as I was walking, I might as well take the opportunity to do so."

Sybilla looked little appeased. "You knew I was visiting there. You could have given the things to me."

"I didn't think of it then, Grandmama." Lizzy's flush, which had begun to die down, flared up again. "As it happens, I — I met Mr Maplewood on the Common. He was walking with his cousin." Her eyes came back to Ottilia. "The bereaved cousin, Daniel."

Ottilia's interest quickened. "Ah, so that is why you came to find me?"

"Yes, indeed, for—"

"I have not done with you yet, my girl."

"Oh, Grandmama, pray—"

"Mama, let the girl speak. She may have discovered something of importance."

Throwing her spouse a grateful glance, Ottilia added her mite. "Indeed, Sybilla, I would like to hear Lizzy's account. Remember what you were saying in the carriage?"

Irritation showed in Sybilla's face. "Of course I don't remember. This child's antics have put everything out of my head."

Lizzy seized one of Sybilla's hands and held it to her cheek. "I am indeed sorry to have given you a fright, Grandmama."

"Don't you try to flummery me, girl."

But Ottilia noted Sybilla made no attempt to retrieve her hand, and her tone was less acerbic. Lizzy kissed the hand, producing a dazzling smile.

"You may ring your peal over me later, Grandmama, and I promise I won't say a word in my defence."

Sybilla grunted. "If I had my way, your uncle would take a stick to you. But I dare say he would refuse the office."

"I should. Emphatically. I have no wish to incur my brother-in-law's wrath, I thank you, ma'am."

"Nor would he dream of such a violent proceeding, Lizzy," Ottilia added, "and your grandmother does not mean it either, I am persuaded."

Lizzy's throaty laugh sounded. "Oh, I know that, Aunt." She threw a mischievous glance at Francis. "As for my uncle, he would have to catch me first."

Sybilla waved her hands. "Enough of this levity. Sit then. Sit, girl, and say your piece."

Nothing loath, Lizzy seized the footstool Francis had been using, plonked it at Ottilia's feet and sat down, by which time Sybilla had taken his vacated chair and he, retrieving his mug of ale, rang the bell. "Wine, Mama?"

"I will take Port, if I must have my time commandeered in this fashion."

"Lizzy?"

"I would be glad of some lemonade, if you please. I am hot from hastening back." She then turned to Ottilia. "Daniel is utterly cast down, Lady Fan. He is convinced one of his family pushed Isabel off that rock."

"Ha! Did I not say so?"

Ottilia could have laughed at her mother-in-law's instant change of face, but the proposition was too intriguing. "Why does he think so?"

The footman entering just then, it was a moment before her niece was able to tell her tale. The order for wine put in, Ottilia listened without comment to Lizzy's lively account of what Daniel had to say, taking due note of the mention of the female Clarissa. Not one of those she had met earlier.

"I could not but feel sorry for the poor man," Lizzy ended, "for he is plainly beside himself with grief."

"And therefore talking a great deal of nonsense, I make no doubt," put in Sybilla with another volte face. "One cannot take the maunderings of a person in such a condition with any seriousness."

Francis snorted. "Make up your mind, ma'am. A moment ago, Tillie tells me, you were convinced of the poor fellow's guilt."

"I am not convinced of anything, I thank you, but I shall air all the opinions I choose without incurring censure from an impertinent son."

His eye kindled. "If you are minded to be this crotchety, Mama, I have a good mind to pack Ottilia up and depart this very day."

Battle was fairly joined as Sybilla retaliated. Lizzy made a comical face at Ottilia, who put a finger to her lips, watching the give and take without interfering. It was plain Sybilla was revelling in the opportunity to disgorge her spleen and Francis was quite as capable as she of holding his own. Ottilia had a sudden vision of her spouse as an elderly gentleman, just as crusty and irascible, and had to bite down on a threatening fit of the giggles.

Before either party could annihilate the other, Tyler entered, bearing a loaded tray and bringing about an immediate silence. Francis seized on it, set the tray down and poured at once from the decanter into two glasses. Dismissing the footman, he took one to Sybilla. "Here. Drink this, for pity's sake, and let us have done!"

Sybilla took it, black eyes still snapping, and sipped. Ottilia watched her spouse throw back the contents of his own glass in one swallow and judged it prudent to break in at last. "Is that Lizzy's lemonade in the jug? Lizzy, why don't you—?"

"I'll do it." Francis poured out a full glass and handed it to his niece, and then refilled his own glass and retired to the seat by the window, turning his gaze upon the Walks outside.

An uneasy atmosphere prevailed. Ottilia tried for a neutral note, returning to Lizzy's encounter. "Which of the Brockhurst females is Clarissa, do you know?"

"I have only spoken to her once or twice. She is Daniel's sister-in-law, Julius's wife. He is the heir."

"Sickly."

Ottilia turned at Sybilla's cryptic remark. "Who is sickly, Sybilla?"

"The Honourable Julius Brockhurst. According to his mother, he has suffered one ailment after another all his life."

"Ah, that would be the mousey little creature I met today. Mary Ann, was it?"

Sybilla's usual dismissive gesture came. "A poor thing she is, too. I imagine Julius takes his constitution from her side."

"And Daniel does not?"

"I have no notion. The Brockhursts have not been in the habit of speaking about him. Until the fracas arose about his marriage at least."

She was sounding much more like her usual self and Ottilia could not but be anxious for her husband, still divorced from the discussion. Sybilla, she noted, cast one or two surreptitious glances in his direction. Would she make her peace? Ottilia's attention was drawn back to Lizzy.

"Aunt, do you suppose Clarissa might have been the conduit for a scheme to eliminate Isabel?"

Ottilia eyed the eager young face. "Why should you think so?"

Faint colour crept into Lizzy's cheeks. "Well, because it was the only thing in which Mr Maplewood took an interest. When Daniel was talking of her, saying she had been kind and advising him to take Isabel out for drives and so on, Mr Maplewood got up — he had been sketching, you know, and paying no attention because he said he had heard it all before — and he asked specifically if it was Clarissa who suggested the visit to High Rocks."

Ottilia's interest quickened. "And was it?"

"Daniel could not remember." Lizzy scanned Ottilia's face. "But don't you think it shows Mr Maplewood is suspicious?"

"Have you asked him?"

"I couldn't. Not with Daniel present. But it is perfectly plain he can't bear his grandmother. He called her a reptile."

A little shiver shook Ottilia. "I have to confess I found her snakelike myself."

"No wonder," came from Sybilla, her tone redolent of ancient enmity. "Protasia was ever a sneaking poisonous serpent, dripping venom. She near ruined my life once and her presence is threatening more damage now, making me vicious." She turned as she spoke and put out a hand towards Francis. "Come here, boy. I cannot be estranged from you too. Bad enough to lose my elder son's affections."

He looked round, the dark eyes sombre, wringing Ottilia's heart. But yet he hesitated.

Sybilla shook her outstretched hand. "Come, Francis. Come and kiss me. I will apologise for the whole."

His features softened at once and he rose, coming across to lean down to her. "It was not all your blame, Mama."

Her hand touched his cheek and Ottilia's bosom filled with emotion at the unaccustomed wetness visible in her mother-in-law's eyes. Sybilla's voice was husky.

"You know well how I value you, my son. Pay no heed to my megrims, I charge you."

The rueful expression Ottilia knew so well overspread his features. "I don't as a rule." He kissed her cheek and straightened, looking towards Ottilia. "I think I have been more overset by this business than I supposed."

"We have all been so," Ottilia soothed. "To be upon the spot when that poor girl fell was unpleasant in the extreme."

Lizzy chimed in again. "Yes, and that makes it even more imperative to find out if it was meant."

To Ottilia's consternation, she found not only Lizzy's gaze upon her in question, but those of her spouse and Sybilla too. As if she knew. She balked.

"Well, don't all look at me."

Francis lifted an eyebrow. "Why not? You need not pretend you have not by this formed an opinion. I have not forgot that when my mother broke in upon us you were about to tell me why you don't think this Protasia ordered the deed."

This brought Sybilla into play. "Indeed? And why not, pray? It has her stamp all over it."

Lizzy was eager. "Lady Fan strikes again! You have a notion who it was, have you not?"

"No such thing. How could I? I don't even know these people."

"But you don't fancy the Dowager Lady Wem for it, do you, my love?"

Ottilia sighed and capitulated. "Very well, if you must have it, I do not. A woman as despotic as she is, it seems to me, need not stoop to murder, vicarious or otherwise."

"Why not?" demanded her mother-in-law. "She is evil enough."

"So she may be. But her rule is absolute. Daniel said to Lizzy she wanted to annul the marriage. I am persuaded she is the type of person who would be confident of carrying through her design to be rid of her grandson's unsuitable wife without recourse to arranging her death."

CHAPTER FIVE

The great hall of the Assembly Rooms was rather too crowded for Ottilia's comfort. With her marriage had come the unfamiliar milieu of the high ton, rich in idleness and bent upon keeping boredom at bay in a succession of pastimes she found tedious. But people were ever of interest and the intelligence, conveyed in great excitement by Lizzy Fiske this Wednesday morning, that a flock of Brockhursts had invaded the Rooms, brought her hotfoot to the scene.

"I don't know what you expect to discover if you don't mean to mingle," complained her reluctant spouse, having found chairs a little removed from the throng, driven indoors with the weather at last breaking out in a storm in the night and leaving the air damp, the skies dull and the Walks still wet with a stack of umbrellas decorating the vestibule to the Rooms.

The Fanshawe's position yet commanded a comprehensive view of the gathering of Brockhursts at this end of the spacious room and Ottilia threw Francis a mischievous look. "I depend upon at least one of their number coming to me."

"Because of your hints the other morning?"

"Just so."

At this point, however, every visible member of the family appeared to be engaged with those intent upon proffering condolences. Or indulging curiosity. Ottilia gave herself an inward chiding for the cynical thought. Was she not just as guilty?

The Dowager Lady Wem, defiant in purple despite her care for appearances, had taken a prominent central seat, the same three women about her. They were accompanied by several males, who stood about in attitudes suggestive of guards ready to fend off untoward attacks. Indeed, each appeared to engage with a constant stream of well-wishers coming up, while others managed to slip through to beard the matriarch.

"They are all under excellent control," Ottilia observed. "She is like a puppet master."

Francis followed the direction of her gaze. "Lady Wem? Worse than my mother, you think?"

"Oh, she is a great deal more commanding. And she has no heart." The reminder sent Ottilia hunting the patrons. "Where is Sybilla? Did not Lizzy say she left her here?"

"Where do you suppose?" Francis's laconic tone held faint amusement. "Not even this stirring event could long keep Mama from the whist tables."

Ottilia had to laugh. "She must have discovered old cronies here then."

"Or made new ones. The place is chock-full of residents of similar years. Here is Lizzy again. She will know if it interests you."

It did, but not nearly as much as the young man who was approaching in Lizzy's company. He was a fellow of middling height, dressed rather more casually than fashion dictated in a brown frock-coat over buff breeches with a red-spotted handkerchief knotted about his throat in place of a neck-cloth and shaggy hair worn loose about a countenance unremarkable but for a pair of interesting eyes, both bright and humorous, that were trained upon Ottilia as the pair came up.

Ottilia noted the breathless sparkle characterising Lizzy as she pushed her companion forward. "This is Mr Maplewood, Aunt. He wanted to meet you."

Francis was rising. "Then present us properly, Lizzy."

The girl blushed a little. "Oh, yes, sir, forgive me." She turned to the young man with a look brim-full of mischief. "See how you have infected me, Mr Maplewood? He is an artist, you must know, which is why he does not think it behoves him to conform to convention."

Mr Maplewood's lip quivered. "And yet it is you, Lady Elizabeth, who is failing in your duty."

"Only because you provoke me into behaving badly, sir."

The indignant note was pronounced and Ottilia's suspicions deepened. Was Lizzy smitten? The object of her fancy gave no sign of discomfiture, but Ottilia saw a twinkle in his eye as he turned back to her.

"Present me, if you please, Lady Elizabeth."

"Lady and Lord Francis Fanshawe. Mr Maplewood."

"A trifle grudging, but it will serve. How do you do, ma'am?" He bowed, ignoring the little snort of annoyance emanating from his victim, and nodded towards Francis. "My lord."

Ottilia was obliged to suppress a giggle at the astonishment in her spouse's face, but he answered in a normal tone.

"I take it you are related to the Brockhursts?"

"For my sins, sir. As a rule, I keep well away, but my esteemed grandmother requires me to exercise my skills upon a family group. Duty thus called me here."

The undercurrent was anything but dutiful. Ottilia recalled Lizzy speaking of his dislike of the Dowager Lady Wem. Lizzy chimed in before either she or Francis could respond. "Tell them about Daniel's suspicions, Mr Maplewood."

He turned an ironic eye upon her. "I thought you had already done so."

"I only mentioned what he said yesterday when we spoke together."

"Then you have heard it all," said Mr Maplewood, turning back to Ottilia. "My cousin is ready, perhaps understandably, to accuse all and sundry of making away with his wife."

"But you don't believe it?"

He shrugged. "I don't know what to believe, Lady Francis. Dan is grief-stricken and incoherent for the most part. One cannot take his ravings at face value."

"I should imagine not," put in Francis. "Would it not better serve him to remove from the vicinity? To remain here must necessarily keep him in misery."

"He won't go, Uncle Francis. Mr Maplewood tried to persuade him, didn't you?"

The young man grimaced. "Worse. He keeps badgering me to take him back to High Rocks. Why he wants to relive the scene, I cannot imagine."

"Because he wishes to undo it," Ottilia said, speaking her thought aloud. She smiled at Mr Maplewood. "I dare say you find it frustrating, sir, but I expect your cousin is suffering from guilt."

Mr Maplewood's brows drew together. He lowered his voice. "Dan didn't push her; of that I am as certain as I stand here."

"If he had, sir, he would rather wish to avoid the place. It is telling he wants to go there."

Lizzy seized the young man's arm. "You see? Did I not say Lady Fan would have it unravelled in a twinkling?" She released him. "Go on, Aunt Ottilia. What else?"

Mr Maplewood did not speak, but his gaze remained upon Ottilia's face in mute question. She spread her hands. "I have no comfort for you, sir."

"But what do you think, Aunt?"

Ottilia sighed. "I think one cannot set much store by Mr Daniel Brockhurst's accusations."

"But the family hated his marriage, did they not, Mr Maplewood?" Lizzy threw a darkling glance towards the Brockhurst ménage, but, to Ottilia's relief, none showed any disposition to notice them.

Mr Maplewood did not answer, only keeping his gaze fixed as if he waited for what else Ottilia had to offer. She felt compelled to say more, reflecting this man might prove a useful foil to Lizzy's impulsive nature.

"It seems to me, sir, your cousin is looking for any means by which he may eradicate the past. Impossible, of course, but a common manifestation of grief brought on by such a violent and sudden taking off. He has to come to terms with it in his own way, do you not think?"

Mr Maplewood nodded, at last relaxing his steady gaze and glancing at Lizzy. "You talk sense, ma'am. Yet Lady Elizabeth is not wildly out either. Dan suffered cruelly at my grandmother's hands for his misalliance. She would not even acknowledge Isabel's presence with so much as a word. Dan's grief is compounded by resentment and the notion of one of our number having pushed Isabel is not as far-fetched as it might at first appear."

He had spoken in a tone even lower than before and Ottilia had to lean forward to catch the words. Interest quickened and she glanced up at Francis.

"Is there another chair or two nearby?" She added, as her spouse moved off, "Sit with me awhile, Mr Maplewood. My husband will find a chair for Lizzy."

A sudden grin split Mr Maplewood's face, bringing light to it in a way that gave Ottilia an inkling of his attraction for her niece.

"Lizzy?" Mr Maplewood turned on her with an unmistakeable tease in his voice. "I was going to make it Eliza."

Lizzy gaped, blushed and giggled. "Why Eliza, for heaven's sake?"

"Suits your propensity for mischief. Lizzy is much too sweet a name for you."

"Odious creature, how dare you? He is too provoking, Aunt."

Ottilia had to laugh. "Well, he is certainly blunt. And he has gauged you with some accuracy, I fear."

Lizzy broke into her infectious peal of laughter and Ottilia was intrigued to see how Mr Maplewood's lips twisted in amusement. Was there warmth in his eyes? This became a game worthy of examination. Did Sybilla realise what was going on under her nose? The fleeting thought her sister-in-law Harriet was unlikely to approve of an untitled suitor gave way to renewed interest in the Brockhurst death as Francis brought two more chairs and Mr Maplewood settled beside her.

Ottilia lost no time. "Which of your family was gathered upon the rock when Daniel's wife fell, Mr Maplewood?"

"I was not there, ma'am, but by the time I reached Dan, both his father and my uncle Godfrey were with him. Also Julius, Dan's brother."

Ottilia liked the ease of response, direct and open. He and Lizzy would suit admirably in that respect. "Do you recall any others?"

"Your cousin Marcus was there," chimed in Lizzy, "for he spoke to us after the rest had gone."

Mr Maplewood regarded her, his expression thoughtful. "I didn't notice him. Nor would I swear to one or two of my aunts being present. Or — stay! I vaguely recall a fleeting glimpse of my Aunt Berta. Yet I cannot now be certain. My attention was wholly on Dan at the time." He returned his gaze to Ottilia as he spoke. "We have long been friends as well as cousins. I have some influence with him."

"But not enough to stop him marrying the wrong sort of female?"

A grunt emanated from the young man. "I was ignorant of his intentions. And I would not have attempted to dissuade him if I had been privy to them. I am not a Brockhurst, ma'am. I do not share the prejudices of the rest of my family."

There was a hard note in his voice and Ottilia had no difficulty in divining his lack of fondness for the Brockhurst milieu.

"You are frank, sir," observed Francis. "The accident of birth may often prove a burden."

Mr Maplewood uttered a short laugh. "You may well say so, sir. In general, however, I do not allow myself to be troubled by them."

Did that argue a selfish streak? Ottilia could not avoid a glance at Lizzy, who sat watching Mr Maplewood with a singularly foolish smile on her face. Wearing her heart upon her sleeve, silly child. Willingly could Ottilia have shaken her. She made a mental note to have a judicious word with the girl.

Before she could put any further question, a violent voice cut across the general hubbub of the Assembly Room.

"Murderers! Devils! You cannot even mourn for her!"

"Oh, my God, it's Dan!"

Mr Maplewood was up even as the wild-eyed man came crashing through the startled patrons, handsome face ravaged, contorted as he yelled his grief to all the world.

"All here carousing while my Isabel lies cold in the dark."

"Damnation, I should never have left him!"

Any further mutterings from Mr Maplewood were lost as he headed for the fray, and then drowned by the uproar erupting from the Brockhurst circle.

"Be silent, sir! Have you lost your mind?"

"Daniel, for God's sake hold your tongue!"

Two of the men started towards the boy as he ploughed through, heedless of the craning necks and avid stares, of the heads and shoulders pulling out of range as he passed, still crying out accusing imprecations.

"You killed her! You pushed her! Everyone knows." He cast a wild gesture about the nearest persons, knocking off a hat in the process. "You know! You all whisper it, don't you? Don't you, eh? My Isabel is dead at their hands. Dead, you hear me? Killed, slain, murdered!"

By this, several hands laid hold on the man. Or tried to. Ottilia saw how his raving condition gave him strength enough to throw them off.

"They would do better to leave him be."

She had not realised she was heard under the continuing cacophony until Francis answered.

"One can't blame them for trying to shut the fellow up."

"Poor man. Poor, poor man!"

The husky note brought Ottilia's head round. "Do you weep for him, Lizzy?"

Lizzy turned swimming eyes upon Ottilia. "He is mad with grief, Aunt. Can't they see that?"

It was apparent this aspect of the matter weighed little with the Brockhursts. There were now three men manhandling the boy in an effort to get him out of the public eye. And failing dismally.

"It looks as if even your Mr Maplewood is to be unsuccessful this time."

"He is not *my* Mr Maplewood." But the indignation was superseded by a groan. "If they would just leave him to manage, he could do the trick."

"They won't," stated Francis. "Too embarrassing and too public."

The hoarse voice was still crying murder, but it was muted now as the initial shock subsided enough for onlookers to begin to murmur amongst themselves. All eyes were yet upon the struggle, however, and Ottilia only caught the flash of purple in the periphery of her vision before she recognised the Dowager Lady Wem.

"Good God, is the woman entering the fray herself?"

Ottilia did not answer, her gaze fixed upon the squat figure which thrust through to confront the boy, still twisting and crying out as he tried to rid himself of his captors. Lady Wem stepped up to Daniel and dealt him a cracking slap upon the cheek. Brought up short, he froze.

So sudden and shocking was the sight those within range fell silent and the ripple of murmurs died away swiftly. Into the hush came the clear commanding voice of the Brockhurst matriarch.

"You will cease this disgusting exhibition at once. Go home. I will deal with you presently."

An eon passed as she held Daniel's gaze. Ottilia could not look away. She saw him blink and thought he was upon the point of capitulation.

Then Daniel Brockhurst flung up a defiant head and, with clear deliberation, spat into his grandmother's face.

It seemed to Ottilia the world held still for a space while young and old eyes fought for supremacy. Then Lady Wem turned short about and strode back to her family group, one for one standing like frozen statues. Intent upon watching the

84

woman, Ottilia did not notice what transpired at the scene of battle until Francis spoke.

"Maplewood has got him away at last."

Ottilia withdrew her gaze from the matriarch, almost obscured now by the women gathering about her. Loyalty? Or merely expedience and quite as lost in the drama as the rest of the chattering world?

There was now no sign of Daniel, but the two older men were in low-voiced conference over by the entrance. Lord Wem and his brother?

"Would you believe it, Aunt? Lady Wem is sitting down again. After such an exhibition?"

Ottilia's glance flew back. The purple-clad dowager had indeed retaken her seat, her expression supremely indifferent. Her female companions were likewise settling again, although Berta Brockhurst and the sturdier of the daughters-in-law looked discomfited. The third was buried in a pocket handkerchief. Daniel's mother? The company had also been augmented by two males.

"Who are those young gentlemen, Lizzy, do you know?"

Her niece made a face. "The tall one is that awful Marcus. The other is Daniel's older brother Julius. You would think he at least might go after poor Daniel."

"That woman who is woebegone is his mother, is she not?"

"The younger Lady Wem, you mean? Only no one in the family ever calls her that. Mr Maplewood says everyone only speaks of her as Mary Ann and she is always weeping."

"Well, if what we have just witnessed is a sample of life in that household, no doubt she has reason."

"Yes, and she worries constantly over Julius's health, Mr Maplewood says. More than Clarissa does."

Ottilia was still taking stock of the young men, but she ran an eye over the women again. "You are talking of Julius's wife? She does not appear to be present."

"Yes, she is." Lizzy indicated a knot of people standing just outside the entrance to the card room. "That's her, the young one talking to Grandmama."

"Ha! I might have known my mother would not miss such a scene. Grilling the girl, I shouldn't wonder."

Ottilia had to smile. "No doubt, Fan. Let us hope she may discover something useful."

"For pity's sake, Tillie! You are not thinking of involving yourself with this crew, are you? After all that?"

"Oh, I think there are bound to be repercussions, don't you?"

"Well, you need not sound so eager."

Lizzy's throaty laugh came. "No less than I, sir. I am positively agog. I can't believe Lady Wem is content to remain in the Rooms after such a spectacle."

Ottilia surveyed the dowager viscountess, regal in her pose of indifference. "It is a testament to her strength of character that she does so."

"Heavens, Aunt, do you say you admire her?"

"Pardon me, but I don't believe I said any such thing. I disliked her intensely, but I admit her to possess a great deal of courage."

"Or is she merely too arrogant to care about the stares of the curious?"

"I think not, Fan. Had that been the case, I suspect she would have left the place in a good deal of disdain. That she remains to face it out argues a sort of defiant valour. She dares us to make an issue of the scene we have all witnessed." Ottilia at last looked away from the group and found her niece's frowning gaze upon her. "Well, what, Lizzy?"

A sigh came. "I shall never be able to emulate you, Lady Fan. How do you contrive to see these things?"

Francis cocked an eyebrow. "You've not taken your aunt's measure, child. She is a student of human nature."

Quick to hear the note of pride, Ottilia felt the usual flush of embarrassment and disclaimed at once. "I have no special powers, Lizzy. It is merely a trick of observation."

A snort came from Francis. "It's a great deal more than that and you know it, Tillie. I don't rate myself a fool by any means, but you leave me standing half the time."

"Oh, poppycock, Fan, if I may borrow from Sybilla." Ottilia was seized with mischief. "What of the other half, pray? Do you not outguess me all too often?"

He grinned. "Because I've learned how your mind works." He turned to Lizzy, who was looking from one to the other in a puzzled fashion. "Pay her no heed at all. She will be deep into this in no time." He pointed a finger. "But you, Miss Nosy, had best keep out of it."

Lizzy waved agitated hands. "It is of no use to say that, Uncle Francis, for I shan't be able to."

"No, because you don't wish to."

Ottilia intervened. "Come, Fan, it is too much to expect poor Lizzy not to be bursting for more. I dare say Mr Maplewood will be happy to satisfy her curiosity in due course."

This brought the flush to Lizzy's cheeks, and Ottilia hid a smile. But the girl jumped on it, nonetheless. "He will, yes. And I shan't hesitate to ask him. He is not like the rest of them, you know."

Francis cast up his eyes, but Ottilia cut in before he could make any remark.

"Why is Mrs Maplewood not among those present, I wonder."

"Because she is as much a rebel in her way as Mr Maplewood. At least, that is what I suspect. She avoids them, it seems to me. I certainly never saw her with the Brockhursts before all this began."

"Did she not attend the Rooms at all? How then did you meet her?"

"I have not met her, not officially. But I've seen her walking on the Pantiles with Mr Maplewood."

Ottilia eyed her. "Did he not think to introduce you?"

Lizzy became airy. "Oh, he could not, you know. I saw them from the window of our parlour."

Another of his snorts emanated from Francis. "You mean you were hanging out of it for the purpose of looking out for the fellow." He bent a mock severe gaze upon his niece, whose cheeks were afire. "If I am to stand in place of your papa, my girl, I take leave to tell you such conduct will not do. A little maidenly modesty would not go amiss."

Lizzy grimaced. "Oh, sad stuff, sir. Would you have me simper like a bread-and-butter miss? I decline to do anything so paltry."

Ottilia found herself the recipient of an exasperated look from Francis. "I am done. Try if you can bring her to reason."

She set a hand on his. "Don't fret, Fan. I suspect Mr Maplewood is rather taken with Lizzy's bold manners."

"Well, he has no manners himself, so he cannot expect any from me," said Lizzy with defiance. "Besides, it is ridiculous of you both to suppose there is anything... I mean, that I — that he — Oh, here is Grandmama," she ended on a note of obvious relief.

Ottilia cast a mischievous look at her spouse and gave a slight shake of her head. He put up his brows, but thankfully Sybilla descended upon them before anything more could be said. She proved to be in triumphant mode.

"Well, now you see what sort of a woman that female is and no mistake. Did you ever witness the like?"

It was some moments before Ottilia was able to break in upon her mother-in-law's animadversions upon the public display, said with clear relish. Ottilia could not but wonder again about the reason for this enduring enmity, but she had a more pressing interest. She put the question as soon as she could get a word in.

"What had this Clarissa to say of it all, Sybilla?"

Sybilla flapped a hand. "Oh, she was bent upon exonerating the wretch."

"Who — Daniel?"

"That too, Francis, but I meant that purple-clad monstrosity. Clarissa will have it she acted out of concern. Yes, concern for what people might think."

"Well, that is understandable," said Ottilia on a soothing note. "It was embarrassing."

Sybilla snorted. "Then she need not have added to it. Although Clarissa protested her brother-in-law needed a shock to bring him back to his senses. 'It is all too, too distressing,'" Sybilla mimicked in a mincing voice, "'and we are all so terribly, terribly sorry for poor Daniel.' Poppycock! They are one and all against the boy, for they have made that clear."

Ottilia frowned her niece down, for Lizzy showed every sign of dissolving into giggles at her grandmother's copycat tones. But Lizzy proved irrepressible, bubbling over as she spoke. "You sounded exactly like her, Grandmama. That is just how Clarissa talks."

"An empty-headed nincompoop she is too."

"Or a duplicitous conspirator." Ottilia then wished she had held her tongue for she came under the suddenly intent beam of Sybilla's stare and Lizzy, sobering at once, picked it up.

"Then you do think they are guilty!"

Ottilia hastily backtracked. "I spoke a thought aloud."

"But Clarissa was the one who pretended to befriend Isabel."

"We don't know it was pretence."

"You just said she was acting when she talked to Grandmama."

"Pish and tush, child! You must learn to distinguish between supposition and fact. Ottilia made no such statement."

Glad as she was to be spared having to say as much herself, Ottilia yet felt sorry for her niece, who looked crestfallen. On balance, best to let it pass. Except she was not permitted to do so.

"Yet I should like to know just what you did mean, Ottilia."

"She told you, Mama," cut in Francis. "You know her mind is lightning. She was making jumps. I dare say she doesn't yet know herself what she means." He turned to Ottilia with a wry look as he spoke.

She had to laugh. "True, Fan. I have not spoken with the woman so it is impossible to tell. But she at least talked with this unfortunate Isabel. She might have some notion of her state of mind."

Sybilla stared. "What has that to say to anything?"

"You are not supposing she did indeed throw herself off that rock, are you, Aunt?"

Ottilia clicked her tongue. "Did I say so? I am merely exploring every avenue. One can judge little without coming to understand the characters of those involved."

"Well, if you want to hear about Isabel, Mr Maplewood knew her," Lizzy offered, not without a faint colour arising in her cheeks.

His name provoked a memory in Ottilia's mind. "Or his mother. She must know them all well. Perhaps I may cultivate the acquaintance of Mrs Maplewood."

CHAPTER SIX

A tapping on the door wove into Ottilia's dreams and drifted away. Vague rustlings poked her mind. And then a whisper and a hand touching her shoulder.

"My lady! My lady!"

Ottilia jerked awake. The young face of her maid hung over her and she recalled it had been too hot to pull the curtains around the bed.

"Joanie?"

"I'm sorry to wake you, my lady, but she says it's urgent."

A question tickled Ottilia's mind, but it was still wreathed about with the mists of sleep and she felt sluggish. She had given in to her niece's persuasions to attend Friday's ball and the late night had taken its toll. She glanced at the sleeping form beside her and then at the shafts of light slipping through the partly open shutters. She struggled up onto her elbow.

"What time is it?"

"Just on six, my lady. I tried to tell her to come later, but she refused. She said as I must fetch you at once."

The low muttered words sent apprehension through her and identity became paramount as Ottilia pushed back the covers and swung her legs out, sitting up. "Is it Lady Elizabeth? Has she come about Lady Polbrook? Is my mother-in-law ill?"

Joanie was fetching her dressing-gown but she hissed across. "It's not young miss, but she's a lady, no question."

Sybilla? No, she would have come into the bedchamber herself. Then who in the world wanted her at this hour? She stood up, still a trifle disorientated, and allowed Joanie to help her into the robe. "Did she give a name?"

"No, my lady. Just said as you was needed straight."

Mystified, Ottilia tied the sash of her robe, scraped her loose hair back as best she could and dropped back down to the bed to shove her feet into the slippers Joanie had waiting.

"What in the world are you doing, Tillie?"

She swivelled to find Francis up on his elbow and blinking at her. Ottilia put out a hand. "Don't trouble, Fan. It is only someone with a message."

He glanced at the window and back. "This early? What, is it Mama?"

She heard the instant anxiety and made haste to disclaim. "Joanie says not, Fan. Let me find out what is so urgent and—"

"Urgent? Who is this person?"

"I have no notion," said Ottilia, rising, "but Joanie says she is a lady. I will have to go and see what she wants with me."

Francis fell back with a groan. "Oh, dear Lord, what now?"

Ottilia thought it prudent to make good her escape before Francis could break into further protest. He was bound to be testy at being woken too early, especially after he had been dragooned into dancing the previous evening, a pastime of which he was never particularly fond, let alone the hint of brewing trouble.

"She's in the parlour, my lady," said the maid, still whispering as she closed the bedchamber door behind Ottilia.

"Thank you." She bethought her of a need for immediate relief. "Can you arrange for coffee, if you please, Joanie? And see that hot water is brought up as soon as possible."

The maid went off towards the stairs and Ottilia glided across the hall and entered the parlour.

A woman was standing by the window, looking out upon what appeared to be a thankfully bright day, but she turned upon the opening of the door, showing Ottilia a face faintly familiar but etched with anxiety.

"Ma'am? You wanted me?" The woman did not move at once, but stood there, her mouth working as if she knew not how to proceed. Ottilia tried again. "Forgive my receiving you thus arrayed. I understood your need was urgent?"

At last the woman spoke, her voice rough with tormenting anxiety. "Urgent, yes. I did not know where else to turn. It is said you understand these things." She came forward then, a hand held out. "You will think me fanciful, I dare say, but I cannot let it pass this time."

Ottilia took the hand, aware this female was in something of a frenzy. She set herself to soothe. "Softly, ma'am, softly. May I know your name first?"

The woman put her free hand to her head. "Oh, how silly. Yes, forgive me. I am so overset I cannot think straight. I am Annis Maplewood."

The features at once clarified in Ottilia's mind. "Ah, of course. We met over your unfortunate niece's body." The words were out before she could stop them. *Wake up, Ottilia!* She squeezed the hand. "Forgive me. That was maladroit."

"It's true for all that. And what you said then could not but rattle away in my mind all these last days. And now — I cannot pass over this. I cannot, I tell you."

The scene at the Assembly Rooms leapt to the fore of Ottilia's mind. But that was three days ago. Naught had been seen of the Brockhursts in the intervening time and gossip had it the Dowager Lady Wem was keeping them all incarcerated until such time as the episode was forgotten or superseded by some other scandalous occurrence. Then that could not have prompted this visit. Nor the agitation and upset in the female confronting her.

"What is amiss, Mrs Maplewood?"

The visitor tugged her hand free and pushed away, fidgeting. "I hardly know how to tell you. How to speak aloud such black suspicion?"

Ottilia went to her. "Will you not sit down, ma'am?"

"I had rather stay on my feet. I am too restless to sit."

"Very well, but speak out, I pray you. What is troubling you to bring you to me thus early in the day?"

Mrs Maplewood threw out a hand. "Oh, because if I am right, you must come at once, must you not? You must see it for yourself, before…" The back of the hand went to her mouth as she gasped in breath.

Ottilia infused a trifle of command into her tone. "Before what?"

Out it came in a rush. "Before they manage to cover up the truth. The doctor has been sent for, of course, but there is nothing he can do."

An inkling of the trouble grew rapidly into a certainty. "Someone has died, is that it?"

Mrs Maplewood's eyes filled and her voice was a rasp. "Daniel."

Horror swept through Ottilia. "The bereaved boy?"

Tears were trickling down the woman's face but she disregarded them. "He was found by a servant who raised the alarm."

"Found how? I mean, where was he found?"

"In his bed. He's lying there, cold and still." Her voice rasped again. "I've seen him. It was horrible. Worse even than Isabel's death."

Ottilia kept her tone as cool as she could although the woman's oppressed condition was affecting. "Do you have any notion how he came to die?"

"None."

"Was there any sign of — pardon me for being frank — of distortion in his face? Of suffering?"

Mrs Maplewood shivered. "That is the worst of it. There is nothing. He looks as if he is sleeping."

No violence then? Poison? Laudanum? No point in questions. It was plain her visitor had no knowledge of what to look for. She was dashing the wet from her cheeks.

"The house is in uproar. They are saying he took his own life."

"Because of Isabel?"

Mrs Maplewood seized her hands. "You must come, Lady Francis. You must see him for yourself. They say he was mad with grief, that he had nothing more to live for, but it isn't true. There is Pretty, after all."

The name was new to Ottilia but she had no chance to ask for Mrs Maplewood's voice, gaining strength, became frantic.

"You can tell these things, can't you? You will know if they are lying. I thought of you the moment I saw him, for you were right about Isabel in every particular." The grip she had on Ottilia's hands tightened enough to hurt. "Lady Francis, I don't believe he died by his own hand."

The extraordinary arrival of her uncle while she and her grandmother were breakfasting took Lizzy aback. "Good heavens, Uncle Francis! I did not think you ever ventured out of doors at such an hour."

"It was not by my choice, I assure you," he said as he came up to the table. "Especially after you and your aunt must needs force me into unaccustomed exertion."

Sybilla gave him her hand. "Ottilia sent you, did she?"

Lizzy, not a penny the worse for last evening's hectic exertions on the dance floor, eyed him with a flicker of mischief as he saluted the hand and then his mother's cheek. "It must be something momentous if my aunt managed to persuade you to come thus early."

"Have you breakfasted?"

"He can't have done, Grandmama."

Francis was lifting one of the silver covers on the table. "I grabbed a bite, but I could do justice to a platter of bacon."

"There is plenty left. Eggs too. Ring the bell, Elizabeth."

Francis took a chair and glanced at the coffee pot. "Is that hot?"

Lizzy leaned across to pick up the hand bell and plied it, then passed him her unused cup. "You can have mine, Uncle. But you get no bacon until you tell us why Aunt Ottilia made you come over."

He was pouring from the pot, but he pointed a finger at her with his free hand. "Behave, Lizzy!"

"Yes, we'll have none of your sauce, Miss. Not but what I am quite as agog. Is something amiss?"

He gave a heavy sigh. "Very much so."

"Well, don't keep us in suspense, boy. Is it Ottilia?"

"No, no, she is perfectly fine. At least, she is well enough, apart from losing sleep."

Exasperation seized Lizzy. "Well, what, sir?"

But at this moment, Sybilla's maid entered and she was obliged to contain her impatience while Sybilla requested Alice to fetch another plate and utensils along with a fresh cup for Lizzy's use. The moment the door closed behind the maid, Lizzy rapped the table with her fork.

"What is it, sir? What has happened?"

An odd look of wariness crossed Francis's face as he looked at her. "I wish you won't fly into a fuss, Lizzy, though I suspect you may. Daniel Brockhurst is dead."

For an instant, the words made no sense. Blank of mind, Lizzy stared at him, hardly aware of her grandmother's exclamatory response.

"No! How in the world did that happen? Dead? When, Francis?"

"Overnight. He was found cold in his bed this morning." Francis's gaze was still upon Lizzy. "Are you going to swoon, Lizzy?"

A sharper note in his voice penetrated the dull cloud and she repeated the fell word. "Dead?"

"I'm afraid so."

Lizzy's pulse began to beat a heavy tattoo in her bosom. "He can't be dead. When we saw him last he was … he was vibrant … wild … how can he be dead?"

"Francis, she is incoherent! Come, child, drink something. Give her a sip of your coffee, Francis."

"A drop of brandy might better serve the case. I was afraid of this."

Francis was up and moving. From some distant place, Lizzy watched her grandmother, also on her feet, pick up the hand bell and the ring of it echoed in her head.

"Lizzy, drink this!"

A cup was at her lip. Without will, she opened her mouth and hot liquid slid onto her tongue, bitter and strong. The fleeting thought she disliked black sugarless coffee sang through her head and was gone. She swallowed and pushed away the cup.

"No more."

"Fetch the brandy decanter, Alice. And a glass. Quick, girl, run!"

But Lizzy desired no brandy. Her mind was clearing, thoughts beginning to form, the image of a face leaping forth. "Mr Maplewood! Oh, he will be anguished! Daniel is his friend, not merely his cousin. All he did to try and help him, and now this. Poor, poor man."

"Poor Mr Maplewood?" Sybilla's acerbic tone cut across the burgeoning distress. "Reserve your sympathy for the poor victim."

Lizzy's heart kicked. "Victim?"

"Steady, Mama. Let us not run ahead of ourselves."

Francis had resumed his seat and Lizzy glanced at him, her mind all at once ticking like a clock. "That is why Aunt Ottilia was sent for. They killed him too!"

Francis held up a hand. "Don't go off at half-cock, Lizzy. Until we know more—"

"But why summon Lady Fan otherwise? They must think it or they would not have done so. Who sent for her? Was it Mr Maplewood?"

A resigned sigh came from Francis. "His mother came. She was in a frantic state, Tillie said. The Brockhursts are saying the boy took his own life, but Mrs Maplewood refuses to believe it. She wanted Tillie to see him before—"

"Before they have a chance to hush it up. And they will. That terrible woman must have ordered it, carried it out even."

"Lizzy, be quiet!"

The sharp command brought her up short and she caught her breath. She threw him a deprecating glance. "I am being impulsive again. Aunt Ottilia would tell me to wait for proof."

"Quite right too," stated Sybilla, retaking her own seat. "Not but what I am entirely of your opinion. After the exhibition we witnessed the other day, I would believe anything of that vile creature."

The door opened again and the maid hurried into the room, carrying a tray upon which reposed a decanter and three glasses.

"Ah, well thought of, Alice. I can do with a tot myself. Do the honours, Francis."

The maid set the tray down by Francis. "I'll fetch the fresh cup and plate for his lordship, my lady. I'm sorry, but I didn't have time before the bell rang."

Sybilla waved this away. "No matter, girl. Off you go and fetch them now."

A glass was set in front of Lizzy. "Get that down you. No need to make a face, child, it's only a mouthful."

Reluctant, Lizzy handled it gingerly. A sip sent fire down her throat, but within a moment the ice in her veins began to dissipate. She held her tongue on the words begging to be uttered and slowly finished the dose, her thoughts concentrating upon the one most to be hurt by this turn.

It was strange to think of Vivian Maplewood in any mood other than the insouciance that characterised him, with the teasing look that infuriated and excited her in equal measure. But this was bound to distress him. The picture could not but obtrude of Mr Maplewood holding Daniel as he wept when

Isabel had fallen off the rock. Another crept in, of that walk and the talk she had with Daniel, convinced as he was his family had done for his wife. Had they now as surely done for him? Did Mr Maplewood believe it? The question threw her into speech.

"Did Mrs Maplewood say if her son thought as she did?"

Francis turned from Sybilla and Lizzy realised she had missed a low-voiced conversation between them. He still had a glass in his hand, but he tossed off the contents before he answered.

"She came alone. Tillie said nothing of Mr Maplewood."

Lizzy spoke her instant thought. "He must be guarding the body."

Her grandmother stared. "Guarding the body?"

"To stop them destroying the evidence."

Francis clicked his tongue. "Talk sense, Lizzy. What do you suppose anyone will do in such circumstances? No one who cared for the boy will be thinking of anything but his loss, including your Mr Maplewood."

"He is not *my* Mr Maplewood." The response was automatic, his earlier words in her head. "Besides, his mother thought of it. You just said so."

"Listen, child, I know what I'm talking about."

"He does," interpolated Sybilla. "He's been dragged into these things time and again."

Francis ignored the interruption. "The house will be at sixes and sevens, for one thing. A doctor has already been sent for, and it is likely he will call in the coroner. If I know the condition of relatives at such times, you may take it they will be huddling in discussion or lost in their grief. None are likely to be either coherent or capable of acting much beyond necessities. And that, I'll wager, includes Maplewood."

Rebellion rose in Lizzy's breast and she could not withhold her objection. "They were not in that condition for Isabel. And you heard how Lady Wem spoke to Daniel."

"But this is a son of the house, Lizzy. He may have transgressed, but his loss will be felt."

"Not by whoever did the deed."

"Elizabeth, that will do!" Sybilla pointed a fork at her. "Have you not listened to a word your uncle has said?"

Lizzy tossed her head. "I have and I hold by my opinion nonetheless."

Alice re-entered, armed with the accoutrements requested and Lizzy was abruptly glad of being stopped from declaring her intention of going up to the Brockhurst residence at the first opportunity. Grandmama would have a fit, and Francis would put his foot down. He was looking perfectly exasperated as he began piling bacon onto the plate the maid had set before him. Lizzy watched him reach to the covered basket for a roll. She passed the butter dish as Alice slipped out of the room.

"I doubt those are still warm, sir, but the butter will be soft from standing."

He lifted an eyebrow as he looked across, his knife poised. "Trying to turn me up sweet, Lizzy?"

She managed a spurious laugh. "I did not mean to be impertinent, Uncle."

Sybilla was engaged in drinking coffee, but she lowered her cup at this and Lizzy received a sharp glance. "What are you up to, child?"

Lizzy essayed her innocent look. "Why nothing, Grandmama."

"Don't tell me. Francis, she is planning mischief."

He glanced heavenwards and proceeded to butter his roll. "Whatever it is, Lizzy, don't do it, that's all. Though I dare say it is useless for me to say as much."

A giggle escaped Lizzy. "Well, at least I am not swooning, sir."

"No, but the alternative fills me with misgiving."

Lizzy let out a resigned breath. "Oh, very well, but it isn't anything dreadful, I promise."

Sybilla snorted. "Heaven help us all! I might have known it was asking for trouble to take you up, Elizabeth."

"So you might, ma'am, but the thing is done now." Francis's brown gaze met hers again. "If you think to beard this Maplewood fellow, Lizzy, I must beg you to have a care. If he is as fond of his cousin as you say, he is unlikely to welcome inappropriate questions."

"Beard the fellow? Gracious heaven, I should think not indeed! I hope you would have more conduct, Elizabeth."

Francis's perspicacity had driven warmth into Lizzy's cheeks, giving her away for sure. She preserved a prudent silence, taking refuge in pouring herself a cup of coffee and larding it with cream and sugar, avoiding the questioning eyes.

"Well?"

She looked across the table. "Well what, Grandmama?"

"Are you going to behave?"

Lizzy sighed. "Of what use to ask me, ma'am? I will take Nancy with me, if that will content you."

Sybilla flung up agitated hands. "Content me? No, girl, it will not. Do you suppose the fellow will welcome you?"

Lizzy lifted her chin. "I don't care if he does or does not, Grandmama. I cannot remain still when I know he is suffering."

She then wished she had held her tongue for a dismaying silence greeted this, her relatives exchanging an odd look. Sybilla's gaze returned to her face and her tone, for a wonder, gentled.

"My dear child, you cannot throw yourself at the man's head."

A sudden tightening at Lizzy's throat prevented her from speech. She struggled to suppress the threatening tears, the protests rising in her mind. Her grandmama had it all wrong. It was not like that. Mr Maplewood was not the usual kind of man, to consider an impulsive act of sympathy as a ploy to gain attention. But the implication she was setting her cap at him served to bring home the uncertain state of her heart. She did like him. Rather too much for her comfort. But she had never before taken the notion further, to consider Vivian Maplewood as her potential life's partner. That was going too far.

Her thoughts had carried her through the upset and she found herself on her dignity. "I consider Mr Maplewood a friend, ma'am. He is not the kind of man to take my approach in this extremity in any other spirit." She rose on the words and dropped a curtsey, crossing to the door.

"Elizabeth, wait!"

"Let her be, Mama. Ottilia is there, remember."

Gratitude towards her uncle flooded Lizzy, but as she gained her chamber and pulled the bell for her maid, her thoughts veered to Mr Maplewood and the happenings at the house on the hill.

The Brockhurst residence was a good deal quieter than Ottilia expected. She felt almost as if she was smuggled in, Mrs Maplewood ushering her through a side door and up a back stair and speaking in a whisper.

"I hope by this they are all dressing in their rooms. Although whether Leo has managed to drag Mary Ann away remains a question."

She hurried down a narrow corridor and halted at the end door. Ottilia saw, as it opened, that it gave into a wide vestibule with several doors off. Mrs Maplewood peered around in a furtive fashion and a little sigh escaped her.

"It looks as if the coast is clear. Come, but tread softly."

Ottilia was almost betrayed into laughter, partly brought on by the other's excessive caution and partly by the inevitable and familiar beat of excitement at the intrigue that could not but begin to grip. If Daniel Brockhurst proved to have been slain, the potential repercussions were legion, never mind finding out the responsible party.

She followed as Annis Maplewood tiptoed through the vestibule and halted again at the last door. Putting a finger to her lips, she signed to Ottilia to move out of sight of anyone within. She suppressed a flitter of impatience as her guide turned the handle and poked her head around the door. Her shoulders relaxed and she looked back.

"We are safe. It is only the footman."

Reflecting that the door ought to have been locked instead of leaving a man within, Ottilia followed Mrs Maplewood into a chamber lit mainly by candles, although the blinds were up, allowing light to filter in about the closed shutters, and the drapes were drawn back from around the bed and tied at the posts. A liveried fellow rose at once from a chair by the wall, but Ottilia's gaze riveted upon the still figure, covered to the chest in bedclothes, the upper torso and head exposed. Had he been left just as he was found? No attempt had yet been made to prepare the body for death. Awaiting the doctor?

"You may wait outside, John."

Ottilia turned to find the servant looking enquiry, his gaze going from Mrs Maplewood to herself. Was he about to make some objection?

"Stay by the door, if you please. Alert me at once if anyone comes."

The footman frowned but bowed. "As you wish, ma'am."

He cast another fleeting glance at Ottilia as he went. Mrs Maplewood spoke only when the door closed behind him, her voice a murmur.

"We don't need him watching what you may do. He has Leo's ear."

"Then he will likely tell him I have been here."

"Oh, they will all know soon enough if you find what I suspect." She then turned to the bed, her voice breaking. "Poor boy! He did not deserve this."

Ottilia wasted no words. Crossing to the bed, she twitched down the bedclothes and looked over the body. Just as Mrs Maplewood averred, Daniel looked as if he slept. There was no disarrangement of limbs to suggest he had thrashed about. His arms were flung, one out to the side, one across his chest. Blood had pooled on their undersides and the nails were pale. Ottilia touched the flesh on his open hand. Stone cold. She tested the limbs for rigor. Stiffening was there, though incomplete. She moved to the bed head and found both jaw and neck locked tight. He had been dead for several hours.

She bent over the boy's face. Was there a faint bruising around the mouth and nose? A trace of froth crept from one corner of the mouth. She pushed a finger between his lips and lifted the upper one, looking close.

"What is it? What have you found?"

The urgent murmur caught her off guard and she spoke without thinking. "Abrasions. The teeth have caused a trifle of bruising. It happens if they are pressed upon too heavily."

Mrs Maplewood gave a gasp. "Then it is as I thought!"

Ottilia looked up. "Not so fast, if you please, ma'am. This is no proof of anything as yet."

She felt the woman's agitation, although Mrs Maplewood said nothing more. Bending again, Ottilia lifted one of the closed lids. Bloodshot. A ripple went through her, but she suppressed the jump in her mind. Had Daniel been drinking, or taken some kind of sedative, that might account for the eyes. Both showed red veined lines across the whites.

Hunting, Ottilia inspected the skin of the dead face as closely as she could. A tinge of blue-grey? It was just visible under the skin. Veins looked to have broken across the nasal area, and a suggestive shadow high on the forehead made Ottilia lift away the dark lock of hair. The edges of the scalp showed slightly blue.

Certainty beginning to grip, Ottilia lifted Daniel's hand as far as the stiffness would allow and examined his fingernails. Pale, yes, but blue too. Faint, but it was there. A caution arose: that might be merely due to the onset of rigor mortis. But the signs taken together indicated otherwise.

She straightened, looking across at Mrs Maplewood's face of alarm. "It is not conclusive, I fear, but Daniel may have been smothered."

The other woman fell back, clutching her garments, a look of dawning horror splaying across her countenance. "It is so. One of them disposed of him. Oh, I had not dared to believe it."

Ottilia moved around the bed with swift steps. "You had better sit down, Mrs Maplewood." Guiding the woman with a hand to her back, she used a voice of quiet command. "Come, take this chair. Put your head down. Good. Breathe gently now."

Presently the matron was able to sit up, pronouncing herself recovered. Her white face belied her and Ottilia hastened to soften the blow.

"You may believe as you choose, ma'am, but as I said, there is scant proof here. What I found may as easily be answered by some other cause."

Mrs Maplewood's look was shrewd as she stared up at Ottilia. "But you don't believe that, do you?"

Ottilia did not gainsay her. "I do not, I confess. Taken together with Isabel's fall, I fear this small evidence is sufficient to convince me there has been foul play here."

The matron shuddered. "Yes. Yes, indeed. But who? Which of them would do this?"

"I imagine you can guess that better than I."

"No! I don't wish to suppose either of my brothers would go to such lengths. No, I cannot bear to think of it."

Ottilia hesitated but a moment. This woman was strong enough. "It is not beyond the bounds of probability for a woman to hold a pillow over a man's head for long enough to suffocate him."

Mrs Maplewood's expression grew fearful. "My sisters? No, no, Lady Francis, that I could not countenance. What, Mary Ann to kill her own son? Impossible!"

"Who, then? Your brother Godfrey's wife? Your sister Berta?" She did not add the one name that leapt to her mind. But Mrs Maplewood was ahead of her.

"Next you will accuse my mother of the deed!"

Ottilia became tart. "I am accusing no one, Mrs Maplewood. Without evidence? Certainly not. I only wish you to understand that if Daniel was indeed killed, the perpetrator could as well have been female as male." She put up a finger as the other opened her mouth. "And I would add, ma'am, you requested my presence here this morning."

Mrs Maplewood's breath left her body in a bang and she slumped in the chair. "You are very right. I beg your pardon. I am overset."

"It is understandable. But you may as well prepare yourself to be overborne if you intend to pursue this line. I cannot suppose any doctor will come to this conclusion. He will merely report his findings to the coroner, who will doubtless schedule an inquest. It is highly unlikely a verdict of unlawful death would be brought in."

Mrs Maplewood stiffened, rising suddenly. "They will not get away with this. Whoever did it will be found out, on that I am determined. Lady Francis, will you help me?"

Lizzy's breast felt taut as she toiled up the hill, immune to a chill breeze, although the skies were presently clear. The fleeting thought she ought to have brought an umbrella gave way to the notion of Mr Maplewood's unhappiness, which caught at her heartstrings. Not even remembrance of his provoking ways could reconcile her to the notion of his suffering as Daniel himself had suffered at the loss of his wife. Who was there to comfort him? Not his mother, who had come for Ottilia.

By the time she came within sight of the house on the hill, set back from the road in its own grounds like several others forming a row across the top of the town, Lizzy's steps began to lag. Her grandmother's admonition seeped into her brain. Was it too forward to be proffering her sympathy in this impulsive fashion? An apprehension, hitherto unacknowledged, attacked her that Mr Maplewood might reject the gesture. Resent it even.

Well, if he did, what of it? The thought of his sorrow was harder to bear than the possibility of repudiation. It was the right thing to do for a friend. The word echoed in her mind as she stepped boldly up the short driveway. Lizzy damped down the sneaking desire for more. Friendship was good. And this was one of its obligations.

On the thought, she approached the oaken front door with its old-fashioned arch and decorative iron bands and grasped the hanging bell to one side, pulling it with confidence and setting a peal ringing inside that quite startled her. Involuntarily she stepped back as footsteps sounded within. The door opened and a scared-looking maid peeped around it. Taken aback, Lizzy blurted out her piece.

"I am here to see Mr Maplewood."

The maid looked uncertain, but she held the door wider. "I don't know as he's receiving. I don't know as any of them are. I thought you was the doctor."

Lizzy lifted her chin. "No, I am Lady Elizabeth Fiske. Mr Maplewood will see me. Pray allow me to enter."

The youthful girl, who was plainly outside her role, hesitated. "Well, it's not a fit time, my lady."

Lizzy dropped into confiding warmth. "Yes, I know all about it. Mr Daniel Brockhurst has died, has he not? I am come to condole with Mr Maplewood."

The maid's face puckered and she let go of the door handle. "Terrible it is, miss. On Mr Lamport's morning off too. And John sitting with poor Mr Brockhurst and all."

Taking advantage of the girl's affliction, Lizzy barged into the house, patting a shoulder and deftly closing the door behind her. "I am sure it is perfectly horrid for you all, but you are doing excellently in Mr Lamport's stead. Pray where may I find Mr Maplewood?"

The maid sniffed, rubbing her sleeve across her nose. "I see him go into the mistress's study. Terrible he looked, miss — I mean, my lady."

An odd shaft went through Lizzy's bosom. Had she not known it? She ran her gaze about the dark hall, panelled throughout and devoid of light beyond that which came down from the gallery above a broad staircase. Could the study be through one of the doors leading off at either side?

"Direct me to this study, if you please."

The maid began to move towards the back of the hall, but stopped, turning in haste so that Lizzy, following, almost cannoned into her. "I don't know as I ought, my lady. No one didn't tell me to let in any but the doctor."

Lizzy smiled, speaking in a conspiratorial way. "I will not tell on you, I promise. Only show me where to go and you may return to your post to await the doctor."

Even as she spoke, the bell clanged again, sounding even louder from within. The maid, jumpy with the events of the morning, threw a hand to her bosom.

"That'll be him now. Ooh, miss, what do I do?"

"Quick! Tell me which is the study."

The girl, her eyes on the door, pointed back into the gloom behind the staircase. "Last one on the right, miss."

"Excellent. Off you go, now." Lizzy gave her a little push towards the front door and herself made good her escape, walking with swift steps in the direction indicated.

It was darker in the lee of the stairwell and she had to pause, peering to locate the door at the end of the hall. She could hear a man's voice at the front door and the maid's relieved response. This was then the doctor. Lizzy was glad of the concealment within the gloom and, her eyes becoming accustomed, spied the back wall and the last door even as the doctor's footsteps began to ascend the stairs. She moved to the study door and carefully turned the handle.

An excess of light from several windows made her blink, half blinded by the contrast. As her eyes adjusted, she saw Mr Maplewood sitting in a chair before a neat bureau. He was unmoving, staring ahead, his head resting on the fingers of one hand which were supported by his elbow on the arm of the chair. The other lay slack upon his knee. She guessed he had not heard the opening of the door.

With caution, Lizzy took a few steps into the room. He did not notice. She felt a catch at her bosom as his face came into better focus. He looked grey and drawn, defeated. So unlike the vigorous animation Lizzy was used to she could almost believe him a stranger. But, no, he was lost in shock and grief. She had come not a moment too soon.

Moving to his chair, Lizzy dropped to her knees beside it. Still he made no move. She stared up into the motionless face, her heart wrung. Without hesitation or thought, she slid her own hand under the slack one resting on his knee and cradled it.

His head turned then. A sharp movement, his gaze going to the joined hands and thence shifting up to meet Lizzy's eyes. He blinked, a crease appearing between his brows.

"Eliza. You came."

His voice was unnaturally low, thick with grief. Lizzy answered from the heart.

"Of course I came."

To her inestimable joy, his fingers shifted, lacing with hers. "Thank you."

Then he fell silent, his gaze shifting again, settling on the desk, although Lizzy was certain he saw nothing of the leather-backed blotter and the inkstand set before the bank of little drawers. Her heart swelled at this quiet acceptance. He understood and he was glad. It was more than she had dared to hope.

It seemed an age to her they remained thus. Her tongue hovered on a myriad words but she forced it to silence. He did not wish to talk — yet. Had he spilled his grief in tears? She searched his eyes for tell-tale redness and found none. She longed to berate him for bottling it up, but an unprecedented instinct bade her respect his wish for quiet. If this was his way of dealing with the loss, it was not for her to force him otherwise. Even if she yearned so to do. Even if her heart urged her to rise, to hold his head to her bosom and encourage him to weep.

His fingers moved, squeezing a little. "You are unusually quiet for a chatterbox, Eliza."

Startled by the ordinary note as much as by his resumption of that teasing quality he used with her, Lizzy fairly gaped. "I didn't think you wanted to talk."

His lip shifted, not quite a twitch. "I don't."

Remembrance of his words penetrated. "Am I a chatterbox?"

"As a rule, yes." He flicked a glance at her. "Oh, don't look so dismayed. I rather like it."

Lizzy's hand under his tightened involuntarily. Mr Maplewood looked at the hands and, with a certain deliberation, let go, removing his from the spot and straightening up at the same time. His tone became harsh.

"You had best get up and take a chair."

A hollow opened up in Lizzy's breast as a wave of disappointment swept through her. To hide it, she made a business of rising and looking about for a chair. He made no move to assist and she felt chagrined. His manners were atrocious. Even in this extremity, he might have made an effort to find her a seat. There was in fact only one other chair to be had, situated at a little distance and facing away from the one at the bureau. Lizzy took it, seating herself with dignified defiance without shifting its position.

Mr Maplewood, rather to her satisfaction, saw fit to shift his own chair around, partially rising for the purpose. He sat again, eyeing her in a fixed manner she found particularly unnerving.

"How did you hear? It can't be all over town as yet."

Hardly conscious of lifting her chin in the defiant way she had, Lizzy met his gaze boldly. "Your mama came to fetch my aunt. I heard the tidings from my uncle."

"And came to succour me? I thank you, Doctor Fiske."

Lizzy balked, despite the circumstances. "If you are minded to be sarcastic, sir, I shall take myself off again."

A spasm crossed his face and he threw out a hand. "No, don't. I need the distraction."

"I did not come to be a distraction, Mr Maplewood."

His mouth twisted. "No, you came to condole with me and bid me get it all out so you might pat me on the back and say there, there and think mere words might soothe the aching breast. Well, they won't, my lady Elizabeth. Don't waste them."

From some dim corner behind the hurt, Lizzy recognised a need he had to hit out. At something, anything. And she was there. Yet the wounding rejection made her feel physically ill. She did not speak. What could she say? But she was not going to look away from the eyes boring at her in that steely way. No longer bright, but hard and dull.

Mr Maplewood broke first, putting up a hand to half shade his eyes, his fingers rubbing at his forehead. The hand fell and he was frowning, his gaze narrowed. With pain this time?

"You should not have come. I am not fit company — for anyone."

Goaded, Lizzy hit back. "I did not expect you to be. Moreover, you thanked me for coming at first."

He looked away. "Did I? I don't remember."

She sat silent for a moment, willing the turmoil of emotion in her breast to quiet. She had come here to help, not to hinder. She must try. "Don't you want to talk of him?"

"No!" Swift and cruelly fierce. "If I talk, I will say things I must regret. Best to keep mum, don't you think?" His mouth twisted again, almost contemptuous. "No, you don't, do you? What was it you said? You hold a contrary view."

Lizzy struggled with the rising fury. "I shall not answer you, sir. I cannot engage to speak with any moderation if I do, and it is scarcely appropriate for me to be haranguing you at such a time."

He jerked his head up. "Harangue me as much as you wish, Eliza. I shall welcome it."

Incensed, she rose. "I see what it is. You wish to use me for your whipping boy. Well, I have no mind to be your butt, Mr Maplewood. I came in friendship. If you will have none of it, there is no more to be said." Seething, tears smarting at her eyes, she swept towards the door.

A violent motion behind her startled her into turning, just as Mr Maplewood came up. He seized her shoulders, his grip intense. "Don't you walk out on me!"

She tried unavailingly to wrench away. "Why should I not?"

"Because I need you!"

She stilled under his hands, her heart melting as she stared into the anguish in his gaze. He sighed out a breath and released her.

"I beg your pardon. Go, if you wish." He grimaced. "I'm not ungrateful." A mirthless laugh came. "I'm a boor at the best of times, and this is the worst. Will you forgive me?"

Lizzy was altogether touched. "Willingly. You are nothing if not honest, Mr Maplewood, and I like that."

"Vivian."

Bewildered, she blinked at him. "What?"

A travesty of a smile came. "I hoped you might dispense with 'Mr Maplewood'. My name is Vivian."

"Yes, I know. But — but I cannot call you so. It would be most improper."

"I didn't think you cared for propriety."

"I do. At least, I try to abide by the conventions. Unlike…"

"Unlike me? But then, as you have so sapiently stated several times, I am an artist. Artists are immune to convention."

The resumption of the teasing note both warmed and alarmed her. He ought to be grieving. Except he had made it plain he had no intention of sharing his grief. Even with her. The prick of the earlier rejection revived. She spoke out of it without realising.

"Yet you will not let a person in, Mr Maplewood, for all your scorn of propriety and convention. I think you are more private a person than you appear. Is it all a sham?"

A frown appeared, deepening the cleft between his brows. "Shrewd? Or are you trying to provoke me?"

Lizzy drew an unsteady breath. "I am trying to be to you what you evidently do not wish for. You have lost a friend this day. I cannot replace him. I should not have tried."

He did not speak, but the deadness returned to his eyes. Lizzy could find no more words. She had fared ill here, perhaps done more harm than good. She dropped a curtsey and turned from him, heading for the door. The hollow in her breast widened as she reached it, for Mr Maplewood made no move to stop her again. Nor did he speak, even to say a word of farewell.

Once on the other side of the door, Lizzy found her vision blurring. She made rather blindly for the light coming in at the front door and half stumbled as she reached it. There was no sign of the maid. With her hand on the doorknob, she paused, looking back towards the stairs. A longing to pour out her heart came over her. Where was Aunt Ottilia?

The silence of the house yawned at her. She was an intruder here, unwanted and useless. With unwonted humility, Lizzy opened the front door and quietly let herself out.

CHAPTER SEVEN

Ottilia was sat in a chair by the far wall as the doctor began his examination of Daniel's body. Mrs Maplewood entered the room with her son, Vivian Maplewood. The doctor straightened, disturbed by the sound of people entering. He turned an enquiring eye upon Mr Maplewood. "You are not Lord Wem, I presume?"

Vivian Maplewood went forward. "I'm Mr Maplewood. Mr Brockhurst is my cousin."

The doctor nodded. "Very well. Pray stand off while I proceed."

"I will remain here, I thank you. Perhaps you will be good enough to explain what you are doing, Doctor—?"

"Heather. I am sorry to be serving the family upon another unfortunate event."

"Another?"

From behind, Mrs Maplewood spoke. "Doctor Heather was present when Isabel fell at High Rocks."

"Ah."

The doctor bent to his task again.

"What the deuce are you all doing in this room?"

The irate tones of a man Ottilia recognised as Lord Wem brought everyone's heads round. Lord Wem looked grey, his long cheeks sunken, the lines between nose and mouth accentuated. His voice was unusually gruff, yet his manner was pompous as he turned upon his sister.

"Annis, you have no business here."

He threw a dismissive gesture towards her and moved to the doctor, who had straightened again. "Well? What say you? Is it suicide?"

Doctor Heather bowed. "As yet, my lord, I have not ascertained the cause of death. Give me leave, if you will. These things take time."

Lord Wem harrumphed. "Get on with it then." He appeared to notice Mr Maplewood for the first time. "You here, boy? What do you want?"

"The same as you, sir. To know how and why Dan lies dead."

Lord Wem flinched. "Don't use that tone to me, boy. You are talking of my son."

Mr Maplewood held his gaze. "I beg your pardon, sir. But you will admit it is of first importance to understand what happened here."

"What happened? What happened?" Lord Wem threw a wild gesture towards the unmoving occupant of the bed. "You can see what happened, can't you? Boy was in a frenzy, out of his senses. And now this!"

The doctor chose this moment to speak again. "My lord, I fear there is little indication of a possible cause to be seen here. A post mortem will be necessary. I will be obliged to report my findings to the coroner."

Lord Wem's gaze seared him. "Findings? You've just said there is nothing to see."

Doctor Heather coughed in a deprecating way. "As to the cause of death, my lord. There is question about his pallor, although it is customary for the extremities to turn blue. What I can tell you is the unfortunate gentleman has been dead some hours."

Mr Maplewood cut in. "How many hours?"

"From the state of rigor at this moment, I should say somewhere between five to eight, perhaps a little less or a little more. The present warmth may well distort the usual inferences. In these matters, there is ever a margin for error, my lord."

Lord Wem's agitation showed in his infuriated response. "This tells me nothing, sir. What I wish to know is what he took? He must have taken something, the Lord knows what."

The doctor cleared his throat. "We may know more, my lord, when the contents of the stomach have been examined."

Revulsion showed in Lord Wem's face. "Must it come to that?"

Doctor Heather became apologetic. "Without it, my lord, I fear the coroner will be unable to decide whether an inquest should be held."

"Oh, good God, this is intolerable! Inquests and coroners? Has not my wife borne enough?" Lord Wem threw a glance at the body on the bed that verged upon a glare. "Very well, if you must. But do the business as swiftly as you may and let us be done with it." With which, he turned his back upon his son's remains and stalked out of the bedchamber.

A silent witness to the interchange, Ottilia noted the doctor's sigh. He addressed himself to Mr Maplewood, who had been staring after his uncle in a manner that struck her as peculiarly belligerent.

"I fear his lordship is displeased with me, but there is nothing I can do."

Mr Maplewood turned a hard gaze upon him. "Yes, there is. You can tell me exactly what you have seen. Did you not speak of blue? Of his pallor?"

"It is faint in the face, particularly under the hairline. One cannot set much store by it. Indeed, as I told his lordship, there is no immediate visible sign to indicate conclusively why the gentleman died."

"No immediate sign? What does that mean?"

Doctor Heather pursed his lips. "A more thorough examination is needed." He lowered his voice, casting a glance at Mrs Maplewood, who was standing near the door. "I will say, however, I do not suspect poison."

"That is my uncle's supposition, not mine. Why don't you suspect it?"

The doctor spread his hands. "Poisons readily available are not in general palatable. But there is no contortion in the face. If he has ingested some substance for the purpose of taking his own life, I would expect to find a narcotic of some kind."

"Laudanum? He might have access to that."

"It is a possibility. I will know more once the post mortem is carried out." The doctor leaned down and carefully drew the sheet over Daniel's head. "Now, sir, if you will forgive me, I must go. My fellows will come for the body as quickly as I can arrange for its disposal."

Ottilia watched the doctor leave the room and rose, moving to join the Maplewoods, both of whom looked irresolute and anxious. Annis Maplewood spoke at once.

"You see? Did I not say my brother is determined upon suicide?"

"I dare say it is the only way he can make sense of it," Ottilia said on a soothing note. "Lord Wem is a good deal upset, and no wonder."

She was interrupted by the woman's son, his tone harsh.

"Is it true you think Daniel was smothered?"

121

She met his gaze. "There are signs he may have been."

"That doctor did not think so."

Ottilia kept her gaze steady. "He did not say so, no. Yet I cannot think he will have missed the indicative signs. He was thorough."

"Not as thorough as you were," cut in Mrs Maplewood. "He did not look at the boy's fingernails as you did. Nor did he check the inside of his mouth. I noted that particularly."

Ottilia caught a look of revulsion in Mr Maplewood's face as she turned to the mother. "But he did look under the eyelids. He cannot have missed the broken veins."

"Doctor Heather mentioned none of these things."

"Doctors are always cautious, Mr Maplewood. My brother rarely talks of his findings to relatives. They are apt to jump to conclusions before all is known."

"Like my uncle."

"Just so."

"Oh, Leo will force his opinion upon the fellow if he can."

"But Lord Wem will not influence a coroner, Mrs Maplewood. This is not his own ground and we must hope the local justice is not susceptible to family pressure."

"Or bribery." A cynical curl marred the young man's mouth. "The Dowager Lady Wem will not hesitate to use any weapon to hand if she wishes to hush this up."

"Vivian, for shame!"

"Well, she would, Mama. Lady Francis may as well know what she is up against. The crocodile will move heaven and earth to have her way and you know it."

Mrs Maplewood bridled. "I can be quite as ruthless as my mother, I will have you know, and I am equally determined Lady Francis will find out the perpetrator."

"If there is one." Ottilia was obliged to enter a further caveat. "And if no one is willing to speak to me, I fear there is little I can do."

"She's right, Mama. None of them will take kindly to questions, especially from an outsider."

Mrs Maplewood's eye became steely. "You underrate me, Vivian. As do they all. I will set the cat among the pigeons, if I have to, but I will not let this pass."

CHAPTER EIGHT

Partaking of a makeshift breakfast as she gave Francis an account of her visit to the stricken Brockhurst household, Ottilia became conscious of a degree of relief. She sat back and pushed away her plate, leaving a half-eaten roll and the remains of the sliced ham with which her spouse had supplied her. The action drew a frown from him.

"You can't survive on that, Tillie. Finish it."

"I have had more than enough, I thank you, Fan." She cast him a mischievous look. "I do not share your gargantuan appetite, my dearest dear."

He snorted. "I carved you a tithe of what I would eat."

"All I want is coffee, I promise you."

"If you didn't fill your stomach with that stuff, you'd have room for more food." But he replenished her cup all the same.

Ottilia took a satisfying swallow. "That is so much better." She smiled as he cast his gaze heavenwards. "Not the coffee so much. Just being here with you and out of that dreadful atmosphere."

Francis took a pull of his tankard. "With that lot in there? I'm not surprised."

"Well, I only saw the Maplewoods and Lord Wem, but the gloom was perfectly stifling."

"I imagine it might be. One cannot blame them, I suppose."

"Yes, but it is not merely that poor boy's demise. There is no light in that house."

Francis picked up her fork and speared one of the leftover pieces of ham. "If it is as dark-panelled as you say—"

"No, I don't mean that, though to be sure the hall is dimly lit and the shutters had not been opened in Daniel's chamber. It is as if a heavy weight descends upon you even as you enter the place." She gave an involuntary shiver. "Like a tomb."

"Well, with two dead in the space of a week, it practically is one," said Francis, making short work of the ham she had left. "What have they done with the girl's body, by the by?"

"I did not ask. I imagine she must long have been coffined. There was no need for a post mortem in her case."

Francis drained his tankard and Ottilia found his gaze upon her in a questioning look she knew well. She sighed. "It is of no avail to ask, Fan, for I have no slightest notion of where to begin. Moreover, I strongly doubt I will be permitted to ask any questions at all, despite Mrs Maplewood's determination."

"You think this dragon of a matriarch will hush it up?"

"I suspect they will all seek to do so. Lord Wem is intent upon his son having taken his own life. And if the family is ranged against her, I doubt Mrs Maplewood will make any headway."

He said nothing for a moment and Ottilia wondered if he was glad to think she might not be further involved. For herself, she was not certain whether to be relieved or disappointed. She could not help but be intrigued, although the prospect of dealing with the Brockhursts did not recommend itself to her.

Francis looked up abruptly. "Lord, if I had not forgot to tell you! Lizzy came back from seeing Maplewood looking hangdog. I've never seen her so subdued."

"Seeing Maplewood? Do you say she was in the house while I was there?"

He leaned in a little, setting a supporting elbow on the table. "She insisted on going up to offer her condolences. Mama warned her not to throw herself at the fellow's head, but Lizzy would have it they were friends. Only it does not appear to have gone well."

Concerned, Ottilia probed for more. "What did she say? I can vouch for it, Mr Maplewood is affected, but he appeared to me to be in command of himself."

Her spouse made a hopeless gesture. "She didn't say. At least, she said she thinks he was too raw to be susceptible to any comfort she might offer."

"Dear me, this is sad hearing. She is certainly smitten, but this does not augur well for his returning her regard."

"Just as well. Harriet won't care for the connection and I doubt Gil will be satisfied with a mere gentleman for a match. You know how he dotes on Lizzy."

Ottilia could not help bridling. "Well, if he does, Dalesford ought to be the more anxious for her happiness than to be marrying her off for the sake of a title."

Francis groaned. "I'm not pursuing an argument about this, my love, so for pity's sake don't start on one of your crusades for the underdog."

"Mr Maplewood is hardly an underdog. He has decided views and is, I suspect, a man of strong common sense. I think he would match well with Lizzy."

"Tillie!"

She waved the cup she was bringing to her lips. "Oh, very well, I am dumb. Although if he was not willing to accept Lizzy's proffered sympathies, the business is unlikely to come to anything."

An exasperated noise came from the other side of the table. "I thought you said you were dumb."

Ottilia let out a laugh. "I shall desist, O impatient one. What said Sybilla, by the by?"

"About Lizzy? She's whisked her away to the Tea Room to take her mind off it."

"I meant about the fresh murder, but that sounds a sensible move."

She came under the inspection of Francis's brown gaze. "You are certain it was murder then?"

"Oh, there can be no doubt." She set down her empty cup. "The traces are faint, as I told you, but they are there. It needs only for the post mortem to discover no sign of poisoning to confirm it. For me at least. The coroner may take a different view. Indeed, if there is evidence of a narcotic, which is likely for he did not struggle, it may well prove validation enough for a verdict of suicide."

As the day wore on, Lizzy's naturally buoyant spirits began to creep back. After all, Mr Maplewood had not been uniformly dismissive. And he had at first taken her proffered hand and been glad of her presence. She could hardly expect him to be thinking of her feelings at such a moment and it was scarcely surprising he had not welcomed her efforts to cheer him. Her conscience was clear. She had followed her instinct and that must content her.

These thoughts warred a little with the smart in Lizzy's bosom, dulled by the afternoon when she strolled out to idle under the colonnade while her grandmother took a nap. Several others were taking advantage of the renewed sunshine, but Lizzy avoided them. There was no saying when the news might be out and she dreaded talking of it with her special knowledge.

She dawdled along the row of little shops, peering through the windows in search of distraction. She could not conjure much interest in Pelton's the bookseller or Booty's, but there were several toy shops sporting knick-knacks of all kinds: snuffboxes, thimble-holders and pincushions; metal buckles, candlesnuffers and scissors, corkscrews, needle and bodkin cases and a profusion of gilt jewellery. A pretty writing box made of Tunbridge ware took her eye and she was about to enter this establishment when someone hailed her.

"Lady Elizabeth!"

It was not the voice she secretly yearned to hear. Turning, she beheld the dandified Marcus, dressed in garments unusually sober but not, as was fitting with his cousin but just dead, funereal. Lizzy's instinctive dislike of the man made her greet him with a little reserve, her dipped curtsey scarcely fitted to the elegant bow he made, sweeping off his hat.

"Mr Brockhurst, how do you do?" Recalling the unpleasant circumstances of the day, she hastily retracted. "Oh, I beg your pardon. How can you do at such a time? My heartfelt condolences, sir."

He assumed a suitably sorrowful mien which Lizzy at once suspected to be spurious. "Indeed, ma'am, it is a sad day for us all. If only dear Daniel had not been so deeply bereft. I fear he was frenetic to the point of madness."

With difficulty, Lizzy refrained from a scoffing retort. So this was how they meant to play it, just as Mr Maplewood had foretold. She tried for a sympathetic note. "Yes, indeed. The poor man was deep in melancholy, and no wonder."

"A terrible thing." Marcus pursed his lips. "I could scarce believe my poor cousin could be driven to such an extreme. We are all cast down." He produced a sad smile. "So much indeed, I was obliged to escape for a space." He waved a vague hand. "Fresh air, you know. So efficacious. I wish I might have persuaded my mother to do the same, but she professed herself too occupied with my poor aunt."

"Mary Ann, you mean," said Lizzy unguardedly.

He looked surprised. "The younger Lady Wem, yes. She is, as you may imagine, almost out of her senses with grief."

"I imagine she must be." The words were mechanical as Lizzy eyed him with growing suspicion. Why had he accosted her? Did he know of Ottilia's involvement? Was he bent upon securing her belief in his innocence, and his mother's too? It struck her Marcus might have the most to gain from Daniel's death. If the sickly Julius did not survive either, did he stand to gain the viscountcy in due course? It became imperative all at once to discover if the heir had any sons. But how to phrase it without alerting Marcus to her suspicions?

"I am sorry for your other cousin. Julius, is it not? He must feel this loss terribly."

Marcus shook a heavy head. "Utterly cast down. Clarissa worries this may bring on one of his turns. The poor fellow has never enjoyed robust health."

Lizzy leapt in, pleased with this ready allusion to a matter which ought to be strictly private. How fortunate Marcus had a gossiping tongue. "So I understand. I do hope he has not bequeathed his unfortunate constitution to his offspring."

Marcus responded to the interrogatory note without an apparent qualm. "Oh, his girls enjoy perfect health. Much to Clarissa's relief, I may say. The poor woman has a deal to bear."

"I dare say it is a worry for her," said Lizzy, eager to pursue the subject. She dared to probe further. "And the boys?"

His brows rose. "Boys?"

Lizzy feigned confusion. "Oh, I beg your pardon. You spoke of Julius's girls, and I wondered... But I should not ask."

He waved a hand in a delicate gesture more suited to a female than a man. "Ah, yes. It is a grief to our dear Clarissa to have lost the boys."

"She has no sons then?"

"Two, but neither survived infancy." He gave a somewhat enigmatic smile. "There is time. She is young yet." He then raised a hand to his head and struck himself a slight blow on the forehead. "I had not thought, but this business must provide a spur."

Lizzy agreed to it, but doubt began to creep in. Was it an act? He was altogether too smooth and she could discern no real sign of grief. Yet if he had indeed disposed of his cousin, would he be thus frank? To her, of all people. Foolhardy to talk so freely, if he knew there was a suspicion of Daniel having been done away with. And Marcus, she was convinced, was anything but foolish. She took the bull by the horns.

"I dare say you know my aunt was requested to go up to the house this morning?"

Was there a flash of annoyance in his eyes? If so, it was fleeting for he took it head on, curling his lip. "Ah, poor Aunt Annis. Deluded, I fear. My father thinks she took our Daniel's ravings to heart. Inevitable perhaps, since he and Cousin Vivian were so close. She is bound to support his interests at such a moment."

"His interests? But—"

"Oh, mothers, you know, are apt to protect their chicks. But to be setting the family at outs, today of all days!" He gave a scornful laugh. "My father will have it Annis was ever an odd one. There is never any saying what absurd notion she might take into her head."

Lizzy seized on the pertinent point. "Oh, dear, is the family indeed at outs?"

He made a wide gesture. "What would you? Dragging a stranger into our midst and making unfounded accusations."

"How can you know they are unfounded?"

The lip curled again. "My dear Lady Elizabeth, what possible reason could any one of us have to put poor Daniel out of the way? Merely because he had temporarily lost his reason through grief? Indeed, my uncle Leo was talking of having him confined for a space."

Shock ripped through Lizzy. "Confined? He was not a lunatic, sir!"

Marcus gave an eloquent shrug. "Debatable, ma'am, but be that as it may, his father merely meant he should be taken to some tranquil spot where he might regain his senses in peace. I believe Uncle Leo meant to request Vivian to accompany him." He heaved a sigh. "A vain scheme as it chances, since poor Daniel was a good deal more disturbed in mind than any of us thought for."

"Disturbed enough to take his own life?"

Marcus shuddered. "It does not bear thinking of. My hope is it will be found to be an accident."

Thoroughly roused by his insouciant attitude, Lizzy did not hesitate. "How, pray?"

"My dear ma'am, nothing could be simpler to explain. My aunt Mary Ann was dosing him with one of her witch's brews. Daniel likely took more than he ought in an effort to quieten his mind. I am persuaded it will be found to be so."

Convenient for him if it was, no doubt. "Let us hope so, for all your sakes." Her words felt as spurious as the ones Marcus had spouted. Not for an instant did she believe him sincere. If he was disinterested, he would embrace every possibility, would he not? She was abruptly on fire to know what Ottilia

131

might have discovered. She was about to excuse herself when Marcus spoke again.

"I understand you also paid a visit to the house, Lady Elizabeth?"

His eyes held a distinct challenge. Lizzy met it without hesitation.

"Indeed, sir. I wished to offer my condolences to Mr Maplewood."

"Ah, did you? I had not realised you were on such terms with my cousin."

"We are friends, Mr Brockhurst, that is all."

He smiled, but his gaze held a calculating look. "How quaint. A hardened case is my cousin. It is entertaining to see his armour pierced a little. I wish you all success, ma'am."

He bowed again and walked away before Lizzy had a chance to respond. She was glad of it, for she could think of nothing whatsoever to say. The warning was implicit. A feather brushed her heart. Coming as it did on top of the morning's fiasco, the words could not but revive a half-acknowledged thread of anxiety.

A welcome interruption came in the voice of her aunt. "Lizzy, there you are! I was expecting to be obliged to hunt for you in the Assembly Rooms."

"Easy enough to find me there, Aunt Ottilia," she said as she turned in some relief to greet her. "It is usually thin of company at this hour."

Ottilia's smile warmed her. "That was Marcus Brockhurst with you, was it not?"

Lizzy's dissatisfaction with the man rose up. "Hateful creature. He is convinced, or so he says, Daniel took more than he ought of his mother's concoction."

She received a shrewd look. "You don't believe him?"

132

"I don't believe anything he says."

Ottilia laughed. "Dear me, as bad as that?"

Worse, but Lizzy was not going to mention the last exchange. She warmed a little as Ottilia tucked a hand into her arm.

"Come, Lizzy, walk with me."

Lizzy willingly allowed herself to be drawn out into the paved walkway to stroll gently in the weak sun. The day was close but clouding over again, presaging more rain. A breeze fanned her cheeks and she recalled her aunt's earlier words.

"Were you looking for me?"

Ottilia gave her a direct glance. "I was. Francis told me you were not happy when you came back from seeing Mr Maplewood."

The smart returned with a vengeance and Lizzy blurted it out. "He was quite horrid to me, Aunt. Not at first. And he did apologise, in a way. He used me for a whipping boy. It was — uncomfortable."

"And hurtful too, I imagine."

The instant comprehension was balm, but it pricked so accurately her throat ached. She strove to keep her voice steady. "I presumed too m-much. He wasn't kind. You will say I could not expect him to be, and you are right."

"No, I won't say that. I dare say you took him by surprise."

"Yes." Lizzy was remembering it all. The harshness, her own grudging responses. "He seemed to wish for me, and yet he rejected me too. I don't understand, Aunt Ottilia."

The hand in her arm squeezed a little. "Take comfort, my dear. A man is never so open as when he is vulnerable."

"But he wasn't open. He closed himself against me."

Ottilia clicked her tongue. "I don't mean that, Lizzy. It sounds to me as though Mr Maplewood showed you more of himself than he would towards someone for whom he cared nothing at all."

A flicker of hope sprang up. "You think he does care?"

"More perhaps than he knows as yet. If I am any judge, you touched him on the raw, going as you did. He was unprepared. Shocked and grieving to boot. You likely saw more of his real feelings than you would at any other time."

Considerably cheered by this view of the matter, Lizzy replayed snatches of the interview in her mind and found less reason for despondency. "He did say he needed me. And he thanked me for coming."

"Well, that is excellent." Ottilia paused and Lizzy held her breath. "If you value my advice—"

"You know I do, Aunt Ottilia. I would be glad of anything."

Lizzy found herself at a standstill at Ottilia's urging.

"Don't wear your heart on your sleeve, Lizzy. Let him see you are strong enough to do without him."

"You think I did wrong to go then?"

"No, I don't. I think you did right. But it may serve you better to hold a little aloof. Let him come to you."

Lizzy was conscious of a fillip of apprehension. "What if he doesn't?"

Ottilia smiled. "Oh, he will."

"How can you be so sure?"

"Because a show of indifference will pique him. It is human nature, you must know."

Lizzy remained unconvinced. "But he's grieving. He won't think of me."

Ottilia's smile held mischief. "Your uncle Francis thought of me despite all the horror and upset of your Aunt Emily's death. If the spark is there, my dear, nothing will keep it from taking fire."

"But is it there?"

Ottilia laughed. "My dear Lizzy, you must be the judge of that."

Lizzy sighed. "I don't feel competent to judge of anything where Mr Maplewood is concerned."

A hail from above the colonnade caught her attention and she looked up to see Francis leaning out. He called down even as Ottilia waved to him.

"You're wanted, Tillie!"

The atmosphere in the Brockhurst dwelling was quite as oppressive as it had been in the morning, although there were sounds indicative of normal life. Ottilia heard voices coming from beyond a door to the side of the gloomy hall and a pair of whispering female servants, burdened with full trays, came down the stairs and slid away to the nether regions behind. The butler who had admitted her, back on duty this afternoon, began a stately climb and Ottilia followed.

She had with difficulty persuaded Sybilla against bearing her company. Sybilla was found to have arrived in the lodging just before the footman who had brought Mrs Maplewood's missive, hastily scrawled by the ink blots, and folded without a seal. It was brief and to the point.

"My mother wishes you to come and say to her face all that you said to me this morning. Pray make haste if you can. Matters are desperate."

Sybilla aired her views even as Ottilia was making herself mistress of these words.

"I don't see why you should obey such a rude summons. How dare that woman send to you in this fashion? Are you a lackey?"

"Oh, hush, Grandmama, of course she must go. Must you not, Aunt?"

Francis snorted. "Try if you can stop her, ma'am. She is itching to get her teeth into this, aren't you, my love?"

Ottilia had to laugh. "I cannot say I am looking forward to an encounter with Lady Wem, but I will admit to a deal of curiosity."

Sybilla threw up her hands in a gesture exactly like her son's when he was exasperated. "Well, if you insist upon going, I had best come with you. I must make a visit of condolence in any event. Moreover, I am loath to leave you to face that dreadful female alone."

But Ottilia had no desire to be hampered by Sybilla's presence. The enmity between the two women was bound to cause ructions just when she needed to employ all the tact at her disposal. "I think I will do better to be private with her if possible, Sybilla. She cannot eat me after all."

"I would not be too sure," said Sybilla darkly. "I have long suspected Protasia of practicing some form of witchcraft. One cannot else account for—" She broke off abruptly, her black gaze daring anyone to question it. "Well, that is neither here nor there." She wagged a finger at Ottilia. "Do not underestimate the woman. She is poison through and through."

Lizzy gave an audible groan and Ottilia made haste to respond. "I will be careful, ma'am, but I am in hopes she may be more forthcoming if I see her alone."

Francis, to her relief, backed her up. "Make your condolences at another time, ma'am. Lady Wem will not easily intimidate my woman of wonder."

He gave her an encouraging smile on the words and Ottilia had taken it as tacit permission to pursue her enquiries. Indeed, she suspected Francis was secretly interested despite his alleged dislike of the Brockhursts. Besides, he must know nothing untoward was likely to come of a visit to the Dowager Lady Wem. She was presently able to set forth with only Hemp for escort since she chose to walk. He was awaiting her outside, preferring to enjoy the rare English warmth, balm no doubt to a fellow brought up in Barbados.

The main stairway rose to a wide corridor and as the butler turned into it, Ottilia detected the sound of distant lamentation which grew louder as they proceeded. She glanced at closed doors as they passed, wondering which of the women was weeping. There was no sign of Annis Maplewood. Was she waiting with the senior Lady Wem?

Her guide went on by the door to the grand parlour Ottilia remembered from her first visit with Sybilla where the dowager viscountess had received them in state, and instead halted at one a little way beyond. Ottilia entered on the announcement of her name and found herself in a much smaller apartment, its décor quite as gloomy as the rest of the house. Chintz-covered chairs rendered the dark panels no more kind, although the beam from the window enabled her to make out a Chippendale card table with cabriole legs, a heavy secretaire filled with books set against one wall, and a gold-framed pier glass over the mantel of mottled marble.

There was only one occupant, seated in a chair by the window embrasure, the small figure silhouetted against the light. Ottilia could not tell whether Lady Wem was looking her way, but there was rigidity in the way she sat, upright and perched forward in her seat. She did not speak.

Ottilia moved towards her. "You sent for me, ma'am?"

A claw-like hand came out, gesturing to a chair opposite. Still she did not look at the visitor.

Ottilia was beset with a mixture of irritation and faint amusement. The woman's arrogant regality was almost theatrical. Then she recalled the woman had just lost her grandson and a wave of compassion loosened her tongue.

"I feel for you, ma'am. You have sustained a tragic loss."

A shudder shook the small frame and at last Lady Wem's gaze caught hers as Ottilia took the indicated chair. From this angle, with light falling on her face from the wide sash window, she was seen to be suffering. Her eyes were red-rimmed, her skin blotched and pasty, and the suppressed malevolence was missing from her demeanour. Was she human after all? Her voice, when she spoke at last, rasped a little.

"You made an observation this morning."

No appellation? No greeting? Was it to be thus? Ottilia groaned in spirit. Dealing with this woman was going to prove as tricky as she had anticipated. She answered in kind. "I did."

"Well?"

Ottilia hesitated, eyeing the woman with a resurgence of dislike. She was tempted to bat it out without preamble, but the woman had sustained shocks enough this day. "I am not sure what you are asking me, ma'am. Do you wish to hear my findings or my conclusion?"

Lady Wem's chin came up. "All of it."

"Very well, if you prefer the naked truth, I believe your grandson was smothered."

The woman flinched, but her gaze held on Ottilia's, becoming narrow. "Your reasons?"

"A blue pallor, coupled with damage from the teeth in the mouth, broken veins in the eyes and elsewhere which, taken together, are indicative of his being deprived of breath for long enough to succumb. He did not struggle, but I doubt the presence of a narcotic in his stomach will prove to have been strong enough to kill him."

Lady Wem had listened to the recital without expression, though Ottilia noted a hardening to the line of her jaw. She was far from indifferent. For a moment she did not respond, her gaze never leaving Ottilia's face. Then the rasp came again. "Not suicide then."

"No."

Lady Wem set an elbow on the arm of her chair and leaned her head on her hand, her gaze shifting to the rug adorning the embrasure where the chairs were set. "My son desires an answer of suicide."

Ottilia sighed. "He may well get one."

The woman did not raise her head but flashed a glance at Ottilia. "How so?"

"The signs are faint. The doctor did not speak of them all and he ascribed the blue to a natural result. His report to the coroner is like to produce a verdict of accidental death. It rather depends what is found at post mortem."

Lady Wem's hand dropped and she straightened. "Something will be found."

"Undoubtedly. He was drugged."

"With one of Mary Ann's brews? Phooey!"

It was the most normal remark Ottilia had heard from her. "What is in these brews, do you know?"

The woman shrugged. "Herbs, she says. Julius appears to derive benefit from them. Lord knows what she puts in them. Fancies herself a healer."

"Well, if she has knowledge of herbs, she likely is one. Has she said what was in the mixture she gave Daniel?"

A rude sound exploded from Lady Wem. "Who can say? She will do nothing but wail and weep. Try if you can get any sense out of the ninny."

Ottilia could not withstand a protest. "She has just lost her son, ma'am."

"So also has Leo. So also have I. A grandson."

"It is different for a mother, do you not think?"

A bitter note entered the woman's voice. "What I think is that someone has taken advantage of my boy's state of mind. And of mine too."

Ottilia did not hesitate. "That is why you sent for me. You believe he was murdered?"

All at once the serpent look was back. "I believe they are all in a plot to harass and mortify me. It is all of a piece. Daniel has come by his desserts, but that does not exonerate the rest of them. The end will be they will drive me into my grave. Only then will they be satisfied."

The tirade ended, she glared at Ottilia as if she was herself responsible for the unhappy state of affairs. Was the woman unhinged by the happenings of the last few days? Or was this merely the ravings of grief. Ottilia gave her a tiny smile.

"Forgive me for saying so, ma'am, but you sound much like your grandson did that day in the Assembly Rooms. I am persuaded you do not mean all you say."

A wry look came. "Don't I? Perhaps not. But I will have the truth for all that."

Ottilia balked. "If you are expecting me to find it, ma'am—"

"You have already begun. Annis can help. This is her doing."

"I highly doubt that, Lady Wem. She is perhaps the one person above suspicion."

A shrewd look came Ottilia's way. "Because she raised a hue and cry? Don't be fooled by that. A devious thing she has ever been. She plays the dutiful daughter and despises me in secret. She thinks I don't notice, but I have her measure. She would be glad enough to see me confounded. They all would."

Ottilia began to despair of making any headway. The woman was bitter to the point of obsession. If grief there was on account of the boy's passing, it was superseded by Lady Wem's determination to imagine herself a victim, beset by the machinations of others. Difficult to see her conniving with any one of her unfortunate relatives since she trusted none of them. Ottilia opted for the direct approach.

"Which of them might have a reason to do away with your grandson, do you think?"

Lady Wem's mouth thinned as she compressed her lips, the slant eyes staring unblinkingly at Ottilia. She persisted.

"Annis, for example. Why would she do such a thing?"

"How should I know? I told you she is devious."

"But that does not constitute a motive for ridding the world of her nephew. Come, ma'am. You said you wished me to find out the truth."

The woman's mouth twisted. "You would have me condemn them out of my own mouth? That is your task, not mine."

Incensed, Ottilia let fly. "I have not said I am willing to undertake it, Lady Wem. Nor am I subject to your command. You have no jurisdiction over me whatsoever and I will not be spoken to as if I am one of the unfortunates obliged to pander to your every whim. Either you answer my questions or I remove from this house and leave you to fry in your own grease!"

She ended on a shrill note that shocked her into silence, the more infuriated to have been provoked into losing her temper.

But the outburst proved salutary. Lady Wem's hard gaze did not waver, but a grim smile curved her mouth. "I am glad to think Sybilla is obliged to contend with you. I dare say you drive her up the wall. None of my lot would dare speak to me so." She sniffed. "I wish they might show backbone enough to do so."

Unable to help herself, Ottilia hit back. "Yet when your grandson did so, you faced him down and slapped his face in public."

Lady Wem blew out a scornful breath. "Of course I did. But that don't mean I didn't admire his spirit. I had to slap the boy down. What, allow him to make an exhibition of me? I could not have that."

Ottilia refrained from pointing out she had made an exhibition of herself. Despite her still smouldering annoyance, the evidence of feeling intrigued her. She probed it.

"You cared for Daniel?"

A shadow crossed the woman's face. "He was my favourite. That, if you must have it, is why his defection rived my heart. And there you have it, if you wish for reasons. They all knew it. Any one of them would be glad of an excuse to grieve me."

Exasperation seized Ottilia. "Will you have me believe that one of your family would destroy this boy's life merely for the purpose of making you suffer?"

"Why not? It's the purpose of all their lives. Ingrates and parasites, the lot of them. Take Leo. Bleating on about his fury with the boy when his failure to control Daniel's quirks is to blame for this shambles."

"You mean he might have stopped the marriage?"

"He indulged the boy disgracefully. Should have bought him a commission instead of giving him an allowance. The weak-minded fool gave in to his silly wife's whims, I don't doubt. She couldn't endure to expose her babe to the dangers of soldiering. No surprise he ran wild."

Ottilia sifted out the pertinent issue. "An indulgent father would not kill his own son, ma'am, however much he sought to harass you."

Lady Wem gave her a glare. "Did I say Leo did the deed?"

"You implied any of your family might have done it."

"Do you think I want to believe that?"

"I do not, ma'am. But I cannot imagine there is any possibility of an outside agency having committed such an act. Which leaves every inhabitant of the house suspect."

The serpent look became pronounced. "Including me, I dare say."

Ottilia did not balk. "Why, yes. You are slight, it is true, but Daniel was too drugged to struggle."

Lady Wem gave a grunt. "And you will throw at me I was angry enough to do it too."

Ottilia was betrayed into a wry smile. "I have yet to find anger a sufficient motive to kill in cold blood. In all likelihood, this was premeditated. You might, in a fury, swat the boy with a candlestick. It is a different matter to plan and carry out a murder in the secret hours of the night. We must look for a more cogent motive."

The woman was silent for a space, as if she cogitated, her gaze shifting to the window. It gave on to the front of the house, beyond which the Common and the bank of buildings forming the main drag of the town below was visible. Ottilia was half inclined to hope the woman might abandon the project and dismiss her. The hunt for a murderer looked to be pretty hopeless. Unless someone had heard or seen something, she must be dependent upon tripping the murderer into making a slip. This, in turn, requiring her to find means to question everyone. Unless the dowager viscountess so instructed them, would anyone bar the Maplewoods even be willing to talk to her?

At length the woman gave vent to a long sigh. "I would let it be if I could. Don't wish to know any spawn of mine might do such a thing. Godfrey? No, he doesn't covet the title. He's got more money than is good for him already. Lilian now. She'd supplant Mary Ann if she could and lord it over me. Marcus? Namby-pamby do-nothing is what he is. With Daniel gone, he's next in line if Julius succumbs to his pernicious ailments. Mary Ann quacks him, of course. Always has."

Committing these details to memory, Ottilia probed for the rest. "You have another daughter, I believe?"

"Berta? Jealous as sin." The cynical reptilian look became pronounced. "Hates dancing attendance on me. Thinks I don't see it, but I do. Pinches at the others and pretends it's on my behalf, but I know better. She'd see me crushed if she could. If this is her revenge, she's missed the mark."

The woman's self-absorption was total. Ottilia could not but pity the daughter obliged to live in her orbit, despised and bullied. A wretched existence. But would she take such a cruel method of repaying the mother's unkindness?

"Well, that is comprehensive, ma'am. Do you permit me to talk to these people?"

Lady Wem sniffed. "You'll have to, won't you? Not that any will confess. I'll flay whoever did it and they know it."

Which would not make her task any easier. "I must warn you I am liable to come up blank. Moreover, the coroner's verdict is likely to make any investigation superfluous."

"It's not superfluous to me." The hard gaze raked Ottilia. "Don't neglect Mary Ann or Annis, no matter the song and dance they are creating, one way and another."

Ottilia had difficulty believing any mother would do away with her own son, but she had no chance to say so.

"There's Clarissa too. I might acquit Julius, but that pert little piece dared to befriend the other wench. In the face of my prohibition. I gave her a piece of my mind. Advised Julius to take a stick to the girl, but he's a lily-livered weakling." The bitterness returned full force. "See it now, do you? Poltroons, the lot of them. Only one who dared defy me was Daniel, and he's dead. What have I got to live for now? I'd be happier in my own grave, but I wouldn't give them the satisfaction."

Thoroughly disgusted, Ottilia could find nothing to say. All at once, Lady Wem turned on her.

"Well? What are you waiting for, girl? Get on with it, can't you?"

Her ire rising, Ottilia got up. "I will leave you, ma'am. But I am going home. When you have recovered your temper, send to me. I will then consider whether or not I am willing to oblige you."

A rasping laugh came from the other. "Oh, you'll oblige me. Heard a great deal about you, Lady Fan. You won't be able to resist."

CHAPTER NINE

"And the worst of it is, the horrid creature is right. The wretched business is disastrously intriguing."

His back propped against the mantel, Francis had listened to his wife's recital without comment. Annoyed though he was at the rudeness to which she had been subjected, he yet had to smile at this last.

"I knew you'd be into the thick of it in no time, my dear one."

From where she sat in the chair she favoured, sipping her perennial beverage, his wife threw him one of her mischievous looks. "You are so disobliging, Fan. Why could you not have taken one of your pets and forbidden me to have anything to do with it?"

"Because for once it doesn't appear to offer you any danger." On reflection, he amended this. "Or none beyond being obliged to endure that ghastly woman's appalling lack of courtesy."

"Oh, I didn't. I gave her word for word and took no prisoners."

He broke into laughter. "There's for her then."

"For a wonder, she liked that."

Francis set down his empty tankard. He had quaffed ale in a bid to counteract the rising heat of the afternoon, stuffy despite the poor showing of the sun. The windows were open as wide as they could go and he had abandoned his coat, but even in shirtsleeves, he felt sticky and hot. And irritable.

"If she could be said to like anything. At least I am glad to know you gave as good as you got. She'd have got short shrift from me."

Tillie smiled. "I know, my darling champion, and I don't think it would have answered. She lords it over her men."

"Like my revered mother."

"But Sybilla has a heart, Fan. This woman is embittered to the core. To be truthful, I don't think she has a heart. She sees everything as it relates to herself. It is excessively wearing and I am astonished none of her downtrodden brood has taken her off instead of wasting that poor young man's life. Not to mention his unfortunate wife."

Francis's attention veered. "You hold by that also being a murder then?"

"Do not you? Now the boy has also been killed, it is hard to believe the first death was an accident."

"Perpetrated by the same hand?"

"Or another who took advantage of the boy's disturbed condition."

He watched her slide into reverie and knew at once she was mulling the possibilities. For himself, he would much prefer to have nothing to do with the Brockhursts. With the exception of young Maplewood perhaps, assuming Lizzy's preference for the fellow came to anything. He had toyed with the notion of alerting his brother-in-law, but the reflection his mother had the girl in charge deterred him. It was rather her place to curb the business. Besides, he suspected his darling wife approved the boy and he trusted her judgement. Although any association with the Brockhurst clan was frankly anathema, even remotely. With luck, the affair would fade away.

"What are you thinking, Fan?"

He blinked and looked across to find her gaze upon him. He balked. "You're the one who went off into one of your daydreams."

She did not take the bait. "Were you wondering about the murders?"

He sighed, capitulating. "No, I was reflecting on this cursed fancy of Lizzy's for the Maplewood boy. Do you suppose this business will cause him to sheer off? He was fond of the dead man, as I understand it."

His wife's clear gaze remained on his face. "Is that what you hope?"

He shrugged, discomfited. "It's not my concern, Tillie."

"But you are concerned. Is it that you fear Dalesford will disapprove?"

"Likely he will, but that's not it. The boy is too closely involved with these ghastly Brockhursts."

"You hold that against him?"

"It's an accident of birth, I know, but I for one would balk at being associated with them in any way whatsoever. I'm tempted to warn Gil of what is in the wind because of that." She was regarding him with a frown and Francis cursed. "Don't look at me like that, Tillie. These things matter."

"His being untitled, you mean."

Her tone was flat and hard. Francis felt his temper rising. "I didn't say that."

"But it is what you believe."

He could not contain the spurt of anger. "Yes, if you must have it. But that aspect pales against the worse prospect of Lizzy marrying into that family."

She let out a sound of exasperation. "For heaven's sake, Fan! Would you turn this into Romeo and Juliet? We do not live in the middle ages. Besides, by Lizzy's account, the Maplewoods in general have little to do with the Brockhurst family. And if you wish to know my mind, I imagine this murder will serve to bring them closer. After all, it is just what happened with you and me."

Brought up short, Francis stared at her, the memory surfacing of the terrible week of his sister-in-law's murder. He had met his wife on that very day. The murder had indeed precipitated them both into an alliance that grew rapidly into intimacy. His ire died and he laughed.

"So it did indeed." He moved to her chair and leaned down, capturing her face between his hands. "I forget sometimes how blessed I am."

Her eyes rimmed with wet and her hands came up to clasp his wrists for a moment. "So too do I."

Francis kissed her and released her, straightening up. "Shall we agree to differ?"

She looked uncertain. "Will you write to Dalesford?"

He shook his head. "I won't put a spoke in Lizzy's wheel, but I hold by my opinion. The Brockhursts are a sorry lot and I pity anyone connected with them."

Tillie's eyes scanned his face. "Does that mean you won't help me, Fan?"

His brows rose. "Did I say so? I might dislike them, but I am perfectly ready to hound them for disposing of one of their own. Whom do you wish me to tackle?"

Primed, and more importantly, stoked with a full stomach from an excellent dinner, Francis sauntered into The Duke of York tavern on the hunt for any sign of a Brockhurst male. He thought it unlikely any of the clan would make an appearance in the Assembly Rooms, although Ottilia, unusually keen, had accompanied his mother and Lizzy there.

"I may glean some useful little titbit from one of the permanent residents. Those who are acquainted with Lady Wem may have insights into the various relationships."

Francis was retying his hair in a queue, but he turned to survey her. "Does that mean you want me to do likewise if I find no Brockhursts?"

She had given him one of those tantalising smiles, moving to him and setting a hand to his chest. "If you please, my darling lord. I know it goes against the grain with you to engage in gossip, but you are become adept at ferreting out just those details I need."

He had quirked an eyebrow. "Flattery, Tillie?"

"Truth, Fan." She laughed. "And a trifle of cajolery."

"At which you are adept, you rogue."

Mischief gleamed in her eyes. "There is an excellent meal awaiting you, Fan."

He gave a shout of laughter and kissed her. "In that case, you may command me in anything."

They had dined in perfect amity, gathered up the dowager and her charge and parted at the Assembly Room doors. The half-threatened rain had not materialised but the air had turned chill. Francis was glad to enter the tavern, already thick with smoke from a plethora of pipes, and murmuring from many tongues assailed his ears as he scanned the taproom for faces he knew as he moved to the counter.

The tapster took his order for a glass of claret and Francis searched a little more closely, passing over one or two customers who eyed him with interest. Two men hunched over a table in a corner caught his attention. They looked to be in earnest conversation, both nursing glasses of wine. As if he felt himself under scrutiny, one of the men glanced up.

Shock ran through Francis. Lord Wem? On the evening of the very day his son had died? An unlikely chance, but not to be wasted.

He took his glass from the tapster, threw a couple of coins on the counter, and casually shifted a little closer. From a better angle, he saw the fellow's companion was also of middle years. The brother? What was his name? He searched his memory and found it. Godfrey Brockhurst. He had not been introduced to the man, but this must be he. Francis could call acquaintance with Wem, however, and the pretext was easy enough. He approached the table.

"I hesitate to interrupt, sir, but I must beg to offer my condolences."

He received a glare that astonished him. "You must, must you?" Lord Wem rose from his seat. "You are Fanshawe, yes?"

The tone was accusatory and Francis bristled. "I am, and I object to your attitude."

"You object, do you? Then hear this. Call off your lady wife, or you will know more of objections than you care for!"

Furious, Francis squared up to the man. "You dare to threaten me, sir?"

A look of disdain was cast upon him. "Threat? Nothing so paltry. I will be writing to my lawyers at once."

"To what purpose?"

"That you shall discover in due time. I repeat. Order that bloodhound of yours to desist forthwith." With which, he pushed past Francis and the staring eyes around them where men had fallen silent to listen and headed for the door. His temper at full stretch, Francis would have followed, but for the hand that grasped his arm and held it in a vice-like grip.

"Let him go, man! He is overwrought."

151

Turning, he found his captor was Godfrey. Francis growled a protest. "I care nothing for his state of mind. No man speaks of my wife in such terms."

The other's grip held and he spoke in lowered tones, urgent and anxious. "It was bad indeed, but make allowance, I pray you, Lord Francis. My brother has had a bellyful of a day."

Still seething, Francis was yet able to appreciate the justice of this. But he could not let the matter pass. "It was by no wish of my wife's that she has become embroiled, sir, I promise you."

"Yes, yes, I know. I have heard it from all sides, I assure you."

The soothing note rankled and Francis was unable to stop harping on his grievance. "Mrs Maplewood — your sister, yes? — begged my wife's intervention early this morning. Moreover, your mother the dowager all but commanded her visit. Which, let me tell you, I take in strong objection."

"And who shall blame you, my dear sir?" Godfrey took the glass out of Francis's hand and he found himself ushered into Lord Wem's vacated seat. "Pray allow me to make my apologies on behalf of my poor brother. I fear he is sorely beset. Drink up, my lord, and I will procure you a refill."

Francis allowed himself to be mollified, taking up his glass and tossing off the contents. He felt inescapably aggrieved, but the fellow was making such efforts to placate him, he felt it churlish to persist in complaint. Before he could even turn his mind to the advantage he began to perceive he had, his glass was refilled and Brockhurst was making soothing noises.

"A fine claret they serve here, sir. Just what one needs in these trying circumstances."

Lord Wem's abandoned glass was on the table before Francis. With an irritated gesture, he pushed it away. Godfrey removed it out of his reach and leaned in, nursing his own glass between his fingers.

"I must tell you, my dear sir, I for one am grateful for your wife's attendance and interest."

Surprised, Francis eyed him. "Why should you be?"

He was treated to an earnest look in a countenance that bore a resemblance to the brother, though softer and a little fleshy. Testament to good living? Had not Ottilia said Godfrey was alleged to be plump in the pocket?

"My sister Annis is not the only one to cherish suspicions, sir."

"Indeed? Yourself then?"

He nodded, casting a rather furtive glance at the other patrons of the tavern who had thankfully returned to their own interests. "One dare not voice such notions too freely. My brother desires to believe my poor nephew committed suicide."

"So I understand. But you don't believe it?"

Godfrey spread his hands, sighing. "I do not know what to believe, but my heart misgives me, I confess."

His evasiveness could not but annoy. Francis pushed for more. "Be plain with me, sir. What do you really think?"

The fellow's gaze met his boldly. "I cannot think it coincidence. What would you, sir? The girl falls from that rock. Pretty convenient, would you not say? Within a matter of days, Daniel follows her to the grave."

"Which your brother takes to be an expression of grief."

Godfrey wagged a finger. "No, no, you mistake. Not grief. Leo thinks it was an act of defiance that went awry. That is why he is so angry with the lad."

"What, he supposes the boy meant to punish him, or the family? How could that be?"

A faint laugh lightened the seriousness of the other's face. "I did not say it was rational. This is Leo's effort to make sense of a terrible tragedy. He has Mary Ann on his hands, you see."

"His wife?"

"Exactly so." A grimace came. "She is a trying female at the best of times. Quite useless in this crisis, I fear. A devoted mother, I grant you, for she dotes on those boys. One must make allowance for a mother's grief, but Mary Ann is like to lose her reason, as Lillian says."

"Lillian?"

"My helpmeet. Poor woman. She is bearing the brunt of Mary Ann's lamentations. Leo has no patience for them, I fear."

That he spoke so freely to a relative stranger was a surprise. Or was the unburdening needed after a difficult day? Francis nevertheless returned him to the main issue.

"If you don't believe Daniel killed himself, what do you think, sir?"

The man's eyes flared. "Oh, it is obvious!"

"Is it?"

Godfrey leaned in again, lowering his voice to a murmur. "Who was the most enraged? Who suffered the gravest disappointment in her favourite? Who had the least to gain, but was the most humiliated?"

Considerably startled, Francis could only stare at him for a moment. To gain time, he took a swallow from his glass. But it had to be said. "You accuse your own mother?"

Godfrey put up a hand in a defensive gesture, a laugh escaping his lips. "Gracious me, where had you such a notion? Pray do not bandy it about!"

Bewilderment wreathed Francis's brain. "What other construction can be placed upon your words, sir?"

Godfrey took up his glass and sipped, giving Francis a sly look. "I put a few questions to you, Lord Francis. I take no responsibility for any conclusion you may choose to draw."

Francis began to fume. "This is ridiculous. You wish me to understand you are suspicious of the cause of your nephew's death, but you won't openly state your case? Faugh!"

An enigmatic smile was cast upon him. "You read me aright, sir. What would you? Only consider my position vis-à-vis this probing of your wife's. I also have a son. My other nephew is sickly." Both gaze and tone became meaningful. "Need I say more?"

Francis eyed him measuringly. Was this altogether a ploy? Had he meant to come to this point all along? Throw suspicion on his mother in order to divert it from his own son? He would catch cold at that. No need to say so, however.

"I understand you, I believe."

Another sly smile. "I thought you would."

Francis became urgent to quit the fellow's company but bethought him of the one person who had not yet been mentioned. "What of your other sister?"

Godfrey's brows rose. "Berta?"

"Where does she stand in all this?"

His lip twisted. "Poor Berta. So unfortunate she failed to find a husband. Still, she has proved a dedicated daughter." The man's gaze became meaningful again. "Extremely dedicated. Obedient too."

Exasperated, Francis gave tongue. "For pity's sake! You wish me to understand, I suppose, that your sister Berta made away with your nephew at the instigation of your mother."

He was treated to a pained look. "My dear Lord Francis! Have I said a word to give you such an impression?"

"Yes," returned Francis flatly. "Very deliberate have your words been, Brockhurst." He tossed off the rest of his wine and stood, looking down at the fellow's now smiling features. "I prefer your brother's direct dealing, sir. At least he has the courage of his convictions."

Sybilla's two cronies were willing enough to talk, the elder a trifle more discreet than her gossipy friend. Mrs Trefnant no sooner grasped Ottilia's purpose than she launched into the subject with avidity.

"Shocking, is it not? Sinister too. We were saying so only a moment ago, were we not, dear Lady Countersett?"

The aged dame addressed, a bony woman who looked to Ottilia's eye to be suffering from rheumatism, let out an impatient sound, shifting in her chair and wafting a hand across the cards, dealt and discarded upon the table.

"You were saying so. I was trying to play whist."

Ottilia had already apologised for interrupting the game, although her mother-in-law was the real culprit. Sybilla had barged into the card room, spied her quarries, and broken in without compunction, dragging away the two elderly gentlemen who were playing against the pair. Lady Countersett, on a winning streak, was disgruntled, but Mrs Trefnant had abandoned the cards with alacrity.

"Oh, you and your whist! At such a time, dear Lady Countersett, one cannot be thinking of cards."

"I had rather think of cards than waste my attention on That Woman and her abysmal brood."

"Oh, do not say so," her companion exclaimed, plump cheeks quivering. "They are not all as beastly as Lady Wem. And that poor young man was so extremely handsome."

"Handsome is as handsome does. His conduct left a deal to be desired."

"But he had lost that lovely wife of his, dear Lady Countersett. One must make allowances." She turned excited blue eyes upon Ottilia. "And that was sinister too."

Ottilia eyed her with interest. "What makes you think so, Mrs Trefnant?"

The eyes widened. "Well, it is obvious, is it not?" She leaned in a little, lowering her voice. "None of them liked her, poor girl. I had some speech with her, you must know."

"Did you indeed? What was she like?"

"Quite harmless." Mrs Trefnant threw a hand to her bosom and sighed. "I can hardly bear to think of it. So pretty she was, but terribly shy. I met her on the Common, walking with her little girl."

It was the first Ottilia had heard of a child. Her heart gave a little flip. "They had a daughter?"

Mrs Trefnant sighed again. "Oh, yes. A pretty child. They called her that, you know. Pretty. What in the world will become of her now, I dread to think."

A memory clicked in Ottilia's mind. Who had spoken of Pretty? Ah, yes, Annis Maplewood. She had no chance to question the matter for Lady Countersett made an explosive sound.

"Don't be a fool, woman. There is family enough to look out for the child."

"If they choose to do it," said the other darkly. "It would not surprise me if they disposed of her as well."

Lady Countersett groaned. "You have the wildest imagination of anyone of my acquaintance, Lavinia. Pay no heed to her, Lady Francis, I charge you. She will have it the whole is a concerted plot by the family to be rid of a sorry business."

Ottilia was tempted to retort that Mrs Trefnant might well be right, but it was politic to keep her opinion to herself for the present. She was forestalled.

Mrs Trefnant leaned in again. "But you think it too, do you not, Lady Francis? Dear Lady Polbrook said you desired information about the Brockhursts. Why else should you wish for it?" The childlike eyes took on a look of admiration, laced with cunning. "It is your forte, is it not, enquiring into murders?"

A little sigh escaped Ottilia. "You have that, have you?"

This was greeted with a simper. "Oh, your fame goes before you, dear ma'am."

Lady Countersett was staring at Ottilia as at a rare specimen. "Lady Polbrook said nothing of this."

Triumph lit the other lady's glance. "Oh, you are behindhand, dear Lady Countersett. I had it from your charming niece, Lady Francis."

Grimness settled in Ottilia's breast. "Did you indeed?"

Pudgy hands fluttered. "Oh, you must not blame dear Lady Elizabeth. I confess I badgered her until she confirmed the rumours."

"What rumours?" demanded Lady Countersett. "The only rumours running around this town concern That Woman and her acolytes."

"No, no, not here. I am not speaking of Tunbridge Wells. You do not come to Town now, dear Lady Countersett, or you would have heard them too. Everyone was talking of it in the Spring."

Ottilia groaned in spirit. But at least she need not hold back. She made up her mind. "You are right, Mrs Trefnant. I have been requested to look into this matter. I hoped, as you both know Lady Wem and her family well, you might be able to enlighten me."

"As to what?" demanded the elder dame. "We know no more than anyone. It is all conjecture. Excessively silly conjecture too," said with a reprimanding glance at her companion, "talking of murder and such. A tragedy it is, I grant you, but no more."

Mrs Trefnant did not look to be chastened by her friend's severity, but Ottilia intervened before she could retaliate.

"Unfortunately, ma'am, there is a deal more. But mum for that. Will you tell me, if you please—"

"You know something!" The plump woman leaned in, eager now. "Pray tell, Lady Francis!"

Ignoring an exasperated sound from the other, Ottilia made a deprecating face. "I fear I cannot speak out at this time, ma'am. It would not do to bandy it about. That is how rumour begins."

Mrs Trefnant pouted. "Well! It is too bad if we are not to know your mind."

Ottilia smiled. "But you may still participate, if you choose. What can you tell me of the ladies of the house? Miss Brockhurst, for example. Or Mrs Lillian Brockhurst."

The ploy had an instant effect. Mrs Trefnant brightened. "Oh, Berta? A copy of her mother."

"She tries to be, you mean," cut in Lady Countersett. "And a sorry job she makes of it. She has not half the backbone."

"Well, but one cannot help feeling sorry for her, dear Lady Countersett. Rubbed and harried as she is and obliged to live under Lady Wem's despotic rule." She turned to Ottilia. "If you ask me, she is quite as embittered as her mother, and no wonder. She hates the woman."

Ottilia balked. "How do you know that, ma'am?"

"She does not know at all. Conjecture again."

"I do know, dear Lady Countersett, for I have had speech with her on several occasions."

"What, and she told you as much? Balderdash!"

"No, but I could tell. She looked quite daggers whenever her mama was mentioned. Moreover, she spoke of a scheme she has of taking a tour upon the continent and visiting Italy."

"I dare say she did, but what has that to say to anything? Not that That Woman would permit her to go."

"Exactly so, and that is what she said. Or rather, she said she would come into an independence when her mama died and she meant to use it to accomplish her dream." A hushed thrill entered Mrs Trefnant's voice. "Moreover, she intimated it might not be long before she was free of all restraint. What do you think of that, Lady Francis?"

Before Ottilia could answer, Lady Countersett snorted. "What should she think? I have no doubt any of that brood would be glad to see That Woman in her grave, but you are letting your imagination run away with you again."

Recalling Lady Wem's conviction of much the same sentiment, Ottilia took up the point with Mrs Trefnant. "You would wish me to understand that you believe the daughter would go so far as to dispose of her own mother?"

This bluntness brought a tide of red to the woman's cheeks and Lady Countersett regarded Ottilia with approval for the first time.

"You call a spade a spade, Lady Francis. I like that. You see now, Lavinia, where your nonsense has led you?"

Flustered, the other tried to backtrack. "I did not mean — I had not quite thought of it in such terms, you see."

Ottilia relented. "It does not sound well when one puts it into words, do you not think? Nevertheless, your reading of Berta's character may be helpful." She became brisk. "Tell me about Lillian Brockhurst."

Surprisingly, it was Lady Countersett who took this. "A secretive woman. Or perhaps I should say reserved. She has a complacent air about her that makes one itch to slap her."

"Ah, you do not like her?"

"Don't like any of them. Giving themselves airs the way they do. At least, they do so when That Woman is not by. Wem is bad-tempered and his brother preens himself on his wealth. That all came from her, of course."

"Lillian, you mean?"

"Oh, she was a considerable heiress," broke in Mrs Trefnant, but the light of gossipy excitement flickered in her gaze as she dropped her voice. "She was not of the first stare, you must know. A merchant's daughter, they say."

Startled, Ottilia caught at this at once. "If that is so, I am astonished Lady Wem sanctioned the match."

Mrs Trefnant was fairly bubbling. "Well, but that is what made her so wild with poor Daniel."

Another snort escaped the elder dame. "You can't know that, Lavinia. I wish you will not jump to conclusions." She turned on Ottilia. "Don't you believe all she says. Lillian may have been born into the middling class but she was educated at a select school and took her place in good society."

"Although not in the most tonnish circles," averred the irrepressible Mrs Trefnant. "But Godfrey was glad enough to take her, I'll be bound, He sold out of his captaincy before he had seen active service."

For which the man could scarcely be blamed. Aware her own husband had benefited from his first marriage in a similar if more modest fashion, Ottilia could not decry a man's taking the opportunity to better himself. Not that Francis had married for other than love, but he had been widowed all too soon, just as she had been when her husband Jack was killed in the American war. That they had found each other years later was a blessing for which she never ceased to be thankful.

But this aspect rather lessened the possibility of either Godfrey or Lillian having eliminated Daniel and the unfortunate Isabel. A thought which brought to mind the orphaned child.

"May I return you to the matter of the little girl, Mrs Trefnant? Pretty, did you say?"

"It was a pet name, I believe."

"So I should imagine. How old is she?"

"Oh, a very babe. No more than two or three, poor little mite."

Poor little mite indeed. Her heart wrung, Ottilia tried not to think of the infant's future, to be raised among those who had regarded her mother with enmity. A loveless future too, if she was any judge. Who in that family would stand to her in place of a mother? A thought surfaced and she spoke it aloud.

"What of Clarissa? Might she take the babe under her wing?"

The response was immediate. "Good heavens, no. She has two little girls of her own and has not yet fulfilled her duty."

"You mean she has no living sons. Yes, that I had heard. But I understand she befriended Isabel."

Lady Countersett stared. "Behind That Woman's back? I don't believe it."

Ottilia regarded her with interest. "Why not?"

"Because she is a selfish little madam. Two-faced into the bargain. Don't be fooled by that simpering innocent air, I charge you. If you ask me, she is quite as ruthless as That Woman, only she hides it better."

Yet what advantage could it be to Clarissa to rid the world of her brother-in-law? Never mind his unfortunate wife. But Ottilia did not say so, her mind busy as she listened with only half an ear to Mrs Trefnant's vehement refutation. She, for one, had not taken the girl's true measure, assuming Lady Countersett read her aright.

"A sweet girl, I always think, with a proper respect for her elders. She is perfectly deferent to you, dear Lady Countersett."

"I don't care for deference. It merely demonstrates adherence to the social conventions learned at her mama's knee. Yet I have heard her speak slightingly of That Woman, in a manner meant to be taken for a pleasantry. I would not trust her sayings if you paid me." She gave a comprehensive snort, turning her gaze on Ottilia again. "If you wish to know my true mind, ma'am, I would trust nary a one of them."

Ottilia cut into Mrs Trefnant's twittering objections. "Not even Mrs Maplewood?"

Lady Countersett pursed her lips. "Annis Maplewood began a Brockhurst. The taint is on her too."

"Taint?"

The elder dame pursed her lips. "Her mother's blood. What is bred in the bone, Lady Francis…"

Lizzy had not expected to find any of the females of the Brockhurst family in the Assembly Rooms on such a day. At sight of Clarissa entering quite alone, she abandoned her grandmother on the instant. Truth to tell, she was glad of the excuse. Her grandmama had been buttonholed by that tedious old Mr Richard Cumberland, boring on about his plays to any who would listen.

Lizzy glided away and intercepted Clarissa, who was hovering near the door and looking purposefully about. "Mrs Brockhurst?"

The woman blinked, her gaze shifting to Lizzy's face. "Oh. Lady Elizabeth. How — how do you do?"

She appeared dazed and Lizzy smiled. "More to the point, how do you do, ma'am? May I offer you my heartfelt condolences?"

Clarissa stared at her a moment without answering. Was she too distracted to respond? This blankness was decidedly out of character. Abruptly, she spoke, casting another glance across the knots of visitors. "Have you seen Marcus?"

"Not since the early afternoon. I met him on the Pantiles."

Clarissa clicked her tongue. "He is the most provoking creature."

She was definitely jolted out of her usual manner. Lizzy at once took advantage. "What has he done, ma'am? Is he wanted perhaps?"

Clarissa gave an exasperated sigh. "We are all wanted. My father-in-law is in one of his furies and my husband is in such a taking, I said I would come to find him in Julius's stead."

Lizzy took her arm in a deliberate gesture of spurious friendship. "I don't think he is here but let us make a circuit to be sure."

The woman made no demur, clearly too overturned by the day's events to use the manner habitual to her. Which rather argued it was largely assumed. Intrigued, Lizzy probed a little as she drew her in an unobtrusive walk about the spacious room. Aware of narrowed looks nevertheless, she took care not to meet anyone's gaze.

"I imagine the whole household is at sixes and sevens?"

"It is perfectly dreadful and I don't think I can bear it." This was said low-voiced, but with a shrill edge. "They are all beside themselves, every one of them, and I just want to go home."

"I don't blame you. It must be quite horrid."

"Oh, you can have no notion. It is vile at the best of times, but this has…" She faded out, throwing a look of consternation sideways. "Oh, what am I saying? Don't heed me, pray."

Agog, Lizzy had all to do to keep from bursting out. Mindful of her aunt's strictures on her impulsiveness, she bit her tongue on the myriad questions leaping in her mind and managed a neutral tone. "I do not think your cousin is here. Let us leave this place, ma'am."

Clarissa followed where she led, even picking up the pace a little, as if she could not wait to be gone. Lizzy escorted her out into the deserted vestibule and there halted.

"That is better." She released her hold on Clarissa's arm and instead grasped her hands, infusing sympathy into her voice. "I feel for you, ma'am, I promise you. It must be an impossible situation."

The woman's eyes rimmed with moisture. "Oh, it is dreadful. The atmosphere is dismal and Mary Ann's incessant wailing is enough to drive everyone demented. Not that I blame her. You must not think I blame her. She doted on Daniel. They all did."

"Well, they did not behave as if they did," said Lizzy on a tart note before she could stop herself. "The poor fellow was in utter despair and no one but Mr Maplewood sympathised at all."

Clarissa wrenched her hands away. "But we did, we did! You are wrong. I was terribly upset for Daniel. Julius too. We both tried to comfort him, to no avail. He would keep insisting one of us had pushed Isabel off that rock. As if I would! I liked her. She was a sweet girl."

"Then why in the world did you behave as you did in public?"

Clarissa drew back. "I had to, don't you see? We all have to do as she desires. If I go against her, she makes life intolerable for Julius. His papa too. Lord Wem is severe upon both his sons if they enrage his mother." She caught herself up, throwing a hand to her mouth. "What have I said? Daniel is gone and now my poor Julius will bear the brunt of it all and he is not strong. Oh, if only we could go home!"

The heartfelt sob in her throat convinced Lizzy she was speaking the truth. Sympathy flooded her and she said the first thing that came into her head. "Why don't you?"

Clarissa fairly blinked. "Go home?"

"Yes. What is to keep you?"

A somewhat hysterical little laugh escaped the woman. "You know little of my husband's grandmother if you imagine we may do as we choose. Besides, Julius will never go against his papa. He is not like Daniel."

Forgetful of caution, Lizzy blurted her thought aloud. "Who do you think killed him?"

Clarissa's gaze registered horror. "You too? Oh, dear heaven, what will become of us all?" The look in her eyes changed all at once, becoming fierce, and she seized Lizzy's arm in a painful grip. "That female is your aunt. If you value her at all, you will persuade her to leave us alone. It is perilous to interfere in Brockhurst affairs. Believe me, I know." Upon which, she released her hold and scuttled away.

Lizzy watched her vanish through the doors to the paved way beyond, her mind all chaos. What manner of warning was that? Did she think Ottilia could be in danger? And she had not answered directly. In one breath she seemed to decry the notion of murder, and yet indicated the family might harm Lady Fan.

She was about to turn back into the Rooms when the street door opened again and Mr Maplewood walked in. He stopped short on seeing her and stood irresolute, his hand still around the door handle.

All the horrid symptoms of the morning rushed back into Lizzy's bosom and she found herself stiffening. The temptation to flounce away into the Rooms attacked her, but instinct bade her remain and face him out. She determined not to be the first to speak. Not that she could have uttered a word, for her skittering pulses and the thickening at her throat.

At last Mr Maplewood shut the door and took a couple of steps into the vestibule. "I gather you were talking with my cousin's wife."

Disappointment swept through Lizzy and the discomforting sensations subsided, giving way to annoyance. "What if I was?"

His brows drew together. "Nothing. She just passed me and, finding you here, I drew that conclusion."

Lizzy lifted her chin. "Well?"

With a sigh, he swept the hat off his head. "I have not come to quarrel with you, Eliza."

"Don't call me that!"

He bowed in a resigned fashion. "I beg your pardon — Lady Elizabeth."

Lizzy wanted to hit him. Controlling herself with difficulty, she dropped a curtsey. "You must excuse me. I have to attend my grandmother."

She turned to go. His voice arrested her.

"Wait!"

Lizzy paused, glancing over her shoulder. "Yes, sir?"

He hesitated, shifting his hat in his hands in a manner that suggested uncharacteristic discomfort. "I owe you an apology, ma'am."

Lizzy turned. "I agree. But since it obviously chokes you to make it, I suggest you refrain."

He threw his gaze heavenwards. "For God's sake, woman, must you be so naggy? I am trying to make amends."

Not in the least appeased, Lizzy hit back. "Yes, I must. And if you wish to know, I don't care for your amends. I have no desire to talk to you."

Again she made to leave the vestibule, but a quick footstep sounded, her shoulder was seized and he swung her about.

"You will listen to me, Eliza, if I have to kidnap you and tie you down to make you."

Lizzy's temper flared. "Oh, indeed? Manhandling women is your style, is it? Well, let me tell you, Mr Monstrous Maplewood—"

"Be silent, you silly girl! I am just trying to—"

"How dare you? Don't imagine you can lord it over me, sir!"

He showed her an exasperated face. "You are an impossible female, did you know? Will you please calm down and let me say my piece?"

Lizzy began to feel a trifle foolish. The memory of his bereavement tapped remindingly on the walls of her mind. Yet she could not suppress the sulk in her tone.

"Very well, if you must."

He grimaced. "Grudging, but I'll take it." His features softened. "You meant well, coming to me. I hurt you. It was not well done of me."

The blunt admission could not but affect her. She answered from the heart. "You were grieving. One is not master of oneself at such a time."

His mouth twisted, not quite a smile. "Generous of you. May I hope—?"

"For what, sir?" The hurt he spoke of leapt to the fore. "Hope for nothing from me, Mr Maplewood. You made your position clear, despite this olive branch. You do not welcome intrusion into your deepest feelings."

He looked taken aback. Yet his response did not help matters. "Not as a rule, no."

The pain of the morning's rejection echoed in her breast and Lizzy had difficulty controlling her voice for the tumult within. "Well, I am not of your ilk, Mr Maplewood. I c-cannot be forever h-held at a d-distance. It is better we remain mere acquaintances."

Unable to meet the frowning puzzlement in his gaze, Lizzy curtsied and turning, hurried into the Rooms where it must be impossible for her feelings to overcome her.

CHAPTER TEN

The morning found Ottilia distrait. She slept ill, disturbed both by her spouse's tirade against Lord Wem and the trouble she detected in her niece. Lizzy's relation of her talk with Clarissa had lacked her usual spark. Ottilia refrained from making enquiry in the presence of Sybilla, and any opportunity was lost when Francis, bursting with spleen, came upon them as they were crossing the Walks on the way to the lodgings.

He began low-voiced even before they had attained refuge from public ears. "I no longer wonder at your loathing, Mama, if the son is anything to go by. Yes, I am talking of Wem. The dratted fellow had the gall to threaten me."

"Ha! You see it now, do you?" exclaimed Sybilla in triumph.

Ottilia cut in fast. "Threaten you how, Fan?"

"He ordered me — ordered me, if you please — to call you off and said I would hear from his lawyers if I didn't. You may imagine how I answered that."

Ottilia had no difficulty in so doing and her heart sank. She broke into Sybilla's instant reiteration of her opinion of Lady Wem with its rider 'like mother, like son'.

"Say no more until we are private, ma'am, I beg of you. You too, Francis. We have all much to tell each other, I think."

But there was no relating her findings, nor enquiring further into Lizzy's meeting with Clarissa, until Francis had delivered himself of a comprehensive indictment of Lord Wem's manners, attitude and general character. Once she grasped he'd had speech with Godfrey, Ottilia paid less heed to this, beyond attempting to soothe, and managed at last to steer her husband into giving an account of the meeting.

Not without difficulty, for her mother-in-law was relishing the details and her acerbic comments were not readily silenced.

"What else can one expect with such a poisonous female for a mother? Did not I warn you how it would be?"

"Don't talk to me of warnings, ma'am! As for that blustering fool having his lawyer approach me, I wish I may see it. I shall know how to act."

Ottilia gave an inward groan. "Fan, calm yourself, pray. This is getting us nowhere. Have some more brandy."

"If you think brandy is going to mend matters, you may think again." But he nevertheless went to the table and poured himself a second measure.

Ottilia seized opportunity. "We have hashed over it enough tonight, do you not think, Sybilla? Everything will look better in the morning."

"Yes, if one can sleep with all this going on." But Sybilla at once began to harry her grand-daughter, who had been markedly silent throughout. "Come, Elizabeth. High time you were in bed."

"I am rather tired, ma'am."

Lizzy's yawn added colour to her words, but Ottilia, observing her narrowly, noted the wan cheeks and the lack of sparkle in the eyes. While Sybilla said her farewells to her son, she contrived to find excuse for a whispered word in giving the girl a hug.

"You are upset, Lizzy. Is it Mr Maplewood?"

A tiny sob sounded in her ear. "I met him. Say nothing, Aunt, pray!"

Ottilia contented herself with a reassuring smile and murmur. "We will talk tomorrow. Try to sleep."

Lizzy nodded, a tremulous smile on her lips. She raised her voice. "I am ready, Grandmama."

171

Francis thankfully held his peace while the servants were in the room as they both readied for bed. Once Diplock and Joanie had gone, however, he reverted to the subject as he climbed into bed while Ottilia sat to her nightly hair brushing routine.

"I have a good mind to go up to the house tomorrow and tell that fellow exactly what I think of him."

"I beg you won't, Fan. What would it achieve, beyond making it impossible for any discourse to occur between our two households?" She paused in her task and looked round as a thought occurred. "Or is that what you wish? Would you have me halt this enquiry?"

He snorted. "Halt it? At his bidding? Most certainly not. You will pursue it to the end if I have my way."

She could not repress a laugh. "Here's a new come-out, Fan. I thought you wanted nothing to do with these Brockhursts."

"Oh, I've not changed, Tillie. I can't bear them. But I won't be dictated to. Especially with regard to my dealings with you, my dear one. Call off my bloodhound indeed!"

"Is that what he said?"

"Exactly that. Bare-faced too. I nearly planted him a flush hit to the jaw."

"Well, you have called me a bloodhound before, Fan."

"So I may have done, but that does not give him the right to say it. It was nothing short of an insult."

Ottilia set down the brush and rose from the dressing-stool. "I dare say it is not the only insult likely to be levelled at me. The Brockhursts are not noted for the courtesies."

She spoke lightly in hopes of keeping Francis in this better frame of mind. He became a good deal calmer once she was ensconced in his arms and Ottilia made an effort to be particularly loving. Yet when he slept, she remained wakeful, worrisome thoughts churning in her mind.

The task she had set herself was beset with difficulties. Never had she tackled a more recalcitrant set of individuals than the Brockhursts. With the exception of Annis Maplewood and her son. Although his dealings with poor Lizzy left something to be desired. She was conscious of a wish they had gone rather to Weymouth as planned since Tunbridge Wells was proving a hotbed of complications. Yet could she, in all conscience, leave the matter unsettled?

There was a question of justice here. That lovely girl, cut off in the flower of her happiness. And poor Daniel, lost in grief, sent to his maker within days. Was it fair? Was it right? The memory of Mrs Trefnant's revelation leapt to mind, scorching her heart. The child! Left motherless and fatherless both. Ah, cruel. If there was a place for vengeance, it was here. What life was there for a babe despised? If the Brockhursts could not tolerate the mother, how would her little girl fare at their hands?

Ottilia fell asleep weeping silent tears and woke to the landlady's chambermaid making up the fire. Heavy headed and cloudy with exhaustion, she lay staring at the tester until she could no longer endure it. Slipping out of the semi-curtained bed with care so as not to wake Francis, she donned her dressing-gown and went in search of refreshment. She found Joanie setting the table for breakfast.

"Oh, thank heavens!"

The maid started, turning sharp about. "Gracious goodness, my lady, you did give me a fright!"

Ottilia put out a conciliatory hand. "Forgive me, Joanie. Would you ask Tyler to bring coffee, if you please?"

"Of course, my lady, but what are you doing up so early? There won't be no hot water yet for washing."

Ottilia took her favoured chair. "I could not sleep. When his lordship wakes, I will get a powder from my dressing case. The hot water can wait, Joanie. But coffee, pray. I am gasping."

"It'll be here in a winking, my lady," the girl promised, dropping a curtsey and hurrying away.

Ottilia rested her head against the cushioned back and closed her eyes. The light coming in at the window was harsh, promising a hot day. She put a hand to her brow, massaging away the trace of threatening headache.

"Milady?"

Her hand fell as she opened her eyes to find her steward standing by the chair. "Oh, it's you, Hemp? Where is Tyler?"

He proffered a cup and saucer. "Your coffee, milady. I brought it up myself." His dark gaze raked her. "What is it, milady?"

Ottilia was sipping the fresh brew with enjoyment, but she lowered the cup and sighed. "I am troubled, Hemp. His lordship is upset."

The steward looked grave. "Is there anything I can do?"

To relieve her spouse? She doubted it. But a possible avenue glimmered. "There may be. I don't suppose you have encountered any of the domestics from the Brockhurst house, have you?"

Hemp shifted his stance, a shade of consciousness entering his dark features. "One, milady. While I waited for you there, I met a nursemaid."

Ottilia's heart leapt. "Was her charge with her? A little girl of two or three?"

Surprise flickered in his eyes. "She was, milady. Pretty, she called her."

A stab attacked Ottilia's bosom. "Oh, Hemp, that is the poor orphaned little mite. What is to become of her?"

He looked grave. "That is what the girl Hepsie was asking. I found her weeping, milady, and tried to give comfort."

"She was weeping before the child?"

"I believe she was trying to hold back. Pretty was busy with a butterfly, chasing it from flower to flower. Hepsie cried because the little girl keeps asking for her mother. She does not know both her parents are dead."

Ottilia was obliged to swallow a lump in her throat. She could not speak and took refuge in sipping the hot coffee. Presently, her throat soothed, she was able to put the question in her mind. "Does this Hepsie have any notion what the family intends by Pretty?"

Hemp shook his head. "She fears she will be dismissed and then the girl will have no one of familiarity."

Ottilia balked. "They won't do that. It would be foolish beyond permission as well as cruel."

Hemp's gaze clouded. "Hepsie maintains they are cruel, all of them. She says it would be better for Pretty to go to her mother's family, but she believes there is no hope of that. The Brockhursts are too proud."

To allow the child to be brought up under the aegis of a tradesman? Probably. Yet would the Dowager Lady Wem wish to succour the daughter of a girl of whom she had thoroughly disapproved? She suppressed a wistful utterance born of her own loss.

"Well, I dare say the business will be settled by Lord Wem. She falls under his responsibility, I imagine."

Which, if her husband's experience was anything to go by, was not likely to prove an enviable position. She made an effort to dismiss the matter for she had a task to perform and her steward was ever willing on her behalf.

"Hemp, could you, do you think, contrive to infiltrate the downstairs ménage?"

His rare smile came. "Nothing easier, milady. Do you mean to go today?"

"I must, I think." She could not hold off merely because it was Sunday. The sooner she began, the better. Unlikely the Brockhursts would attend church today.

"If you will allow me to escort you, milady, I may seek refreshment in the right quarter while you are occupied."

Gratitude flooded her. "I can always rely upon you, Hemp. You are a great comfort to me." She added, unwontedly deferent, "And a friend, I hope?"

The steward's mouth twisted. "As far as that is possible, milady. You have my loyalty."

"And you have my trust."

His gaze met hers and Ottilia read in it a measure of something more than loyalty. Inwardly, she cursed the misfortune of position that prevented the warmer relationship, existing, but which must remain unacknowledged.

Hemp bowed. "I will be ready when you are, milady."

He withdrew and Ottilia was startled to find her spouse standing there in his dressing-gown. There was a sombre look in his face that caused an instant thread of guilt. Ottilia did not prevaricate.

"You heard all?" He neither moved nor spoke. Tears sprang to her eyes and she put out a hand. "Oh, my darling, don't look at me so! You have no need to be jealous, I promise you. Fan, you have all my heart."

His face changed on the instant and he came to her, dropping down to his haunches, seizing the hand and kissing it.

"I know it, my dear one. Forgive me, I am being selfish. I can't bear to share you with anyone, least of all Hemp Roy."

She set her cup down out of the way and leaned to stroke his face. "There is no question of sharing. Never think it. If you wish to know the truth, I regard Hemp much in the light of a brother perhaps. Oh, not in the way of the affection I have for Patrick. But in feeling I may ask of him what I would not expect from a servant."

Francis sighed. "I am aware you don't think of him as a servant."

"No, I don't. I never have."

"What then?"

Ottilia clutched his hand. "An equal, if you must have it. In everything but station. I try not to despise a system that prevents my treating him as such, but I was not born to the trappings of rank, Fan."

He released her and rose, looking down with a frowning gaze. "You dislike it, I know."

"I don't." Mischief glimmered in her breast. "It has its values."

A reluctant grin appeared. "Yes, you wretch, I am well aware of your machinations when it suits you to flaunt your title."

She could not withstand a gurgle of laughter. "Not flaunt, Fan."

"Use, then. I am thanking God for mine in the present predicament, for at least it gives me some armour against that blasted Wem." He sauntered to a chair and flung himself into it. "Speaking of which, what is your intent?"

Ottilia blew out a frustrated breath. "I wish I did not have one, but I must engage with them all today if I mean to do it at all. I have set Hemp to tackle the domestics."

"Yes, I heard."

"But first," continued Ottilia, unheeding as her mind became busy, "I must speak to Lizzy. Something untoward occurred between her and Mr Maplewood."

Francis groaned. "Oh, Lord, must we have that on our hands as well?"

Ottilia tutted. "Do you forget our purpose in coming to the Wells? We are pledged to help Sybilla with Lizzy."

"You are so pledged. I can have nothing to do with arranging my niece's love affairs, I thank you."

She laughed and got up. "Then I had best get dressed and begin."

He rose likewise. "What made you wake so early?"

The anxieties of the night rolled back. "I slept ill."

He was following her through to their bedchamber as he spoke. "Because of all this?"

Ottilia hesitated, moving to pull the bell-pull to signal the servants to bring up the jugs of hot water. She slipped off her dressing-gown and reached for her hairpins before she answered, unwilling to speak of the plight of the little girl that had distressed her more than anything else. Aware of the deeper wound that prompted it, she was reluctant to remind her spouse of those dark days. She compromised.

"I was worried for Lizzy. And for you."

"Why in the world, Tillie?" Francis was combing his lush hair, tousled from the night, but he looked round at this.

"Because of your encounter with Wem, of course."

"That? I discharged my spleen last night. Besides, I am confident the fellow will not carry out his threat of dragging a lawyer into the business. It was all bluster, no doubt brought on by grief and frustration, as Brockhurst suggested."

Relieved, Ottilia would have said so but for the entrance of Diplock and Joanie, armed with the accoutrements for their ablutions.

By the time she and Francis partook of breakfast, Ottilia's feeling of exhaustion had given way to an eagerness to confront the Brockhurst ménage. She had taken one of the powders to which she rarely resorted, even though Patrick had prepared them, her doctor brother having provided her with a supply upon the occasion of her miscarriage. They relieved her feeling of malaise and took care of an incipient headache so that she was able to swallow a fair portion of baked eggs and bacon. Another cup of coffee did much to restore her to her usual buoyancy.

She was about to propose going in search of her niece when an explosive sound came from her spouse who had opened a sealed missive brought in by Tyler, which had arrived by special messenger.

"What is it, Fan?"

He looked up from the paper in his hand. "Damn the man to hell! I was wrong. He has done it."

"Who has done what?"

"That blasted Wem! This is a cease and desist letter from his lawyer."

The younger Lady Wem was different from the woman Ottilia remembered from that first meeting. Mousey and fearful she had been in the presence of the all-powerful dowager. Now, sitting with Godfrey's wife in the front downstairs parlour, Mary Ann bore all the marks of a bereaved mother. Her face was blotched, her eyes red and swollen and her restless fingers travelled from her lap to her bosom, up to her face and down again.

Her air was at once hunted and eager as she acknowledged the introduction effected by Annis Maplewood. "Oh! You are the one. Leo does not wish ... oh, what shall I do?"

Lillian, a stolid matron with a squarish face and large bosom, set a hand on hers. "You need not speak at all, Mary Ann. No one can make you."

Ottilia noted the other's hand shrink away, curling into a fist. Her gaze remained upon the newcomer.

"But I want to speak. At least ... oh, I must, don't you see? My Danny..." She dissolved into sobs, hastily putting up a crumpled pocket handkerchief to her eyes. Lillian lifted a disdainful gaze to Ottilia's face.

"She is not fit to be questioned. Would you wish her to incur her husband's wrath?"

Annis cut in before Ottilia could answer. "Leo is not present, Lillian. Let Mary Ann be. If this business is not cleared up once and for all, there will be no peace for her."

The handkerchief fell. Mary Ann raised swimming eyes to Ottilia, vehemence in her tone. "Yes, that is it! I cannot rest. I have not slept since..." She hesitated, glancing at her sister-in-law. "Lillian, pray understand. You are so good and kind to me, but I need to know what has been discovered. Let this woman tell me all." She turned again to Ottilia. "I will help you in any way I can, but you must promise me not to tell Leo anything I may say." She rose on the words, seizing Ottilia's hands. "Promise! He is beside himself, but he does not see how desperate I am. He wants it all to go away, you see. That is his method, but it is not mine. Not mine, I tell you! How can I bear...? My Danny, my Danny... I only wanted him to be at peace, but ... oh, pray help me!"

She collapsed again and Ottilia made haste to utter reassurances, cutting across Lillian, who immediately entered another protest.

"You see how it is with her? Have you no pity? Cannot you—?"

"I will keep your counsel as best I can, ma'am. I cannot promise your husband will not discover you have spoken, but it will not be from me."

"If you cannot be discreet for her, Lady Francis, you had better—"

"I will not disclose anything you tell me to Lord Wem," Ottilia said, ignoring the interjection and directly addressing Mary Ann. She was grateful when Annis intervened.

"Lillian, go away, do! You are not helping."

The buxom dame took instant umbrage. "I will not be ordered out by you, Annis. This is all your fault. You began it by bringing this female here. If you had not stirred the coals, Mary Ann would never have been so alarmed."

"Better she is alarmed than Daniel's murder is allowed to be passed off as suicide."

A wail from the afflicted woman induced Ottilia to cut in, her tone sharp. "That is enough, both of you. There can be no profit in throwing your tongues at one another. What is done is done. I am here at the Dowager Lady Wem's behest and there's an end."

Lillian closed her lips though her eyes looked daggers, but Annis softened at once.

"She is right, Lillian. Come, we will both retire. Let Lady Francis talk to Mary Ann alone. We will get nowhere else."

Ottilia thanked her and watched as the other matron, still huffing, was drawn out of the room. She made no immediate attempt to cajole the weeping Mary Ann into discussion, hopeful the ensuing quiet would do the trick.

She had approached the Brockhurst residence with reluctance, her disaffection with its inmates increased by her niece's sorry tale. It was plain Lizzy cared a deal more for Vivian Maplewood than he did for her. Or perhaps more than he knew he did? But that was not a possibility to be proffered to Lizzy.

"You did the right thing, my dear, to extricate yourself before your affections become irrevocably involved." They likely already were, but best not to say that either. "It is bound to be hurtful but try to bear up. Don't allow him to see how you are suffering."

Lizzy was doleful, but willing. "I won't do that." A tiny flicker of hope showed in her eyes. "You said he would come to me, Aunt, and he did."

"I will allow that is a good sign."

Her face fell. "But you don't think I should get my hopes up."

Ottilia had to smile. "My dear Lizzy, nothing I can say will prevent you from hoping. It is entirely natural. All I will advise is you do not wear your heart upon your sleeve."

Lizzy's agreement had been wholehearted and Ottilia was satisfied. Nothing could be more prejudicial to her chances with the young man than to demonstrate how much she missed his company. A show of indifference was much more likely to set him a-hunting.

Yet that did not stop Ottilia wishing she might meet him for the purpose of giving him pepper. Not that she would, of course, but it was difficult not to think of him as hardly as she did the rest of the clan.

She parted from Hemp when he had rung the bell for her, hopeful of what he might discover from the household servants. The door was opened, rather to her surprise, by Annis Maplewood.

"I have been on the watch for you. I mean to bring you at once to Mary Ann while Leo is out of the way."

"He is not in the house?" As well, considering the state of mind in which she had left her spouse. Incandescent, he had sped her on her way with a recommendation to bring the deed home to Lord Wem himself.

"He is, but closeted with Godfrey and the sons. It is of no use to ask me what they are about, for I don't know. But the opportunity is not to be wasted. He has forbidden Mary Ann to speak to you."

"His son too, no doubt?"

"Julius, yes. Clarissa too. I expect he is doing the same by Godfrey and Marcus, although his authority is less absolute there." Annis had moved as she spoke to the nearest door off the gloomy hall. With her hand on the doorknob, she spoke in a lowered tone. "You will find her lachrymose in the extreme, but I dare say you will be able to manage her."

Saying which, she had opened the door and Ottilia followed her into a room with a sunnier aspect than any other she had yet entered in this house. Two wide sash windows, partially open, faced the town below, a couple of chairs set before them. A sideboard table with a decorative frieze was situated to one side, its surface bearing several ornaments and an unlit candelabrum, and a pair of matching sofas, upholstered in flower-festooned tapestry, were placed either side of the fireplace. Upon one of these Mary Ann and Lillian sat side by side.

In a few moments, Mary Ann's sobs subsided. Wishing the windows might be opened more to let in much-needed air, Ottilia took the place vacated by Lillian beside her on the sofa and sat at an angle, watching the woman's face as she dabbed with the now damp handkerchief at her stained cheeks.

"Do you feel up to conversing with me?"

The woman's glance met hers, an eager look observable at once. "Oh, yes, if you please. I am ready. Forgive me if I weep, but I will answer you if I can."

Ottilia kept her tone friendly. "Excellent. What I chiefly had in mind to ask you concerns the preparation you gave Daniel that night."

Mary Ann's gaze faltered, dropping to the mangled square of linen in her fingers. "I meant only to calm his mind, to sleep sound, so he would not feel so acutely."

"Just so. What did you give him, Mary Ann — if I may?"

She jerked at the edges of the handkerchief. "It is a recipe of my own." Her gaze returned to Ottilia, an earnest note creeping in. "I do know my herbs, ma'am, despite what anyone says. I have studied Culpeper religiously and I've had years and years of practice. My elder son … Julius suffers so. He has done from a babe. Leo does not agree, but I lost hope with the medical men long ago. Nothing they did for him sufficed. But Leo cannot deny me that success. Has he not grown to manhood? Is it not my care, my attention to his needs that has enabled him to come thus far?"

A rising note of threatening hysteria made Ottilia hasten to soothe. "Indeed, I am sure your efforts have been eminently valuable. But let us, if you please, concentrate on this present concoction you administered to Daniel."

The handkerchief fluttered. "My poor boy… I wish I had not … but it is too late. Too late." She turned eyes abruptly fierce upon Ottilia. "But it was not my herbs. That I will swear to, whatever Leo says. It was not my doing, but his! He threatened to shut poor Danny away. He told him so and Danny was beside himself with rage and chagrin. As if grief had not sufficiently destroyed him! What else could I do, I ask you? What else could I do?"

Ottilia brought her ruthlessly back to the point. "What was in the drink, Mary Ann? Tell me precisely the ingredients."

A frown appeared between her brows and she shied a little. Lost in despair? "The drink? Yes ... yes. I am trying to recall. Oh, I know. Mandrake, to bring him sleep. What else? I think motherwort and melancholy thistle to lessen the grief. I wish I might be certain, but I have been so overset, I cannot remember."

"Come, Mary Ann, you know your herbs, you said. This is a preparation you have been used to make for Julius, did you not just say so? Think of that instead."

Mary Ann's luminous orbs came back to her face. "But it was not exactly the same. Julius's needs are different. Besides, I have given his care over to Clarissa for the most part. With careful instructions and receipts for each condition. She comes to me for the herbs, for I have my own garden and a stillroom for the drying and mixing." A trifle of enthusiasm entered in. "I act for a great many of my friends and acquaintants, you must know. My remedies are much requested. Danny was used to tease me for a witch..."

She faded out, present memory returning, and her face dropped. Ottilia cut in swiftly.

"Impressive, ma'am. Let us leave the concoction for the present. Tell me instead—"

"Oh, I remember! There was one last ingredient. I slipped it in especially as I was boiling up the mix. Black hellebore it was and a little wine to warm the whole. I remember because Leo would keep saying poor Danny had gone mad and hellebore calms the spirits."

She looked so triumphant at the recollection, Ottilia was tempted to remove her at once from suspicion. But it would not do. Far-fetched it might be, to think a mother would smother her own son, but the possibility Mary Ann's woeful demeanour was an act could not be discounted.

"That is excellent, ma'am. Thank you. Was that why he slept too soundly, do you think?"

"Oh, no, that was the mandrake. It has a singularly soporific effect." She became vehement. "But it would not serve to kill anyone! And for Leo to accuse me of carelessness is the outside of enough."

"Did he so do?"

She fidgeted with the piece of linen. "Well, not precisely that. But he threw it in my face I had given our son means by which to take his own life. And I did not, I swear it! That drink could not have killed him. It was not by my Danny's hand! I know it, I know it!"

Not much to Ottilia's surprise, the outburst ended in another bout of sobs. She waited, mulling the evidence of dissension between Lord Wem and his wife. Was she quite as cowed and obedient as one had been led to expect? She tested the theory as soon as the woman quieted again.

"Are you afraid of Leo, Mary Ann?"

Her head came up. "Afraid of him? No! Oh, he will bluster and shout, but he is never deliberately unkind. He is always sorry when he reduces me to tears."

Ah, that was her weapon, was it? A useful ploy. Ottilia changed tack. "What of Isabel?"

A cry issued from Mary Ann's throat. "That poor girl! I warned Danny not to bring her. I knew how it would be. Such a sweet girl. She did not deserve such harshness."

"You knew her?"

Mary Ann looked astonished. "She was my daughter-in-law."

"Indeed, but I understood Lord Wem would not countenance the match."

"Leo? Heavens, no! He refused to have anything to do with the poor thing. I was obliged to visit them in secret."

Ottilia stared at her. "Then you knew of the marriage?"

"Of course. We all did. I do not know if Lillian or Godfrey knew, but Marcus had it from Clarissa, I believe. Or was it Julius? In any event, Leo ordered everyone to keep silent. And to have no truck with the wife, although Danny was still welcome at our home."

"Were you the only one of the family to visit them?"

"Except for Vivian Maplewood. But he has ever gone his own way. Leo deplores his attitude. He disapproves mightily of Annis too."

Ottilia swept this aside. "Tell me this, Mary Ann. If the Dowager Lady Wem's disapproval was not in question, do you suppose your husband would have relented towards Daniel and Isabel?"

Mary Ann gave a little shudder. "I wish it had been she who died rather than my Danny. There is a witch, if you will. I hate her!" This came out low-voiced, vicious in intensity. That it was said at all in her presence spoke volumes for Mary Ann's wayward state of mind. She must have realised her error, for her hand came up to her mouth and she looked fearful. "I should not have said that. Forget it, pray. Leo warned me to be circumspect, but I am so overset…"

"Have no fear, ma'am. Your admission is safe with me." Ottilia was tempted to leave it there, but the question pressing on her heart begged to be uttered. "What will happen to the little girl, ma'am? Pretty, is it not?"

A change came over Mary Ann. Her face lit and she gave a spontaneous smile. "And she *is* pretty too! An adorable child. I saw her first when she was quite a babe. I made Isabel a tonic for the colic for little Pretty was prone to suffer from it. She is the most delightful grand-daughter, poor sweet thing."

"But what is to become of her, ma'am? Will you take her?"

"I?" Immediate shock. "How could I possibly do so? Leo would never allow it."

"Clarissa then?"

Mary Ann waved agitated hands. "You do not understand. Yes, yes, it is very sad and I have wept for the poor little thing. But to bring her up as one of the family? It cannot be. You can have no notion how my mother-in-law would react. If she were dead too … but, no. No, impossible. Leo says we will have to hide her away somewhere."

With difficulty, Ottilia suppressed the urge to voice her shock and disapproval. Hide the child away? A guilty secret to end as the skeleton in the family closet? Abominable. It was not as if she was Daniel's natural daughter. She could not help a trifle of protest. "Who is to comfort her then, ma'am? Have you seen her since her parents died?"

"Oh, I could not bear to. I would weep if I did and she must not be told."

"What has she been told?"

"Nothing. She has her nurse. For the present, that must suffice."

Ottilia's opinion of the woman veered. Was she callous? Or merely too self-absorbed to think of anything but her own tribulation?

Before she could say or question anything more, the door opened to admit Annis Maplewood. "The meeting is over. I came to warn you, Mary Ann. Leo is looking for you."

The younger Lady Wem uttered a shriek and leapt up. Without a word to Ottilia, she scuttled from the room in a fashion that leant little colour to her assertion she did not fear her husband.

"Did you find out anything useful, Lady Francis?"

Ottilia got up. "Perhaps. At least I have a better understanding of Mary Ann." She braced. "Now for Lillian. Do you think she will talk to me?"

Hemp Roy's appearance at the rear door did not elicit quite the usual response, although the cook eyed him askance. The kitchen maid who let him in shied a little, looking a trifle scared, but a footman seated at the big deal table greeted him with a mere nod.

"You'll be serving that Lady Francis, I reckon."

Hemp nodded. "Her steward. My name is Roy."

The fellow waved at a chair. "Take a pew, friend Roy. If I read it aright, she won't be out for an age. Cook'll rustle up a jug of ale, if that's your fancy."

"I would prefer coffee, if it is not too much trouble." This to the buxom dame who was engaged in kneading pastry at the other end of the table.

His deferent manner had an effect. The cook visibly softened, dusting floury hands and gesturing her skivvy towards the range. "Bestir yourself, Milly. Get the man a cup of coffee."

Hemp threw a smile at the girl. "Black, if you please. With sugar."

"And open those doors, girl," put in the footman. "We'll bake as brown as Cook's pastry in here." He took a pull from his tankard and set it down as the kitchen maid ran to comply. "John's the name. Take it your mistress is come about the business with our young master?"

No surprise the domestics were privy to the whole affair. Milady had known how it would be. Glad to be spared the necessity of bringing the subject up, Hemp took instant advantage. "That is correct. My mistress has much experience of such matters." He added for good measure, "She has never failed to identify the culprit."

The cook paused in her labours and the girl Milly turned from the range where she had just taken hold of a steaming pot. John expressed the consternation in all three faces.

"Culprit? She thinks one of 'em did for young Master Daniel?"

"She thinks he was murdered, yes," Hemp agreed, with flat deliberation.

This brought about a silence and an exchange of looks between John and the cook, whose hands were still poised on the lump of dough she had just pummelled. Hemp caught her eye and she looked quickly away to the kitchen maid.

"Don't stand dreaming, Milly. Pour that coffee, girl!"

John shifted his tankard to and fro. Then he looked across. "That's what she was doing then when Mrs Maplewood brought her in that morning. Not that I minded being chucked out of Master Daniel's chamber. Can't say it was any pleasure to me having to sit there with his corpse."

Hemp thanked the girl Milly who set a mug of coffee before him. "Sugar?" Milly stretched to the middle of the table and dumped down a bowl of sugar lumps within his reach. He adopted a deprecating tone. "I have a sweet tooth. I was born and bred on a sugar plantation."

Milly blinked. "Where's that then?"

"Barbados. It is an island in the Caribbean. A long way away."

The girl grew round-eyed. "Across the sea? Well, I never did!"

Hemp picked up the tongs and slipped several lumps into the mug. Milly found a spoon and gave it to him. Amused by her awe, he would have spoken more of his homeland if he had not pledged himself to ferret out information for milady. He addressed himself to the footman. "Did you know him well, John? Your Master Daniel?"

The footman, a fellow of middle years, shook his head. "Don't know none of 'em that well, nor I don't want to. I'll be off soon as I can secure a better place." He added on a laconic note, "She can't keep a servant, the Empress can't. Except Mr Lamport."

"Don't forget old Janet," put in the cook, taking up a rolling pin. "Them two is the only ones as'll stay with Mistress. And me o'course. Long as she don't come in my kitchen, which she won't, I can bear it. I won't take no nonsense from that Berta, neither, hoity-toity though she makes herself."

"She means the mistress's daughter. The one who ain't married." John rolled his eyes. "A right sourpuss she is an' all."

Hemp took this without comment. "Who is Janet?"

"Mistress's old nurse. Can't hardly get about much now, but she knows all of 'em through and through. Nursed each one, she did, 'til they got to be having lessons and the boys went off to school. So Mr Lamport says."

"Mr Lamport?"

"Butler. Been with the mistress nigh on twenty year. But Janet, she's served her since the Ark seemingly."

"She is here in Tunbridge Wells?"

The cook, vigorously plying her rolling pin, took this. "Stays here now. Too old and decrepit to travel, she says. Mistress goes up to Wem Hall but old Janet won't go no more. Stays in her room mostly, less'n Milly here helps her go down to take the waters."

Hemp returned his gaze to the footman. "It seems odd no one in the house knows what happened that night. Whoever went in your Master Daniel's room could easily have been heard or seen."

John gave a snorting laugh. "Heard? You've to cover your ears in this house if you don't wish to be deafened by the rumpus. If it ain't the Empress herself, it's his lordship. He and young master were going at it hammer and tongs."

Hemp seized on this. "Lord Wem went into his son's room?"

"He were there all right, kicking up fit to take the rafters off."

"Did Master Daniel shout too?"

"He were fit to bust himself, saying as how his lady wife were pushed off that rock and a-blaming of his pa for it. His lordship comes back at him as young master ought to be confined. 'And I'll do it too,' he says, 'don't think I won't. You are mad, sir,' he says, 'and if I have to, I'll thrash you back to your senses.' Then he comes out of there at such a lick, I had to belt off around the corner so's he wouldn't catch me. His lordship slams the door fit to bust it off its hinges and marches away, cursing his head off."

"It sounds as if you all had a rough night."

The cook pointed her rolling pin at John. "Don't forget young master's mama."

"That was later," said the footman.

The cook turned to Hemp, using the wooden implement for emphasis. "Invades my kitchen, that one. She came down for to boil one of her potions. Had a handful of them little bags she uses, full of dried up herbs. Puts in a bit of this, a bit of that and mutters over the pot. Incantations they may be for all of me. Pork jelly is good enough for most if a body's under par, but not her witching ladyship, oh no."

"Ellen saw her going into Master Daniel with a steaming brew," put in John, taking up the tale. "Nor she didn't leave for an age, for she were still there when Ellen came back from her errand. And," added the footman with an air of triumph, "Miss Berta were listening at the door." He sat back, looking smug. Waiting for Hemp's admiration? Astonishment? He would find himself disappointed.

"Who else went near the room?"

John frowned. "Why d'you want to know?"

Hemp gave a faint smile. "Would you prefer if my mistress asked you?"

"Ah, a witness, am I?"

"To some extent. Although, except for hearing the argument with Lord Wem, what you have told me is hearsay." He showed his teeth in a grin. "Still useful, however."

The footman slapped a hand on the table, emitting a raucous laugh. "You're a fine one, you are. Barbados, you say? That's slave country, ain't it?"

Hemp repressed a rise of irritation. "I was never a slave, if that is what you imply."

John threw up a hand. "Meant no offence, friend." He turned his head as the kitchen door opened and an aproned girl came in. "Here's Ellen herself. She'll tell you. She saw it all."

The cook once again used her rolling pin to gesture the newcomer across. "Sit down, Ellen. This here is Mr Roy. He's servant to that lady as came to look at Master Daniel. Tell him what you seen the night before."

The maid Ellen, looking both startled and scared, sidled away from the cook's implement and hovered near the footman's chair. He pulled out one next to him.

"Sit you down, girl. He won't bite." He flicked a wry look at Hemp. "He ain't no bogey-man, for all he's dark as the night."

Hemp gentled his tone, leaning in a little, mug in hand. "I should be grateful for anything you can tell me, Miss Ellen."

The girl blushed, visibly flattered by this form of address. The cook, setting her pastry aside, dusted off her hands and called upon Milly to give her a cup of coffee. While the kitchen maid complied, she sat herself down and rapped the table, looking at Ellen.

"Come on, girl. You see her ladyship Mary Ann going in to Master Daniel. And you see Miss Berta with her ear to the door, ain't that right?"

Ellen at last spoke up, sounding scared. "I see Master Vivian and all, when I was answering the mistress's bell for to help her undress."

"Did he go into the room?"

Ellen nodded. "I didn't see him come out."

"Do you know if Miss Berta went in?"

A shrug. "Not as I saw, sir. I were in a rush like, for as there's only me and John for the mistress and Miss Berta, and Mrs Lillian never brought no maid this time so's I had to do for her and all."

"A mean piece, she is," put in John. "Not as if she can't afford to bring a score of maids, aye, and house 'em elsewhere like they have to. We ain't got room for 'em all here. Valets and maids. They board out when the Empress sends for the lot. Good for them. Wish I might spend my off time away from this madhouse."

"I see Miss Berta, I did," piped up Milly as she supplied her senior with a large mug.

The cook gave her a glare. "You never did! Why didn't you say so afore?"

The chambermaid's eyes were on Hemp. "I see Mrs Brockhurst too."

"Where?" demanded John.

Hemp intervened. "Which Mrs Brockhurst?"

"That Lillian, she means." But the cook was dissatisfied. "What was you doing up there? You ain't got no business in the bedchambers."

Milly tossed her head. "I was helping Ellen with the warming pans."

"She was, Cook. They was all ringing at once and I couldn't manage."

The cook entered a protest at her skivvy being taken off her kitchen duties without permission. Hemp broke into the threatening argument as both girls defended themselves, his deep voice easily taking precedence. "Hey, hey, ladies! Give me leave!" He smiled at the cook. "May I ask Milly what she saw and when?"

The stout dame sniffed and nodded towards the girl. "Tell him then."

Nothing loath, Milly launched into her story. "I were coming along that corridor and I see Miss Berta at the door."

"Was it open?"

195

"Just a bit. She were holding the handle. I kept meself back for as Miss Berta might give me a tongue lashing if she sees me, an' a good thing I did for along comes Mr Godfrey's missus—"

"Lillian?"

"That's right. An' she goes a-whispering with Miss Berta, an' I wish as they'd go away for as I've got hot coals and the pan is heavy, an' it were Mr Godfrey's missus as took Miss Berta off at last."

"At what time was this, Milly?"

The girl screwed up her face. "Musta been more'n ten o' the clock."

"Nearer eleven, Milly. Might have been after even." Ellen turned her gaze on Hemp. "There was ever such a lot of to-ing and fro-ing all evening. Stamping about all over they were."

Hemp backtracked. "Let me see if I have got this right. Lady Wem was in the room while Miss Berta was at the door, before or after eleven, yes?"

"Yes," chorused both girls, and broke into giggles, hastily choked.

Allowing himself a smile, Hemp pursued his course. "You saw Master Vivian go in, Ellen. I take it that was earlier?"

"Must've been, for the mistress 'ud be mad as mad if I didn't go in to her first."

"Thank you." He turned to the footman. "Can you place the time, John, when Lord Wem was arguing with Master Daniel?"

John rubbed his chin. "Danged if I know. Like I told you, it were all rush and bother and I'd Master Marcus's coat in hand to take down for his valet to iron first thing. He took hisself off soon as he'd done it, as if I hadn't enough on my hands."

Hemp persisted. "Ellen didn't see Master Vivian come out, but we may take it he was not there when Lord Wem went in."

"Couldn't have been, now I think of it. He and Master Marcus had a nightcap in the breakfast room, for Master Marcus said so when he rang. He were the last and his lordship's valet had been in to him and gone off by then." He slapped the table. "That must be it. I'd forgot, for as I scarpered so quick, but I think his lordship was wearing his dressing-gown."

"Who discovered the body?" Shocked faces greeted this question. Hemp tried to mitigate his blunder. "I beg your pardon. Who was it found Master Daniel in the morning?"

John recovered first. "His lordship's valet again. He was acting for Master Daniel too. He come in with the rest to have his cup first thing like we all do, then went off up with the tray for the masters. He come back down quick, I can tell you. So I went up with him and when I saw—" He paused, swallowed something in his throat, and continued less smoothly, "Well, it took a minute, I don't mind saying, as to be sure he were gone. He just lay like he were sleeping. But he were gone all right. So I stayed and sent the valet off to fetch his lordship."

Ellen was shifting in her chair, her gaze fixed on Hemp. He eyed her a moment.

"Something else, Miss Ellen?"

Pinkness entered her cheeks and she grew flustered. "I don't rightly like to say, only…"

The cook opened her mouth. Hemp quickly forestalled her. "Anything you have to tell me, any little detail, may be of help."

The maid appeared to make up her mind. "Well, you see, I … I thought I heard summat. In the night."

"Ah, you did, did you? And I suppose you got up out of your bed and went down to see," scoffed Cook.

"I did too. I crept out of my room—"

A chorus of disbelieving protests drowned her out, but Hemp's attention was caught by another female entering the kitchen. The nursemaid Hepsie whom he had met before, with the orphaned child carried in her arms. The little girl looked half asleep, her head resting on the nurse's shoulder, one finger tucked into the neckline of Hepsie's gown. The child wore no cap, red-tinged golden locks curling against her cheek.

To his secret consternation, Hepsie met his gaze and came over, a slight furrow between her brows. Her tone was hushed. "Are they talking of it? Is that why you are here?"

Hemp gave a nod. "My mistress bade me find out if anyone saw anything."

Hepsie looked round at the still vocal argument and raised her voice. "I did. I saw something."

The announcement brought about a silence, all eyes turning on the nursemaid. She did not flinch, nor flush like the other girls, Hemp noted with a rise of admiration. A sturdy female, this Hepsie. Her grief for the child's plight notwithstanding, she kept faith with her charge's needs. Her pansy eyes were edged with shadows, her features drawn, yet she cradled the babe in strong arms, rocking her even as she talked.

"Ellen's right. There was someone about in the night."

The chambermaid threw the cook a triumphant glance. "See, I didn't imagine it neither."

"But you ain't gone down to look, I'll be bound. Hid under the covers more like."

"I did not! I got up and listened at the top of the stairs. I heard a pattering of feet, I swear."

"And then you ran back to bed and hid under the covers," said John.

Hemp cut into the laughter. "May we hear what Hepsie has to say, if you please?"

The nursemaid again became the focus of the rest, but her attention was on Pretty, disturbed by the commotion. Hepsie hushed her into quiet, dipping to kiss the little face. When the child's eyelids drooped, she turned to Hemp, speaking in a quiet tone.

"She was wakeful that night. She'd not been at peace since … you know."

Hemp nodded, glad the rest of the kitchen company had the sensitivity to remain silent.

"I came down to the kitchen to warm up some milk for her. On the way back…" She drew a visible breath. "I had to pass the master's room. I waited a bit, wondering should I call him to come to Pretty. Only if he'd wept, it would upset her more. So I went on past."

She paused, casting a glance across her auditors. Each one rapt, Hemp noted, such was the power of her hushed telling.

"Well, go on," urged Milly. "Did you see summat?"

Hepsie shifted the child closer to her bosom, as if the shadow of that night lay across the babe. "I thought I heard the master's door, but I can't be sure. It might have been another. I thought maybe he was coming out and I could ask him … but when I looked, it was someone else."

"How could you tell in the dark?" demanded the cook.

"There's a trifle of light in that corridor when the moon is up," put in John. "Who did you see, Hepsie?"

The nursemaid shivered a little. "I don't know. It was just a figure in a nightgown, flitting away too fast to tell. But I'm certain sure it was female."

CHAPTER ELEVEN

Lillian was found in the grand but dour parlour upstairs where Ottilia had first been received, along with Sybilla in that now seemingly far-off visit of condolence. Seated on a sofa by an open window, which thankfully provided a modicum of fresh air as well as brightness to the pervading gloom of the dark-panelled walls, Lillian was flicking through a periodical. She looked up as Ottilia entered on the heels of Annis Maplewood, glancing from one to the other.

"My turn, is it?" Setting aside the magazine, she folded her hands in her lap and fixed Ottilia with a challenging stare. "Go on. Accuse me."

Mrs Maplewood erupted. "Oh, for heaven's sake, Lillian! Lady Francis merely has a few questions."

Ottilia put up a staying hand, her gaze on the Brockhurst female, and moved to shift the nearest chair to a position close enough to be able to read the woman's expression. She sat, aware Lillian watched her with belligerent eyes.

"Of what should I accuse you, Mrs Brockhurst?"

Lillian looked taken aback. "That is what you are here for, is it not?"

"I am here to ferret for the truth of your nephew's death. Believe me, it is no pleasure to me to be here."

"Then why do it?"

Ottilia gave her look for look. "For justice, ma'am." And for the orphaned child most hurt by the deeds of the perpetrator, but that was her secret now.

"I thought you said my mother-in-law ordered it."

Ottilia bridled. "I am not subject to the orders of the Dowager Lady Wem."

"Then desist and go home. Leo doesn't want you here."

"It has nothing to do with Leo," Annis cut in. "He is not master here. Mama calls the tune, as you well know."

Ottilia turned to the woman, who was standing over Lillian, intent upon ensuring her cooperation. It was not likely to prove helpful. "Pardon me, Mrs Maplewood, but I believe we will do better alone."

Lillian said nothing, and Annis hesitated. "Are you sure? I doubt she's prepared to answer anything."

"That is Mrs Brockhurst's prerogative. I cannot force her tongue." Ottilia glanced at the woman as she spoke and noted a faint lessening of the rigidity of her pose. She'd found the right tack. "Pray give us a little time to ourselves, Mrs Maplewood."

"Oh, call me Annis, for the love of heaven! There is altogether too much formality in this house already."

Ottilia smiled. "Thank you. I am usually reduced to Lady Fan, but Ottilia will do, if you wish."

A warm smile creased Annis's mouth. "Lady Fan. I like that." She nodded at Lillian. "Treat her well. She is doing us all a favour, you know."

Ottilia observed Lillian's gaze follow her sister-in-law as she left the room. When the door latch clicked, she turned a wry face upon Ottilia. "She is an odd one, Annis. The odd one out. She and that son of hers make a pretty pair. They have no respect."

"For Lady Wem, you mean?"

"For anyone. They despise us."

"For what, ma'am?"

"Kowtowing to Protasia's decrees. I can't bear wrangling. The sort of brouhaha Leo kicks up. He is no docile son, so don't think it. He won't argue with her in front of the rest of us, God knows why, because we can hear them going at each other like woodpeckers."

Relieved the woman's tongue had loosened, Ottilia took immediate advantage. "Your husband does not similarly fight back?"

"Heavens, no. Godfrey is a peaceable fellow. His policy is to keep mum and act the dutiful son, as he told me at the outset. Once we are away from here, we may do as we please."

"And Marcus?"

A change came over Lillian. Her features softened and her lip quivered. "My handsome boy. A sensible fellow, too. He would never dream of creating difficulties for us." The maternal note vanished. "Besides, I hold his purse-strings. He knows I have his interests at heart."

How much at heart? Enough to dispose of a barrier to his advancement? Ottilia knew she must tread with care. The slightest hint of such a suspicion would send this woman back up into the boughs.

"Was there anything unusual that occurred that night?"

There was an instant wariness in Lillian's eyes. "Unusual? The whole affair was unusual. We are not in general obliged to endure public accusations of murderous intent."

"Just so. But think back, if you please."

Lillian tossed her head. "The boy was out of his senses. Anyone could see that. For my part, Leo has it correctly. He took his own life. Mary Ann supplied him with the means, I have no doubt." A hand flew palm up. "Not that she had any such intention. She doted on the boy. We have that in common at least. We dote on our sons."

202

Ottilia went for the jugular. "I am afraid that theory will not hold, Mrs Brockhurst. There can be no doubt Daniel was murdered. He was smothered, likely with one of his own pillows."

Was that alarm in her eyes? Or was it shock alone?

"Smothered?" Lillian set a hand to her ample bosom, which began to rise and fall as her agitation increased. "You must be mistaken. The doctor…"

"Doctor Heather is, I understand, waiting upon a post mortem."

"Smothered?"

The repetition set up a tremor in her fingers as they travelled from lap to mouth, lingered there, and then dropped to be clasped tight in her lap again. Ottilia observed these motions with mixed feelings. They argued for innocence and guilt both. The shock of hearing it was known? Or merely that of realising there was more to the business than suicide?

"Now do you see why I ask if anything untoward occurred that night?"

Lillian nodded. "Yes. Yes, I see."

"Well?"

She released one hand again, putting it to her brow. "Let me think. You have set my head in a whirl."

No doubt. Ottilia tried not to let suspicion grow uppermost. Aware of her own dislike, she must strive to remain neutral in judgement. She remained silent, waiting. Either for Lillian to recall some little detail, or to make something up.

The hand fell, a frown appearing. "Yes. Yes, it was unusual, now I come to think of it. We were all exercised over what to do. Protasia held we must remain aloof until something was settled about Daniel. Not that she participated in the discussions. She made her decree as ever and left the rest of us to find the way."

"Was a way to be found?"

"Not immediately. Godfrey and Leo were at one in the need to get Daniel away. Berta, however, was adamant it would infuriate Protasia the more. Vivian maintained Daniel would refuse to leave." Her gaze had darted about as she spoke, but with this it came back to Ottilia's face. "He was right, of course. Leo went in to Daniel and there was a fearful row. Myself, I suspect Vivian had advised Daniel to stand firm."

"This was the night before he died? You are sure of that?"

Lillian waved a restless hand. "Yes, but it had been going on since that dreadful public exhibition. Protasia's temper was so rubbed, she hit out at anyone and everyone if they so much as opened their mouths. She harangued Daniel several times. He was quite maddened, you know. It is no stretch to think he would wish to end it all."

"But he did not end it, Mrs Brockhurst. Someone ended it for him."

Lillian uttered a cry and clutched her brow. "There you go again! It cannot be. I refuse to believe it. Who would do such a thing?"

Ottilia struck hard. "The same person who would push Isabel off that rock."

Lillian's mouth fell open. Her eyes bulged. Her voice came out a croak. "You are as mad as he is."

Ottilia held her gaze. "You believe it was an accident?"

"Accident? Of course it was an accident. What possible reason could I have — could anyone have, to do such a thing?"

Ottilia caught the slip. "You, Mrs Brockhurst? You said 'I'."

"Did I?" Was it consternation? Bewilderment? Was her face growing a trifle flushed? "I didn't mean … it was a figure of speech. You cannot suppose I pushed that girl. Why in the world should I?"

"To curry favour with your mother-in-law? To settle the family dispute? You dislike wrangling, you said so. Was it not politic, and simple, for someone to be rid of the problem?"

Lillian threw up exasperated hands. "Oh, this is nonsense! Protasia had already determined on an annulment of the marriage."

Ottilia quashed this without hesitation. "I fear that will not hold, ma'am. Anyone with the smallest knowledge of the law must know there would be no annulment granted. There is a child. Clearly consummation had taken place."

"Well, divorce then."

The woman was beginning to sound desperate. Ottilia remained relentless. "With the scandal that entails? I hardly think the Dowager Lady Wem would have countenanced that path."

Lillian smacked her hands together. "Then she would have become reconciled. In the end, I believe she must have been."

"Indeed? As she became at last to your marriage, ma'am?"

That hit the mark. Lillian went white. Her eyes spat fury.

What she might have said remained unknown, for the door was flung open, banging back against the wall.

Startled, Ottilia turned to find Berta standing in the aperture, eyes blazing and pointing an accusing finger. "You! How dare you come here? My brother forbade you the house!"

The oddest change came over Lillian. She started up, annoyance in her tone. "For the love of heaven, don't start your play-acting, Berta! Have we not had enough of dramatic alarums and fighting? Shut that door, woman, and come and sit down!"

To Ottilia's utter astonishment, the woman complied, closing the door and hurrying across to plonk down beside Lillian. The latter leaned to pat her hand.

"That's better. Now just sit there quietly while Lady Francis asks her questions."

At that, the woman's head reared up and she gave Ottilia a nasty look, giving the woman an aspect all too reminiscent of the reptilian slant of the mother.

"I shall answer nothing."

The voice was high and querulous, matching the willowy figure. She was taller than her mother and thin, her cheeks sunken, mouth pinched. She looked, Ottilia guessed, a good deal older than her years.

"Lady Francis is here because your mama ordered it."

"Requested," Ottilia cut in. She would not countenance this notion Lady Wem had the slightest dominion over her actions.

"Oh, well, *requested*, if you insist." Lillian's tone was a sneer. "You are here, are you not, though you profess to dislike it?"

With difficulty, Ottilia controlled a rise of temper. "As I told you, I am here for justice."

It bore repeating for Berta's benefit. Not that she got much by it. The woman continued to watch her with a regard Ottilia could only interpret as malevolent.

"Justice? You seek for justice in vain in this house. Where is justice for me? I have seen none these twenty years."

Was this play-acting, as Lillian would have it? Or had the woman a genuine complaint? A lasting grudge, that was certain. Could it have led to revenge? Yet what satisfaction might it grant to be rid of her own nephew? He was not responsible for the ills of her life. The thoughts swept rapidly through Ottilia's mind and she resolved to be wary in her approach.

"I was asking Mrs Brockhurst about the night before Daniel died. You are perhaps better placed to say if there was anything unusual toward."

Disdain entered Berta's features. "You seek to lure me with flattery? It is no compliment to me to refer to my chains."

This was play-acting indeed. Ottilia was afflicted with an inappropriate desire to giggle. She quashed it. "Pardon me. I should have rather said I trust in your familiarity with this establishment, little though you appreciate being obliged to live here."

Surprise flickered in Berta's cold eyes. "Shrewd."

No, obvious. But Ottilia did not say so. She pursued the tack. "Was it more or less discomforting that night?"

A high-pitched laugh escaped the woman, mirthless but telling. "Discomforting? Do you suppose my comfort has ever been regarded? Do they, any of them, think of me?"

"Berta!"

She turned on Lillian at her side. "Don't you Berta me. You most of all. You have the means. A splendid house, a life of ease, anything you wish for at your fingertips. Do you ever think to invite me?" She put up the flat of her hand as Lillian opened her mouth to respond. "No, do not speak. Do I wish to hear a mouthful of excuses? Selfish. Selfish, all of you." She looked back at Ottilia. "None of them ever thinks of me. It is all Mama this, Mama that. Never Berta. No one cares if I am buried here or in the ground. It is all one."

The tirade reminded Ottilia irresistibly of the Dowager Lady Wem. No surprise Berta was her copy. She had no doubt learned her catalogue of complaint at her mother's knee. Was

207

there any way to break through the obsessive self-absorption? She tried a different approach. "Were you fond of Daniel?"

"Fond? Why should I care for Leo's boy? He was fawned upon enough."

"Not latterly, as I understand it."

"He crossed the line. What did he expect? He ought to have known how it would be, but had he a thought for any but himself? A grain of sense, did he have one, must have told him what I would be obliged to endure once the truth was out."

Ottilia pounced on this. "You knew of the marriage then?"

"Who did not, except the one person it could hurt?" Berta became shrill as she emitted another of those high-pitched laughs. "I could have enjoyed how she was confounded when she discovered it, if it had not brought a whirlwind of discontent upon me." She leaned in, thrusting her pointed chin at Ottilia and looking remarkably like a witch. "Always I must bear the brunt of her storming rages. They were not here to endure the ravings, the screams, the vile epithets heaped upon them all in their absence and falling upon me. All, all I endured, I alone." She sat back, a sour smile creasing her thin lips. "No, my fine lady, I was not fond. Not of my nephew, nor any of them, leaving me here to rot while they carouse. Selfish, all."

Feeling battered, Ottilia began to wish for air and light, for the balm of her spouse's affection. Most of all, for a legitimate reason to abandon this appalling family to drown in their own stew pot. But there were two victims to be accounted for, and the innocent most wounded by their taking off. She gathered her courage. "You can tell me nothing of that night then, Miss Brockhurst?"

Berta threw her a mocking glance. "Oh, I could tell you much, if I so chose."

"But you don't, I take it?"

"I told you at the outset I would answer nothing. I stand by it."

Yet she had told Ottilia a great deal. Enough to arouse suspicion of a possible motive. It would not be the first time she had met with jealousy of an order sufficient to kill. But where was the profit in it? Lillian might be ambitious for her son. Berta would only heap more ignominy upon her head from the mother she loathed with an all-consuming passion.

She had no time to indulge these thoughts further for the opening door brought about a visible change in both women as they looked towards it. Berta sat up straighter and her face became a mask, utterly free of the viciousness she had so far exhibited. As for Lillian, an ingratiating smile appeared on her lips, though it was not reflected in her eyes which showed a trifle apprehensive.

Ottilia's back was to the door. She twisted in her seat and found herself staring into the irate features of Lord Wem.

The expected explosion did not come, but his tone was distinctly unamiable. "You here, Lady Francis? After my express prohibition?"

Ottilia rose from her chair and faced him. "As you see, sir."

His gaze turned on the ladies. "I am astonished you submitted to be questioned, Lillian."

The woman simpered. "You know me, Leo. I am a peaceable being. Besides, I had nothing of value to offer Lady Francis. As you are aware, I am at one with your belief."

Lord Wem's smouldering look was next cast upon his sister and he marched across the room to confront her. "And you, Berta? Have you betrayed me?"

In a flash, the woman was up. "I betray you, brother? Heaven forbid! Any more than I would betray our dear mother." The unctuous tone made Ottilia feel physically ill. Such hypocrisy.

"So I should hope," said her brother austerely. "You are, after all, beholden to Mama."

Did Berta stiffen? She moved towards the door. "Speaking of whom, I must go and see how she does. She ate poorly this morning."

With which, she whisked out of the door without sparing so much as a glance for Ottilia, never mind bidding her farewell. Not that any such courtesy could be expected from a female of her ilk.

Lord Wem shifted to the fireplace and turned there, his inimical gaze falling upon Ottilia. She braced. His aspect reminded her of an angry swan, regal but looking ready to hiss and spit if politeness did not decree otherwise. Or was he merely reluctant to show his true colours before a stranger? He was allegedly practiced at concealment in his mother's presence.

"I will be obliged, ma'am, if you will remove yourself forthwith. You have no business here."

Ottilia's ire rose and she struggled not to fly out at the wretch. As it was she could not prevent a clipped tone. "I am here, as I have been obliged to point out several times, at the request of the Dowager Lady Wem. If you object, I suggest you take up the matter with the mistress of this house."

He looked nonplussed, if irritated, champing for a moment and clasping his hands behind his back. Ottilia caught Lillian's gaze slipping from Wem to herself and back again. He spoke at last, by the stiffness of his jaw experiencing difficulty in holding in his temper.

"This is your answer? Even with my lawyer's letter in your husband's hands, as I have no doubt it is by this time."

"Yes, it is, sir. And yes, this is my answer." She added with relish, "If you care to enquire of my husband, you will find him adamant I should continue my enquiries in despite of such a letter. My husband, sir, does not take kindly to high-handed interference."

Lord Wem's breath came in snorting harrumphs and Ottilia almost felt sorry for him, obliged to contain his spleen. She adopted a tone of spurious courtesy.

"Your mother, my lord, was wishful I should make enquiry of all in this house. That, I believe, includes you."

She had gone too far. Wem exploded, taking a couple of strides in her direction.

"Question me? An insult of the first order, madam. I to be accused of bringing about my son's death? An event, mark you, which bears all the marks of suicide, little though I savour the implication."

"You would prefer if it were murder then?"

"Emphatically no, madam. The notion is absurd and ridiculous."

Ottilia grasped the edge of the chair back, feeling in need of support as he towered before her. "Would you be willing to hear why it is neither absurd nor ridiculous, sir?"

He put up a staying hand. "I have heard it. I have also heard of your alleged qualifications for making such claims. I prefer to trust in an accredited medical man's opinion."

She faced him down. "Yet your medical man did not supply you with the diagnosis you wanted, did he? I was there. I heard what he said to you."

Lord Wem's eye flashed fire. "You were there, yes. Upon the urging of my deluded sister. Annis had no right to interfere."

Weary of the constant questioning of rights, Ottilia let this pass, returning to the main thread. "I suppose you have had no word from the doctor of the results of the post mortem?"

"None." There was dissatisfaction in the word, and he added with bitterness, "Not that it is any concern of yours."

Ottilia eyed him. Would a conciliatory manner work? "How if we wait upon that result, my lord? If you do not get the answer you want, perhaps you may yourself become anxious to discover who could have smothered your son."

His expression altered. "Smothered?" The word choked out of him. "That is what you believe?"

"The signs were indicative of such. Did your informant not tell you as much?"

Bafflement flitted across his features. "Not that, no. They spoke of … murder."

Another word that seemed to soil his mouth. Ottilia was once again moved to pity. She was forgetting he was a man in grief, if unexpressed, as in the manner of his wife. She dared a step towards him. "Come, sir. Do you not owe it to your son to find out the truth?"

The soft approach proved vain. Lord Wem pokered up again. "I owe the boy nothing. After such disruption as he caused? Setting the family at outs and the household into chaos. No, madam, he has come by his desserts."

Shocked, Ottilia forgot to mind her tongue. "You cannot mean that, sir. All the boy did was to snatch at happiness. Will you condemn him on account of your mother's prejudice?"

His features contorted. "Are you daring to tell me my business? Who are you, madam, to lecture me about my own?" He strode past her to the door and threw it open. "Enough of this! Get you gone, Lady Francis, out of my house!"

Ottilia was all too ready to leave, despite the pattering of her pulse as fury rose at the manner of this speech. She would have stalked out but the way became blocked by the diminutive figure of the Dowager Lady Wem abruptly appearing in the aperture.

She did not look at Ottilia, instead addressing her son in a scorching tone. "Since when, Leo, do you eject visitors from this establishment? This is not yet your house."

Lord Wem did not speak, his stance more that of a waxwork effigy than anything else. Only the eyes gave away his baffled fury as he stalked towards the door.

His mother's gaze turned from him to the Brockhurst female, a silent spectator of the futile battle. "Where is my daughter?"

Lillian's tone was subservient in the extreme. "Berta? She went to find you, dear Protasia."

"Well for her she did not succeed. Leave us, Lillian."

Lord Wem had already departed. Lillian rose on the instant and hurried out. The Dowager Lady Wem went to the chair placed centrally with the fire to one side. Her throne? It was where she had sat on that first day. She pointed to the chair by which Ottilia was standing. "Bring that close and sit."

Little though she cared for the command, and rather disappointed than otherwise at not being able to escape, Ottilia complied. As she sat down, Lady Wem's gaze raked her face.

"Well?"

Ottilia could not withhold a sigh. "I take it that is a request to hear what progress I have made?"

"Well?"

The repetition rankled, but Ottilia let it go. "Very little, if you must have it."

Lady Wem gave a nod. "They will not co-operate? As I expected. Recalcitrant fools."

"On the contrary. I found both Mary Ann and Lillian willing enough. However, nothing they told me has brought me nearer to the truth."

Lady Wem seemed to accept this. She jerked her head towards the door. "He won't speak of it to you. Bent upon thwarting me. A stubborn fool, my son. He wants to be rid of the business. So do we all, I told him, but there's a traitor in our midst. I won't have traitors about me." She pierced Ottilia with a stare. "Find the culprit."

Ottilia let out an overcharged breath. "How, ma'am, when every word must be dragged out? I understand Lord Wem has enjoined half the family at least not to speak to me."

"I will see to Leo."

Losing patience, Ottilia told her the truth. "Like all despots, Lady Wem, you imagine you control all tongues because they are silent in your presence. People are not so readily controlled." Especially your foul brood, she might have added, but managed to stop the words from escaping her lips.

The reptilian sneer appeared. "Do you think I don't know? Disobedient, the lot of them." She banged a fist on the arm of her chair. "But I will not tolerate treachery. They will pay."

Exasperated, Ottilia rose. "Enough, ma'am. It is not you who must endure the rude treatment to which I have been subjected. I will stay no longer." She turned, heading for the door. The woman's taunting voice followed her.

"No backbone, eh? No appetite for a challenge?"

Halting, Ottilia turned in fury. "Do not think to browbeat me, Lady Wem. I do not choose to embroil myself further in this business. What is it to me, after all?"

There was satisfaction in the woman's slanting eyes, a mocking curl at her lips. Triumph at having provoked Ottilia into losing her temper?

"Come tomorrow. I will engage for it there will be answers from any you choose to question."

Despite her annoyance, Ottilia was conscious of a flitter of amusement. Admiration too. If one could admire cunning. But she was not to be deprived of choice.

"I will give it some thought, ma'am. That is all I am prepared to say."

Having spent a disconsolate hour or two dawdling in the shade and examining the little shops along the colonnade, Lizzy welcomed the relief afforded by Ottilia's request. Ottilia had hailed her from the window of the lodging as she crossed the Pantiles with the intention of re-joining her grandmother in the Assembly Rooms.

"Wait there, Lizzy! I am coming down."

Lizzy waved acquiescence and wandered to the little musicians' gallery, empty of players during this period of quiet while the visitors, church duty done, were at chat, play being postponed on the Lord's Day, ensconced either in the Rooms or the coffee house. Anxiety rose up. What had happened at the Brockhurst residence? She knew of Lord Wem's disapprobation for her uncle had been voluble on the subject. Lord Francis had vented his outrage once Ottilia had departed.

"I don't wish to trouble Tillie any further. She is upset enough as it is. But this wretch, instead of decently mourning his son, must have sent directly to this lawyer of his — for he resides in the town—"

"It must be his mother's man, I should think."

"—and enjoins the fellow to write this stink to me! Overnight. Such impudence! I tell you, Mama, I am minded to call Wem out."

Sybilla, predictably, lost no time in attributing Lord Wem's attitude to the influence of the poisonous Protasia. But her advice was sound.

"Send to Jardine, Francis. Let him deal with the business. Heaven knows I cannot abide the man, but there is no denying he will quash this nonsense in no time. He will have this lawyer of Wem's quailing in his boots."

Lizzy knew the family's man of business to be a formidable legal opponent and it came as no surprise when Francis seized upon the suggestion with alacrity, removing to his own lodging with the intention of sending an immediate express to the capital. Lizzy was left to miserable reflection, tempered by frustration at being excluded from the hunt for Daniel's killer.

She was therefore ripe for her assigned task when at length her aunt appeared and they sat together on one of the benches shaded by the trees along the edge of the Pantiles.

"Lizzy, I need your help."

"For what, ma'am? If it is this Brockhurst affair—"

"It is, but I am not asking you to approach Mr Maplewood, never fear."

A little fillip of hope, of which Lizzy had scarcely been aware, subsided. "How did you fare, Aunt? Were they horrid?"

Ottilia let out a weary sigh. "For the most part. They are all quite different when you catch them alone, however. Mary Ann was forthcoming, in between bouts of tearfulness. Lillian had a great deal to say, but little to the purpose. Berta was…" She hesitated and Lizzy saw a gleam of amusement appear in her eye.

"Berta was what?" she prompted, intrigued.

A laugh escaped Ottilia. "She was next door to demented, poor woman. One cannot help but feel sorry for her, despite the rude treatment she meted out. Still, it was no worse than what I endured from the obnoxious Leo."

"Heavens, Aunt, how did you bear it?"

Ottilia looked mischievous. "I did not. I gave no quarter and told Lady Wem I did not wish to pursue the business."

Lizzy was conscious of disappointment. "You have abandoned it then."

"Of course I have not, though I was sorely tempted." She sighed. "How could I leave it? There are two grossly wronged victims demanding justice. More, there is an innocent in the case left to the Lord knows what sort of future."

Ottilia sounded tremulous all at once, puzzling Lizzy. "Innocent?"

"Little Pretty." There was a distinct break in her aunt's voice. "A daughter, Lizzy. She is left an orphan."

Memory leapt in Lizzy's head. "Daniel spoke of her. I had forgot. When he was grieving, he asked how she would fare without her mother. And now he is dead too. Oh, Aunt, that is so sad! Poor little thing."

"Just so. It is in this connection I desire your help, Lizzy."

Moved, Lizzy grasped one of her hands. "What do you wish me to do?"

Ottilia's fingers squeezed hers for a moment and then she disengaged her hand, straightening up and looking Lizzy directly in the face. "I trust you, Lizzy, to keep mum on my reason for asking this of you."

"I shall say nothing, Aunt Ottilia, but what in the world is the matter?"

She watched in consternation as her aunt took a visible breath, her clear gaze a trifle luminous. "I cannot trust myself,

Lizzy. I do not wish to encounter this waif and the nurse must be questioned."

Lizzy gazed at her in bewilderment. "Why don't you wish to? I thought you doted on children. Mama says you were practically a second mother to your nephews."

Ottilia waved this away. "Tom and Ben are different. They were sturdy little fellows from the outset. And they had not lost their parents. This little mite…" She shook her head as if to rid it of unwanted thoughts. "You may question the nurse for me, Lizzy. You will be able to keep your attention fully on her, while I… Pray do this for me, my dear, and we may make a little progress at last."

Acutely troubled, Lizzy was yet loath to pursue the burning questions in her head. It was plain Ottilia was cast down by Pretty's plight, but it was not like her to shirk a task for such a reason as that.

"If you wish me to do it, of course I will, Aunt. But why must this nurse be questioned?"

Ottilia became brisk. "I set Hemp to talk to such domestic staff as he could find. Hepsie, the nurse that is, saw a female form flit along the corridor in the night. People usually see a lot more than they realise at the time. If you press her, I am in hopes there may be more to it."

Burgeoning interest drove through Lizzy's inner discontent. "What of you, Aunt? Will you go back there?"

"Tomorrow. But after I catch a retainer referred to as old Janet. Hemp is pledged to arrange with a kitchen maid named Milly to bring her to drink the waters in the morning."

Her natural sparkle was beginning to flow through Lizzy's veins and she laughed. "Lady Fan at work, and she needs me at last. I could not be more delighted."

Ottilia got up. "I must go back. Francis is fretting and we cannot have him tangling with Lord Wem."

Lizzy got up too. "Does he know how they treated you there then?"

Ottilia sighed. "We have no secrets. At least, none of any significance. But do not mention all I have said of Pretty, I pray you, Lizzy. Fan will think… No matter for that. Only do your part. As soon as you may, if you please. I must go."

She was off on the words, leaving Lizzy prey to uncomfortable conjecture. The felicity of her aunt's marriage was a byword in the family. Was there a bone of contention? A memory surfaced. Before the couple arrived, had not her grandmama issued a warning?

"Whatever you do, Elizabeth, do not ask your aunt about babies, do you understand?" To a query as to why, she had only given a vague response. "It is a sore point with Ottilia, that is all."

The mystery sprang back into being. A sore point indeed if she could not bring herself to question this Hepsie for fear of finding herself in the company of the orphaned child. What had she called her? A waif? Aunt Ottilia had been near to weeping, and she was always so assured and capable.

While these thoughts revolved, Lizzy was walking in the direction of the Assembly Rooms. Best to let her grandmama know what she was about or she would be scolded for vanishing again.

The Dowager Lady Polbrook was deep into a discussion with Lady Countersett, Mrs Trefnant and several of the elderly male inhabitants of the town concerning the alarming news filtering in from France about the benighted King and Queen whom, it was said, had taken refuge with the Legislative Assembly for fear of the vengeance of the rebels. For her part,

Lizzy was the more exercised by matters closer to home, although she could not but be momentarily horrified on hearing one of the gentlemen speak of the outrage as signalling the overthrow of the French monarchy.

Sybilla made no objection when she knew whence came her errand. "Your aunt asked it of you? In that case, you may go. But take Nancy."

Deciding it would be no bad thing to have her own maid become acquainted with this Hepsie, Lizzy lost no time in returning to the lodgings to collect Nancy before starting up the Common towards the Brockhurst residence on the hill. Her maid might well be better placed to locate the nurse. She could hardly ring the bell and ask for the girl herself. Not without raising question.

As luck would have it, as Lizzy approached the house, she heard a child's treble voice. Glancing about, she caught sight of a little girl running in a garden to one side. Standing close by was a young female in motley attire but wearing a comprehensive apron that spoke of the nursemaid. This must be Hepsie.

Elated, Lizzy looked for a way into the garden. It was shady with trees and enclosed by iron railings. "Can you see a gate, Nancy?"

Her maid pointed. "Looks to be up by the side of the house, my lady."

Sure enough, a path led around from the entrance and the gate was just visible from where they stood. It did not take more than a moment for Lizzy to make her way to the entrance point. She unlatched the gate, bidding Nancy follow and close it behind her.

The nursemaid had spotted them, although the little girl was still in pursuit of a rolling ball. She moved in front of the child, in a protective attitude, lifting her chin at the newcomers.

Lizzy produced a smile. "You are Hepsie, I believe? And this must be Pretty."

The nurse frowned. "Yes, ma'am. I don't know you though."

There was no subservience. Even a touch of belligerence. Lizzy wondered at it but made haste to introduce herself. "I am Lady Elizabeth Fiske and this is my maid Nancy. I am niece to Lady Francis Fanshawe. I believe you know her steward, Hemp Roy?"

A change came over the girl and she visibly relaxed. "He's a kind fellow. He understood."

Lizzy had little acquaintance with Hemp, but she knew her aunt valued his services. She took advantage of the girl's approval. "I am glad he was of help. It is a difficult time for you."

Hepsie shifted her shoulders. "I don't care for that. It's the babe as will suffer. She calls for her mama and I don't know what to say to her. I can only tell her Hepsie's here. Nor I can't promise I will be for I don't know what they intend."

"I am so sorry. Has not anyone talked to you since these terrible losses?"

The nursemaid's gaze darkened. "I hoped as the master's mama might have come up, though she's the one most affected. She's the only one as knows the babe and the rest of them don't care. Nor they've not said nothing, nor even asked how my little darling does. I tremble for her future and that's a fact."

Shocked and considerably dismayed, Lizzy made a mental resolve to tackle Mr Maplewood on the subject. He at least, who was his cousin's friend, might have shown regard for the welfare of Daniel's daughter. Horrid and callous of him to neglect the child.

But this had no bearing on her commission. She must be glad Hepsie was so ready to talk. She plunged in. "Hemp says you saw someone that night. A woman?"

The nursemaid's brows drew together. "Are you asking for that black fellow's mistress and all?"

"Yes, I am. Lady Francis, or Lady Fan as she likes to be called, is trying to find out the truth."

A wail from the little girl sent Hepsie scurrying to Pretty, who had fallen in her chase. While the nurse stood her up again and soothed her into quiet, Lizzy took occasion to observe the child. The name was apt. She was clad in a white lawn gown tied with a blue sash; curls of pale gold, escaping from under her frilled cap, framed an adorable little face with the plump cheeks of babyhood and a pink rosebud of a mouth. Lizzy's mind leapt to Ottilia's half-expressed fears and she experienced a glimmer of understanding. Before it could be fully formed, Hepsie was back, having set the ball rolling again and sent Pretty on her way.

"She is well named," Lizzy remarked.

Hepsie brushed this aside. "Yes, ma'am, but you were asking about that night."

An anxious note caught Lizzy's attention and she spoke without thought. "Do you believe someone killed him? Your master?"

"I can't think he'd be dead else. Mr Daniel wouldn't have done it himself like his lordship says. Not when there was the babe to think of. Oh, yes, he was stricken for losing the mistress, who wouldn't be? But he come to Pretty most nights, and he held back his tears, and he read her a fairy story like he used to and kissed her goodnight, and now my little darling don't even have that."

Here Hepsie's voice became wholly suspended. Lizzy's immediate impulse to set an arm about her was forestalled as Nancy slipped from behind her and did just that, hushing the girl and thrusting a pocket handkerchief into her fingers.

"Now, now, you stop that crying," she murmured low. "You don't want the little one to hear you." Hepsie nodded and gulped down her tears, making use of the square of linen and scrunching it in her fingers. "There, that's better. Tell you what. I'll go and play with your babe there while you talk to my lady."

Hepsie thanked her and watched as Nancy went to the child, picked up the ball and threw it gently. Pretty stared at her for a moment and then looked for the familiar face of her nurse.

"Catch the ball, my pretty. Nancy will throw it for you. Hepsie is here, never fear."

The child looked uncertain for a moment, but upon Nancy repeating her throw and encouraging her again, the lure of the ball won and she consented to be distracted.

Lizzy watched the little piece of byplay with a lift of admiration for her maid. For the moment, she had the nurse's full attention.

"Pray tell me exactly what you saw, Hepsie."

The nurse fiddled with the handkerchief she held. "It's what I told the man Hemp. I had to go down for milk for Pretty—"

"What time was this?"

"I'm not rightly sure. Must have been one or two in the morning. Might have been later, I can't say for certain."

But it was a time when the household was quiet and abed. Excitement burgeoned and Lizzy pushed for more. "What happened exactly?"

Hepsie's brows flickered as she concentrated. "I come up from the kitchens with the glass. I had to pass the master's door. There was a little light so I could see it was shut."

"Did you hear anything?"

Hepsie jerked the handkerchief between her hands. "I wish I had. I did listen for as I thought of going in and waking the master to come to Pretty. But it was quiet."

"In the room, you mean?"

All at once, the nurse's gaze lit with realisation. "Too quiet. No sighing, nor yet a snore. The master never slept that quiet."

"Then he was already—" Lizzy bit off the final word, but Hepsie said it for her.

"Dead. He must have been."

"But you couldn't have known. What did you do then, Hepsie?"

She blew out a breath. "I went off towards the stairs. That's when I heard a door opening. Or so I thought. Might have been his, but there's several along that corridor. Could have been one of the others."

"Who sleeps in those other rooms?"

"Mr Marcus is in one. Miss Clarissa and Mr Julius in the other."

That was no use if the figure was female. Lizzy had reason to believe Clarissa had not done the deed. But it might have been she who came out of her room. Only where was Vivian?

"Is not Mr Maplewood in one of those rooms?"

"Yes, but it's on the other side of the house. He wouldn't hear anything."

"I see. What happened when you heard the door?"

"If it was a door I heard. I drew back and kept still. It went through my mind as the master might have got up, but of course he couldn't have done, could he? He were gone already by then."

Hepsie's conviction was total. Lizzy returned her to her story.

"But what did you see?"

"Someone walking along the corridor, quiet like. A ghost nearly, for all I knew."

"In which direction? Was the person making for the stairs like you?"

"Not the back stairs as I use. She went down the main stairs."

"It was definitely a she?"

Hepsie hesitated. "I thought I was sure of that, but I don't know. The nightgown went to the ankles, which it wouldn't for a man. But I might've been mistook. The light was faint. It was more a white shape than anything."

Lizzy picked up another point. "But it went down the stairs?"

"Yes, I'm certain sure of that, my lady."

"Are the principal bedchambers on the floor below your master's room? Or is that only the parlours?"

"That's right, my lady. Leastways, I don't know which room is which, but my Lord Wem and his lady are down there, besides his lordship's brother and his wife; and there's Mrs Maplewood as well as the mistress of the house. That's beside the parlours. It's a big house and I haven't been all over it. I've mostly kept to the upper floors and the kitchens. Nor I don't bring Pretty out by the front for the garden. I keep her out of their way. Out of sight, out of mind, I hope, for as they won't think to send me away too soon."

While sympathetic to this view, Lizzy's mind was turning on the story. It was scant enough, especially with the uncertainty of gender. If only she had her aunt's knack of asking just the right question.

"Is there anything else you remember, Hepsie? Any little detail?"

The nurse shook her head in a regretful way. "I've thought on it and thought on it, my lady, and the more I think the less certain I feel."

Lizzy made haste to reassure. "What you have told me will be most helpful to Lady Fan. If you do remember or think of anything else, please come forward. Nancy will tell you where we are lodging." She set a hand on the nurse's arm. "Try not to fret, Hepsie. Something will be done for Pretty, I am certain."

Hepsie looked unconvinced. "But what, my lady? I know well as the mistress weren't wanted here. None of them took her part. They won't want nothing to do with Mistress Isabel's daughter."

The blunt utterance had a bitter edge. Lizzy was ashamed to realise she had almost forgotten the tragic fall and her initial conviction it had been no accident. Her aunt was right. There were two victims here. No, three. She had become lost in her preoccupation with Mr Maplewood, forgetful of what counted in this tangle.

She had no comfort for Hepsie's prime concern, but at least she could offer a crumb. "My aunt will solve this mystery, I promise you. Whoever did this will be found out."

The nursemaid nodded, but her mouth was tight, her tone clipped. "It won't help Pretty, but I won't deny I'd like to see the finger pointed. Cruel and evil it is. And I know who made it happen even if she didn't do it."

Lizzy did not pretend ignorance. "Quite so, Hepsie. But pray don't say it to anyone else."

"I know when to keep my tongue, my lady. You learn fast in this house."

A shrewd female, this nurse. Lizzy called to Nancy and made her farewells, with one last admonition to Hepsie to bring anything she remembered to the right quarter.

"Or indeed anything you may hear that could aid us."

Hepsie agreed and went to relieve Nancy of her charge. Lizzy turned for the gate and stopped short. Mr Maplewood was standing on the other side.

Lizzy called to her maid. "Nancy, wait here for me, if you please." She stepped up to the gate, meeting Mr Maplewood's gaze.

He opened the gate for her. "Walk with me?"

Lizzy did not answer but stepped through. Mr Maplewood indicated the wide pathway leading towards the back of the house. "There is an orchard just along here. You will be within sight of your maid."

Lizzy glanced round. "How did you know I was here?"

"I saw you from the window. That room I like to use overlooks the garden."

Mr Maplewood moved ahead of her and unlatched a second gate, waiting for her to go ahead. Lizzy passed through, glancing about at the ordered rows of trees, just now heavy with cherries, plums and apples. She turned and faced him, unable to help an accusatory tone.

"Why have you not been to see that child? How could you, who profess to love her father, neglect her in these terrible circumstances? Poor Hepsie is at her wit's end, worrying what will become of Pretty. You at least might have reassured her."

Mr Maplewood met her glare. "Judging me again, Eliza?"

Lizzy lifted her chin. "Yes, I am judging you, sir. Do you know no one in the house has gone near the child since her papa was killed? Hepsie is certain she will be dismissed and little Pretty sent away and then the child will have no one at all to love her. It is pitiful, Vivian."

He captured one of the hands with which she had gestured. "You are not as indifferent to me as you would have me suppose, are you?"

Astonishment drove away Lizzy's wrath. She made no attempt to withdraw her hand from his hard grasp. "You are the strangest creature, Mr Maplewood."

"Not that. Use my name, woman. You just did."

"I didn't mean to."

"But you did."

Lizzy wrenched her fingers out of his. "This is singularly stupid. I'm trying to bring you to a sense of your callousness and all you can do is—"

"You may resume your dressing down in a moment," he interrupted. "Let us settle this once and for all. We are not strangers. There is something between us and I won't let you dismiss me out of hand, do you see?"

Her confusion intensified. "You have an odd way of telling a person you like them, sir, if that is what you are implying."

"Like? I don't know if I like you. You infuriate and amuse me both. Or you did. I can't say what it is, but I do know I don't want your enmity. Will that suffice?"

"No, it will not suffice, you stupid man! Why did you come out? What do you want of me?"

Exasperation sounded in his tone. "I've just told you, Eliza. I want you back. The way it was. Or better. I don't know."

Her gaze wavered, the fierceness in her bosom dissipating. She looked towards the garden again, and the movement drew his eye as well to the small figure holding up a flower for her nurse's inspection.

"Heaven help me, you are right to reproach me, Eliza. I had not thought of Pretty. The vultures won't spare her." His gaze shifted back. "I'll talk to Mama. She will know what is being mooted."

"Thank you! Do you suppose Mrs Maplewood might have a solution? I know my aunt is troubled by the thought of what will happen to Pretty. She could not bear to come face to face with her, you must know, and sent me to question Hepsie in her stead."

"Hepsie? About what?"

"It is the most telling thing, Vivian. She saw someone in the night hours who may have been coming from Daniel's room. She thinks it was a woman."

Mr Maplewood's brows snapped together. "Then it's true. One of them did smother him."

"Yes, but which remains a question."

"Has your aunt no clue as yet?"

"No, for she has been treated so badly. Only a couple of your aunts were willing to talk. Lord Wem was rude and so was Berta. Aunt Ottilia thinks Berta is a little touched."

Mr Maplewood blew out a contemptuous breath. "That wouldn't surprise me. She's as bad as the crocodile. But this Lady Fan of yours doesn't mean to give up, I hope."

"She never does. I wish I had her intellect. She is extraordinarily clever. She believes in justice, though in this case I think it is compassion which drives her."

"You admire her a great deal, I perceive."

"Oh, I do."

"And would emulate her?"

Lizzy laughed in a self-conscious way. "Alas, it is an empty aspiration. I am far too impulsive. Nor do I have her ability to make such connections as lead Lady Fan to the truth. I do love her. She is a wonderful person and your horrid family does not deserve her."

"You need not tell me. I am no advocate for the Brockhursts. Who, then? Could it have been Mary Ann?"

"I had not thought of that. She might have gone in to check on Daniel, might she not? She gave him a potion."

Mr Maplewood wafted a hand. "That's what I was thinking. I don't believe she would have murdered Dan. Lillian now. Though what could she hope to gain? Dan wasn't the heir."

"Which leaves Berta or Clarissa."

"You are forgetting the crocodile."

"The Dowager Lady Wem? Would she go so far?"

"She is eminently capable of it."

Lizzy was unconvinced. "Then why insist upon Lady Fan finding the culprit?"

"To throw off the scent. To cause ructions among her descendants. That is her forte."

"Yes, but it doesn't make sense, Vivian."

Mr Maplewood frowned. "Why not?"

"You can't see it for prejudice. She had only to accept Lord Wem's conviction of suicide. Why stir the coals?"

"You are persuasive, Eliza, I'll give you that." He paused as Lizzy eyed him. "What is it?"

She looked away and back again. "How are you faring?"

He did not pretend to misunderstand. "I cannot say the worst is over. I think it has dulled rather, superseded by this notion of murder. I can't feel it, Eliza. At least, there are moments when…" He faded out.

Lizzy did not prompt him, instead keeping her gaze fixed on his face. He did not meet her eyes. Could he not endure the sympathy? He spoke again.

"There are moments when it hurts acutely. It is a real physical ache. I had no notion grief could do that. I have more understanding of Dan's state, I think." His gaze came back to her. "You read him better than I did, Eliza."

"I am glad I was able to help him, even a little." She became brisk again. "Now the best service we can render him is to find out his killer." She scanned his face. "For Pretty's sake too."

Mr Maplewood winced. "I will do my part there, Eliza. Will you allow me to find you out to hear how your aunt progresses?"

"I would certainly prefer you to find me than to be obliged to come seeking you in this horrid house."

CHAPTER TWELVE

Old Janet was a wizened woman, shrunken with age. Although she must, Ottilia thought, have been sturdy in youth for she still walked without the aid of a stick, using instead the arm of the kitchen maid Milly who had obliged Hemp with the introduction. Janet's face was criss-crossed with wrinkles, but the bright pair of orbs looking up at Ottilia held a good deal of shrewdness.

"Heard of you, I have."

"Indeed? How so?"

"Not much goes on aroun' these parts as I don't hear of it. You'll be wantin' ter ask about them children, I fancy."

Ottilia guessed she meant those Brockhurst children now adults. "If you are willing."

"Not before this 'un." The old dame tugged at Milly's arm. "You bring me ter Betty's and leave me and the leddy ter talk."

Milly nudged her back. "You can't take the lady there. It's not fit for the likes of her."

"You leave me ter judge that, girlie." An appraising glance ran over Ottilia. "She ain't one to balk at keepin' company wi' lesser folk, I can tell that."

Ottilia at once agreed. "I am in your hands, Mistress Janet."

"You can leave off mistress. Janet will do."

"Then you must call me Lady Fan."

The civility appeared to please the old nurse and she urged the kitchen maid onward. It took a little time to weave a passage through the morning habitués, out in force after Sunday's quiet, taking advantage of the continuing balmy weather and chattering without cease. At length the party proceeded out of the Pantiles, passing the church on the corner, and into a little alley off Chapel Street, fetching up at a hostelry which bore the simple legend *Betty's* in flowing characters above the entrance, and whose clientele proved to be tradesmen and domestics. A long table occupied the main part of the small establishment, smoky with trails from a number of long pipes. Along the sides were set a few smaller tables for clients preferring a cosy atmosphere.

Several pairs of eyes marked Ottilia's progress as she followed Old Janet and Milly past the crowded central table to a secluded corner. Secure in Hemp's discreet presence, Ottilia took a seat with a word to her steward.

"Would you keep Milly company and supply her with refreshment, if you please?"

He gave a small bow and addressed the maid. "I am at your service, Milly."

The girl blushed, giggled and allowed herself to be drawn off to a different part of the coffee house. Old Janet watched her go.

"A downy one he is, that dark feller."

"He is indeed." Seeing a bustling woman approaching the booth, Ottilia added, "Allow me to procure you refreshment also, Janet. What shall it be?"

The nurse opted for chocolate. "Need it arter them nasty waters. Waste of time drinkin' 'em."

"Then why do it?"

A twinkle entered the old woman's eye. "Fer a bit of fun and gig. Gets me out of that there house. Like to see what the world is a-doin', don't I?"

Ottilia laughed. "I cannot say I blame you."

Janet leaned in with a confidential air. "Troublesome lot they are and no mistake. Allus was, allus will be."

"The Brockhursts? You nursed them all?"

"All, top to bottom, 'ceptin' young Marcus. Highty-tighty didn' wish fer me, spite what the mistress said. Got gingerbread enough ter turn up her nose, never no mind Master Godfrey didn' want no argy-bargy with his ma. Allus one fer peace he was, snivellin' little rascal."

Amused, but intrigued, Ottilia probed this aspect of Godfrey's character. "Why snivelling?"

Old Janet snorted. "He were that kind as run to complain of bein' bested, tellin' tales of his brother and sisters. Mind, he were better after he went ter school. Learned how ter keep outta trouble and made sure as Master Leo paid him no mind. Didn' surprise me when he made that match. Weren't fitted for the army, that one. He weren't no fighter, Master Godfrey. Nor it ain't no puzzle who rules the roost in that family."

"Lillian?"

"O'course. Her pa tied up that fortune so Master Godfrey couldn' get at more'n the dowry what was agreed. Mind, she'd give her last groat fer that namby-pamby boy of hers, and a right wastrel he is."

Gratified to have her impressions solidified, Ottilia pressed the point. "Do you believe Lillian's partiality extends to jealousy on her son's behalf?"

The elderly dame narrowed her gaze, but as her chosen beverage appeared at this point along with Ottilia's ubiquitous coffee, she made no immediate reply. Once the waiting woman had departed, she lifted the lid, set her nose over the steaming cup and sniffed the pungent aroma. "Ah, that's good, is that." She spooned sugar into her cup and stirred. Then settled the spoon in the saucer and looked across at Ottilia. "Yer thinkin' Master Daniel were in the way and Master Julius won't last ter take his pa's place, is that it?"

The blunt recognition of what was in Ottilia's mind took her aback, but she did not hesitate. "It is a possibility, do you not think?"

Janet made no reply, instead lifting the cup and sucking noisily, and with gusto, at the hot chocolate inside. Patient, and not unhopeful, Ottilia poured coffee from the pewter pot and laced it with cream and sugar. The brew was of inferior quality, but it was worth the drinking to plunge the depths of Old Janet's intimate knowledge of the inmates of the Brockhurst household.

"Good is that." Janet eyed Ottilia over the cup. "Lady Fan, you say?"

"It is a pet name derived from my husband's name. I find it saves trouble and I dislike formality."

Another snort came and Janet set down her cup. "The mistress wouldn' have any other. Like it from a child she were."

"You are talking of the dowager? You nursed her too?"

"Nursed her, maided her, saw her through tantrum after tantrum. No one don' understan' her like I do. Thwarted she is, or she thinks so. Allus one ter take a pet if things didn' go her way. Nor they didn' most times fer as no one don't like bein' nagged at and fussed at and told as they was all wrong no matter what they did."

"Yes, I rather gathered she feels betrayed and bitter for it."

Old Janet became unexpectedly fierce. "But don' you go a-thinkin' as she done away wi' that boy, fer I'd stake my life as she never would."

"How can you be so sure?"

An odd smile creased the old dame's mouth and cunning entered her features. "She'd be afeared."

"Afraid of what?"

"The rope. She'd not risk bringin' that fate on herself, no she wouldn'. She's afeared of dyin'. She's afeared of many things, but most is dyin'. When she were a little 'un, a bitty girlie, she'd ask me over an' over when she were goin' to die. Today, tomorrow, next week. Prayed every night she did, askin' the Almighty ter spare her one more night. Every time she were poorly, she were sure as sure she were goin' to die. No, my Protasia wouldn' risk the rope, I know that."

Ottilia digested this in silence for a moment, sipping her unsatisfactory brew. The nurse's dictum marched with the conviction Lady Wem had expressed that her family would be glad to see her in her grave. Yet she need not necessarily fear the rope herself. Ottilia would not wager against the woman throwing one of her family to the lions. She tested this out. "What if she need not fear the rope, Janet? What if she assigned the task to another?"

The nurse was enjoying gulps of chocolate, but she lowered the cup at this, giving Ottilia an intent stare. Then she put the cup to her lips and drained the last of the dark liquid. The cup, its sides running with drips, was set back in the saucer.

"You've not asked about Master Leo. Nor yet Miss Annis and Miss Berta."

This woman was adept at ignoring any question she chose not to answer. Resigning herself, Ottilia accepted the change of subject.

"Pardon me. Which of them would you like to talk of?"

"Which of 'em do you want ter know of?"

Ottilia suppressed a sigh. "Let us begin with Leo."

Old Janet tossed her head. "Nasty-tempered little brute, allus was. Mistook he did, marryin' that bread-'n-butter miss. Too easy ter bully the way he bullied his sister. Do anythin' fer

Master Leo she would. Not fer love, don't think it, fer as 'tis my belief she hates him. Mind, she hates everyone she does."

"You are talking of Berta."

A cackle escaped the old dame. "Well, I ain't talkin' of Miss Annis. Wouldn' take none of Master Leo's bombast, she wouldn'. Allus went her own way. She were of Godfrey's bent in that. Kept outta the way of the fights unless she couldn' avoid 'em, and then she give as good as she got."

"Why does Berta hate everyone?"

Janet looked surprised. "Fer as her ma wouldn' let her go free, never no mind the rest of 'em escaped. Used ter run aroun' the house nights, she did."

Alert to a possible implication, Ottilia probed for more. "Why?"

"Fer as it were only time as she could run free. Many's the night I had to go chasing roun' to find her and drag her back to bed."

"Does she still do that? Wander about at night?"

Old Janet shrugged. "If she do, I'd not know it. These old bones ain't made fer stompin' up and down them stairs."

Ottilia tried a different tack on the earlier question. "You say Berta would do anything for Leo despite hating him. Would she do as much for her mother?"

A gleam entered the old woman's eye. "I see what you'd be at. What d'yer think? Protasia wouldn' spare her fer bein' disobedient, never no mind the girlie tried. Leastways, she did as a child. Never got no praise fer it neither. Hating is as hating does, eh?"

Cryptic, to say the least. Ottilia might make much of it if she chose, but she let it go. So much for the older generation. She was glad to think she had gauged the characters of Leo, Annis and Berta fairly accurately. She shifted her focus. "What can you tell me of Master Julius? I have only heard he was ever sickly, but I know nothing of the type of man he is."

It did not seem as if Janet approved the switch. She clearly preferred to lead the discussion. But she answered, if with a trifle of unwillingness.

"Not much ter tell. Master Julius never give his pa no pride in 'im. His ma's boy through and through he is. Sickly in body, weak in mind."

"Do you mean he is backward?"

Janet shook a vehement head. "Nothing of that. A reed he is, sways with the wind, this way and that. Says yay to nay and the other way about, dependin'."

"On what?"

"On who's sayin', who's askin'. Yes to his ma as she warns him ter take care. No to his pa if his pa's askin' is he ill again, even if he is."

Ottilia tried for a more cogent response. "What was his relationship with Daniel?"

Old Janet shrugged. "They was brothers. Danny were the tough one, looked out fer his brother even as he were younger."

"Was Julius jealous that Daniel was his grandmother's favourite?"

"Who told you that?" The straight look was accompanied by an accusatory gaze.

Ottilia produced her ace. "Lady Wem herself. She believes they were all jealous of her partiality for Daniel."

This provoked an explosive sound. "No, she don't. Lyin' she is. It's her as is jealous. Of the pretty one he caught. Nor it's no manner of use sayin' it's all on account she were born wrong."

"Isabel? I understood Lady Wem could not approve of a merchant's daughter."

"She didn' take no account of that," scoffed Janet, "never no mind she said it were so."

A glimmer of light began to dawn in Ottilia's mind. "What, then?"

Janet leaned in close, dropping her voice. "There's only one thing as she can't abide and that's any man of hers lovin' another wench more." She sat up again and tapped the table with a bony finger. "She's top, she. Must be first oars with all. Not even held to her own neither, fer I've seen her choke with rage as a feller she fancied had eyes fer another girlie."

A wayward notion flickered in Ottilia's mind but she failed to capture it, intent upon the implication here. "She was jealous of Isabel because Daniel loved her?"

"Hating jealous. Good at hate, she is. Told you. It's tantrums when she don't get her way. Holds all of 'em afeared as she'll go into one of they fits, shoutin' and screamin', lashin' out with slaps and curses. I see it all, from when she were a bitty girlie, and she won't stop til' she's old as I or dead. Oh, she hated that Isabel all right, she did. Now if you'd been askin' me did she get rid of that one, 'tis a diff'rent tale."

Fretful still at his wife's report of her treatment at the hands of Lord Wem, Francis prowled the Walks where parties in dishabille, engaged in amicable chat, were shifting towards their respective lodgings. Where had Tillie disappeared to? His worry was only partially damped by her assertion she meant only to tackle this aged nurse. Any one of these blasted Brockhursts might waylay her and subject her to further insult.

If he could, he would do the whole business in her stead. But that was no use. He hadn't his wife's insight and would bungle it. Not that he cared which of them had committed the vile act. But Tillie did. He was of a mind to forbid her to continue, despite his fury at Wem's daring to command it, only he knew well any such attempt would invoke a wearing argument. Which he would undoubtedly lose. Tillie had her teeth into this, her wretched conscience in play again.

"How could I, in all honour, leave it now, Fan? I wish I might, but where then is justice for that poor boy? Isabel too. Accident forsooth! How can we now take that for other than a fairy tale?"

Even as she spoke, she seemed preoccupied. Holding back? "Is there more to this than you're telling me?"

"Of course not, dearest."

But she did not meet his eyes, busying herself with the coffee pot. He let it go, resuming his breakfast, but could not withstand a pointed query. "You're willing to endure more of this boorish bully then?"

She shrugged. "It is all hot air and bluster, Fan. It cannot hurt me."

He had perforce accepted this, aware of having been instrumental in pushing her to keep at it only to throw down his gauntlet before Wem. Tillie's motives were more worthy and Francis was torn by that knowledge. Ridiculous and contrary to be forbidding her now.

An express from Jardine, arriving just after Tillie left him, proved of some comfort. As expected, his man of business had quashed Wem's threat readily enough.

"Do not let it worry you, my lord. I shall engage with the lawyer in the case at once. Letters to and fro may prolong the argument until her ladyship has concluded the affair. There will be no action at law."

This was balm, but with his wife out of his sight, Francis grew prey to anxiety. Not least because of a nagging suspicion she was concealing some notion or other. That in itself was not unusual when she was involved in solving one of these puzzles,

240

but instinct told Francis this was distressing to his darling wife. At least he might watch over her, for though she had Hemp with her, the steward could not intervene if a Brockhurst accosted her. By the time he reached the pump where the waters were dispensed, however, Tillie was not to be found among the various persons milling about as they drank from thick tumblers, chatting in a desultory fashion before drifting off to dress suitably for the day.

Francis nodded to a couple of acquaintances and shifted back towards the main drag of the walkway, looking into windows beneath the colonnade without seeing anything and moving out again to pace in a restless manner and watch for his wife's reappearance.

"Lord Francis Fanshawe, is it not?"

Francis turned to find himself accosted by a slim young fellow, vaguely familiar, with a sallow complexion and shadows about the eyes. His hair was dark under a beaver hat, worn tied back in a way that made his already thin face more hollowed. He was dressed in sober garments and wore a black neckcloth. A flittering notion of his identity was confirmed even as it formed.

"I am Julius Brockhurst, sir. I beg your pardon if I offend, but I have a great desire to speak with you."

Francis eyed him with a lift of interest superseding the hackles that had arisen at the name. If this was Lord Wem's elder son, he was as unlike his father as he could be.

"How may I serve you, sir?"

A weak smile formed. "I should not think you could, my lord, nor would I expect it."

"Yet you wished to speak to me?"

The young man cleared his throat. "Your lady wife, sir."

Francis bristled. "What of my wife?"

241

A pale hand was raised. "Pray do not misunderstand me. I have no intention — I do not wish to — in short, sir, I beg to ask if it is true Lady Francis found signs indicative of..." He faded out and Francis saw his eyes darken, heartache visible in his features. Sympathy stirred.

"You are asking about your brother's condition, I take it?" The fellow nodded, and it was evident he was unable to speak without emotion. "I will be plain with you, Brockhurst. The signs were faint, but according to my wife, conclusive."

Julius's chest caved as if struck by a blow, a sighing breath escaping. His voice was hoarse. "I feared it. My father will not have it so, but Vivian — my cousin, you know — says his mother watched her motions. My aunt told me she was thorough, more so than the doctor."

"Has there been no word from the post mortem?"

"None. It is Vivian's belief the doctor is afraid to come forward because my father does not wish for the worst outcome."

Francis quashed this at once. "My dear sir, no physician worth his salt will balk at supplying the truth. It is more likely there is uncertainty. My wife said at the outset the coroner was likely to bring it in as accidental death."

The young man looked bewildered. "Then why does Lady Francis persist?"

"Because your grandmother requested her intervention. And because," Francis added with deliberation, "she believes your brother deserves justice." He refrained from mentioning the dead girl. As well, for his words appeared to have a profound effect upon Julius.

He blenched even under the already pasty complexion. "Justice. Yes, if it proves out. Dan did not deserve such a fate. My brother was a good man, sir, if misguided."

Which seemed to indicate Julius was not the perpetrator. Nevertheless, Francis pushed for more. "His marriage?"

Julius let out a heavy breath. "It was foolish. It does not do to thwart my father."

"I had remarked that," Francis said, unable to help an acid note.

"Yes, yes, I am aware of the breach with you, sir, but you do not understand, I fear."

With what he had endured from Lord Wem, this rankled. "What should I understand?"

"I have no son, Lord Francis." Julius's gaze registered sadness. "Perhaps you have heard of my unfortunate constitution?"

"It has been mentioned."

"Well, you see?"

The fellow's gaze was earnest, almost pleading for approbation. Was this meant to exonerate Wem? "I don't quite see, sir. Would you wish me to understand Lord Wem expected Daniel to succeed him?"

"Oh, no, no." Julius ran a restless hand across his smooth chin and dropped it again. "I am speaking of the marriage, sir. If the worst should happen — not that this horrific event may be classed as anything less — then Daniel's sons, had he chosen aright, would take the line."

"They must still have taken it in law, sir, regardless of the status of his wife."

Julius began to look decidedly embarrassed. "Well, that is the matter in a nutshell. Without means to prevent that, my father could only trust the marriage might founder."

A wash of suspicion attacked Francis's breast. "Let me understand you, sir. This marriage was so unpalatable, Wem would go to any lengths to end it?"

Horror leapt in the other man's eyes. "Not such lengths as I surmise you imply. How would that serve? There is now no alternative to my cousin's claim, unless my wife and I prove luckier than we have been."

Francis whistled. "I believe I have it now. Wem's prime concern is to keep your cousin Marcus from inheriting?"

Julius sighed again. "My father does not deem him worthy. He must wait upon my uncle's turn, of course, but there is no saying it would come to that."

"It may not come to it at all, sir. You may yet survive."

"Against the odds, sir. I do not expect to see my middle years."

Such a defeatist attitude went so much against the grain, Francis was tempted to shake the man out of it. He compromised. "You take a pessimistic view in a philosophical spirit, I will give you that."

The young man's sad smile appeared. "I prefer to call it realistic. If you knew how many narrow escapes I have endured! And here is Dan, as robust as I am weak, gone from us forever. I weep for my mother, sir. She is inconsolable."

But not, Francis noted, for his father. What Julius revealed had shifted Wem out of the running. Not that he had been first choice with Ottilia. She was prone to take this matter of a flitting ghost-like female figure for her most pertinent marker on the trail.

At this juncture, a different drawling voice cut into the thoughtful silence that had fallen.

"My dear Julius, what in the world are you doing? Do you wish to send my uncle off in an apoplexy? Are we not burdened with funerals enough?"

The mocking note set Francis's teeth on edge, but Julius's pallid countenance flew a touch of unnatural colour and he closed his lips firmly together. Marcus Brockhurst, his neckcloth conspicuously white though his coat was of dark maroon, took up a negligent pose, setting one leg across the other and leaning on a cane as he looked the pair up and down.

"Is this wise? Is this politic, dear coz? You know we are forbidden to engage with the enemy."

Disgust rode Francis. "Your levity, sir, is ill-timed and misplaced."

"Marcus, you mistake," broke in Julius. "The prohibition was for Lady Francis."

"And by extension, his lordship here. I fear that excuse will not weigh with my uncle."

Francis eyed him with hostility. "Then don't tell him. Your cousin had a sufficient reason to talk with me. It is not for you to judge."

Marcus gave an amused and gentle laugh, in which Francis placed not the slightest belief. "Oh, I am no tattletale. I would not wish to bring down my uncle's wrath upon poor Julius's head. My cousinly concern is purely altruistic, you must know."

Francis made no answer, feeling his hand itch to form a punishing fist. One could scarcely blame Wem for not wishing to see the man take his place, however distant the eventuality. Instead, he seized the chance to rattle Marcus. "You might more profitably use your time in my company to exonerate yourself from any involvement in your cousin Daniel's demise."

To his chagrin, Marcus did not turn a hair. "I? My dear Lord Francis, what possible reason could I have for such a morbid undertaking?"

Before Francis could wither him, Julius took this. "Pray don't be obtuse, Marcus. You stand to gain, just as my uncle Godfrey does."

His cousin wafted a dismissive hand. "Upon such a remote contingency? Dear coz, I fear you rate your chances too low. Why, with Clarissa and your mama protecting you from every wind that blows, I am confident you will outlive us all. Besides, I don't doubt Clarissa will present you with the boy we all desire in short order."

Disingenuous beyond belief. How could he treat so lightly the seriousness of his cousin's prospects? Francis yearned to flatten the fellow. Before he could formulate a way to express his disaffection, Marcus turned upon him with a spurious look of interest. "Since we are conversing, albeit against all care for the consequences, how fares the hunt? Has the inestimable Lady Francis found out the villain of the piece? Setting aside myself, of course."

The veiled contempt in his allusion to Ottilia put Francis into a flame, but he suppressed the urge to retaliate in the only way Marcus deserved.

"Your complacency is premature, sir. I doubt you are out of the frame. As to any other, my wife prefers to keep her findings close to her chest until she is certain."

"Oh, but surely, sir, you must be her confidant?"

"If I am, it would hardly be in keeping with the role to be bandying any notion to which I chanced to be privy."

Marcus gave an elaborate sigh, turning to his cousin. "As close-mouthed as bedamned, dear coz. Alas, I fear we must remain in ignorance until the finger is pointed."

"Which it will be, make no mistake," Francis snapped before he could stop himself. "My wife does not fail."

Marcus's lips twisted into something like a sneer. "You mean she has not yet done so. To my understanding, though, we Brockhursts have proved singularly uncooperative. Setting aside my uncle, whose reluctance goes without saying, I gather my aunt Berta became perfectly wild. I can only suppose my dear mother's calm good sense must have come as a welcome relief to Lady Francis. I should not myself care to run the gamut of Mary Ann's hysteria — saving your presence, coz — let alone mad Aunt Berta."

Infuriated, Francis was about to hit back hard with a tirade upon the treatment meted out to Tillie, when a further interruption occurred. Godfrey appeared at his son's side, all apology and soothing words.

"Come, come, boys, this will not do. Lord Francis, I must beg your indulgence. This meeting is inappropriate. I will remove them at once." He began ushering the two young men in the direction of the Assembly Rooms.

Francis took advantage of his arrival and called out after him. "A moment, if you please, sir."

Godfrey glanced back, hesitated, and then murmured to the other two. Marcus sauntered off, but Julius paused, looking towards Francis. Godfrey spoke again, giving him a slight push that sent him on his way. Then he retraced his steps as Francis came to meet him. "My lord?"

"One question, sir, if you will."

Godfrey's bland expression did not falter. "And that is?"

"What is your opinion of your nephew Julius's state of health? He seems to believe himself doomed."

Godfrey's brows drew together. "Ah, a possible motive for me, is that it? Or do you favour my son?"

Neither, if Tillie held by a female. Francis tried to read the man's expression, but Godfrey gave nothing away. "You will admit it is a consideration under the circumstances."

A shrug. "Certainly. That was obvious from the first. I dare say my brother had the same thought, which is likely the thing that put him most against the notion of murder. Leo would not

247

like to think his nearest and dearest could contemplate such an act."

"But someone did contemplate it, sir. And carried it through."

Godfrey grimaced. "So it would appear. Well, if you value my opinion, as I have had occasion to tell you before, you will advise your wife to look at my mother. She is quite ruthless, you know, when she wishes to gain her own ends."

He turned on the words and walked away, leaving Francis thoroughly taken aback to think a man would casually name his own mother for a killer.

CHAPTER THIRTEEN

Ottilia approached the oncoming confrontation with a degree of trepidation. She had sent word to Lady Wem to appoint a meeting with all the women of the family, stressing the "all". As she told her spouse while they partook of a light luncheon, the time had come for a bold move.

"You are convinced of the perpetrator being a woman then?"

"Not entirely, Fan, but it looks that way."

He quaffed from his tankard and set it down, pushing aside the plate now empty of the ham and cold pie he had consumed. "I would stake my money on Marcus. A slippery fellow, too smooth by half."

Ottilia turned the glass in her fingers, still half-full of lemonade. She had eaten sparingly, a trifle on the fidgets but knowing she must fortify herself for the coming ordeal. She looked across at Francis. "This is the difficulty, Fan. It is all to do with the characters of those involved. We have little to go on by way of who may have done what."

"Except this business of the female wanderer of the night."

"Just so. It is sketchy, to say the least. There is no proof of anything."

Francis's brows drew together. "Are you stumped, Tillie?"

Mischief crept into her breast. "Losing faith in me, Fan?"

His features relaxed and amusement showed in his gaze. "Go on then, my woman of wonder, confound me. What do you mean to do?"

"Rattle their cages."

He laughed, and then frowned heavily. "Be careful, my dear one. I don't trust those Brockhursts. Not an inch. Least of all the women. If you ask me, they are one for one as devious as the devil."

"Then it behoves me to flush out the truth. I will not get it by questioning."

"Well, whoever did it isn't going to tell you directly, that's sure. What is this strategy you have dreamed up?" He whistled when she told him. "I had best accompany you then."

Ottilia declined his escort. "Your presence would hamper me, my dearest. Besides, it won't help for Lord Wem to find you in the house and kick up a dust."

"Let him try, that's all."

"Fan, of what use will it be if you engage in fisticuffs with the man? Or worse, call him out."

Francis snorted. "It won't come to that."

It took time and patience to convince him to allow her to go on her own, with Hemp in tow to see to her safety. She succeeded at last and left him grumbling, but her courage began to fail as she climbed the hill, glad of a light breeze wafting away the heat. She bolstered it with the reminder Lady Wem might be trusted to keep a strong hand on the reins. None would dare molest her in the dowager's presence.

The women were found in the grand parlour upstairs, Lady Wem senior enthroned in her high-backed chair, surrounded by the rest. Annis and Lillian sat together on the dark red upholstered sofa, Berta in a chair with matching cushioned seat a little behind her mother's, while Mary Ann was ensconced in another, opposite the sofa, to which her daughter-in-law Clarissa had pulled a straight chair close for the purpose, it appeared, of cradling the afflicted lady's hand.

Ottilia was met with a distinct lack of greeting, none daring to speak unless urged thereto by the Dowager Lady Wem.

"In good time. They are all here. You know everyone already."

Ottilia took a moment to let her gaze travel around the room and halted upon Clarissa. "I have not had the pleasure of making acquaintance with the Honourable Mrs Julius Brockhurst."

Lady Wem snapped her fingers towards the girl. "Make your curtsey, Clarissa."

Thus adjured, Clarissa made haste to rise and comply. "How do you do, ma'am?"

Ottilia inclined her head. She threw an apologetic glance around. "Do any of you object to it if I use your given names? I should much dislike to confuse things with this plethora of Brockhursts, whether Mrs or Miss."

"Call them whatever you wish. I will engage for it they will make no objection." Lady Wem cast a menacing glance about the assembly as she spoke. She then fluttered a hand in Ottilia's direction. "Sit, sit. There will do."

She pointed to a chair set a little apart from where Mary Ann was seated. Ottilia crossed to take it and was gratified to find she had a good view of each of the women. Was it deliberate on the part of the matriarch? She was able to see the door also without turning towards it, which was an advantage should any of the gentlemen choose to enter. Although she could not but suspect they had been forbidden so to do.

"Well? Ask your questions. They will answer, I shall see to that."

Ottilia took a breath, priming her guns. "I have no individual questions, ma'am."

The woman's features grew more reptilian as she narrowed her gaze like a lizard. "Is this a jest? I commanded them here for your convenience."

"Yes, and I am glad of it, ma'am, but the only questions in my mind are unlikely to be answered in this assembly. Or any other, come to that."

Ottilia glanced round as she spoke, noting both puzzlement and apprehension appearing in several faces. Only Lillian seemed unmoved and Berta looked merely contemptuous.

Annis broke the silence. "Will you have the goodness to explain, Lady Francis?"

Ottilia glanced across. "I intend to."

"Then?" Lady Wem, her tone a snap.

"Patience, if you please." Ottilia took time for another circuit around the faces. Then she fired her first broadside. "This whole affair hinges on two things. First, which of you was seen wandering the corridor next to Daniel's room on the night he died."

She got no further. Lillian's pose of disinterest shattered.

"Seen? What do you mean, seen?"

Ottilia looked at her, as did all the rest, including Berta, whose already hollow cheeks became the more pinched.

"I mean what I say. A female figure was observed in the area during the early hours of the morning."

A flicker of movement from Annis Maplewood caught Ottilia's eye. Her lips were pursed but there was no surprise there. Was she already aware of it? It did not take much thought to follow the shift from Lizzy to Vivian Maplewood and thence to his mother. Not that it mattered since she was not under suspicion, despite her mother's insistence she should be included.

"Who saw it?" This from Lillian again.

Ottilia gave a spurious smile. "I cannot tell you that."

"Why not?" Berta now, her gaze sharp. "I detest secrets."

"Because," said Ottilia with deliberation, "I would not care to put that person's life in jeopardy."

Two gasps came from the women closest to Ottilia, while the rest sat mumchance, stunned, to judge by their faces. The Dowager Lady Wem took the floor. "Two things, you said."

There was a concerted shift and Ottilia felt the battery of eyes upon her even as she turned to the dowager. "The second thing I would like to know is who suggested the excursion to High Rocks."

The shot found its mark in every single face. None had expected her to hark back to Isabel's demise. The hush in the room was total for a matter of seconds. Then several voices spoke over each other.

"What has that to say to anything?"

"That was an accident!"

"I don't understand."

"But that was me! I mentioned it to Isabel."

This last, from Clarissa, brought Lady Wem's gaze to bear upon the youngest of the females. She had not joined in the chorus, but she spoke now, and with venom.

"You dared to hobnob with the woman? After my prohibition?"

Ottilia intervened swiftly. "I must beg your indulgence, ma'am. This is not the moment for recriminations." Without waiting for a response, she addressed the now trembling girl. "Clarissa, you say you told Isabel, but was it your notion?"

Looking frightened, Clarissa shook her head. "I only suggested Daniel should take her for a drive. Everyone had decided upon High Rocks."

"And you were detailed to tell Isabel?"

"Well, I asked her if she would like to go." Her voice started to shake and Mary Ann clutched her hand, the ubiquitous tears starting to fall. "I s-said we were going to make a day of it and perhaps it would be p-pleasant to be out of the house. B-but I never thought— If I'd known…"

She faded out and Ottilia took up the pertinent point. "If it was not your idea, who did suggest it?" She glanced about them all, hoping for some little giveaway.

"I don't remember." There was protest in Clarissa now. "It is all such a muddle, and after… It was so horrid, I could only think how sorry I was that I persuaded poor Isabel to go at all."

Ottilia softened her tone. "It was not your fault, my dear."

"No, dearest Clarissa, you could not have known," said Mary Ann on a husky note. "You must not blame yourself."

"But Lady Francis blames someone, don't you?"

Ottilia made no answer, glancing from one to the other of those who remained silent. "Cannot any of you recall who mooted the expedition in the first place? Clarissa speaks of a family discussion. Were the men part of it?"

Annis put her hands palm up. "Do not look at me. I was not there. Vivian told me of it."

"Who was there? Lillian? Berta? Mary Ann?" Ottilia allowed her glance to fall on the Dowager Lady Wem. "You, ma'am?"

A sneer crossed the woman's face. "I? What have I to do with such foolish pastimes? Wem spoke of it to me at breakfast."

"Then Lord Wem was of the party when the idea was discussed?" Again, Ottilia regarded the three older women, one after the other. She saw Clarissa fidgeting and gave her a penetrating glance. "You have something more to say?"

She looked ready to weep, but Ottilia was not going to let her off the hook. All at once, it burst out of the girl. "My papa-in-law was not party to it. Nor yet his brother Godfrey. Marcus was there. And Julius came in while we were talking of it." Clarissa threw a fearful glance at the others. "The rest of us were present."

"Thank you. You then, Lillian? You too, Berta? And Mary Ann?"

The latter waved agitated hands. "Yes, yes, but I did not approve. I told Clarissa it was too much exertion for Julius, but you paid no heed."

"Julius didn't suffer," Clarissa declared. "Isabel did. And poor Daniel." She dissolved into sobs, which were at once echoed by Mary Ann beside her.

Ottilia heard an exasperated sound from the women on the sofa and quickly turned her gaze that way. Lillian was looking bored. Highly inappropriate. Was it feigned? Then Annis must have expressed annoyance. The dowager's darting gaze appeared to take it all in and Berta sat as if carved in stone.

Ottilia went for the jugular. "Well now, perhaps your memories may furnish a more pertinent detail."

Once again, all eyes trained upon her, all but the dowager apprehensive, some downright fearful. The matriarch's snake-like look became accentuated as she thrust her head forward.

"I told you to find out who disposed of my grandson. I have no interest in the other incident."

"But I have, ma'am. It was after all the spur to what followed." Ottilia waited, but the woman merely stared her out. She shifted focus, her gaze flitting across the rest.

Annis broke. "Is this not distressing enough? If there is something more, say it, for the love of heaven!"

"It is quite a little thing, but crucial. Which of you was up on the summit of the rock that day?"

The ripple of shock could be felt. Now she was getting somewhere. The youngest of them again fell prey to protest.

"But why us? All the men went up too. I did not, for I detest heights. Nor did my mama-in-law, did you, Mary Ann?"

"No, no, no. I would have warned Isabel to keep away from the edge. I told Danny." Near hysteria sounded in Mary Ann's voice. "You should not have let her near the edge, I said, but he would not listen. He said she was safe enough until — until…" Her tears were falling again. "What could I do? He was obsessed. Obsessed, I tell you!"

Ottilia glanced quickly at the two women who had not spoken. Not Annis. She had been below. Then Berta and Lillian, both of whom were wearing expressions too indifferent to be true, must have been the only two women on the rock. The net was closing in.

Before she could formulate any further thrust to break the true culprit, the door opened and the butler walked in. Ignoring the prevailing atmosphere of heaviness and surmise, he addressed his mistress.

"You requested refreshments after half an hour, my lady."

The Dowager Lady Wem stared at him without speaking, and Ottilia could not tell if she had or had not given such an order. Had someone done it on her behalf? Or to break up Ottilia's questioning? If so, the ruse succeeded. The procession of footman and maid coming in behind the butler at once reduced the scene to one of prosaic domesticity. The opportunity to force the issue was lost.

Ottilia seethed in silence. Now it would be all to do again and they would have leisure to prepare. Defence or counterattack? Either way she had lost the advantage.

Absently, she watched as the accoutrements for tea were set upon a large side table at one wall. Both Annis and Lillian rose and moved to the table as the servants gave place. As Lillian busied herself with the kettle and the pot, Annis began upending cups upon their saucers. Ottilia caught the dowager turning to address some remark to Berta, who got up, her expression turning sulky the moment she had passed her mother on her way to the table, presumably to assist. Neither Clarissa nor Mary Ann, who had their heads together, whispering, made any move.

Ottilia watched the servants filing out, trying to think how to recover her advantage. As she brought her gaze back from the closing door, a movement behind a vacant chair close to the sofa captured her attention. Her eyes focused on a small pair of shoes.

The heart fluttered in Ottilia's breast. As she watched, the shoes vanished, but in a moment, a curly head appeared in their stead. Under golden locks, an enchanting little face peered into the room. Ottilia became riveted. The entire purpose of her visit went out of her head. She had no attention to spare for any of the women, or what they might be doing. Pretty! It must be.

As the thought flitted through, the child caught her looking and ducked back, not quite out of sight. She smiled as Pretty peeped out again, her bright eyes fixed on Ottilia. The smile won an answering one that hovered, vanished and came again. Pretty crawled around the chair and sat with her back to it, little feet in their small shoes protruding under her baby gown, her eyes holding Ottilia captive. One tiny finger came up, hooking into her mouth.

Warmth flooded Ottilia's bosom and she would have beckoned the little girl to her, but that a shriek of rage made the child jump. Fury erupted from the Dowager Lady Wem.

"What is that brat doing here? Where is the nurse? How dare she allow it to escape? Somebody ring the bell! Get it out of here! Out! Out! Get it out, I say!"

The little girl shrunk away, looking terrified as well she might while the tirade continued. Ottilia was on her feet, moving to the chair with the intention of picking Pretty up. But one of the women pushed past, scooped the child from the floor and headed for the door just as it opened and a girl, looking quite horrified, rushed in. She was clad in a plain bronze gown covered with an apron, a mobcap imperfectly concealing dark locks. She seized the infant and scooted out of the door. It slammed behind her just as a pathetic wailing broke out in the corridor.

Shaken, Ottilia sank back into her seat, her ears assailed by the echoing cries as Pretty was borne away. The cruelty of it struck at her and she could barely endure to be in the same room as these terrible people.

A hand produced a cup and saucer before her. Ottilia took it automatically, without looking up, her mind too benumbed even to utter a word of thanks. Vaguely in the background she was aware of talk, voices urgent, pleading, attempting to soothe the still vibrant complaints of that hideous voice.

"How many times must I repeat myself? Does no one care for my wishes in this house? If the brat cannot be kept out of sight, I want her gone from here. Out of my house! Out!"

Ottilia tried to recover control over the tumult in her breast, aware she had still a task to perform but with no present memory of what it was. Recalling she had been supplied with a drink, she picked up the cup and sipped. Tea. Not as efficacious as coffee in these circumstances, but it would serve. She had downed the better part of the liquid before she achieved a modicum of calm, the image of the petrified little face dancing in her head.

Wicked of them. Unkind and cruel. None took the child's part, so beaten down by that terrible woman they dared not take one step against her. Ottilia recalled Old Janet's dictum from the morning: of screaming tantrums, of jealousies, of a ruthless determination to get her own way.

At last Ottilia looked up, glancing across at the huddle of females about the dowager's chair. She felt curiously lightheaded. The aftermath of shock?

An abrupt desire to be gone from this dreadful house overcame her. She felt in no fit state to deal further with the inhuman Brockhurst clan. No one was looking her way. They were variously grouped about the matriarch. As if she deserved such attention!

Ottilia set down her cup and saucer, rose up from the chair and quietly left the room.

Francis regarded his wife with dismay and concern as she sat, a trifle slumped, one hand kneading at her forehead. Tillie had gone off brave and come back defeated. A temporary condition, he hoped. She had said little, but what she did say was unusually severe.

"They are a horrible lot, Fan. Horrible. I pity anyone obliged to live under the aegis of that woman. Or her dreadful offspring. And their spouses. They are all unkind and she is cruel beyond belief."

It was unlike his darling wife to be so vehement in condemnation. Was she more discomposed than the occasion warranted? He hovered over her, surveying her face. "You look pale, my dear one. I will ring for coffee. I think you need it."

She waved him off. "Not now, Fan. I had tea there. To tell you the truth, I feel a little queasy."

"I am not surprised. Keeping company with that crew is enough to give anyone bellyache." He stood back, leaning an elbow on the mantel. "I take it they reacted badly to your bombshell?"

She glanced up at him, a faint frown between her brows. "Bombshell?"

"You said you meant to flush the murderer out. Did you, do you think?"

"Oh. Yes, perhaps. Or, no. I don't know."

Her manner was distrait and his concern deepened. "What is the matter, Tillie? Does it pain you? Your head, I mean."

"Not that." Her hand dropped and she set it against her stomach, grimacing. "I really feel quite ill, Fan."

He straightened. "What sort of ill? Are you faint? Or just queasy? Do you need a physician? Shall I get you a powder?"

There was time for no more questions. His wife's hand went to her mouth and he heard a muffled cry.

"I am going to be sick!"

Galvanised, Francis glanced round, spotted the brass spittoon set upon the hearth and seized it, placing it square into his wife's lap. "Here, use this!"

She grasped its sides and bent over it, retching. Francis leapt for the hand bell and plied it with vigour, at the same time yelling for the servants.

"Joanie! Tyler! Here to me, now!"

Then he got back to Tillie just as the contents of her stomach deluged out, landing partially in the receptacle and spilling over her gown. Francis sat on the arm of her chair and held her as she vomited over and again, until there was nothing left but a trickle of sputum.

By this time, the servants were in the room, exclaiming and muttering. Francis had no attention to spare for anything but his wife as she sank against his supporting arm, exhausted. He thrust the spittoon at the hovering maid.

"Take this." He extracted his pocket handkerchief and wiped Tillie's face as best he could. "Fetch a wet flannel, girl. And get the bed ready for her ladyship. Tyler, a physician. As fast as you can." He caught sight of the steward in the doorway. "Hemp, go and fetch my mother."

The servants despatched, he shifted his position, allowing his wife to lean back in the chair so he could more readily survey her and assess her condition. She looked grey and worn. And this was not unprecedented. He spoke his thought aloud. "Are you pregnant, Tillie?"

Her eyes flickered open. "Am I?"

"Well, it occurs to me you were sick like this the last time. But in the mornings."

Her voice was a murmur. "I was moody, though. I haven't been. Have I?"

"Just now you were a deal more so than usual."

She made a weak gesture of dismissal. "Those Brockhursts upset me."

He did not pursue the matter as Joanie came in with a damped cloth. He took it from her and performed the office of freshening Tillie's face himself. She sighed as he did so. "Thank you, Fan. That is much better."

But her eyes were closed and she still lay in a semi-stupor. A fillip of apprehension went through Francis. She had not been this affected during her last pregnancy. If that was the cause here. The maid cut into his worrisome thoughts.

"I've turned down the covers, my lord."

"Thank you." He leaned down again. "Come, Tillie, let's get you to bed."

It seemed to Francis she opened her eyes with an effort. "Presently. I don't think I can walk quite yet."

"You don't need to. I will carry you. Arm around my neck, my dear one." She tried, but the arm slipped down again. Francis picked up the arm and placed it for her. "Hold on."

He tucked his arms under her and lifted, not without difficulty. In her present debilitated state, she was almost a dead weight, unable to help at all. Francis shifted her weight as he rose and began to carry her into the bedchamber. Just as he reached the door, her eyes suddenly flew open and she clutched his coat lapel.

"Fan! The tea!"

For a moment, Francis made no sense of this, intent upon reaching the bed where Joanie, running ahead, was already pushing the covers further off the sheet.

"What about the tea?"

"I drank tea there." Her voice was growing stronger, urgent. "Someone gave me the cup, I don't know who. I drank it. I didn't think, Fan. And Mary Ann is a herbalist."

CHAPTER FOURTEEN

The implication hit. Francis felt his insides grow cold. On automatic, his mind and heart flying fury, he set his burden down on the bed. Leaning in, he spoke in as soothing a tone as he could muster.

"I'll see to it, Tillie. Don't fret. Mama will be here in a moment to look after you."

She seized his hand. "The teacups. Let them not wash the teacups."

"I have it, my darling." Francis kissed her forehead, holding in the burgeoning rage with difficulty. "You have nothing to do but rest." He rose on the words, aware Tillie's eyes followed him. He addressed the maid. "Joanie, help her ladyship to undress. Give her nothing except water until the doctor arrives."

To his heartfelt relief, his mother's voice sounded without. "Where is she?"

He raised his voice. "In here, Mama. The bedchamber."

One glance towards his wife of, he hoped, sufficient reassurance, and he moved to the door, almost colliding with Sybilla coming in.

"In good time, ma'am. Pray take care of Tillie until I return."

His mother was already on her way to the bed, but she paused at this, turning. "Where are you off to, pray?"

"I have urgent business with the Brockhursts."

With which, he walked out, ready to let the bubbling rage come to the fore and was instantly obliged to suppress it upon catching sight of his niece.

"What is it? What has happened, sir?"

He did not beat about the bush. "Your aunt has been sick. She was likely given poisoned tea."

Lizzy's eyes registered horror. "By the Brockhursts?"

"Who else? I am off to call them to account. Go in, Lizzy. I dare say they can use your help in getting your aunt undressed."

Lizzy shot off towards the bedchamber and Francis, not even troubling to stop for his hat, went into the hall, calling for the steward. Hemp appeared so fast, Francis thought he must have been waiting just out of sight.

"Milord?"

"I need you, Hemp. You know the domestics at the Brockhurst house, correct?"

"Yes, milord."

"Then come with me."

The bustle by the bedside kept Lizzy's hands busy as she did as her grandmother directed, but her mind was in turmoil. Poison? How could they do that? Why? And who? There was no asking her aunt at this point.

"She has fainted, Elizabeth. Quickly, untie her stay-laces. It will help her to breathe."

The three of them had managed to remove Ottilia's soiled overskirt as well as her bodice, already unpinned at the bosom by Joanie, while she was still able to move her arms. But as the top half of the cotton chintz gown came off, she had collapsed back against the pillows. While Sybilla and Joanie held her on her side, Lizzy climbed on the bed and, fingers unwieldy with panic, wrestled with a stubborn knot.

"Hurry, Elizabeth!"

"I am trying, Grandmama." It gave at last. "There, it is free."

The stays immediately loosened and she was able to whip the laces out of the holes. The stays clear, Ottilia was laid flat again and Joanie was quick to nip them out from under her back, what time Sybilla began untying the under-petticoat from about Ottilia's waist.

Between them, she and the maid managed to slide the fulsome garment down, leaving only the shift while Lizzy began untying the strings to which her aunt's pockets were attached. She was about to set the objects aside when her grandmother checked her.

"Elizabeth, wait! See if she has a vinaigrette handy. I know Ottilia has one."

Lizzy dove a hand into one of the pockets and brought out a little silver box. "Here it is. Shall I—?"

"Yes, yes. Wave it under her nose."

Lizzy opened the box, taking care to avoid smelling the aromatic contents herself. She held it to her aunt's nostrils and jiggled it a little to stir up the sal volatile inside while the maid made haste to drag the covers over the still figure in the bed.

She stirred in a moment, shifting her head away from the pungent aroma. Her eyelids flickered open and she spoke, her voice a trifle hoarse.

"Is that smelling salts? Did I swoon?"

"You did indeed, my dear. Take them away, Elizabeth." Sybilla moved to perch on the edge of the bed, picking up one slack hand and chafing it. "How do you feel, Ottilia?"

The patient moistened her lips. "Thirsty."

"Water, girl." This to the hovering maid, who produced a full glass from the side table. Sybilla took it. "Hold her head, Elizabeth."

Lizzy made haste to obey, biting her tongue on the questions jumping in her mind, over the top of a suppressed terror. What if Ottilia had died?

She was sipping at the liquid in the glass held to her lips. In a moment or two, she seemed to grow stronger, struggling a little.

"Lie still, my dear."

"I need to sit up."

"Elizabeth, bank pillows behind her."

She set the glass down and turned to the maid. "That will do for now, girl. Go and wait for the doctor and bring him here the instant he arrives. Stay, open the windows wider first. And find me a fan."

Aware Joanie obeyed and then curtsied before leaving the room, Lizzy watched as Ottilia sank with a sigh and a murmured word of thanks against the pile of pillows she had made. Lizzy tucked her legs to one side to make herself a little more comfortable and eyed her afflicted aunt.

"You don't look quite so pale, Aunt. Do you feel a degree better?"

A faint frown appeared between Ottilia's brows. "I am trying to remember."

Sybilla, as she busied herself plying the fan to cool the sufferer's face, tutted. "No need. Wait until the doctor has seen you."

Ottilia paid no heed, her gaze shifting between Lizzy and her grandmother. "One of them handed me a cup and saucer. I was distracted by something." Her eyes grew dark. "Pretty! She came in when they brought the tea. Oh, she is adorable! You've seen her, Lizzy. Is she not the dearest little thing?"

Dismay shot through Lizzy. "She came into the parlour? How? Did Hepsie lose her?"

"She must have given her the slip."

"Did Lady Wem see her?"

A shadow crossed Ottilia's face, but Sybilla cut in before she could answer.

"Of what are you talking? Who is this Pretty?"

"She is Daniel's daughter, Grandmama."

"Heavens above!"

"She looks like Isabel and they have all of them neglected her, poor child." Lizzy turned back to Ottilia. "I cannot imagine she was welcomed."

"Far from it, Lizzy. It was quite dreadful." Her gaze found Sybilla's. "You were right, Sybilla. She is poison. I have never in my life witnessed anything half as cruel. The way she ranted at that child, screaming like a madwoman!"

"Ha! Did I not warn you? The woman is insane."

"Indeed, I think she is. At least, she behaves insanely when she loses her temper." She put a hand to her head. "I wanted to go to Pretty, to protect her, but…"

"You could hardly interfere, Ottilia. It is not your concern."

Ottilia seemed not to have heard. "One of them was before me. Then the nurse came in and took Pretty away. It was perfect chaos. I was too appalled, too upset to be sensible, for I should have been paying attention. I did not see who gave me the tea." She shifted her head from side to side in an agitated fashion that wrung Lizzy's heart. "So silly. So foolish. Had I been in my senses, I should never have drunk the stuff."

Sybilla closed the fan with a snap, becoming brisk and autocratic. "Cease this nonsense, Ottilia! We all make mistakes. I will not have you berate yourself. You are in no fit state to be worrying your head over what cannot be mended."

"But I should have—"

"Enough. Francis will discover who did this to you, never fear."

Ottilia was not appeased. "He will go after Mary Ann, but it may well have been another. Hemp had it from the cook she has little bags of herbs aplenty. Any of the women could have appropriated a pinch of one or other, or Mary Ann might have given it to them."

"What, does the woman physic them all? I thought it was this sickly boy of hers she sought to cure."

"It can't be, Grandmama, for she gave Daniel a drink to make him sleep on the night he died."

Ottilia was muttering to herself, but she added to this at once. "She ministers to friends even, she told me. It is far more likely Berta or Lillian put something in my tea. They were both dispensing it. Annis too, but I doubt she wished to frighten me off."

Lizzy stared, while Sybilla exclaimed.

"Frighten you off? Is that what you believe?"

"Well, I can't think anyone would dare attempt to murder me. Only think of the consequences. I suspect it was an emetic, designed to make me ill, no more."

"Well, that is bad enough."

A thought occurred to Lizzy and she gave it voice. "Could it have been Lady Wem herself?"

"No, for she was in the middle of a hysterical fit at the time. Besides, she does not do her own dirty work."

At this moment, the discussion was interrupted by the sound of a male voice asking for Lord Francis. Joanie was heard to reply.

"It's her ladyship as is needful of your services, sir. Pray come this way."

Sybilla became brisk, rising the better to greet the physician. "Get off the bed, Elizabeth. And you go off home. There is no necessity for us all to remain. Nancy will take care of you."

Lizzy scuttled off the bed but she was reluctant. "Can't I wait in the parlour?"

"No, no. I daresay the doctor will give her something to make her sleep. I will join you presently."

"Thank you, Lizzy," said Ottilia with a smile. "We will talk later."

There was nothing to do but retire. In any event, a middle-aged man Lizzy recalled seeing about the town was already being ushered into the room. She slipped out and paused for a space in the hall. She was not minded to go back to the lodgings. What could she do there, with all this upset in her head? Almost without knowing she had made up her mind, she took the stairs and walked across the lane to the Common. There was one person in whom she might confide. This would make Vivian even more hot against his relatives, but at least she could sift the questions. Perhaps even discover on Ottilia's behalf the perpetrator of this horrid act.

The churning mix of anxiety and wrath propelled Francis up the hill path through the Common at a great rate, unmindful of the rising heat of the day. No one targeted his precious Tillie and got away with it. Someone was going to pay.

"Milord?"

"What is it?" He answered on automatic, intent upon reaching Lord Wem. He, if anyone, was to blame for this. He had repudiated—

"What do you wish me to do with the domestics, milord?"

With difficulty, Francis brought his attention back. "Teacups. Her ladyship was drinking with the women. Stop them from washing the cups."

"You think there may be traces of something?"

"Herbs of some kind. One of them — Mary Ann, she said—"

"She uses herbs in little bags, milord," Hemp cut in, "so the servants told me."

"Then you know what to do."

"I have it, milord."

Hemp kept pace right behind him, only veering off towards the back premises as they entered the short driveway before the entrance.

Francis stepped up and rang the bell with vigour, his mind winging forward to the coming meeting with Wem. Words tumbled in his head. Violent words. He struggled to contain them. His fingers curled into fists and he envisioned the pleasure of driving one of them into Lord Wem's face. A pleasure he must forego if he was to discover who in this vile household had poisoned his wife.

An elderly butler opened the door, his austere expression giving notice of disapproval. He did not care for the manner of the bell being rung, was that it? He might count himself fortunate not to receive a blast of invective.

"I am Lord Francis Fanshawe and I am here to see Lord Wem on a matter of urgency. Lead me to him on the instant."

The fellow's brows had lifted at the name, but he continued to hold the door half open. "His lordship is occupied, my lord."

"I don't care if he's in the middle of his ablutions. Take me to him at once! And open the door if you don't wish to be thrust back into the house."

"My lord!"

The belligerence at least made the man start back and Francis was able to push into the hall. "Where is he? In one of the saloons?"

Francis started towards the stairs, but the butler, showing surprising agility for one of his years, managed to arrive before him, barring the way.

"My lord, I have just conducted the doctor to his lordship."

Francis could not but pause at this. "What, is he ill too?"

The fleeting thought of an error that might have affected more people in the house went through his mind.

"I believe Doctor Heather has come with the results of the post mortem, my lord."

At any other time, this news would have engaged Francis's immediate interest. But his darling wife was laid down upon their bed in a debilitated state. The deep-seated fear she could have died superseded any other consideration.

"So much the better. If you won't lead me to him, I shall find him myself." He sidestepped the butler and began to mount the stairs.

The man at once followed, though the pace he set made the fellow breathless. "Very well, my lord, if you insist."

Once he reached the top, Francis halted and waved an impatient hand. "After you."

Lord Wem was found in a small parlour to the front of the house. It was dark except for the light coming in from one wide window, which fell on two chintz chairs and threw a shaft across the room, in the middle of which the viscount stood, confronting a youngish fellow with the inescapable mien of a physician. He had the physical wig and wore a dull-coloured coat over country breeches and his aspect was redolent of the obsequious pomposity Francis associated with every doctor except his brother-in-law.

On Francis entering, Lord Wem turned upon him a countenance devoid of the aggression he recalled from their previous encounter. He looked grey, almost defeated. But his eyes nevertheless took fire as he recognised his visitor.

"What the devil do you want, Fanshawe?"

Francis wasted no time. "I want to know who gave my wife poisoned tea. By God, Wem, you and your despicable brood will pay for this!"

The man gave him a blank stare. "Poisoned tea? What in God's name are you talking about? Who gave her poisoned tea?"

"Are you deaf? That is what I'm here to find out. One of your women — your wife, in all probability, isn't she the one who dabbles in the apothecary's art? — handed my wife a cup of tea which she drank and was promptly vilely ill. I have left her in my mother's care. Now do you understand?"

Lord Wem appeared stunned. "My wife? But this is ridiculous. Absurd. Why should Mary Ann do such a thing? I don't believe it."

Francis stepped up to him, ignoring the doctor who had moved back a pace or two, looking bewildered. "You may believe what you like, Wem, but this has gone far enough. Too far."

All at once, Lord Wem gave ground, half staggering to a chair and collapsing into it, setting a hand to his chest.

Balked, Francis watched him. What in the world—? Was it feigned? He glanced at the other fellow. "You are a medical man. What ails him?"

The doctor was already moving towards the sufferer, but he paused at this. "I fear the news I gave his lordship is responsible, rather than — er…" He faded out, a vague hand offering the rest.

Francis had no difficulty in interpreting this. His advent, coming hard on the heels of whatever the doctor had said, had cost Lord Wem his equilibrium. He lost sight of his mission for a moment.

"What did you tell him?"

The doctor paid no heed, addressing himself to Wem, whose breath was dragging. "My lord, I suggest you lie back. Here, I will set a cushion behind your head. There. Allow me to feel your pulse."

He took the man's wrist and Francis waited, impatient, his mind alive with conjecture. The news must be the worst. Had Wem been deprived of his wish for a verdict of suicide? It seemed likely. In which case, a further accusation of poisoning might well have a deleterious effect.

Lord Wem was regaining a little colour, although his eyes were closed. The doctor set down his wrist and proceeded to unbutton his waistcoat and unwind the neckcloth from about his throat.

"There, my lord. You may breathe easier now. With your permission, I will ring the bell and ask your fellow to bring my bag from the gig." At a nod from the patient, he moved to the bell-pull.

Francis followed him, dropping his voice. "You came with the results of the post mortem? What were they? Pray don't look at me in that fashion, sir. My wife has spent the last days investigating this matter, to her cost. It is imperative I know what was found. You may as well tell me your name while you're about it."

The man looked pained. "It is Heather, sir. I believe I am acquainted with your wife, if it is she who was present at High Rocks, and again while I was examining the body here."

"Correct. The results, if you please." The politesse of the words were negated, he knew, by his tone. But he was past caring. If it was not typical of a Brockhurst to thwart him with a dramatic collapse!

Doctor Heather glanced across at Lord Wem, who still lay with his eyes closed, his breast rising and falling in an unnaturally exaggerated fashion. Satisfied at length, he matched the low level of voice Francis had adopted.

"There were various substances in the stomach, most of which we identified to be harmless. But my colleague and I were forced to the conclusion there had been interference with the natural progress of death."

"Cut line, sir. Enough of this rigmarole. You are saying he was murdered?" He just managed to stop himself from mentioning his wife's conclusion. "In what manner?"

A despondent sigh escaped Doctor Heather. "I fear it looks like asphyxiation."

Ha! Bravo, Tillie!

Doctor Heather put up a staying hand. "It is not conclusive and I must beg you will not spread it about until the inquest has been held. The coroner may well protest there is insufficient evidence to come to a verdict of unlawful killing. I was telling his lordship so when you — er — came in upon us."

But the suspicion, coupled with this tea business, was enough to do for Lord Wem. A faint thread of satisfaction ran through Francis. This was better than he might have hoped for. His quarry could not deny culpability in one of the females of his afflictive family. Before he could act on the thought, the door opened to admit a footman. Doctor Heather put in his request for his bag. Francis waited only for the door to close before crossing back to Lord Wem.

"I trust you are satisfied, sir, as to the veracity of the findings of my bloodhound, as you rudely chose to term my wife."

The doctor appeared at his elbow. "My lord, I must protest. His lordship is not well."

"Nor is my wife, thanks to the machinations of somebody in this house." Francis turned back to Lord Wem, who was blinking dazedly. "I demand an apology, sir, for a start."

"Apology be damned!" Lord Wem's voice was rough, but rife with regaining passion. "Don't imagine I am convinced of this nonsense."

Francis snorted. "Not even with two medical men concurring on their findings? Not to mention what my wife saw at the outset. You are obstinate beyond words, Wem."

Lord Wem remained half slumped against the chair back, but he raised a shaky hand and gestured wildly. "But it is absurd. Heather here says my boy was dead for hours by the time they found him."

"At least six hours, my lord," the doctor agreed.

"Six hours, and my wife was with him until after midnight. The thing is impossible."

Arrested, Francis stared at him, making a rapid mathematical calculation. "Then the timing must be wrong. I happen to know from my brother-in-law, who is also a doctor, that it is difficult to estimate an accurate time of death."

Doctor Heather at once chimed in. "That is so, my lord, but the signs were indicative of such an interval."

"Indicative. Not conclusive, I suspect."

"No, my lord." The fellow sounded regretful. "But even allowing for a margin of error, the deceased cannot have been alive much beyond one or two in the morning, if that."

Time enough for a determined individual to do the deed while everyone in the house was asleep. And a female had been seen in the early hours.

"The deceased." Lord Wem almost spat the word. "You are talking of my son!"

Francis paid no heed to this, his mind fixing on the nursemaid's testimony. He tackled Lord Wem again. "How do you know your wife was with Daniel until after midnight? How long after midnight?"

Lord Wem gave a heavy sigh. "I was wakeful. I had dozed a little. I remember feeling frustrated when I heard the clock chime."

"Which clock?"

"The long case clock downstairs. It has a deep tone. Normally I sleep through it, but that night—" He broke off.

"What about that night?"

"Why the devil should I tell you?"

He was reviving along with his irascibility. Francis gave no quarter.

"Because one of your women has rendered my wife incapacitated. It behoves me to act on her behalf. Why were you wakeful, sir?"

Lord Wem sat up in a bang. "If you must know because I had fallen out with Mary Ann. Satisfied?"

"No. Far from it. Upon what occasion?"

"Not that it is any concern of yours, Fanshawe, but we were in disagreement about the proper course of action to take with my boy. Something had to be done."

Something drastic was indeed done. But Francis refrained from stating this truth. "And when you heard the clock chime?"

"Mary Ann had not yet returned. She left me with the intention of dosing the boy with one of her infernal remedies."

"So she was in fact absent until an early hour of the morning."

"Did I say so? She came back a few minutes after I heard the midnight chimes. It cannot have been long. I had only just dropped off."

Francis kept the pressure on. "Did you converse? What did she say of Daniel?"

"She waited to ensure he was sleeping soundly. She wanted to be certain he had a good night's rest. She was adamant that was all that ailed him."

What ailed him at the time was inconsolable grief. Anyone could see that. Lord Wem had neither sympathy nor patience with the poor fellow's terrible loss. But all that was beside the bridge.

"Are you enough recovered to accompany me, sir?"

"To where?"

"I want you to question your women. Who handed my wife that cup of tea?"

Lord Wem let out an exasperated sound and fell back. "Are you at that again? You must be out of your senses. Why should any of them seek to poison your wife? Not that I believe for a moment any of those ridiculous herbs my wife imagines to be efficacious has the power to poison anyone."

To Francis's surprise, Doctor Heather entered a caveat. "Oh, indeed, my lord. There are any number of herbal substances that may be lethal, even in small quantities."

Lord Wem eyed him with a baleful stare. "Your opinion was not sought, Heather."

"But, my lord—"

"Enough!" Francis waved the fellow to silence. "I have no desire to engage in an argument on this subject. The facts speak for themselves. My wife drank tea in this house and vomited within a few minutes of returning to our lodging. Two and two make four, Wem, the last time I counted."

The doctor put his oar in again. "With your permission, my lord, if your lady wife survived, one may assume the substance was not poisonous."

Lord Wem snorted in his turn. "So much for your theory, Fanshawe."

Francis ignored him. "Then why was she ill?"

"I would be more inclined to put it down to a substance designed to induce vomiting. I cannot think why such might be served in a cup of tea, however."

"Can't you? I can, with ease." Derisive, Francis turned his gaze upon Lord Wem again. "My wife was closing in on the truth. The guilty party obviously hoped to put her out of action. Or to dissuade her from pursuing the matter."

"She would have done better to have dropped it at my request," said Lord Wem on a sour note.

Francis allowed himself a twisted smile. "It is plain you have no understanding of the character of my Lady Fan."

Lizzy followed Vivian Maplewood as he strode into the large saloon and stopped short. Amongst the shrieking throng was Mrs Maplewood. She was standing at bay near the crocodile's chair while the other women pressed around, clucking like hens and talking over each other, so that it was hard to make out what was said.

"Why must you persist with—?"

"It is of no use saying I must take her—"

"Nor I, for Julius—"

"Cannot you see how upset Mama is?"

"—Leo will never allow it."

"I don't care." This from Mrs Maplewood, in a harassed but determined tone. "We must settle this."

Mr Maplewood raised his voice to be heard above the cacophony. "Ladies! Will you all be silent?"

Either he went unheard or they chose to ignore him. Lizzy slipped past him, ran to a sideboard table between the windows, picked up a heavy marble ornament and brought it down on the wooden surface with a resounding crash. Once, twice. The noise ceased like magic.

All eyes turned to the source and Lizzy moved to confront them. "One of you here tried to harm my aunt." Her voice was shaking. "I do not stir from this room until I know who it was."

No one spoke, but Mrs Maplewood shot Vivian a glance of question. He stepped in.

"Thank you, Eliza. Drastic, but effective."

The Dowager Lady Wem was crouching in her chair, a malevolent toad, her slit eyes darting from Mr Maplewood to his mother and sweeping over his female relatives.

"What does Lady Elizabeth mean, Vivian?" Mrs Maplewood was approaching.

"I will tell you. She came to me in great affliction. Lady Francis, who was lately with you all in this room, has been struck down by a violent sickness. She ascribes it to the tea she drank here."

Mrs Maplewood's shock was palpable, but Vivian's aunt Lillian demurred in no uncertain terms. "What utter nonsense! We all drank it and we are perfectly well."

Lizzy chimed in, "That proves nothing. One of you may easily have slipped something into her cup. She might have died! She was trying to help you and this is how you serve her."

"Oh, this is all so horrid." Clarissa delivered these words, and then dissolved into tears, drawing the attention of the matriarch.

"Pull yourself together, girl. Or get out."

Clarissa jumped up, but Vivian put up a hand. "No one leaves. Lord Francis is even now in the house, seeking vengeance."

"Where is he then?" This from Berta. "Not that I care. I have more important matters to attend to."

Lizzy chimed in again. "My uncle meant to find Lord Wem. I don't doubt he will be here at any moment."

"Do you see us shaking in our shoes?" Lillian scoffed. "If he is of a mind to cast wild accusations, I shall refer him to Godfrey. He will know how to answer such impertinence." She flounced to the sofa and plonked down, radiating defiance.

Mrs Maplewood took up the argument. "Even supposing it was possible for one of us to contaminate the tea without changing the taste, what would one use?"

Lizzy had been over this with Mr Maplewood before they came up. "A herb of some kind. It would be easy enough to add it to tea."

At this, Mary Ann, who had been standing like a stock, came abruptly to life. "Herb? Oh, heavens, I shall be blamed!" She became predictably tearful. "It is not fair. I try only to do good. I use them to help people. Why does everyone call me a witch and say I am wicked?"

Mrs Maplewood sought to soothe. "No one is saying anything of the kind, Mary Ann."

"Yet it is easy enough to make a mistake," came from Lillian in a measured tone.

"Mistake? I never make mistakes. I know my herbs, I tell you!"

"I am not talking of you, Mary Ann. These wretched little bags of yours are all over the house. You are forever brewing up your potions in the kitchens. One of the servants might have put the herbs into the tea caddy, or—"

"Stuff and nonsense!" Scorn dripped from Berta's voice. "I keep the key to the caddy."

"But the caddy was open today," Mrs Maplewood put in quickly. "You made the tea, Lillian. You did not have to unlock the caddy."

"True, but—"

"If herbs had been in the caddy, we would all be ill," Clarissa cried. "It can't have been anything in the tea."

Stalemate. A silence fell, the women glancing one to the other.

Lizzy was baffled. It certainly began to appear unlikely a substance had been administered to Ottilia. But a niggle of uncertainty refused to be shaken off.

Mrs Maplewood broke the impasse. "One thing is certain. Mama could not have done it."

"I?" The Dowager Lady Wem, haughty. "I commissioned this Lady Fan. Why should I seek to do away with her?"

"Do away?" Clarissa turned scared eyes on Lizzy. "Is that what she thinks?"

The denials came thick and fast.

"Ridiculous. To what end, as dear Mama so rightly says?"

"But I answered her questions. I have no quarrel with her."

"I said nothing. Why should I care enough to hurt the woman?"

Mrs Maplewood cut into them all. "I did not imply any such thing. Mama, you mistake. I was merely establishing you could not have touched the tea. Both Lillian and I were serving. Berta helped."

Lizzy jumped on this. "Serving how? Who passed the tea around?"

"We all did. At least, I think so. I brought my own cup."

"Aunt Berta gave me mine," said Clarissa. "And she handed one to you, ma'am." This to the Dowager Lady Wem, who made no reply, her gaze trained upon her other daughter Annis. But Mrs Maplewood, if she had been about to speak, was forestalled by Mary Ann, almost hysterical.

"How can one be expected to remember? I am so put about I cannot even think. Lillian, did you give me tea?"

"I was pouring."

"But you brought your own, did you not? You might have given me a cup at the same time."

"The point, Mary Ann," interrupted Mrs Maplewood, "is not who gave you a cup, but who handed one to Lady Francis."

"I don't know, I don't know," protested Mary Ann. "There was such a fuss and bother, don't you remember? Pretty came in and—"

"You dare to mention that name again?" The Dowager Lady Wem rose. "Enough of this! Annis, you have caused sufficient trouble for one day. Be silent!"

Mrs Maplewood did not buckle. "I will not be silent, ma'am."

"Do you desire me to strike you?"

"If you do, I will strike you back, and so I warn you."

The issue hung there for a moment. Then the Dowager Lady Wem let out a harsh laugh. "You are more my daughter than this other ninny, that I swear."

Berta looked venom at her sister but closed her lips tightly together.

"Be that as it may, ma'am, I admit Pretty's fate has slipped a trifle at this juncture but be sure I will return to it. Mary Ann is the properest person to take care of her son's child, and I shall tackle Leo on the matter myself. But more important—"

She got no further for the door opened to admit, as Lizzy expected, an irate Francis, but led in, surprisingly, by Lord Wem. The viscount was dishevelled, his cravat loose about his neck, his waistcoat unbuttoned, and his countenance pallid. He came into the room without his usual confident stride, almost shambling, his limbs shaky.

"Leo!" Mary Ann was up, her woes forgotten. "You look dreadful, my dear. What is the matter?"

He waved a vague hand and almost staggered. A third man leapt forward, setting a hand to his elbow. "Steady, my lord!"

Lord Wem was helped to a chair, Mary Ann hovering by it, repeatedly asking after the reason for his debilitated condition. Once settled, he put out a hand to silence her and glanced across the watching women.

"Heather has given me the post mortem results. Daniel suffocated. He could not have done it to himself. He was slain by someone in this house."

There were muttered expletives and shocked gasps.

Then Mary Ann uttered a strangled cry and swooned where she stood.

CHAPTER FIFTEEN

Ottilia had endured the kindly doctor's questions as best she could, her mind swinging between what Francis might be doing up at the house on the hill and the plight of the unfortunate little girl.

"Tea, you say? Have you reacted in this manner before?"

"No. At least, only when I was with child."

The doctor had pounced on this, making much of her faint and Ottilia, only to be rid of him, had agreed it was possible she was indeed enceinte. She allowed no examination, however, and refused the laudanum, for which Sybilla took her to task as soon as the physician had departed.

"I need my wits about me, Sybilla. Besides, you ought to know I disapprove of the use of laudanum. We have seen its effects, remember?"

Sybilla snorted. "Don't harp on about that Tamasine girl, for heaven's sake! I wish I might wipe that episode from my mind."

"Because it occurred on your doorstep? Well, but you have better neighbours now, Sybilla."

"Yes, and thank the Lord! Not but what they are dull enough to send me to screaming point."

Ottilia had to smile, reflecting she had not the luxury of entirely forgetting the events at Willow Court, Hemp's presence inevitably keeping them alive. But she had no leisure now for those memories. "Never mind that now. It is more to the point to unravel this present puzzle."

Her mother-in-law, who was seated in a chair by the bedside, leaned forward and laid a hand on hers. "Leave it, Ottilia. The doctor told you to rest."

"How can I rest? I feel a deal better and my mind is churning." She turned her hand and gripped the thin fingers. "That child, Sybilla."

Sybilla's black eyes narrowed. "What of it?"

Ottilia drew a breath. "I believe she may be in danger."

"Poppycock!" Releasing her hand, Sybilla gestured wildly. "Do you tell me this so-called murderer would go so far?"

Ottilia regarded her steadily. "Why not? She disposed of Isabel without compunction and put a pillow over Daniel's head. She is poison. You have said it yourself countless times."

Sybilla held her gaze for a moment in silence. "You truly think Protasia is responsible for both these deaths?"

"Yes. Oh, not directly. I don't think she killed Daniel personally, and she was not at High Rocks. But she nevertheless bears responsibility."

"You think she ordered it? Even her grandson's death?"

Ottilia remained staunch. "She may have ordered neither. But her browbeating rule seeded the ground, indeed precipitated these events. Whoever pushed Isabel off that rock did so either at Lady Wem's instigation or, which I think more likely, in a belief it would solve an impossible situation which was making everyone miserable."

Sybilla looked both irritated and intrigued. "And Daniel? You ascribe the same motives to the guilty person in his case?"

Ottilia sank back into her pillows. "By no means. That was an altogether different proposition. I am not even sure that crime was perpetrated by the same individual."

Sybilla emitted a sound of frustration. "Now you have lost me utterly. Where in the world do you find these notions,

Ottilia? And the worst of it is, I end by believing you when I know it must be nonsense."

A ripple of amusement lightened for a moment the dark place in Ottilia's bosom. "I admit it sounds unlikely. You would think differently if you had heard Old Janet talking of the siblings. She was exceptionally enlightening as regards this Protasia of yours too."

"She is not *my* Protasia, I thank you. I cannot bear the woman."

Ottilia looked her in the eye. "Why, Sybilla? Was it jealousy on her part? Janet said she cannot endure to be eclipsed."

The closed look appeared on her mother-in-law's face. "That is between Protasia and myself."

Ottilia regarded her for a moment, wondering. But the matter closest to her heart rose up again and she gave it voice. "I could believe anything of her after the way she addressed that child. Or rather, she did not address her. She virtually denied Pretty's right to exist. It haunts me, Sybilla. I do not think she would turn a hair if the child was disposed of."

"All very well, Ottilia, but you have said she was not directly involved in either of these killings."

Urgent, Ottilia sat up again. "But don't you see? If the person — the woman, for that I think is now in no doubt — if the woman who took it upon herself to rid Protasia of Isabel thought to please her by it, why would she balk at ridding her of the child too?"

Sybilla wafted a hand. "The child is not Protasia's problem. Responsibility devolves upon the son, the girl's grandfather."

"True, but I had it from Mary Ann's own lips that Leo has determined to shut the child away somewhere. Pretty will be nothing more than the skeleton in the family closet. Heaven knows to what sort of existence she will be condemned. Now do you see?"

Sybilla snorted. "I see you have a bee in your bonnet as usual. There is nothing you can do about it, Ottilia. Nor is it your affair."

"You suggest I ignore it? And how do you propose I salve my conscience?"

"Don't you get uppity with me, my girl. I know you and your crusades. For heaven's sake, think!"

"I cannot stop thinking about her and that is the difficulty. If I could spirit her away, I would."

Arrested, Ottilia stared at her mother-in-law's face. The enchanting little countenance with its frame of gold-red curls superimposed itself in her mind upon the much older countenance. Why not? It would serve several purposes to admiration. For the moment. But what of the future? Pretty's future. An innocent little girl, motherless and fatherless both, with only her nursemaid to fulfil both roles — if indeed this Hepsie female was permitted to remain with her — condemned to a lonely, isolated existence. Deprived of family affection. Not that such affection could be relied upon even were she brought up among the Brockhursts. Worse perhaps, subjected to the sort of treatment meted out on a regular basis by the matriarch of the clan. Except the matriarch would not even tolerate her presence. Which brought her full circle to the question of safety. To keep the child alive was of the first consideration.

"What are you thinking, Ottilia?"

The stern demand pulled her out of her reverie and she uttered unwise words. "I am thinking I would like to take Pretty myself."

Sybilla's face was a picture. "Have you taken leave of your senses?"

"Drat you, Sybilla. I did not mean to let that out."

"It is too late now. Ottilia, what can you be thinking of? Francis would never consent."

Fan! Her heart plummeted. Sybilla was right, of course. Her darling husband loathed the Brockhursts. It would prove a piece of work to persuade him. If she could. If she *should*. Guilt swamped her. She was a wretch even to think of foisting the child off onto him. Unless…

She was dragged from a myriad of contradictory thoughts by her mother-in-law's voice.

"Ottilia, I most earnestly beg of you to think better of indulging such a whim. The child's situation may be as pitiful as you please, but she comes of the worst possible stock."

Ottilia's heart rebelled. "What has that to say to anything? A child need not be forever tainted by heritage. Environment and upbringing play a major part in—"

"Do not be foolish, my child! The girl is bred in that woman's bone. Have any of her brood turned out well?"

"Yes, there is Annis."

"And there is also Berta."

"Trapped in a terrible proximity to her mother. Of course she is rubbed raw."

"She is vicious, just like her mother. Leo is vile-tempered. I cannot speak for the younger generation, but I guarantee there will be shades of Protasia in all."

"You are too prejudiced to judge. Forgive me, Sybilla, but your hatred makes you blind."

Sybilla's black eyes snapped. "Blind, am I? Let me tell you, that woman made it her business to seduce my affianced husband. Not, mark you, for the pleasure of it. But with the intention of securing Polbrook for herself."

Diverted, and secretly appalled, Ottilia regarded her with rising admiration. "And yet you still married him."

Sybilla waved a dismissive hand. "As to that, she did not succeed. I walked in on them before matters had proceeded to the worst extreme."

"Good heavens! You mean you actually caught them in flagrante delicto?"

"Very nearly. They were both dishevelled and the posture in which they were together engaged told its own tale." Sybilla fairly glared. "I have never told a soul until now. You will take it to your grave, Ottilia. I should never have said a word, but you made me fume with your nonsense about this Pretty."

Ottilia seized her hand. "I won't say a word, I promise. But how could you know Protasia intended marriage?"

"She told me outright." Sybilla slumped a little, as if the memory crushed her. "Polbrook retired from the scene in a hurry. What would you? He was embarrassed. I gave Protasia a piece of my mind. She retorted that she was not done, she would have him in spite of me, that I would not be the marchioness above her, and all manner of things besides. I do not recall the half of the insults she threw at my head. Suffice it, I let her rant for a while. Then I slapped her face for her and walked out."

"Did she try again?"

"If she did, she had no success. Polbrook was abject in apology. Said he had been carried away. I told him if he succumbed again he might expect to be carried away in a coffin and that was the end of it."

Ottilia could not hold back a burst of laughter. "That is priceless, Sybilla. Typical of you too."

A reluctant smile was drawn from her mother-in-law. "He was a good man at heart. He knew his conduct was disgraceful. Let a gentleman keep a mistress by all means, but only a scoundrel takes his pleasure of an innocent girl."

"Innocent?"

"She was genteel, of excellent birth and ought — I say ought advisedly — to have been unsullied. Besides, I was worth a great deal of money to Polbrook. Well for him he did not saddle himself with Protasia. He would have led a dog's life. I felt sorry for Wem when she managed to secure him instead."

"But she has never forgiven you, I surmise?"

"It is mutual." Sybilla straightened. "You see now, my dear girl, how foolish it was of you to dream of taking that child under your wing?"

Ottilia did not see at all. To leave the little girl within reach of such a woman was anathema. But she said nothing of it to Sybilla, who reached for her hand and squeezed.

"You will have a baby of your own and bring it to term with success."

A pang shot through Ottilia and she tried to smile. "Perhaps."

"There is no perhaps about it. You are young enough to bear several children."

The encouraging tone failed of its intent. But Ottilia thrust away the doubts and memories that plagued her every so often, becoming brisk.

"Well, that is for the future. I must at least ensure this child has one."

There was also the unfinished matter of two lives whose futures had been cruelly cut off. But for this present, she needed the services of her steward. Hemp could be trusted to ensure little Pretty's safety.

Ottilia rose from her bed, declaring herself sufficiently recovered, and seated herself at the table with the rest of the family to dine, although she partook sparingly of the viands on offer.

Hemp, summoned at Ottilia's request, told her he had questioned both the footman and maid in a bid to discover if anything might have been inserted into the tea at source, but he drew blank. Neither could either servant state how the tea had come into Ottilia's hand, having left the room after depositing the accoutrements on the table. But he had gleaned one fact of possible interest. "The maid Ellen states Miss Berta took possession of one of Lady Wem's linen bags."

"She had one of Mary Ann's bags of herbs?"

"So Ellen says, milady."

"Did Mary Ann give it to her?"

"Ellen could not say. Miss Brockhurst came out of Lady Wem's bedchamber with it in her hand."

At this, Francis broke out. "Then there's your answer. The woman is nasty enough to do you a mischief."

"Yes, but it was done with intent, Fan."

"To warn you off, yes. But it's vicious nonetheless."

"What I mean is, if Berta put something in my tea — and that she had one of Mary Ann's herbal bags is no proof — it is an indication of guilt."

Sybilla set down her fork. "You are saying Berta killed Daniel?"

"I am saying whoever tried to warn me off today killed Daniel."

"And we failed dismally to find out which of them it was," came from Lizzy.

Francis soothed. "At least you narrowed it down, Lizzy." He looked across at Ottilia. "Everything points to Berta or Lillian, don't you agree?"

Ottilia did not answer for a moment, then she said, "They were both on the rock."

Francis queried her with a touch of annoyance. "What has that to say to anything?"

Ottilia's gaze turned on him. "I asked them about Isabel's death. No one could remember, if it was not pretence, who proposed the expedition. Clarissa confirmed it was not the men."

Sybilla made a gesture of exasperation. "But you have already said the murderer was a woman."

"True. A woman who certainly pushed Isabel. But did she also smother Daniel?"

"Two murderers?" Lizzy's voice was a squeak. "You think someone else took advantage of the first death?"

"I begin to think there is little connection between them, beyond the fact Isabel's death sent Daniel into a frenzied state."

"I don't understand, Aunt. Lady Fan has gone beyond me this time."

Francis laughed. "Count yourself lucky it's only the once."

Sybilla became irritated. "Enough! Explain, Ottilia."

Ottilia gave an apologetic smile. "I wish I could, Sybilla. I am sifting thoughts merely." Then she became suddenly brisk. "Hemp, I need your help."

He had retired into the background, but at once stepped forward. "Milady?"

"I fear for the safety of the orphan. I would have you secure both Pretty and the nurse."

"Ottilia! We discussed this."

"Trust me, Sybilla. I do not mean for Hemp to bring them here."

"Bring them here?" Francis was alert and questioning. "Are you serious?"

"A moment, Fan, if you please. Hemp, tell Hepsie to lock her door. Then keep watch, if you will be so good."

"All night, milady?"

"Dear Lord, why, Tillie?"

"Because persons are all too prone to wander about in the night hours in that house."

"But do you honestly suppose one of those females would seek to harm the child?" demanded Sybilla.

"I believe it, Grandmama. They none of them care about poor Pretty, except Mrs Maplewood. I believe she was trying to arrange for Lord Wem and his wife to take her. There was an argument in train when I arrived with Vivian — I mean, Mr Maplewood." Lizzy cast a fearful glance at her grandmother, but the latter was too intent to notice.

"Ottilia, it is too bizarre."

"I told you I meant to keep the child safe, Sybilla."

Francis looked from one to the other. "Wait. You've discussed this? You said nothing of it to me, Tillie."

"There has been no time, Fan." Ottilia turned swiftly towards Sybilla. "If you had witnessed the fracas when that child was discovered in the drawing room, Sybilla, you would not question it."

"What do you mean, Aunt Ottilia?"

Ottilia's tone became deliberate. "I mean, Lizzy, the woman who was prompted to remove Isabel may all too easily make the exact same decision regarding her daughter. And if she does, Hemp will discover who it was."

Hemp had not told Hepsie he meant to guard her door, not wishing to frighten her unduly. She was scared enough by the instruction, delivered in the little garden the nurse had made a refuge. She had regarded him with perplexity in her eyes.

"Why should I lock my door?"

Hemp turned his gaze upon the child. Pretty was seated on the grass beneath a shady tree, piling small stones in one place and then carefully rearranging them, one by one, in another. The golden curls escaping from beneath her white cap brought buried images to the forefront of his mind. Of another such infant in the heat of Barbados, pulling at strands of sugar cane with concentrated attention. The ache, never far away, returned to plague him. Had milady guessed he would move heaven and earth to prevent a like tragedy? Not that this child was cursed as Tamasine had been. But her double loss was quite as heinous a burden.

He turned back to the nursemaid. "For Pretty's sake, Hepsie."

"I don't understand."

Hemp grew impatient. "Don't you? Then think, girl. Does the mistress here welcome her? Is Pretty any more acceptable than was her mother?"

Hepsie's eyes grew dark, her voice hushed in response. "They wouldn't! Not a child."

"Milady is not so sanguine."

"Lady Fan thinks they mean Pretty harm? But, why?"

"Not all, Hepsie. It is not they, but she. Which she remains a question, though I suspect milady already knows."

Her reaction prompted him to take John into his confidence instead. The footman was sceptical but did as he asked so Hemp was able to slip into the kitchen after the rest of the servants were abed. John gave him a lighted candle.

"I'll show you the chamber."

Walking through alien corridors in the night hours proved eerie and a trifle unsettling. Hemp was glad of the candle, although he must douse it once he found a suitable place of concealment. The child was housed in a chamber on the nursery floor, just below the attics where most of the servants were situated.

"Hardly used these days," John told him in his laconic fashion. "The young ones are all terrified of the Empress, so the nobs don't bring 'em unless she orders it. Which she doesn't mostly. This here's the schoolroom. The girlie is in there."

He pointed to the door next to the one he was holding ajar. Hemp pushed past him into the schoolroom and held his candle aloft, looking about.

A couple of desks stood at one side before a blackboard. There were two or three straight chairs, a bookcase and a large rug which gave evidence of use by the current occupant. A couple of dolls lay discarded upon it and wooden blocks were scattered about, together with an open picture book.

This would serve his turn. He had not expected to derive comfort in his vigil, but he seized one of the chairs and placed it beside the door.

"You'll wait in here then?"

"It will be best, I think. I will wedge the door slightly open."

John's face flickered in the light of his candle as he grinned. "Better you nor me. I won't wish you a good night. Should think you'll perish of boredom."

"I have done worse."

He thanked the footman and watched him walk off to the stairway at the end of the galleried corridor. John went up and

Hemp glanced downwards to the floor below. He would see any approach readily from this vantage point.

The spill from the footman's light disappeared and Hemp snuffed his candle and waited for his eyes to adjust to the sudden gloom. Odd how the noises of a house grew louder in the pitch of night. Footsteps above him. John's in all likelihood. A muffled snoring, a cough, the creak of settling wood, and then a distant chime. One only, which gave Hemp a welcome indication of the time.

The shadows began to separate into forms he could recognise. Faint light filtered in from somewhere. A skylight above? Enough for him to be able to make out the balustrade, the stairs and the turn before the corridor below became obscured by the wall. He would see anyone coming up before they could spy him waiting. His natural dark colouring was a distinct advantage in this situation.

Hemp retreated into the schoolroom. He removed his shoes and set them aside, adjusted his chair so he could set his foot just inside the doorway and closed the door as far as this would allow. He settled down to wait.

The hours wore on. No disturbance occurred, however, and his mind clouded over, drifting with long-forgotten faces under a cloudless sky in the stifling heat presaging heavy rain. He was walking through the tall canes, her hand in his as he threaded a path and rapidly lost his bearings. The rain came on a whisper and he woke, momentarily confused about where he was.

Hemp shook himself awake, taking in the sounds of the first stirrings of the early morning. Creaking beds. The swish of a curtain. A throat clearing. A soft patter of feet coming down the stairs.

He came alert in a bang. Too close, all of it. Reorienting in his head, the sounds came from below, not above where the servants slumbered. There was grey light seeping in through the door from which he hastily removed his foot, instead putting an eye to the narrow opening and craning to see along the galleried corridor. A shadow crossed his vision.

He drew back, training his gaze on the door behind which Hepsie and the babe were sleeping. The shadow reappeared, forming into a figure, stealthy and quiet. It stopped before the door.

His pulse quickened and Hemp tensed, holding still in both body and breath. Shrouded in a dressing robe, the figure was undoubtedly female, a dark pigtail forming a thick line protruding beneath a cap. As Hemp watched, a hand grasped the doorknob. Turned it. Leaned in and pushed. The door resisted. The hand was removed. A moment passed and she tried again. Baffled by the need for stealth? The door held.

A low mutter came. "Locked. Curse the wench."

She stood for a moment that twanged on Hemp's nerves as it lengthened. Then she turned and glided away.

Hemp waited for the tell-tale sound that said she was on the stairs and then rose, letting his breath go at last. He opened the door with caution and peered out. The figure reached the bottom of the stairway and slipped into the corridor, vanishing from sight.

Hemp followed as swiftly as he dared, making no sound in his stockinged feet. He gained the lower level in time to catch sight of the woman as she reached the end of the corridor. Was she making for the main stairway to the next floor down? Hemp put on a burst of speed.

Arrived at the main gallery, he was in time to see her take the stairs. Instead of following, he moved swiftly along the side balustrade, seeking to catch a glimpse of the woman's face. He must have made some noise for she halted on the stairs. Hemp

297

drew back into the shadows, trusting his complexion would keep him hidden.

The woman raised her head, looking this way and that, her countenance a pale oval in the seeping grey of dawn. An oval Hemp was able to identify.

She held no weapon that he could see. But her robe was belted, a serviceable ligature for a strangling. Or had she planned to use a pillow? One hand held her slippered feet clear of the long nightclothes. The other was clenched. Or was she holding something?

A sudden chime from the downstairs case clock shattered her stillness. Her hand shifted, the thing within it gleaming in the light. Then she was moving, hurrying down the remaining stairs to the floor below and gliding off into the dark of the passage leading to the principal bedchambers.

Hemp saw again in his mind's eye the glimpse of whatever object she clutched in her hand. Made of glass? A paperweight? Milady had judged aright again. Berta Brockhurst had meant mischief indeed.

CHAPTER SIXTEEN

"Berta? Are you certain, Hemp?"

"I saw her face clearly, milady."

Ottilia felt a weight lift away. She had gauged it aright then. One thing remained to establish and then she could be rid of this troublesome affair. A reminding pang prompted a question.

"How does the babe fare? Did you have speech with Hepsie?"

"Milady?"

Hemp was standing by the mantel where she'd found him after Joanie came to awaken her. He must be tired for his attention was drifting. Ottilia repeated her query.

The steward's gaze flickered into life. "I thought it better not to remain in the house to be seen by the servants. Nor did I wish to disturb the child's rest."

Ottilia suppressed a sliver of disappointment. "You did right."

"Would you wish me to tell Hepsie the truth?"

"By no means. Locking her door is quite enough. We do not want to frighten the poor girl out of her wits."

Hemp straightened with an obvious effort. "She is strong, that one. I think she does not take fright easily."

"Get to bed, Hemp. You are exhausted."

A faint smile flitted across his face. "I did doze a little."

Ottilia touched his arm. "Thank you. You are invaluable. But go now. I won't keep you any longer."

She watched him go and turned for the bedchamber. At the door she changed her mind and instead went to the open window and took a seat there. Tyler or Joanie must have raised the blinds and opened the shutters to let in the early morning sun. It was intermittent today, the sky thick with drifting clouds. She glanced at the clock on the mantel. Not yet six? No use going back to bed. She would not sleep again now. Her gaze idled over the deserted Walks below, but her mind stayed with the twin dilemmas. How to present her findings and whether to pursue the dictates of her heart.

That itself posed another dilemma. She was not, could never be, sole mistress of that decision. Without the consent, indeed support, of Francis, there was no hope of pursuing it. The guilty certainty she ought not even to ask it of him had threaded into her dreams. Better to concentrate on the other and contain the yearning as best she might.

Hemp's discovery confirmed what she had suspected. Yet there remained the problem of Lillian. But for one circumstance, she slotted perfectly into the picture. The trouble was the picture was by no means perfect. It was distorted, unkind even. And not one of them would believe it. Least of all Annis Maplewood, who retained a certain naivety in the face of owning a particularly unpleasant set of relatives.

"Tillie?"

The thread of half-acknowledged guilt made her start. She turned quickly. Her husband was standing just inside the door, his dressing-gown, carelessly dragged on, left open over his nightshirt.

"Did I wake you?"

"I don't know. I worried when I found you gone." He came towards her. "What's to do?"

Ottilia looked away to the window, beset with a rise of anxiety. She was a wretch to be keeping secrets. She tried for a neutral note. "Hemp came back. He saw Berta trying the door."

Francis reached her, setting an arm about her shoulders, driving in the anguish. "She was after the child, do you think?"

"She was armed with a glass paperweight. If she had got in, I must guess she would have disabled the nurse first."

His face changed. "You're trembling, Tillie. Are you taking this to heart?"

Her throat ached. She met his troubled gaze. "She's just a babe, Fan. The sweetest little thing." Her tears spilled over and the words husked out. "I want her, Fan! I want her so much!"

He did not speak, but his arms folded about her and she wept into his chest. The balm of it warred against her raging conscience. Presently the sobs subsided and she was able to pull away. Francis dug into the pocket of his gown and produced a square of linen. Ottilia took it from him and made use of it, wishing he would say something. She felt him holding back and his silence compelled her to make shift to explain.

"I have not dared to speak of it to you."

He leaned against the windowsill, his brows drawing together. "Why? Do you think I don't know you still hanker for a child? Still feel the loss?"

She found his hand and held it tightly. "But I have not fallen, my dearest."

"Not yet." The twitch came at his eyebrow. "Despite my best efforts."

A watery chuckle escaped her, but the amusement was short-lived. "Fan, I may never conceive again. Patrick warned me it might be so."

"He told me there was no reason why you shouldn't fall pregnant again. The only warning was to give you time to heal."

Ottilia released his hand. "He did not want to worry you."

Her spouse's tone became brusque. "Yet you say he chose to worry you."

"He is my brother, Fan. Patrick would never lie to me."

"Did I say he lied?"

"You implied it. Or do you think I am making it up?"

He let out a breath. "I don't know what to think. Is it a ploy to bolster this whim of yours?"

Ottilia's heart shied. "Pray don't be angry with me, Fan. I did not want to tell you."

"That is well seen."

He turned, striding off to seize up the bell, plying it with a touch of violence. Ottilia swallowed on the words begging to be spoken. She must not say more. Not now. It was plain her husband was striving to keep his volatile temper in check. Had she not known how it would be?

Joanie hurried in and she was relieved to hear Francis order coffee.

"And shut the door behind you, if you please."

Privacy? Ottilia's heart sank. He meant to have it out with her. She remained where she was, gazing out upon the Pantiles where one early walker was now strolling and a couple of maids hurried along, burdened with heavy baskets.

"Were you serious?"

She was tempted to renege, only to avoid the coming storm. But remembrance of the terrified little face steeled her to the truth. "Yes, Fan."

He stared across at her for a moment, the dark eyes sombre. "You realise what you are asking? It is not like taking on Hemp Roy. You can't succour every waif and stray you meet, Ottilia."

Ottilia? Oh, Fan. She felt alienated. Which was precisely what he must be feeling. She softened on the instant and rose, going to him. She met the latent hostility in his eyes and set a hand to his chest. "I am not asking, Fan. I know I have no right to do that."

His gaze remained hard. "Then why mention it?"

"Because it has been festering inside me, my darling, and I cannot endure to have secrets from you."

His mouth twisted. "Don't spare the dagger, will you?"

Her hand fell. "I am trying to be truthful with you, Fan."

His tone was clipped. "I know. It doesn't help."

She stepped back, instinctively giving him space. "It is because she is a Brockhurst, is that it?"

"That, but not only that." His tongue lashed her. "You always do this, Tillie. You work upon my love for you and twist me to your wishes. Well, not this. I'll not take up the burden of another man's child. Not even for you."

The hurt ran deep, but Ottilia welcomed it, assuaging her conscience. She knew better than to answer him.

Relief came in the opening of the door, bringing Tyler bearing a tray with the coffee pot and the necessary accoutrements. Ottilia sat in her usual chair, feeling filleted. No sooner had the footman set the tray down than Francis pounced on it, dismissing Tyler with a word. Ottilia watched him pour, his jerky motions redolent of frustration.

Her affections surfaced. With confession, the yearning desperation had subsided a little. She received her cup and saucer from her husband and essayed a tentative smile.

"We had best talk no more of this matter, do you not think?"

He let out a snort. "Do you take me for an idiot?"

"You know I don't."

"Then don't talk like the fool I know you are not. You know well there is a great deal more to be said." He turned on the words and fetched his own cup, taking the chair opposite and downing several mouthfuls.

Ottilia sipped, her nerves shredding despite every wish to remain calm. As she waited for what he might say next, it dawned on her he had grasped her desire all too swiftly. What had she said? She thought back. Did she speak only of wanting Pretty? She had said nothing of taking her. The implication hit.

"Sybilla betrayed me to you!"

Francis set down his cup and looked across. "Mama was troubled."

"Troubled? For me or for you?"

His shoulders shifted. Discomfort? Well might it be so.

"You have every right to be furious. I told her you would be."

"You might well. I must suppose you have been mulling this ever since. You have already made up your mind against me."

He set down his cup. "What did you expect, Tillie? You rave about taking on a random child—"

"Scarcely random. She has lost both parents and her relatives loathe her."

"You don't know that."

Ottilia sat up, setting aside her coffee, urgent now. "None of them want her, Fan. Lord Wem talked of shutting her away somewhere, out of sight of the family. Why not with us? At least she would be loved!"

"By you?"

Ottilia was brought up short. She hesitated. No, say it, Ottilia. No more secrets. "I could not love you less, Fan, even if I grew to love a child."

He sat up in a bang. "What, you suppose me to be jealous? Don't be ridiculous."

"Well, what then? You said you won't be burdened with another man's child, but what if we never have one of our own?"

"Early days, Tillie. We have time enough."

She slumped a little. "You are quoting Sybilla."

He ignored the charge. "Even if I were willing, I can't see Wem agreeing to it. The child is his responsibility and he can't abide either of us. Besides, Lizzy says Mrs Maplewood is determined to persuade that Mary Ann woman to take the child."

Ottilia's heart chilled. The words came unbidden to her lips. "That will not be possible, I fear."

"Why the devil not? She's the girl's grandmother."

Ottilia spoke with a certain deliberation. "Would you wish to live with the woman who killed your father?"

His brows snapped together. "What? That can't be, Tillie."

"Yet it is so. Mary Ann is the one who smothered Daniel."

A knocking at the front door below took Ottilia's attention from her husband's expletive response. She glanced at the clock. "That can't be Lizzy or Sybilla. What is amiss now?"

Francis was up, moving towards the door. "Not more alarums, for pity's sake!"

He opened the door, and Ottilia listened to the footsteps and low murmurings coming from below, a patter rising in her bosom and a clutching fear. With Hemp out of the way, had Berta succeeded after all?

"Damnation," came from Francis as he moved back into the room. "This nurse of yours has brought the child here."

But Hepsie's errand proved to have no bearing on the acrimonious discussion. She came into the room, bobbing a curtsey, the infant clutched in her arms. "Begging your pardon, my lady, but I had to come."

Ottilia had risen on her entrance, her eye going at once to the sleepy little girl's head resting on the nursemaid's shoulder. "What has happened, Hepsie?"

"It's the master's mama, my lady."

"Mary Ann?" A dread premonition shot through Ottilia.

"Yes, my lady. His lordship couldn't wake her. She's dead."

The hush was palpable. It was not the quiet of a sleeping household. Nor were there the usual sounds of early domestic activity. The maid who answered the door looked terrified.

Ottilia strove for a calm she did not feel, finding a smile from somewhere. "Mrs Maplewood, if you please."

The girl fidgeted with the door handle, glancing back into the house. "I don't know as she can see anyone."

"She will see me." Ottilia set a hand upon the maid's. "Come, my dear, I know what has happened here and I have come to help."

At that, the girl gave a strangled sob. "It's terrible, ma'am. I can't stay here no more. I told Mr Lamport."

Taking advantage, Ottilia pushed her gently into the house, setting an arm about her and giving her a squeeze. "It must be dreadful for you all, but I am sure Mr Lamport needs your support at this difficult time. Come, my dear, dry your eyes. Where is Mrs Maplewood, do you know?"

The maid sniffed, drawing her sleeve across her nose. "They are all of them in the breakfast parlour. We took up tea and coffee and Cook is preparing hot rolls. Not as anyone will eat them, and so I told her. I couldn't swallow a morsel, I know that."

While she talked, Ottilia urged her towards the stairs, making soothing noises. She could not help wishing she might soothe her own sore heart, but that must wait. Francis, the more brusque for the presence of little Pretty, had opted to inform his mother before following Ottilia.

"There is no need, Fan. I am in no danger now."

"I am coming. I will be moments behind you." He spoke with finality, the tone feathering hurt in her bosom.

"As you wish. You will not object to it if I leave Hepsie and the child in Joanie's care?"

He had not glanced at her, intent upon his neckcloth. "I am not a Brockhurst monster, Tillie. Do as you think best."

She felt it as grudging, but at least it was to be done with his assent. The nursemaid was obviously relieved to be spared having to return immediately to the stricken household.

"Thank you, my lady. May I give the babe a little milk?"

"Of course, my dear. Joanie will provide you with whatever you need. Pray remain here until I return."

Ottilia had wished very much to relieve her of Pretty for a space, to hold the little girl just once. But there was no time. She must dress at speed. And Pretty would undoubtedly balk at being parted from her nurse, to whom she clung, big eyes taking in the alien surroundings, the strange faces, a look in them of bewilderment and fear. No wonder, poor little mite.

At the insistence of Francis, Ottilia was accompanied by Tyler, instructed to remain until her husband joined her at the Brockhurst home. She left him in the hall, making her way with the maid up to the first floor and into an apartment she had not before seen.

It was crowded, but one glance served to inform Ottilia not every member of the family was present, all who were there one for one in dishabille. The women were present, but there was no sign either of Lord Wem or his brother Godfrey. Ottilia caught sight of Julius, now doubly bereaved, seated in a chair by the windows, his wife Clarissa beside him. Marcus was at the big round table, drinking from a cup and talking in low tones with his mother Lillian. Berta and Annis were striving to deal with the Dowager Lady Wem, who was in a chair near the table and engaged in a muttering monologue that sounded, to Ottilia's ears, perilously close to hysteria.

No one noticed her entrance, and the maid was far too distracted to think of announcing her. She took a moment before drawing attention to herself, regarding more closely the trio that included the Dowager Lady Wem. The only Lady Wem now, Ottilia reflected.

She did not appear to be affected by whatever her daughters were saying, seemingly enclosed in her own little world. Ottilia tried to tune in and made out snippets.

"Me next, I know it … you will none of you be satisfied … eat nothing, drink nothing…"

The gist was much as one might expect. This third death had rendered her terrified. Had not Old Janet spoken of it as her greatest fear? In truth, she was in no danger. Ottilia was about to move to her to say so when someone spoke beside her.

"Inevitable, I must suppose, you would materialise, Lady Fan. Are you omniscient?"

"Mr Maplewood!" She had not before spotted he was not among the rest. She regathered her focus. "No, indeed, sir. Hepsie came to tell me."

His light gaze met hers. "I trust Lady Elizabeth will not be following you."

"Not so far as I know. My husband will be here shortly."

"This is no place for Eliza. I wish she would keep away from the Brockhurst clan."

Ottilia became tart. "Then I suggest you tell her so, Mr Maplewood."

She left him on the words, moving to accost his mother instead. But Annis had already seen her. She beckoned, moving a pace to meet Ottilia. She was flurried and red-eyed. "I don't know how you found out, but I could not be more relieved to see you, Lady Francis. What, I ask you, is to be made of this? First Daniel. Now Mary Ann. I cannot bear it!"

Ottilia took the hands held out to her and pressed them, wasting no words. "Tell me, was any note found?"

"From Mary Ann?" Mrs Maplewood's gaze sharpened. "You think it was suicide?"

Ottilia released her. "Without doubt."

The son cut in, brusque and rough. "Because of Daniel? She couldn't live with the grief? But that's what they said of Daniel himself, and it proved a futile belief."

Ottilia eyed both intent faces. Was this a good moment? Was there point in waiting? She made up her mind. "She could not live with the guilt."

Shock spread across the faces of both mother and son. Doggedly, she pursued it. "Moreover, once the post mortem results were in, Mary Ann knew she would be found out."

Ottilia became aware the various hushed discussions in progress had died away. Had they all heard?

A glance found Marcus staring open-mouthed. Lillian had gone white. Berta, predictably, glared. Even the Dowager Lady Wem's muttering had ceased, a frown dragging at the slanted orbs. Only Julius, bowed down with woe, had missed it, although Clarissa, engaged in comforting her spouse, was now gazing blankly at Ottilia.

She turned back to the Maplewoods. "That is why I asked about a note."

Annis had a hand pressed to her chest. "A confession?"

"Nothing was found. Or, if it was, Uncle Leo said no word of it."

"But why do you say Mary Ann…?" Annis faded out and tried again. "I cannot say it. It is too horrible. Her own son?"

All at once, other voices cut in.

"I don't believe it."

"More of your nonsensical suppositions."

"You are raving, Lady Francis."

There was more in the same vein, growing louder. And then the dowager came in across them, querulous. "Be silent! All of you!" She pointed a finger at Ottilia. "You! Sit. Sit there." The finger indicated a chair opposite.

Ottilia balked. "I think, with your permission, Lady Wem, I should prefer first to examine Mary Ann's body."

Berta swished forward, spitting rage. "You will do nothing of the kind! This is all your doing. Ever since my fool of a sister brought you in, this family has been falling apart. You, with your questions, your accusations. Who in the name of heaven do you think you are, marching in here without so much as a by your leave and uttering such words?"

"Berta, be quiet!"

But the woman was beside herself. "I will not be quiet. Certainly not at your bidding, Sister! Have we not borne enough? This woman has put everyone at outs."

"We were at outs long before she came, Berta," Annis protested. "Will you at least let her speak?"

"Speak? Speak? The dratted woman has not ceased speaking from the moment she entered this house." Berta turned suddenly on the Dowager Lady Wem. "You gave her leave. You let her probe and poke into our private affairs. You are to blame. Mary Ann would be alive now but for you!"

The truth of this could not but strike Ottilia, but the subject of it rose out of her chair, eyes blazing, an avenging hand flying out to land a violent blow on Berta's cheek. The scream the daughter emitted was echoed in the scoldings of the mother.

"You dare curse me, do you? Take that! Wishing it were me lying there cold instead of Mary Ann, I'll lay my life. Oh, you want me dead, I know that well enough."

Berta fell into violent sobs, crying out through them. "I do wish it! I hate you! You have ruined my life."

"Ruined your life? Pshaw! It's you have ruined mine. I don't know why I bear with you."

"Because I do your bidding. Well, no more, I tell you! You began it all! You began it all!"

Ottilia heard this with a leap of satisfaction. Her pulse, already jumping with the vicious attack she had endured, lost its rhythm. There was no time to indulge her senses, for the combatants, shrieking imprecations, closed one with the other, scratching, hitting, biting even.

It took the combined efforts of the two young men and both their mothers to drag the screeching women away from one another. Ottilia found herself elbowed out of the way. One glance sufficed to tell her both Julius and Clarissa were shocked into leaping up and joining the fray.

Useless to try to expound her understanding in this maelstrom. She opened the door and discovered a bevy of servants in the passage, listening to the uproar within.

They began to scatter as she came out, but Ottilia called out, "Stay!"

Two maids, a footman and a fellow dressed like a valet each hesitated, glancing back.

"Would one of you be so kind as to conduct me to Lord and Lady Wem's chamber, if you please."

The footman hesitated at the door. "I'd best go in ahead, my lady. No saying how his lordship may react."

"On the contrary." Ottilia essayed a tiny smile. "I think I may confidently predict he will not be pleased to see me. It is necessary that I go in, however."

The man's expression became resigned and he knocked. No answer came from within. "Looks like he's not in there, my lady."

"Will you check, if you please?"

He opened the door with caution and peered in. "Not here."

When he would have closed the door again, Ottilia put out a hand to hold it open. "Pray allow me to enter. The body is still there, I presume?"

The fellow glanced back into the room and shuddered. "It's there all right." He pushed the door fully open and stepped aside.

Ottilia walked through and her eye went immediately to the still figure lying in the four-poster bed. She turned back to the footman. "Give me ten minutes, and then find Lord Wem and ask him if I may have the favour of a few words. Come back for me, will you?"

The footman assented and went off on his errand. Ottilia closed the door behind him. If anyone should disturb her examination, she would hear them come in.

She approached the bed with a rise of pity in her breast. The woman had committed the grossest of crimes, but she had suffered for it, burned with remorse and regret. And her motives, if Ottilia read them aright, had been born of affection.

She did not, as her son had done, look peacefully asleep, though her eyes were closed. Her waxen features bore an expression of extreme woe, although there was no distortion to suggest convulsions. A tiny reddish trail was visible, running from each eye and down the cheeks, one tracing along the groove beside the nose to the lip where foam had dried. Blood and tears?

Mary Ann had known precisely what to take. Belladonna? She had almost certainly used one of the soporific narcotics. Adding in all probability the mandrake she had given her son to induce sleep before receiving the full effects of the poison. Time enough for weeping before she sank into coma.

Ottilia straightened. There was no more to be learned from the body. The inevitable post mortem would reveal which herb had been ingested, and any ravages caused within.

Now for the note. If there was one. That it had not been mentioned suggested Lord Wem had not been in any condition to look for one. Mary Ann had not made it easy by leaving the thing in an obvious place. Under the pillow perhaps? She felt about as best she could below the pressure made by the heavy head. Nothing. A pocket? Mary Ann was in her nightgown, so where was the gown she had been wearing yesterday?

Hunting about, Ottilia found a discarded man's nightgown lying on a chest at the bottom of the bed. Then Lord Wem at least had taken time to dress. She spotted a pile of clothes on a chair in the corner. Ottilia lifted off the pieces of a dark-coloured gown, an under-petticoat, stays and a shift. No pockets? Was she still wearing them?

Returning to the body, she felt along its sides at the waist without result. On impulse, she patted about the bosom. A crinkle under her fingers sent a shaft of excitement through her. She slid a hand down the neck of the nightgown, shrinking a little at the touch of the cold flesh, the flaccid skin of the dead woman's bosom. Her fingers caught an edge of paper and she drew it forth.

A folded missive, sealed and addressed in a shaky hand to *My Dearest Leo*.

Ottilia regarded it in a kind of fascinated wonder. Mary Ann had prepared well. A neatly executed end for a woman whose mind had been somewhat unbalanced when she did the deed.

Although Ottilia's fingers itched to break the seal, there could be no justification for so doing. Instead, she straightened Mary Ann's clothing, brought the covers up and drew the sheet over the woman's head, concealing the pitiful condition of her features.

As she left the room, she almost ran into her husband who was just outside, accompanied by the same maid who had let her into the house.

"Francis! You startled me."

"I came directly I had told Mama the news." He glanced from her face to the paper in her hand. "What is that?"

"It is for Lord Wem. How did you know where to find me?"

He nodded towards the maid, whose eyes were riveted on the paper in Ottilia's hand. "This girl told me you had asked to be led here."

Ottilia eyed him, uncertain of his mood. "Then you have not been into the breakfast parlour?"

He frowned. "Should I?"

A fleeting ripple of mischief lit Ottilia's bosom for a moment. "Not unless you wish to enter the devil's domain."

A faint grin lightened the solemnity of his features. "As bad as that?"

"Worse. But where is that footman? I asked him to find Lord Wem and— Ah, there you are!"

The fellow had appeared in the passage behind the maid. "His lordship said he will see you, my lady."

Throwing a glance of surprise at her husband, Ottilia thanked him. At least now she had a sufficient reason to beard the bereaved Lord Wem.

"Is that what I think it is?" Francis asked low-toned as they processed along the corridor behind the footman.

"I hope so indeed," Ottilia returned sotto voce. "It will save me a deal of argument if Mary Ann has told it herself."

Lord Wem was found in the small parlour where Ottilia had spoken alone to his mother days since. It felt like an aeon now. He was sitting in a chair near the window, his brother Godfrey seated close by, one hand kneading at the elder man's arm. Both men were fully dressed, although their attire lacked neatness as if they had scrambled into their clothes.

Leo's face was grey, his cheeks sunken. He did not look up when Ottilia and her husband were announced. Godfrey came to his feet and advanced to meet them, his voice hushed in that bedside manner generally adopted in the presence of the bereaved.

"My brother is suffering, as is to be expected. I trust you will not keep him long."

Ottilia spoke in a normal tone. "I am not here to distress Lord Wem."

"She is here to help, sir." Francis, as usual bristling on her behalf, despite the underlying dissension between them.

Her heart warmed a trifle, but she had something to do here. She moved past Godfrey and took his vacated seat, beginning without preamble. "My lord Wem!"

If she had meant to seize his attention, she succeeded. Leo started, bringing his head up with a jerk and staring at her with hollow eyes.

Ottilia held up the sealed missive. "I found this concealed under your wife's nightgown, sir. It was lying on her bosom." His aspect did not change, but his hand came up and he took it from her, holding it between his fingers. "It is addressed to you, sir. See?"

She pointed to the inscription. His gaze shifted. A rough voice came out.

"Mary Ann?"

"Yes, sir. She meant for you to read it." It was plain he was too numbed to think for himself. Had Godfrey given permission for her entry? "Break the seal, my lord. What she has to say may comfort you."

His brows drew together and he stared at the letter, which began to quiver as his fingers trembled.

Godfrey came in close, leaning down to him. "Shall I do it for you, Leo?"

At that, Lord Wem snatched the paper to his chest, holding his hand against it in a protective fashion. His glance, coming suddenly alive, scorched his brother.

"No one reads it but me!"

Ottilia took a hand. "Open it, sir."

His gaze returned to the missive and his trembling fingers broke the seal. He opened it and began to read. Ottilia itched to look. She could see the words were plentiful, the paper blotched here and there. Mary Ann's tears had likely fallen on the ink as she wrote.

Glancing at her spouse, Ottilia found him frowning, his gaze riveted on the letter. Had he taken in the implications of this fresh death? She doubted it would even occur to him to wonder who of the family might step in with Pretty's grandmother gone. But she must not dwell on that now. The task she had to perform in this house was not yet done.

Godfrey was trying to read the note from his position above his brother's chair. He looked anxious for once. Had he divined his wife was exonerated from suspicion of Daniel's murder by Mary Ann's fate?

Lord Wem came to the end of his reading and looked up, his gaze keener than it had been as it found Ottilia's. "You knew this?"

No use prevaricating. "Only lately, sir. After I learned Mary Ann had not returned to your bed that night until well after the clock struck twelve, it occurred to me your son's demise may well have come earlier than we had all supposed. I know your sister Berta was abroad in the early hours." She glanced at Godfrey. "And I guessed your wife Lillian, sir, from her reaction to hearing a woman was seen, also knew."

Godfrey was frowning now, but Francis demanded clarification. "You mean Lillian thought it was Berta who did the thing?"

"I believe so. She may have seen her too. Earlier Lillian had found Berta at Daniel's door and led her away. At that time, Mary Ann was still with Daniel."

Leo spoke again, his voice stronger now. "But it is preposterous! Why should she do such a thing? Our own son!"

Ottilia glanced at the open paper held loosely in his fingers. "Does she not say?"

Without a word, he passed the letter across. Ottilia ran her eyes down the sheet. The lines were crooked, the words hurried and incoherent for the most part. Much of it read as an attempt to exonerate herself or otherwise beg for forgiveness.

"Do not think too harshly of me, Leo, for I burn with remorse and shame ... could not endure it... My Danny did not wish to live and this was the only thing I could do for him... I must have been mad ... they will punish me cruelly and I meant to be kind ... believe he felt nothing

for I made him sleep … so peaceful he looked at last, my beloved Danny … no one can hurt him now and that is my only balm…"

Nowhere did she specifically state she had taken her son's life, but the words were redolent of the implication. No one could mistake the tenor. Little surprise her bereaved husband could not understand why she had acted thus. Ottilia tried to soften the blow.

"I fear she misunderstood your intentions, Lord Wem. She told me you were determined on shutting Daniel away. I believe the interpretation your wife put upon your words was that you meant to incarcerate Daniel as you would a madman."

Lord Wem covered his face with his hands, emitting an agonised groan.

"But that cannot be all her reason," came from Godfrey.

Ottilia glanced at his frowning visage. "No, it is not all. She was anguished too by her daughter-in-law's accident, by the Dowager Lady Wem's behaviour, but most of all by her son's overwhelming sorrow. I believe she could not bear to see him in the peculiar condition of grief he displayed." She turned again to Lord Wem. "It may perhaps ease you, sir, to realise Mary Ann's mind was at the time unbalanced by these circumstances."

His hands dropped. "You mean she was as mad as Daniel."

"Neither of them were mad in the sense you mean. Grief can do strange things. Mary Ann's grief at Daniel's passing was genuine, you must know. It is now obvious to me that when I spoke to her, she had already begun to persuade herself she had not done it, or she tried to."

"But she was the one who tried to warn you off, was she not?" Francis cut in.

"Yes, because by then she had begun to realise I was closing in on the truth."

"What of Berta with one of these herb bags then?"

"She may have thought of using them on Hepsie or Pretty, but it was certainly Mary Ann who doctored my tea."

"That too?" Lord Wem's face reflected his anguish.

Despite all, Ottilia felt grieved for him. "It was dictated by impulse, sir. As was the act against your son. It was not premeditated." She held the letter out to Lord Wem. "Take it, sir. I don't believe Mary Ann planned what she did. I suspect she intended only to sedate Daniel that night."

"Then why?" It was a plea. "Why go her length and smother the boy?"

Ottilia drew a breath. "I wish I might spare you, sir, but it seems I cannot. You fought with Daniel earlier, did you not? Did you speak of the altercation when you returned to your chamber?"

"Did I?" Leo passed a hand across his brow. "I don't recall now. I may have. We had talked a great deal of the business. My mother was—" He broke off, sucked in a heavy breath and resumed. "The situation was intolerable. Something had to be done. I may have said so. I know I spoke of sending Daniel off somewhere until he had learned to master himself. But whether I said it then…"

He faded out and Ottilia said it for him. "Whatever you did say, I fear it lodged in Mary Ann's mind. She went to him with the intention of giving him a sedative drink. I dare say he raved a great deal before he drank it. Mary Ann was in a state of great upset and the various components tipped her too far. She silenced Daniel perhaps in a bid to silence the maelstrom in this house. I cannot answer for her state of mind, but it was not rational."

What little composure Lord Wem had retained deserted him. A sob gusted forth and his tears spilled.

Ottilia rose, addressing Godfrey. "I will leave you, sir. I am sure your ministrations will be more successful."

Godfrey followed her to the door, dropping his voice, although he was unlikely to be heard by the now sobbing Lord Wem. "You are finished here then, I take it?"

Ottilia paused, as did Francis who was holding the door for her. "Alas, no, sir. There is still one death more to be accounted for."

Godfrey fairly blinked. "I don't understand."

"Isabel, Mr Brockhurst. That fall from the rock was no accident."

CHAPTER SEVENTEEN

Francis kept pace with his wife as she hurried along the corridor, his mind winging ahead to the coming confrontation. He was glad he had chosen to follow her. There was no saying how these women would react. Although Lord Wem's demeanour had been tame enough, thank the Lord.

"I take it you know who pushed Isabel?"

Tillie stopped abruptly, turning an anxious gaze upon him. "Have you not guessed it?"

All at once the words she had spoken before the subject of the child came up leapt in his head. "Ah! Yes, I have it now."

A smile flickered on her lips and was gone again. Francis felt bereft as she turned and pursued her course. Agony to be at outs with her. He had been unnecessarily harsh. How to mend it when he could not satisfy her craving? He could but hope this whim of hers might prove ephemeral once she was away from Tunbridge Wells and contact with this afflictive family. Nothing to be done about it now. At this moment, his darling wife was a woman on a mission.

The breakfast parlour proved sparsely inhabited. Had those who created the hell Tillie spoke of removed themselves? There remained the Dowager Lady Wem seated at the table, attired in her regal purple, but in a garment which looked to be a dressing gown. Her two daughters were also seated there, similarly clad in night attire. But that comprised the entirety of the company. Ottilia proved to be rather more glad than disappointed.

"Ah, you are alone. That may well be a good thing."

Mrs Maplewood rose. "The others have gone to dress, but I did not wish to leave Mama." She briefly acknowledged Francis's presence with a nod but returned at once to Tillie. "Did you find anything?"

Tillie moved to join her, glancing at Berta, tight-lipped and sullen, and the dowager, whose aspect was fearful, eyes darting from Tillie to himself and back again as his wife spoke.

"There was a note. I gave it to Lord Wem."

Mrs Maplewood's gaze grew alarmed. "What was in it? Did you read it?"

"Yes. It was largely incoherent, but I cannot think anyone would take it as other than a confession."

"Then she did…" Mrs Maplewood faded out, sinking slowly into her chair and setting a hand to her brow. "It does not bear thinking of. His own mother. Oh, poor woman."

The Dowager Lady Wem reared up. "Poor woman? Say rather poor Leo, poor Julius, poor me! The woman was unworthy of the name of mother."

Francis nearly jumped as his wife erupted in an unprecedented fury.

"Then what shall we say of a grandmother, ma'am? Is she worthy of the name? She who urged her own daughter to be rid of those most dear to her grandson?"

"What are you saying?" came from Mrs Maplewood, but she was drowned by the woman Berta, who leapt to her feet.

"Ah, I knew it! I knew you would blame me!"

Alarmed, Francis moved to flank Tillie. "You attack my wife at your peril, ma'am!"

A sneer crossed the woman's face. "You bring your guardian, do you? I am not afraid of you, Lord Francis."

"You should be. I will have no compunction in dealing with you as you deserve if you attempt to lay one finger upon my wife, and so I warn you."

"Hush, Fan, pray." Tillie set a hand on his arm but kept her gaze on Berta. Her tone was more normal, the outburst at an end. Or had she calmed herself because of his temper rising as she was apt to do? "Berta, it is of no use to rail. I know you went to Pretty's room last night. You were armed with a glass paperweight. Why, if you had no intent to use it? On the nurse, I dare say. And what of Pretty? Did you mean to emulate Mary Ann and smother the child?" She turned all at once on the dowager. "You, ma'am, are to blame for this. Whether you ordered it or not, I do not know, but your attitude and your screaming fit the other day were enough to give Berta the notion."

"No! It cannot be!" Horror in Mrs Maplewood's voice.

The Dowager Lady Wem did not speak, only holding a malevolent gaze steady on Tillie. There would be no confession forthcoming here. Tillie seemed to realise it.

"I don't expect you to admit to anything, ma'am. You must always be right, must you not? However, Berta herself blamed you not a half hour ago, in this room. You began it, she said."

"She did, she did!" Berta's tone was high and querulous.

"Be quiet, you fool!"

But Berta was up. "I will not be quiet! You said I don't know how many times you wished to be rid of the brat. Just as you wished to be rid of its dratted mother."

"Now we come to it." Tillie again, triumphant. "Pray do not attempt to deny your part in that, Lady Wem. I drew blank when I asked who suggested the visit to High Rocks. No one could remember. You denied all knowledge. But you, ma'am, have been living here for an age. Who but you would think of such an outing? Berta would not. She is too busy running the house and catering to your distempered demands. What is more, she loathes and resents her family members, who have done nothing to ease the horrors of her life with you. No, Berta would not think of making up a party to go to High Rocks." Her gaze turned on Berta. "Or rather, not until your mama put the notion into your head, is that it?"

Berta glared at Tillie for several seconds. Francis almost held his breath, bracing to intervene if she made a move. And then the woman collapsed into her chair, weeping in a hysterical fashion.

Mrs Maplewood's horrified gaze came to rest on Tillie's face. "She did do it then? She pushed Isabel off the rock?"

"Well, it was either Berta or Lillian, and Lillian had no reason to do it."

"Oh, dear heaven!" Mrs Maplewood's eyes turned on the dowager, who sat as if made of marble, giving nothing away. "Mama! Is this true?"

Lady Wem, hard-featured now and cold, turned upon her other daughter. "Believe what you wish. I have nothing to say." Then she rose from her chair and stalked to the door. No one made any move to stop her, but Mrs Maplewood got up, looking after her and then turning a distraught gaze on her mother's accuser.

"How can you let her go? She ought to pay for this!"

Tillie set an arm about the woman's shoulders and moved her away from the table, lowering her voice. "There will be no retribution. It is impossible to prove. But I think we have seen enough to be sure it is the truth."

Berta was still noisily crying and Mrs Maplewood eyed her with uncertainty. "What will she do, I wonder?"

Tillie shrugged. "Nothing. I would guess that after an interval, they will go on just as they have done."

Mrs Maplewood straightened her shoulders. "But the rest of us will not. I want them all to know. Will you tell them?"

Tillie released her and Francis was not in the least surprised when she replied in the negative. "Without seeing what we have witnessed here, I should doubt if anyone will believe it."

Francis cut in. "There you have the operative word, my love. *Doubt.* Let Mrs Maplewood tell it. After what has occurred in this house, I cannot suppose any of the remaining members of the family will be much surprised at anything."

Mrs Maplewood regarded him with approval. "You are right, Lord Francis. I will tell them just what occurred here this morning."

When they were safely out of the doomed house, Tillie became a little more forthcoming.

"I am glad you encouraged Annis to tell the others."

Francis offered her his arm. "Let her bear the repercussions. You have done enough. But why does it please you?"

She tucked her hand in the crook of his arm. "Because I hope it may be enough to break Lady Wem's hold over the family. The servants will spread it abroad too."

Francis looked down at her in some amusement. "What you mean is you plan to urge Hemp to let it slip to the domestic staff."

He was gratified to hear a laugh in her voice. "You know me too well. I think they both deserve it, don't you?"

"What, to be ostracised by the gentry hereabouts?"

"Oh, not ostracised. The gossips will be too eager to twit them on it and see how they react. But it will make it hard indeed for Lady Wem to lord it over the neighbourhood as she has done. Nor do I think she will be able to keep the bulk of her servants. The maid was saying she can't bear to remain."

"Ha! Leaving Lady Wem and Berta to stew. What would you wager one of them will slaughter the other before the year is out?"

Lizzy, prevented by Sybilla from chasing after the Fanshawes to the house on the hill, had eager questions as her aunt and uncle settled to partake of a late breakfast.

"But I still don't quite understand, Aunt. How could you be sure Mary Ann did the killing?"

Ottilia smiled. "It was the only answer that fit. It filtered into my head as soon as I knew Lord Wem had heard the clock chime twelve before his wife returned to bed. We heard from the servants which members of the family had gone into the room and Mary Ann was the last. Berta was seen in the corridor in the small hours, too late to be the perpetrator. Daniel had been dead for many hours."

Lizzy balked. "But what of Marcus? He slept in the same corridor. He might easily have gone in after Mary Ann."

"He might, if he was cunning enough or brave enough. From all I learned of him from you and Francis, he seems to be the type who uses his tongue for a weapon. He might be glad enough if someone did the deed for him, but I highly doubt he would dare himself."

"The fellow riles me no end," cut in Francis, "but I think he spoke sooth when he said his succession to the title must be a remote contingency. I agree, Tillie. He hasn't the backbone for it."

Before Lizzy could say more, Sybilla pitched in. "But you did suspect the mother, Ottilia?"

"For some time. With hindsight, I believe Lillian's shock was genuine when I told her how the boy died. Moreover, I believe her love for her son is tempered by shrewd judgement of his character. She holds the purse-strings, she told me. She was not blindly devoted in the way of Mary Ann."

"What of Protasia herself? If she urged that mean piece of a daughter of hers to dispose of the fellow's wife—"

"She made no such error, Sybilla. She is much too clever. She set the business in train with her ravings and she provided the means. She knew Berta's character all too well. She has been manipulating her to do her will for years. Old Janet had it down. Hating is as hating does, she said. Protasia taught her daughter to hate. Rather than pleasing her mother, I suspect she sought to set the family at outs to please herself. She cared nothing for the consequences and she blamed her mother for all."

Ottilia pushed away her plate, the portion of scrambled eggs only half eaten. She threw a deprecating glance at her husband. "Don't scold, Fan. I have scant appetite."

"You eat like a bird, Tillie," he returned, himself disposing of a full platter of both ham and bacon.

"Pish and tush, let the girl alone, boy!" Sybilla, impatient, as Ottilia picked up her coffee cup.

Lizzy paid scant attention, her mind still running on the terrible Berta. Forgetful of her besetting sin, she came straight out with her thoughts. "Well, I think it is too bad if that horrid Berta is not to be punished. After all, she did not stop at Isabel, did she? If you had not been so alert, Aunt, she might have disposed of poor little Pretty too."

A constrained silence greeted this outburst. Lizzy caught a quick exchange of looks between Sybilla and Francis, and Ottilia steadfastly regarded the coffee in the cup in her hands.

Lizzy suffered a kick of conscience and could not think how to undo her faux pas.

Within a moment, Francis, rising from his chair, spoke words obviously intended to break up the party. "You need rest, Tillie. If you are not harrowed, I am. And you were up early too."

Sybilla got up, her attitude a clear attempt to aid him in glossing over the moment. "Yes, and you deserve a period of quiet after enduring the horrors of Protasia and her abominable family. Thank heavens it is over."

Ottilia had not moved. She looked up at Sybilla. "*Is* it over?"

Were her eyes troubled? Sybilla adopted her bracing tone.

"Of course it is. You are done with the Brockhursts, my dear. And an excellent thing too." Her gaze went to her son. "Take good care of her, Francis. This business has been troublesome in more ways than one."

He made no reply and Ottilia was similarly silent, her gaze trained upon her drink once more. Lizzy looked from one to the other, anxiety rising. All was not well.

"Come, Elizabeth. I am for the Assembly Rooms."

At that, Ottilia's head jerked up. "To spread the word?"

Sybilla frowned. "Do you wish me to?"

Francis was looking at his wife. "You said you hoped it would leak out. Didn't you want those monsters discredited?"

"Yes, but I had not thought it might come through Sybilla."

"No, you thought to leak it through the servants. But isn't this a better way?"

"At least it would be truth and not mere rumour," Sybilla put in. "What do you wish, Ottilia? I will keep mum if that is your preference, though it will go much against the grain. I should like nothing better than to poison that poisonous woman's name."

328

It seemed to Lizzy that her aunt struggled with herself. She was looking both worn and troubled. Was it to do with little Pretty? At last she spoke, on a weary note.

"I don't think it is right for us to sully their reputations here. It is enough to say Mary Ann has died, if you must say anything."

Sybilla gave one of her snorts. "Well, that will cause speculation sufficient for Mrs Trefnant to build upon. I shall let it fall quite casually." She moved to pat Ottilia's shoulder. "Leave it to me, my child. I know just how to raise a dust without it coming home to roost."

Francis gave a spurt of laughter. "I'll go bail you do, Mama!"

But Ottilia's smile was perfunctory and Lizzy's anxiety increased. On impulse, she swooped upon her and hugged her close, whispering as she did so, "Dearest Lady Fan, I love you very much!"

A husky whisper came back. "And I you, Lizzy." Released, she rose quickly. "Pardon me, but I find I am very tired. Shall we dine together later?" With which, she hurried out of the parlour.

Convinced she was on the verge of tears, Lizzy longed to go after her. But her grandmama was calling, Francis saying farewell, and she had no business to be nosing out her aunt's affairs. The episode brought her own heart-sore condition to the fore and it was hard indeed to bear with patience the chatter and exclamations of her grandmama's friends when all she wished for was to fly to Vivian's side. Which was quite out of count.

Lizzy escaped at length, on the pretext of discovering at Mr Sprange's which was the next play expected from Mrs Baker's company and took time to dawdle on the Pantiles under the scurrying clouds. Were the days of respite from the rain over, along with the heat of events at the house on the hill?

"I hoped I might find you here."

Lizzy jumped, her gaze shooting in the direction of the well-known voice. Mr Maplewood was walking towards her from under the colonnade. A flurry attacked her pulse and warmth climbed up to lodge in her cheeks.

"Vivian! I did not dream of — did not expect to see you today of all days. How — how are you all faring?"

His grimace said much as he came up. "It's not good."

"From all my aunt says, it sounds perfectly horrid."

Without conscious thought she put out her hand, gloveless against the still warm day. He took it, lifted it to his lips and dropped a light kiss upon her fingertips. Lizzy's heart gave a little flip and she uttered a breathy laugh.

"You are not ordinarily so gallant, sir."

A smile came. "I've missed you, Eliza."

Her breath caught. "Truly? With all that going on?"

"More so." To her disappointment, he released her fingers. "You are the leaven that makes it less horrid, to use your expression."

She gave a laugh that sounded hollow to her own ears. "Well, I am glad you at least have a use for me."

The bright eyes held hers. "I might have more, but this is not the time."

"No, I see that."

He seemed to hesitate, looking away and back again. "I wanted to find you because I have a message from my mother for this Lady Fan of yours."

Hope dropped. "Again? Nothing more dreadful has occurred, I hope. I thought it was all over."

His eye gleamed. "Not between us, Eliza, so don't think it."

It was too much. "I wish you won't be so provoking, Vivian. Must you speak in riddles? I won't listen to you."

She moved to walk away on the words but he caught her arm. "Don't do that!"

Lizzy turned on him. "I may not walk off from you, but you are free to tease and befuddle me as much as you wish? Well, it won't do, Mr Maplewood."

His lip quivered and Lizzy was further incensed to see amusement burgeon.

"Now that's the Eliza I want to remember."

"Remember?" Pierced, Lizzy could only stare.

His tone gentled. "Until we meet again."

"When?" She knew it was forward and foolish, but she said it regardless. "When, Vivian?"

His gaze held but he drew an audible breath in and let it out again. "A good question. Longer than I could wish, I fear." A more natural tone entered his voice. "Eliza, we are going into mourning. I am pledged to escort Mama home and from there we will travel up as a family to Wem Hall for the funerals to join the others. My uncle is arranging for the coffins to be taken by wagon."

Lizzy was at once attacked by a welter of guilt. "Of course. I should have thought of that. Forgive me. It was selfish of me to be—"

"No, it wasn't. If I followed my inclination, I would abandon the scheme. I am doing it for Dan."

"Of course you must go." She seized his hand, utterly forgetful of the proprieties and all her aunt's strictures upon wearing her heart upon her sleeve. "I shall miss you, Vivian, very much."

His fingers closed about hers. "You had better. Where do you go after Tunbridge Wells?"

"Home to Dalesford. Papa's estate, you must know."

He released her hand and leaned back, nonchalant. "I wonder do you receive visitors there, Lady Elizabeth?"

Radiance lit her bosom. "Only respectable ones, Mr Maplewood. Artists who flout convention must consider themselves persona non grata."

"Indeed? Then I will don a suitable disguise."

Lizzy laughed. "Don't trouble. Papa will see through you in an instant."

"You alarm me. Do you suppose he might be fooled if I were to grow a fine pair of whiskers?"

"I should think he would show you the door. As would I. Whiskers indeed!"

His eyes lit with amusement. "Then it is settled. I will brave the lion's den just as I am."

Lizzy hesitated, surveying him with distrust. "Do you mean it, or are you teasing me?"

The old enigmatic look appeared. "That, dear Lady Eliza, is a question of which I will leave you to be the judge."

She slapped at his arm. "Provoking creature! I am done with you."

His smile embraced her. "No, you are not, even if you believe as much, which you know very well you don't."

Lizzy raised her brows. "Did you not have a message for my aunt, sir?"

Vivian struck his forehead. "You made me forget, wretched female. Which lodging? Can you lead me there?"

Ottilia could not but be glad of any distraction. She had dozed only fitfully while Francis lay oblivious beside her. They had not spoken of the bone of contention between them which grew more weighty with the finish of the excitements of the day. In the press of events, she had forgot her mother-in-law's defection until the awkward moment precipitated by Lizzy. In other circumstances she might have taken Sybilla to task, but her conscience probed too keenly to cavil.

In her wakeful moments, Ottilia's mind twisted this way and that in a bid to present a convincing argument to her spouse at least to keep the little girl safe in their lodging for a few days. Aware her desire was rooted deeper than in the fear, largely groundless, that Berta might still act, she could not bring herself to broach the subject.

It was a relief when hunger urged her to abandon all pretensions to this spurious rest and don the bodice and overskirt she had taken off. Her spouse woke while she was tidying her hair.

"What time is it?"

She kept her gaze on the mirror. "I don't know, but I was too hungry to lie there any longer."

He swung himself up and sat on the edge of the bed. "That's what comes of your ridiculously poor appetite."

Ottilia made no answer as he got up and went to drag on the bell-pull. Unable to bear the constraint, she rose. "I will ask them to supply us with a luncheon of some kind."

She glanced at Francis, who had picked up his discarded waistcoat. He dug out his pocket watch. "It had best be a snack only. The dinner hour is not far off."

"I dare say the landlady has bread and cheese to hand."

"Beef, Tillie. A sandwich will do nicely."

"As you wish."

She received a keen glance from under his brows, but he made no remark. Ottilia hastened out of the bedchamber, racked by the uncomfortable warring sensations of guilt and yearning. The usual deflation of the end of one of these adventures was missing, superseded by the prospect of imminent loss.

She met Tyler coming in answer to the bell and put in her request for sustenance.

"And coffee, Tyler."

The footman grinned. "That goes without saying, my lady."

By the time Francis joined her, the makeshift meal was on the table and Ottilia had consumed half a roll, accompanied by a portion of crumbly cheese. The sight of her husband had the effect of shattering all over again any desire to eat, but she forced herself to finish the roll before taking up her much-needed cup of coffee. Francis glanced up from buttering bread as she did so.

"Are you sure you've had enough?"

Ottilia detected a touch of anxiety in his tone, laced with impatience. For the life of her she could not infuse warmth into her voice. "As you said, dinner will not be long delayed."

His fingers paused in buttering bread and his brown gaze became abruptly intense. "Tillie, this cannot go on."

Hurt welled up. "What do you want of me, Fan? Have I said aught?"

"You don't have to." He paused, eyeing her. "But you want to, don't you?"

Of what use to pretend? She set down her cup and cleared an obstruction in her throat. "I don't want Hepsie taking Pretty back to that house."

His brows drew together but he dropped his gaze, resuming his preparations with the food. "She may have gone back while we slept."

Quick suspicion kindled. "You mean you ordered it?"

His eye flared as he caught her gaze. "I've been with you throughout. When did I have time? Moreover, I resent the notion I would do it without talking to you first."

The familiar rise of guilt forced Ottilia to look away. "Pardon me. I should not have assumed…"

He said nothing for a moment and she watched surreptitiously as he set slices of beef on his bread and covered it, cutting the sandwich in two. Ottilia took refuge in her coffee as he chewed for several moments in silence. One half of the sandwich had disappeared before he spoke again.

"Do you truly think Berta might yet attempt to strike at the child?"

Ottilia struggled with herself. She could not lie to Francis. "I will not pretend it is just that, Fan. She is sufficiently unhinged perhaps, but likely too afraid to try now she has been found out."

"Nevertheless, you want the child under your eye," he said on a dry note.

"Under my wing altogether." She flung up a hand. "Don't balk again, pray. I know it is not possible."

Another painful silence fell. Francis finished his sandwich and raised to his lips the tankard supplied by the all-knowing Tyler. Ottilia suppressed an inward sigh. An impasse. How in the world were they to get over this?

A knock came at the parlour door and Hemp entered. "Milady."

"What is it, Hemp?"

"The nursemaid Hepsie asks if she may have a word, milady."

Ottilia tried not to look at her spouse. "Of course, Hemp. Tell her to come in."

She noted how Francis shifted his chair so that he had a better view of the door and her heart sank. But Hepsie entered the room without the child. A circumstance that at once loosened Ottilia's tongue.

"Where is Pretty? You have not left her alone, I hope?"

The nurse curtsied. "Your maid Joanie is with her, my lady. I came only to thank you for allowing me to let the babe rest here."

To Ottilia's surprise, her husband cut in before she could respond.

"Are you afraid to go back to the Brockhurst house, Hepsie?"

It was borne in upon Ottilia the nurse was looking both worn and worried, but she answered coolly enough.

"I intend to lock the door again, my lord. And while the servants are abroad, I don't fear for the babe. I will keep her in the kitchen or ask one of the maids to accompany us if I take her outside. Mr Roy says he will escort us back, my lord, if you are agreeable."

Francis nodded, but Ottilia received a frowning glance as she asked the question burning on her lips.

"How does Pretty now? Has she settled a little?"

Hepsie ventured a step or two towards her. "She's quiet, my lady, but I won't conceal from you she is not herself."

"What, is she ill?"

"No, my lady. She is restless and grizzling mostly. She is happy at this moment for Joanie invented a game with her, but…" She made a helpless gesture and Ottilia's heart twisted. What hope of peace for the child in the unknown future planned for her? But mum for that. She was about to wish Hepsie well when her husband spoke again.

"It may be best if you keep your charge here for a day or two. Go with Hemp and bring back whatever you may need. I dare say Joanie will mind the child for a space."

Astonished gratification kept Ottilia tongue-tied while Hepsie, looking a deal more cheerful, thanked him profusely and hurried away with Hemp, who had waited silently in the background. The moment the door closed, she tackled Francis.

"Why, Fan? I am glad of it, yes, but I don't understand."

A faint smile came and went again. "Don't you? It's not like you to be obtuse, my dear one."

She drew in a shaky breath. "You did it to placate me?"

"To set your mind at rest. Besides, I pity the girl. The nursemaid, I mean. To go back to that hellhole and be obliged to skulk about for fear of those appalling women? I should not care to condemn my worst enemy to such a fate."

Ottilia's feelings threatened to overcome her, but she held them in, aware her voice was husky. "Thank you, Fan."

His look was wry, but whatever he might have said was withheld as the unmistakable voice of Lady Elizabeth Fiske sounded outside the room.

"Is my aunt within, Hemp?"

His deep voice answered in the affirmative, the door opened and Lizzy burst into the room. "Oh, you are both here. Excellent. Aunt Ottilia, here is Mr Maplewood with a message for you from his mama."

A trifle bemused Ottilia watched as the young man came in, exchanging greetings with Francis who rose to meet him. An offer of refreshment was declined, but at Lizzy's urging, she and Mr Maplewood took a seat at the table. Lizzy gave him no chance to greet Ottilia but at once broke into an explanatory speech.

"Aunt, Vivian tells me the Brockhursts are all going up to the Wem estate in Salop within a day or two for the funerals and Lord Wem is arranging for all the coffins to go up, even Isabel's."

Ottilia noted the use of Mr Maplewood's given name, but had no opportunity to reply as her spouse cut in.

"For pity's sake, Lizzy, will you allow the fellow to speak for himself?"

"Quite so, sir," said her companion. "Cease and desist, Chatterbox!"

From the way her niece burst into laughter, nevertheless apostrophising him as a beast, Ottilia inferred there had been a settling of matters between them. Or a truce at least?

"What message have you for me from Mrs Maplewood, sir?"

He was regarding Lizzy with an amused glint, but he turned to Ottilia at once, his air apologetic. "Forgive me, ma'am. As you can see, I am hampered at every turn."

He flashed a grin at Lizzy as she mewled in protest and Ottilia became the object of her husband's raised eyebrows. She gave him a slight, conspiratorial smile and called the meeting to order.

"Mr Maplewood?"

"At your service, ma'am."

"Your mother?"

The amusement vanished. "Yes, it is, I regret to say, not the most palatable news."

Apprehension leapt in Ottilia's head. "Well, sir? Pray don't keep me in suspense."

He waved a hand. "Oh, nothing very dreadful, ma'am. Only my revered Mama is exercised about little Pretty."

Ottilia's pulse jumped and she shot a look at her spouse just as his brows snapped together. She managed just the one word. "Yes?"

Mr Maplewood shrugged. "She had hoped, as I think you know, to persuade my uncle Leo and Mary Ann to take the child. With — er — recent events, she felt it imperative to tackle him directly."

"Did he believe his sister tried to dispose of Pretty?"

"I can't say, ma'am. There was a great deal of argument and protest. Not to mention tears and hysterics in several quarters. In the end, my uncle said he had too much on his hands to be bothered with the matter now."

Lizzy took the words out of Ottilia's mouth. "He finds it a bother? What does he expect poor Hepsie to do? Could he not spare a moment's attention for his grand-daughter's fate?"

"Oh, he gave it a moment's attention when my mother pointed out the child could hardly be left in situ. He said the child and her nurse might travel up with the servants. They are to remain at Wem until my uncle has leisure to deal with the matter."

"And why, if you please," said Francis, entering the fray for the first time, "does Mrs Maplewood feel it necessary to inform my wife of these matters?"

A thrust of dismay attacked Ottilia's bosom and Mr Maplewood looked utterly taken aback. Lizzy's troubled gaze went from Francis to herself and back again. Small hope of either failing to note the dissension.

"Because your lady wife said Hepsie had brought the news of Mary Ann's demise. I knew she would never leave Pretty. The thing is, sir, my mother thought Lady Francis would wish to know the child was not to remain under the crocodile's roof. She hopes she may find an opportunity, while we are all up at

Salop to persuade my uncle Leo to let the child remain in his care."

Ottilia could not prevent the utterance from leaving her lips. "But he won't, Mr Maplewood. Mary Ann told me herself he was adamant the child could not be brought up within the family."

"Ah, but that was, my mother believes, because of the influence of the crocodile. She is hopeful your exposure of my dear grandmama's misdeeds will induce my uncle to show a little backbone in his dealings with her."

Ottilia found her husband's gaze upon her. "You did say you thought her influence would be lessened, my love."

She turned the question back on Mr Maplewood. "You know him best, sir. Would he flout the Dowager Lady Wem so far as to offer a home to a despised child of a merchant's daughter, be she never so much his own grandchild?"

Mr Maplewood did not answer at once, evidently giving it some thought. Lizzy grew impatient, echoing the scepticism in Ottilia's bosom.

"Well, Vivian? Can you honestly suppose Lord Wem has kindness enough?"

A scoffing sound left the young man's lips. "Kindness? I have yet to see him offer kindness to anyone. If I am to judge by his attitude to Dan when he was in the throes of grief, I must return an answer in the negative."

"What of justice then?" Ottilia felt she was grasping at straws, for she knew in her heart there would be no quarter for Pretty in Lord Wem's train.

Mr Maplewood grimaced. "He wouldn't accept Isabel. If he believes the notion Berta pushed her off that rock, I dare say he might possibly conceive an obligation towards her child, but I cannot in all honesty say I am sanguine."

Ottilia had to bite her tongue on the words hovering there. She wished Lizzy and Maplewood away that she might utter an impassioned plea to her spouse to reconsider. Of what use to think of it? If she succeeded in persuading him, she would know he went against his own judgement and wishes. What hope of succouring Pretty in such circumstances, when that knowledge must drive a wedge between herself and Francis? She could not risk it. If she must choose, then her husband came first always.

A combination of pain and relief went through her as Francis himself called a halt to the scene, rising with an air of finality.

"You may tell your mother, sir, Pretty is staying here for a day or two while you prepare for your journey. This is merely to ensure her safety while she is within reach of Berta."

Mr Maplewood got up, recognising his cue. "Why, thank you, Lord Francis. I am sure she will welcome the news. She will, I am persuaded, find a moment to make her farewells in person." He turned to Ottilia. "Her thanks too, ma'am. Those of us with the wit to recognise the value of your services will be eternally grateful." He smiled as he turned to Lizzy, still seated. "Lady Eliza, your servant. I hope to speak with you again before we leave this infernal place."

Francis moved to the door. "I will see you out, Mr Maplewood. I must in any event escort my mother back from the Assembly Rooms."

Ottilia watched them go, noting how Lizzy's gaze remained upon her cavalier, a singularly foolish smile upon her lips. She was smitten indeed. When the door closed, she put aside her deep-seated wretchedness and probed a little.

"Do I take it Mr Maplewood has declared himself, Lizzy?"

Her niece flushed, looking perfectly flustered. "Gracious, no! At least, nothing has been said. Or not that in any event."

"But something is settled, is it not?"

The glow in Lizzy's eyes was answer enough. "Oh, Aunt, he does care! He has not said it in so many words. But he asked if he may visit at Dalesford. And he said it is not by any means finished between us, or some such thing. Oh, I don't recall precisely, but I could not mistake. I am so happy, Lady Fan!"

Ottilia took the hands she put out and held them strongly, smiling in spite of the ache within. "I am delighted for you, Lizzy. I think you will suit admirably."

Lizzy laughed and released herself. "So do I. At this present at least. But I am glad it is not quite settled."

"Because you have a chance to be sure he is the man you want?"

"Heavens, how did you guess? I think I will miss him dreadfully, but I do take Mama's warnings to heart, little though she thinks it. She says it is wise to be certain before committing one's life into a man's keeping. And I believe she is right."

Aware how she plunged into matrimony with Francis before they had a chance to know one another, Ottilia yet felt this deserved applause.

"You are perfectly right. Do not take my example for your model, I charge you. Your uncle Francis and I were exceptionally lucky, I believe, for we chose well despite the haste of committing ourselves."

She found herself the focus of a questioning look from her niece's eyes. "Yet, forgive me, Aunt Ottilia, but all is not quite well, is it?"

Ottilia stifled a rising sob. "You've noticed? Of course you have." She essayed a smile. "I remember Francis saying to me, upon the first occasion when we had a serious disagreement, that we could not hope to be happy all the time. He was right.

The marriage vow says so. *For better or for worse.* If you care enough, you can ride out the worst."

Lizzy was eyeing her. Wondering if she ought to speak? Ottilia willed her to keep her tongue, but in vain.

"It's about Pretty, isn't it?"

The ache widened. She made a deprecating face. "It will pass. I lost our child, you see. I do not know if… Well, enough." She set a hand on Lizzy's where it rested on the table. "Be happy, my dear. I am, I promise."

"But not just at this moment," said Lizzy, irrepressible at ever.

"No. But I will be again."

The door opened and Sybilla's voice smote her ears. "Elizabeth, there you are! Why in the world did you not come to fetch me?"

Lizzy rose. "Uncle Francis said he would do so, Grandmama."

"Oh? I must have missed him. Ottilia, how are you faring, child? I have ordered dinner at my lodging. I could not think you would wish to be troubled with the palaver here today."

Ottilia had almost finished her toilette by the time Francis appeared in their bedchamber. She had fretted at his absence, half fearing her megrims had driven him away. Relief soared when he came in and she at once dismissed her maid.

"Thank you, Joanie, that will be all."

She would have gone to her spouse on the girl's exit, but his valet arrived, bearing a jug of hot water. She sought for innocuous words, trying for a natural tone.

"We are to dine with Sybilla, but I have not changed. She suggested we might dispense with formality for once."

"Excellent. Then I will just wash." He nodded at the valet, who had set the jug in the basin on the washstand and now took the coat Francis shrugged off. "A clean neck-cloth, Diplock, and I will do the rest myself."

Ottilia pretended to prink at her hair, watching in the mirror as he unbuttoned his waistcoat. Once the valet had laid a fresh pocket handkerchief and a pristine white muslin cravat on the bed, Francis signed to him to leave.

Ottilia waited only for Diplock to close the door before moving to her husband.

"You have been gone an age, Fan. Did you need a respite from me?"

Busy untying his neckcloth, he paused, frowning down at her. "What are you talking about?"

She gave a little sigh, setting a hand to his chest. "You know very well, my dearest. It is anathema to be at odds with you and I can bear it no longer."

He took hold of the hand and held it there. "Nor I, my dear one. Were you fretting?"

"Of course I was fretting. I have been wretched ever since this business came between us."

He cocked an eyebrow. "And you've relented because I agreed to let the child remain for a day or so?"

Ottilia had to smile. "Not entirely. I was talking to Lizzy and I recalled how you once told me, long ago it seems to me now, it would never be all roses. I had no notion how true that was until now."

He kissed the hand and released it, resuming his work with his neckcloth. "My loved one, we've had disagreements enough before this."

"But this harks back to the worst and I never want to be estranged from you in that way again."

"After you lost our boy? God forbid!" He chucked aside the neckcloth and went to the washstand, lifting the jug and pouring water into the basin. "I accompanied Maplewood up to the house. I like that young man, Tillie. He will do very well with Lizzy."

Ottilia gazed at him in no little consternation. "You went up to the Brockhursts?"

"I had business there." He dipped his head over the basin and began to wash.

But Ottilia's attention riveted upon his words. "What business?"

"Tell you in a moment."

She dropped to sit on the bed and waited in an agony of apprehension as he dried his face and emerged from the towel. Throwing it aside, he ripped off the ribbon holding back his hair and Ottilia's patience wore away as he dragged a comb through his lush hair and retied it behind.

"Well?"

"Let me finish dressing or you'll delay me and we'll end by sending Mama up into the boughs."

"Not she, not today. She is in alt at having set the rumour mongers in a bustle. She was obliged to let it out that it was suicide, Sybilla said, for Mrs Trefnant's notions became too lurid to be borne."

While she relayed her mother-in-law's words, her mind was leaping with conjecture. At length, his neckcloth tied to his satisfaction, her husband put on his waistcoat and coat again and declared himself ready.

"Yes, but we are going nowhere until you tell me what you have been about, Fan."

His expression changed as he looked down at her. "I saw Wem."

"You spoke to Lord Wem?" The beat of her pulse became irregular. "About Pretty?"

He put up a hand in a warning gesture. "It's only temporary, Tillie."

"Yes, until they go to Wem's estate. So you said."

"I suggested a little more."

"More?" Ottilia's breath caught. "What more, Fan?"

"That we take her until he has had opportunity to settle his affairs. Until, in other words, he has leisure to attend to the child's needs."

Hardly able to believe her ears, Ottilia got up to speak, found her legs too unsteady, and sat down again. Her voice proved as unreliable as her limbs.

"Why, Fan? What changed your mind?"

"You, my obtuse one."

"But you did not want this. You were adamant. I never wished for you to go against your inclination merely to please me. I will feel it all the time, my dearest."

His mouth twisted. "Yes, I know your conscience, but you may rest easy. It was not your misery, nor yet your withdrawal from me."

"I didn't withdraw! At least, I tried not to, Fan. I tried to swallow my disappointment. I never meant to force you to capitulate with upsets and tears. I despise that sort of manipulation."

He took a seat beside her and his warm hands grasped her unquiet ones, holding them steady. "Did you think you were the only one wakeful when we were allegedly resting today? I have had time to think as well as you, Tillie."

"Then what? I don't understand you in the least."

His grip relaxed and he began fiddling with her fingers, looking at them rather than at her. "It occurred to me to wonder, had our son lived, and if, by some cruel trick of fate, we were both taken from him, what I would wish for his future."

She was used to the pang any mention of that loss brought. "The cases are not the same. Our family—"

"There is Harriet, I know."

"And Patrick too."

"Yet if it were not so, Tillie. If it proved to be Randal or Mama? I could not wish my son to grow up under my brother's aegis. And much as I love my mother, she is growing too impatient for such a charge."

"Even so, it could not compare with the situation Pretty is in," Ottilia objected.

"That is just it. Mrs Maplewood has made no move to succour the child. Who else is there? You said it first, Tillie. She has no one." He set an arm about her and leaned his head against hers. "If my son had no one and a well-disposed person, a warm and big-hearted female such as yourself were to offer him a refuge, I would consider him the luckiest little boy in the world."

Ottilia could no longer hold back the tears. Francis held her as she wept, but the words sobbed out of her.

"Why d-didn't you tell me what you m-meant to d-do?"

"Because I could not bear to disappoint you, my darling heart, if Wem had refused me."

"Oh, Fan, I do love you so very much."

"I know and it's a constant struggle to live up to your expectations."

There was a laugh in his voice and Ottilia gave a watery chuckle. "You don't have to try, my dearest dear."

He gave her the handkerchief Diplock had set ready and Ottilia made use of it, a niggle of doubt arising. "What did Lord Wem say?"

Francis laughed. "He is in such a state of panic and despair, I should imagine he would have agreed to anything that took one problem off his hands." He got up, straightening his clothing. "You do realise there is no question of adoption, Tillie?"

She gave a resigned sigh and rose. "I understand that."

"And that it may come to giving the child up if Wem chooses to collect her in due course?"

Ottilia gave a tremulous smile. "If he does so choose. I can always hope, can I not?"

A NOTE TO THE READER

Dear Reader

Setting *The Fateful Marriage* in Tunbridge Wells was rather like going back to visit an old friend. I lived in the town for four years many moons ago, and I had ample opportunity to visit both the Pantiles and High Rocks. Although the town is much more sprawling than it was in the late 1700s, the essential layout remains much the same, with the roads running along the top and bottom of the common. At this latter end, the buildings still stand that fronted the area of The Walks on the other side.

Outwardly, the Walks, or to use the area's more common name, the Pantiles, remain very much as they were in the 18th Century. It is a "listed" area, which in the UK means it has been designated a heritage site. Thus, owners of the various buildings are required to keep the facades in good order but maintaining their original features. You can see the colonnades and the little shops beneath just as they were and there is a musicians' gallery in the middle of the paved area.

The old Assembly Rooms now house a café, art gallery, more little shops around the sides and a small museum where you can find original sedan chairs and other artefacts from the town's period as a popular spa. The shops are quite poky to modern eyes, but delightful if you want to imagine yourself back in the 18th century, browsing the toy shops for Tunbridge Ware.

While I was there, an acting company used to visit every summer for a week of entertainments. The actors dressed in costume and wandered about the Pantiles, chatting to visitors in the lingo of the 18th Century, bowing and complimenting the ladies. They set up various little scenes with each other, which took place throughout the day — advertised so you could go to the right place to watch. As I remember, there were the gossips, talking of the latest scandals of the day; there was an argument between a couple of gentlemen which ended in a duel; and a flirtatious interlude between a lady and gentlemen. It was great fun, and if you could respond in kind when they addressed you, the actors were delighted.

As for High Rocks, it's quite an adventure to climb up the pathway to the highest rock. The rocks, impressively huge, cover a wide area and date back to the last ice age. Now, of course, there are many safety measures to prevent accidents, but in the old days no one would dream of spoiling the natural beauty of a historic site. Your 18th Century tourist expected to be able to view such places just as they were. Although there seems to have been no objection to the messages carved by earlier visitors defacing the natural rock. These are numerous and can still be seen and read.

This is in fact the third story I have set in Tunbridge Wells, two of my historical romances also taking place in and around the Pantiles. But I must say it was especially enjoyable to take Ottilia and Francis to this favourite location where, naturally, someone is murdered in short order!

I do hope you enjoy this excursion to what was for many years a favourite watering place for the gentry, second only to Bath. If you would consider leaving a review, it would be much appreciated and very helpful. Do feel free to contact me on **elizabeth@elizabethbailey.co.uk** or find me on **Facebook**, **Twitter**, **Goodreads** or my website **elizabethbailey.co.uk**.

Elizabeth Bailey

Sapere Books is an exciting new publisher of brilliant fiction and popular history.

To find out more about our latest releases and our monthly bargain books visit our website:
saperebooks.com

Printed in Great Britain
by Amazon

28931664R00198